# THE WARRIOR WITHIN

Brian,

Thank you for buying
a copy. I hope you enjoy
the book.

Brian W. Fisher

# THE WARRIOR WITHIN

a novel

Brian W. Bishop

iUniverse, Inc.

New York Lincoln Shanghai

**The Warrior Within**

a novel

iUniverse, Inc.

For information address:
iUniverse, Inc.
2021 Pine Lake Road, Suite 100
Lincoln, NE 68512
www.iuniverse.com

ISBN: 0-595-28946-0

Printed in the United States of America

# CONTENTS

▼

# ACKNOWLEDGMENTS

I would like to dedicate this book to my wife, Randi. Her encouragement, love and support never wavered as I struggled to make the dream of completing this book a reality. She never once complained about the long hours spent in the seclusion of my writing "cave", as she calls my home office, and always met me with a smile when I did eventually come out of hiding. I could never have done this without her.

I also want to thank my younger brother, Keith, who was the first to read the rough draft and who provided me with a vitally important sounding board for questions and ideas as well as constant support and affirmation. The rest of my family has been incredibly supportive as well and I want to thank my mom, Leona, my brother, Jim, my sister, Sheri and my sister, Jeri for reading the book, pushing me forward and encouraging me all along the way.

Lastly, I want to thank my friend, Caesar, who read the book, constantly encouraged me to keep working and even donated money to help pay for the supplies necessary to keep writing. Thank you all so very much.

# CHAPTER 1

▼

# BETRAYAL

It is a terrible thing to be a warrior born in a time and place of peace. Even worse not to know it; to live your life with a vague emptiness within you, never knowing what it is you hunger for, knowing only that you hunger. With all your soul, you hunger.

The worn, listless young man moving here and there around his spacious, comfortably furnished bedroom had known this vague emptiness for most of his twenty seven years of life. What he couldn't know as he packed his bags for an extended trip was that he would soon learn his hunger's name. And the high price of satisfying it.

Mitchell Harvey stood five feet eleven inches tall and weighed two hundred and fifty pounds. Once broad shouldered and athletic, he was now broad shouldered and what his mother kindly called "stocky." He had a full head of dark brown hair that went well with his equally dark, intelligent eyes. His clean-shaven face was pale, the result of far too many hours spent sitting in front of computer screens or hunched over data pads.

He wore a well tailored suit of dark blue, a white dress shirt and highly polished black shoes. He was in the process of unknotting his necktie, grey with diagonal blue and white pinstripes, when a beep from his Video Message Link alerted him to an incoming call. Glancing at the caller ID strip above the monitor, he smiled and crossed the room to sit down at the VML console.

"Activate," he said, his deep, smooth voice breaking the heavy mood of the silent room. The twenty-four inch, rectangular screen came to life.

"Did I call at a bad time?" the deeply tanned face of Alton Harvey asked with a smile.

"Only if you're calling to borrow money," Mitch joked. His brother had had the foresight to open a small ocean side restaurant and bar on what was then a small time mining planet called Teluride. As the mining operations had expanded, so had Alton. And now, a short seven years later, the hard working miners of Teluride, who made damn good money working sixteen hour days five days a week, enjoyed spending their much deserved weekends and hard earned credits at the newly opened SeaVista Resort Hotel. Alton Harvey wouldn't be needing any loans.

"No," Alton laughed. "Just wanted to wish you a good trip. I hear you're bilking the government out of my hard earned tax credits again."

Mitch laughed. Alton had a way of snapping him out of his dark moods. Always had.

"As a matter of fact, I am," Mitch told him. "The only thing that pays better than working for the civil government is working for the military. I'm signed on with both this trip."

"You make me proud to be a Harvey, young man," Alton said, pretending to wipe a tear from his eye. "Damn proud."

Taxes were one of his pet peeves, especially since he'd moved into the higher tax brackets, and the fact that his brother made most of his money off of the government gave him a small sense of payback.

"Keep up the good work."

Mitch laughed again. When he'd taken the vocational tests in preparation for his mandatory three year hitch in the Traegus Sector Confederation's military, he had tested out as a linguist. He'd had to sign up for a five year hitch instead of three because of the lengthy schooling involved, but when his five years were up, he'd gone back to civilian life with a marketable skill.

Using the government contacts he'd made, he'd turned that skill into a lucrative business translating and interpreting the various languages and dialects of the Confederation's seven member worlds, plus those of any world seeking entrance into the league. He got no real joy from his work, but he wouldn't be needing any loans either. That had to count for something.

"Where you headed?" Alton asked.

"Rittenmere. It's a pretty small planet but it's loaded with natural resources. I think they'll be approved for membership."

"The more the merrier," Alton said with a grin. "Is Sandra going with you?"

Mitch's face visibly dropped before he was able to regain his composure and try to look cheerful. He and Alton had very nearly had a falling out when his older brother had taken him aside and practically begged him not to marry Sandra. That had been a little over two years ago now and Mitch had only just recently been able to admit to himself that his brother had been right. He wasn't quite ready to admit it to Alton yet.

"No, she's staying here," he said with a forced smile. "Previous commitments. You know how it is."

"Everything O.K, Mitch?" Alton asked, concern in his voice. He knew his brother too well not to have seen the pain in his eyes at the mention of his wife's name.

"Yeah," Mitch told him. "Everything's fine. There are a few things I need to fill you in on but it can wait. Business stuff. I don't want to get into it now. We'd have to video conference with Nate and I really don't have time right now."

Nathan Squires was their mutual attorney. Alton raised a questioning eyebrow but didn't push it.

Mitch found that thinking about the arrangements he'd made with the attorney brightened his mood again.

"I see by your peaked complexion that you've been overworking yourself again," he said with a smile. "How many times do I have to warn you?"

Alton laughed. The miners were so jealous of his tan they'd nicknamed him "Toast".

"It's a hard life, little brother," he said with mock solemnity. "A hard life."

"That much is obvious, you lucky prick," Mitch said with a laugh. "I'll give you a call after I get settled in on Rittenmere."

"Very well," Alton said, doing a credible imitation of their father's 'I'm about to give you a lecture' look. "You take care of yourself, young man," he intoned. "And be careful. It would break your mother's heart if you came home with some exotic genital disease."

The screen went blank while Mitch laughed.

Standing, he went back to packing his bags, wondering if his wife would even make the effort to say goodbye. He hoped she wouldn't bother and doubted she would. They had had a nasty fight the night before when he'd refused to transfer more credits into her account.

He'd been a fool, of course. Why Alton had been able to see through Sandra so easily while he himself had been blind to everything but her tight ass and beautiful knockers he would probably never know. But Sandra had been a different woman before the wedding; attentive and affectionate, never too busy to do something for her husband to be and always eager to please in bed. That had all changed the minute he'd said, "I do".

He'd tried to figure out what was wrong at first, willing to do whatever it took to make things work. His efforts had seemed to amuse Sandra then. But her amusement had quickly turned to impatience and then contempt. The only time she was more than civil was when she ran out of credits. And lately, not even then.

He'd wracked his brain trying to figure out what he'd done wrong before finally realizing that he hadn't done anything wrong except marry Sandra. She was every bit the conniving, money hungry leech Alton had warned him she was. There was no sense in kicking himself about it anymore, though. He'd done what he could for now. He'd take care of the rest when he got back.

Fastening the clasp on the last of his three bags, he pressed his right thumb to the lock mechanism in the bag's upper left corner and carried it from the room, down a high ceilinged, brightly lit hallway and set it on the floor beside the front door with the others, then walked back to his bedroom.

He was just beginning to unbutton his shirt when he heard a whisper of sound behind him. Thinking Sandra had decided to say goodbye after all, he turned to face her, hoping she wasn't in the mood for another argument. But it wasn't Sandra he found himself facing. It was three men he'd never seen before and they were definitely in the mood for an argument.

The first one, the largest of the three left his feet just as Mitch turned, lunging at him, trying to get his arms around Mitch's torso and take him to the floor. Jumping back quickly, Mitch jerked his right knee up. He felt it make solid contact with the man's face just as the other two jumped forward and grabbed for his arms.

The first man fell to his knees with a moan but quickly wrapped his arms around Mitch's legs. Then the man on the left got a firm grip on Mitch's left arm. But his friend on the right missed his grab and when he stepped in for another try, Mitch's right hand shot out, seizing him by the throat and squeezing his larynx. Pulling back sharply with all his adrenaline enhanced strength, Mitch just had time to see the shock and fear in the other man's eyes before there was a sharp prick at the back of his neck and his world disappeared into blackness.

*     *     *     *

It had taken nearly three weeks to set up the meeting. Looking at the short, balding little man in the cheap suit, Sandra Harvey wondered if it was worth it. She got right to the point.

"I need to know what you're going to do with him, Mr. Raines," she said.

Captain Demetrius Nester hesitated. He'd given the good looking blonde a phony name, just as she'd given him one. The difference was that he had already found out who she really was. But she must have known he would.

"I'm afraid I really can't give you that information, Mrs. Harvey," he said. Might as well let her know she wasn't dealing with an amateur.

The woman didn't so much as bat an eyelash.

"Then I'm afraid I can't give you this, Mr. Raines," she said, handing Nestor a funds transfer chip.

Taking his scanner from the inside breast pocket of his jacket, Captain Nestor slid the chip into the access port. He showed no outward reaction to what he saw when the data came up on his screen, but inwardly his blood was warmed by avarice. The figure on the chip was fully three times what he was normally paid to make someone disappear. The blonde seemed to sense what he was thinking.

"Does that change your mind, Mr. Raines?" she asked.

Nestor looked at her for a long minute.

"Why do you need to know, Mrs. Harvey? Why isn't it enough to know he'll disappear?"

"Because I need to be able to pass a life insurance company polygraph, Mr. Raines. I need to be able to truthfully say that I neither killed my husband nor hired someone to kill him."

Nestor was impressed. This was one cold-blooded woman. And she knew her business.

"I give you my word, then, Mrs. Harvey. Your husband won't be killed."

"That's not good enough," she snapped. "To pass that test I need to have absolutely no doubts. You know that."

With so much at stake the life insurance companies invested in only the best polygraph technicians and equipment money could buy. But Sandra knew from previous experience exactly which preliminary questions she'd have to get past.

After another long moment's thought, Nestor decided the money was worth the risk. The bitch couldn't talk without putting herself at risk. Besides, she didn't strike him as the kind that was going to have a sudden attack of conscience and spill her guts.

"Very well, then, Mrs. Harvey," he said. "Most of the people I make disappear, unless I am specifically asked to eliminate them," eliminate sounded so much more professional than kill, "are relocated to one of several secluded planets in my possession. The planet I'll be placing your husband on supports human life. In fact, there are several primitive societies living there. Mr. Harvey will be placed in the vicinity of one of those societies. What happens after that is entirely up to him."

Sandra Harvey took her time thinking it through.

"How secluded are we talking, Mr. Raines?" she asked after a moment. "It would be very unpleasant to have someone stumble onto your little planet."

Nestor smiled confidently.

"The planet is also an active mining world," he said. "There are three armed vessels in continuous orbit to protect the mining operation and ensure that unauthorized vessels keep their distance. I assure you, you have nothing to worry about."

"Alright, Mr. Raines," Sandra Harvey said, though she still had some misgivings. This man had come very highly recommended. Besides, she was running out of time. "We have a deal. You can keep the transfer crystal. You'll get the access code when the job is done."

With that she turned and walked away. They knew where to reach her.

Nestor watched with appreciation as she walked away, then went to his shuttle and headed back to the spaceport. Back aboard his ship, the *Mia Luna*, he read over the information his sources had been able to develop regarding Mr. Mitchell Harvey. There was nothing particularly interesting or surprising. Five years military service, four years spent building a successful business, nice house in Sylvas City, no known adulterous affairs. Nestor wondered idly what the man could have done to earn such hatred from his wife.

But no, not hatred, he corrected himself. He doubted Sandra Harvey hated the man. Actually, he doubted she had any strong feelings either way. Something told him that to her this was nothing more than a business decision. He could respect that. Business was business. No sense letting emotion cloud your judgment.

Scanning the file on Harvey, he tried to decide where to place him. Triton, the name he'd given to the little planet he planned to use for this job, had seven large landmasses, numerous smaller ones and several large island chains. The landmass he normally used for his relocation runs was situated in the middle of the raging seas of Triton's western hemisphere, seas that gave the place a greenish tinge when viewed from space.

It was a fertile, mountainous continent, populated by four primitive societies. He had a feeling none of them were indigenous to Triton, though he couldn't say exactly why. They'd been there when he'd stumbled onto the place, due in large part to a drunken navigator and pure chance. He'd been rather angry at the time. In fact, the drunken navigator had been the first person he'd ever deposited on Triton. Looking back, he could see he owed the man an apology. Too late now, though. He seriously doubted Simmons or Timmons, or whatever his name had been, was still alive. But Triton had turned into a very profitable discovery.

Sooner or later the trade routes and jump-gates would move out to that end of the sector or someone would catch on to him and he'd be forced to sell out and move on to new opportunities. Until then, his three ships should be able to keep anyone from getting too curious. And he could keep himself amused.

He enjoyed making people disappear. It made him feel a little bit like a god: deciding where another human being would struggle through what was left of their existence or where a corpse would return to dust. He found it exhilarating. Intoxicating almost. And it paid well, too. Damn well.

For this trip he had three passengers, a good load. Two of them, one man and one woman, were already sedated and on board. He sometimes felt a little guilty about the women. Triton was a nasty little place, full of predators, primitive living conditions and harsh weather patterns. But, business was business.

Checking the time, he punched his secure audio link.

"Giles, this is Nestor."

"Giles here, sir," the reply came back.

"How are things coming?"

"He's still in a meeting, Captain. I was thinking it might be better to tail him home before making our move."

"Whatever you think is best, Giles," Nestor answered. He could trust his second in command to use discretion. "Call me when you have him."

"Yes, sir."

Switching off his link, Nestor turned back to his data pad. Where should he place these three? Should he flip a coin? Or close his eyes and point blindly at the map? Or maybe just leave them in the middle of some strange city or small village wearing nothing but a confused look? He laughed at the thought. It was good to be a god.

His mood was still light when his audio link chirped a little more than an hour later.

"Captain, this is Giles."

"Do we have him?" Nestor asked, not liking the sound of his second's voice.

"Yes, sir, we have him," Giles answered. "But there were…complications. Penn is dead, or he will be shortly."

"What the hell happened?" Nestor exploded. "Is the mission compromised?"

"No, sir, the mission is not, I repeat, not compromised. If it's alright with you, sir, I'll fill you in on the rest when we get back. What should we do with Penn?"

"Bring him with you, of course. We don't want Mrs. Harvey coming home to a corpse."

"Yes, sir, we won't be long."

"I'll be waiting," Nestor hissed. "Make sure you're not seen."

He snapped the link off and paced around his cabin angrily. How the hell could Penn have gotten himself killed?

He forced himself to control his emotions. In the four years Giles had been working for him he had carried out hundreds of missions without incident. If something had gone wrong this time, there was a good explanation. He owed it to Giles to hear him out.

When his men got back, he waited while Giles and Cage placed Penn's corpse and the unconscious Harvey in the med-bay.

"What happened?" he asked, looking in disbelief at the blood on Giles' battered face and the walnut sized hole in Penn's throat.

"Harvey tore his fucking throat out!" Giles spat angrily, his words sounding slightly slurred due to his swollen lips. "Just reached out, grabbed him by the throat and ripped his larynx out."

Nestor absorbed that for a minute then sighed deeply.

"I apologize," he said, surprising both of his men. Neither of them could remember ever having heard the captain apologize for anything. "His file mentions his interest in the martial arts but I didn't think it was important."

Giles looked at him. Penn's death was hitting Nestor harder than he would have thought. But there was no way it was the captain's fault.

"It's not your fault, sir," he said. He and his team had taken out their fair share of dangerous people; mercenaries, professional assassins, body guards, even top of the line military personnel. Knowing that this guy spent a couple of hours a week dressing up in a silly outfit and beating up on a virtual opponent wouldn't have made them any more cautious. They'd gotten overconfident. *He'd* gotten overconfident. And Penn had paid the price.

"Is that what I should tell his wife?" Nestor asked, motioning toward Penn's body, "that it wasn't my fault?"

He put up a hand to silence Giles' reply, then walked over and placed a clean white sheet over Penn.

"Get us underway please, Giles," he said. "I'd like to be rid of Mr. Harvey as soon as possible. Take care of Penn first. Prepare his body and put him in cold storage. We'll deliver him to his widow when we get back."

"Yes, sir."

Captain Nestor spent the majority of the five day trip in his quarters. On the rare occasions that he did come to the bridge, he was quiet and withdrawn, preoccupied and lost in thought. Giles knew he was considering his options regarding Harvey.

If he had his way, they'd just kill the bastard. Slowly. In the end they would leave him on Triton alive, though. Nestor would keep his end of the bargain he'd made with the big titted blonde in hopes of doing business with her again. In the end, money always won out with Captain Nestor.

After arriving at Triton, they remained in orbit for a full day before the captain finally came to the bridge; a full day being thirty hours. Triton's cycle was thirty hours in a day, thirty-one days in a month, fifteen months in a year.

"I've given this Harvey situation a good deal of thought, Giles," Nestor said as he stood gazing out at Triton through the forward view screen. "I want you to place him on that wide plain on the southern edge of the western landmass. And I want you to withhold the usual clothing, footwear and supplies. I can't kill him without breaking my contract with Mrs. Harvey. But that doesn't mean I have to make it easy for him to survive."

"Yes, sir," Giles said with a grin. There wasn't a drop of water anywhere on that plain. Harvey would be lucky to last a day. If the sun didn't kill him, the cold would. Or one of Triton's predators. Either way, the prick was as good as dead.

"I know I can sometimes be hard, Giles," the captain continued, still gazing out at the planet, "but I don't like seeing my people killed. I wish I could do more."

"This seems like a pretty good solution, sir," Giles said. "I think Penn would approve."

Nestor nodded.

"Place the other two at the foot of the mountains to the north of the plain," he said. "Keep them together and give them the usual clothing and supplies."

"Yes, sir."

"Then set course for Sylvas," Captain Nestor concluded as he turned and walked off the bridge. "We have an access code to pick up. And a widow to visit."

# CHAPTER 2

▼

# CHOICES

Wanchese Hawkins moved stiffly across the small, windowless hovel that was her home. She had slept poorly, the memory of her parent's death coming to her in her dreams. It had been happening more and more often lately and she wondered why. That had been more than eight years ago now.

Taking an earthen jar from beneath a crude wooden table in one corner of the room, she poured cool water into a shallow wooden basin. Reaching behind her head, she untied the thin hide thong that held a round cloth patch over her right eye, removed the patch and washed her face.

She'd lost the eye in the same attack that had taken her parents from her. Thinking of it now, her right hand unconsciously moved to the mottled flesh within her eye socket and traced the long scar down across her cheek to where it ended behind her right ear.

She wished again that the tall, ugly Inchasa had driven his knife just a little deeper, just a little further. Then her life's blood would have spilled out along with that of her parents and she wouldn't have been left behind alone. The ugly Inchasa could have given her that at least. But he hadn't.

Secotan Samuels and some others had come and forced the ugly one to retreat before he could finish what he'd started, leaving her mother and father dead on the ground and young Wanchese dead inside.

Secotan had taken her into his arms then and spoken to her gently, telling her that everything was going to be alright, that the healer was going to take care of her and stop the pain. But nothing had ever been alright again. And no had ever stopped the pain. Not the pain that mattered.

Remembering her father's anguished eyes looking at her as he fell to his knees, the tip of the ugly Inchasa's lance sticking out of his chest, silently begging her forgiveness for having failed her and her mother, she whispered, "I forgive you, father," and hoped he could hear her.

Then she retied the patch over her eye and pulled her heavy sleeping robe off over her head and slipped into a sleeveless, knee length dress. The dress was made from the thin but rugged hide of a banebull, a big, slow moving beast named after the first man to domesticate one of them, Lyman Bane.

The dress was fairly new, Wanchese having made it and two others just like it when her body had undergone a sudden change that had left her old clothing feeling tight and uncomfortable. The change had taken her by surprise and she was still not completely comfortable with her new body. Or the added attention it was drawing from the young warriors of her village.

She had reached her sixteenth year several months earlier, an age by which a young woman was normally fully developed, New Roanoke's year consisting of fifteen thirty-one day months. It was also the age by which a young woman was required by tradition to be wed. But no one had shown any interest in her and nothing had been said when she'd reached her sixteenth year and was still unmarried.

Then her body had changed and the same young men who had either ignored her or called her cruel names all of her life were suddenly finding excuses to run into her and awkwardly trying to engage her in conversation. She didn't want anything to do with them. She wasn't so young that she didn't know it was only her body they were interested in. She had no intention of spending the rest of her life taking care of a man who wanted her only for what he could do to her in his bed. The fools didn't respect her. They didn't really even know her. They'd never taken the time.

She had just slipped on her lightly colored moccasins when the tri-colored blanket that served as a door to her hut was thrown aside and a tall, thickly muscled young warrior stepped into her room. The smile on Hunter Kane's sharp, hard face was not a friendly one. His cold, emotionless, black eyes poured over her body in a way that made her feel terribly unclean.

"Don't you even have manners enough to ask permission before walking into someone's home?" she asked, trying to sound confident and unafraid despite the cold finger of fear that was making it's way up her spine. She had seen the way Kane looked at her and had instinctively avoided him. Until now.

"Be quiet and take off that dress," Kane demanded evenly.

"What?" she asked in disbelief.

"I said, be quiet and take off that dress. Now, do it!"

"Get out!" she demanded angrily. "Get out or I'll tell Secotan of this."

"Go ahead," Kane said calmly, stepping closer, a cold, mirthless smile on his face. "You are well past your sixteenth year, you little bitch. Tradition says that I have only to demand it and you are bound to give yourself to me."

He took another step.

"You should have let one of those young fools take you as a wife," he continued coldly. "Now you will belong to no one and be used by everyone."

Stepping back, Wanchese grabbed her knife, a long, very sharp hunting knife that had once belonged to her father, from where it lay on the table.

Kane laughed.

"Put that down," he said. "Or when I'm done with you I'll show what a warrior can do with a knife."

When the girl said nothing he added, "This doesn't have to be unpleasant."

Wanchese laughed, surprising herself. Having a man force himself on her didn't have to be unpleasant? Did this fool really believe that? She could see that her laughter made him angry. Sensing that that could be to her advantage, she smiled at him. Kane's eyes grew hot with anger and he lunged for her.

She slashed at him and he jumped back with a yelp, a thin, bloody slice across his bare chest. Roaring with anger, he threw himself at her again, this time managing to knock her arm aside and get hold of her hair. He pulled her to him as she tried to twist away and his hand ran up her body until it grasped her right breast painfully.

She could feel his hot breath on her neck as he leaned on her, trying to force her to the floor. Knowing she'd be helpless if he got on top of her, she grasped her knife tightly in her right hand and stabbed down and behind her. The knife sank deeply into the big warrior's muscular thigh.

Enraged and in pain, Kane released his hold on her, spun her around so that she faced him, and struck her hard across the face with the back of his left hand, knocking her into the wooden table and to the floor. She scrambled up quickly, her nose and mouth bleeding, and brandished the knife in front of her, waiting for him to attack again.

Dropping his hand to his waist, Kane drew his own knife from its sheath. Her heart pounding, Wanchese looked desperately for a way to escape. Kane was a powerful warrior, feared even by most of the other men in the village. She couldn't hope to defeat him in an armed struggle. But she would rather die than lie down for a man like him. Maybe if she fought hard enough and resisted long enough, she could force him to kill her. That would be better than what he had in mind for her.

Kane took a hobbling step toward her then stopped when there was a sharp knock from the front of the hut.

"Wanchese, are you home? It's Dare," a woman's voice called.

"Come," Wanchese croaked hoarsely.

The blanket was pushed aside and Dare Samuels stepped into the room. Her friendly smile vanished immediately as she looked at the two of them.

"What's the meaning of this?" she asked, her eyes wide, looking from Kane's bloody body to Wanchese's blood stained knife and battered face.

"That's none of your concern," Kane said menacingly, not taking his burning gaze from Wanchese as he spoke. "Now, get out."

"I will do no such thing," Dare said angrily. "Now, what is going on here?"

"He wants to lie with me by force," Wanchese said, wiping blood from her mouth with her left hand.

"I want to claim my rights as a warrior," Kane spat back. "She's past her sixteenth year and still unwed. You know what tradition says."

He turned and glared at Dare.

"Now, get out. This is none of your concern."

"That is an old and unused tradition, Hunter Kane," Dare told him, trying to control her temper. "It hasn't been enforced in over two hundred years and you know it."

"Old and unused," Kane said, "but still a tradition of our people. It hasn't been enforced in over two hundred years because no woman has been stupid enough to remain unmarried past her sixteenth year. The tradition is valid and I claim my rights!"

"We will see what Secotan has to say about this," Dare shot back. "Now, let her pass. She's coming with me."

"I tell you for the last time, woman," Kane said hotly, "this is none of your concern. Now, get out!"

Dare stood her ground, looking at him defiantly.

"Do not cross me," the big warrior hissed.

"Or what?" Dare asked. "What will you do if I refuse, Hunter Kane? Will you turn your knife on me, too? Is that the kind of man you are, Kane? Do you make war on defenseless women?"

"Silence!" Kane snapped. Then he visibly forced himself to calm down, his body shaking with the effort.

"Very well, woman," he said after a moment. "We will see what your husband has to say about his. And what kind of Councillor he is. I am within my rights."

With a last withering look at Wanchese, he turned and hobbled from the room, brushing roughly past Dare.

"Are you alright?" Dare asked, rushing to the visibly shaken Wanchese.

Wanchese nodded.

"Y...Yes," she stammered. "Thank you," she added, meeting Dare's eyes.

Dare took her by the hand and made her sit down on the bed. Then she dipped a small rag in the washbasin and wiped the blood from Wanchese's face as gently as she could.

"Will you be alright while I go get Secotan?" she asked.

Wanchese nodded and Dare left. Secotan burst into the room a few minutes later, Dare following close behind.

"Are you alright?" he asked, stepping quickly to the girl.

"Yes," Wanchese answered much more steadily.

"Good," he said, patting her hand. "Now, tell me what happened. Everything, please. Don't leave anything out."

Wanchese told him what had happened and Dare added what she'd seen and heard. Secotan's brow grew furrowed and his normally open, pleasant face grew dark with concern as he listened. He'd been afraid of something like this.

As Village Councillor he was responsible for upholding and enforcing his people's sacred beliefs. And Hunter Kane *was* within his rights. But how was he supposed to explain that to this poor girl? He ran a hand through his long, red-brown hair and nervously fingered his necklace of hardened, rectangular pieces of wood. His young wife saw the clouds of doubt and worry in his grey eyes when he turned to her.

"I'm not sure that Kane is wrong," he said quietly. The look of pained disbelief on Wanchese's face hurt only slightly more than the look of shock and horror on Dare's.

"He *is* within his rights," he continued without conviction. Why did this have to happen? Why did Wanchese have to refuse to even listen to any of her young suitors?

"You can't be serious," Dare said when she recovered her voice.

"I'm afraid I am," he said sadly. "It's my duty to safeguard the traditions of our people, Dare. I can't change that. It would have been better if Wanchese had given some of the young warriors who courted her a chance."

He looked at the young woman that had endured so much cruelty already in her young life and who he was now powerless to protect.

"Is there no one you are interested in?" he asked hopefully. "If I could tell Kane that you're betrothed...."

Wanchese said nothing.

"Wanchese?" he asked.

"Leave me," she said softly. "Please. I want to be alone."

"Did you hear what I asked?" Secotan asked pleadingly.

Wanchese raised her head and looked at him, defiance suddenly blazing in her eye.

"Yes, I heard what you asked, Councillor," she said, speaking the title as if it were a dirty word. "I have the choice of spending the rest of my life with one man who wants nothing more than my body or spending the rest of my life with a hundred men who want nothing more than my body. You'll have to forgive me if I need some time to decide. Now, leave me!"

"Alright," Secotan said sadly. "I'll send Dare and my other wives to speak with you, to....tell you what to expect. I'm sorry, Wanchese. Truly, I am."

Then he and Dare left Wanchese's hut and walked slowly up the narrow path that led to the main village. Looking at her husband, Dare knew deep in her heart that he was too good a man not to be tortured by the decision he'd just made. Thinking of what it was going to do to him, and of what Wanchese was going to suffer that night, she knew real hatred for the first time in her life. If she'd been able, she would gladly have killed Hunter Kane in that moment. It was a frightening feeling.

Her heart was still heavy when she and Secotan's two other wives, Virginia and Manta, went to prepare Wanchese for what was coming. The girl sat quietly and listened to all the women had to tell her about the act of mating, seemingly having resigned herself to her fate.

"Do you have any questions?" Manta, the oldest of the three, asked when they were through.

"No," Wanchese answered.

Virginia and Manta turned to go. Dare hung back, reluctant to leave Wanchese alone.

"I'm going to stay a while," she said and the two older women nodded and left quietly.

Turning to face Wanchese, Dare was suddenly overcome with emotion and ran to her, throwing her arms around her and bursting into tears.

"I'm so sorry," she sobbed, thinking both of the girl before her and her husband sitting silently in their longhouse, "I wish there was something I could do."

Wanchese didn't know what to do. She was touched by the other woman's concern, but also confused. She hadn't thought anyone in the village cared what happened to her. She put her arms around Dare hesitantly.

"Thank you for trying to help," she said.

"This is so unfair!" Dare said as she stepped back and wiped the tears from her eyes.

"Yes, it is," Wanchese said softly. "I'll be alright," she added when Dare took her hand and seemed to search for the right words, as if there were any.

"I'll come back after the evening meal and help you bathe and prepare," she said.

"Alright," Wanchese said with a sad smile.

Dare gave her a last hug then turned and walked quickly out the door.

As soon as she was gone Wanchese began to carefully pack food, clothing, some small tools and utensils and what other things she would need to survive, into a large hide pack. She was grateful for Dare's support but if these people thought she was going to let herself be used and degraded just because one of their traditions said she had to, they were even bigger fools than she had thought.

She rolled her thick sleeping robe and her two heavy blankets into a bundle and tied them to the top of the pack. That done she filled her water bag in the nearby river and went back to her hut to wait. She would leave while the rest of the village was eating the evening meal. That would give her some time before Dare came and found her missing.

The morning passed more slowly than she would ever have thought possible and she was tempted more than once to just leave. But if they discovered she was missing while it was still full daylight, she'd never be able to escape. She needed the cover of darkness to have any chance at all.

Unable to sit still any longer, she spent the last half of the morning roaming the forest to the south and west of the village, collecting medicinal plants and herbs that she might not be able to find where she was going. She passed the oppressive heat of mid-day in her hut, grinding the herbs into powder and wrapping them in the large, three pronged leaves of a seli tree.

One of Kane's sons, a young boy of seven named Lake, walked past her hut in the early afternoon and she knew he'd been sent to make sure she was still there. Someone must have seen her in the forest and grown suspicious. She made a point of showing herself while pretending not to notice the boy and he quickly headed back to the village. She went back to waiting.

Finally, the day began to wane and the air began to cool. Walking outside and looking toward the village, she could see that smoke was rising from all of the longhouses. The women were preparing the evening meal. It was time for her to go.

But as she turned to step inside, she saw Kail, one of Geris Quick's wives, coming down the narrow path to her hut. She walked outside to meet her.

"My husband invites you to share our evening meal," Kail said. From the tone of her voice it was clear that she was the obedient but unenthusiastic bearer of this invitation. On any other day Wanchese would have accepted just to spite the older woman. But this was not any other day.

"Please tell Geris I thank him," she said. "But I prefer to eat alone."

Kail turned away quickly, afraid Wanchese might change her mind.

Smiling, Wanchese waited until the woman was out of sight then grabbed her pack and stepped into the forest behind her hut, heading toward the river. She had an idea she hoped would send the searchers in the wrong direction when they started looking for her. If it worked, it would gain her some precious time. And it just might work. Certainly no one would expect a woman alone to go to the mountains. She would have to be insane. Or maybe just desperate.

# CHAPTER 3

▼

# THE INCHASA

Capac stood and watched the small procession come to a halt beside the large roadside shelter, his face betraying none of his hatred as two rows of warriors at the procession's fore peeled off to the left and right, forming a protective wall on each side of the dusty road. Within these protective walls four tall, muscular bearers gently lowered the royal litter to the ground.

The litter, woven from the strong, pale reeds that grew along the edges of Lake Vilca-bamba beside the royal city of Pachacutec, was eight feet long and four feet wide. It had a raised roof of thatch from which hung hand woven panels of deep green cloth that enclosed the litter's occupant, protecting him from the elements. Embroidered on each of the cloth panels was the Inchasa imperial seal, a large golden sun crossed by a warrior's sword and lance, in shimmering gold, silver and red thread. A bearer pulled the panel that faced the roadside shelter aside and the young Cuzco stepped into the fading light of day.

The Cuzco, a tall, thin young man with an erect, noble bearing, had inherited the throne upon his father's death five months earlier. This was his first inspection tour as Cuzco and he found it all very exciting, though he would never allow any hint of his feelings to show. The Cuzco couldn't go around acting like a boy of thirteen. Not even if that was precisely what he was.

Capac watched as the boy walked slowly along the ranks, inspecting his detachment of warrior guards, nodding his approval. The young king took particular pleasure in the idea of himself as military commander of these strong, battle hardened men. Capac knew the boy longed to see them in actual combat, sometimes even wishing idly that someone would be foolish enough to defy him, or better yet, attack him so he could see them in action. Capac hoped the young fool got his wish, and soon.

Tall and gaunt, with a hard, weathered face that could be difficult to read in the best of circumstances and was now further clouded by bruised lips and a left eye that was swollen shut, Capac stood and waited. He wore a white ankle length robe of rough cloth and dark hide woven sandals. The front half of his head was shorn clean, the back covered by long, straight, dark hair pulled back and fastened into a tail behind his head. Burned into his forehead in black ink was an artless representation of two prostrate servants kneeling before a throne, the mark of a Lydacian, servant and interpreter of dreams and visions. It was a mark Capac had once worn proudly. Now it brought him only anger and shame.

"I have inspected the tambo, my Cuzco," he said as he bowed to the approaching king. "Everything is as it should be."

He turned and held out his hand in the direction of one of the men standing beside him.

"This is Tamor, overseer of this Tambo."

The overseer stepped forward and bowed before his king.

"We are honored by your visit, mighty Cuzco," he gushed.

Ignoring him, the young Cuzco stepped past and followed Capac into the tambo and to the room prepared for him.

This was the eighth roadside shelter they had inspected, each sited precisely one day's travel from the last. Tomorrow they would arrive in Atahuallpa, the city the recently deceased Cuzco had ordered constructed on the northern edge of the empire. Everyone in the party was tired of traveling and looked forward to reaching Atahuallpa, the young Cuzco most of all.

"See to the preparation of a meal, Capac," he ordered. "It would please me if there was some fish included." The tambo was situated beside the small half-moon shaped Lake Viracocha. "And tell Manco I invite him to dine with me this evening."

Capac bowed.

"I will see to it, my Cuzco."

The overseer, a short, pudgy little man of questionable intelligence, was beside himself with joy at the mention of the Cuzco's desire for fish with his meal. He scurried off, calling for the cooks to choose the best samples from the day's catch, ordering that they be cleaned and presented for his personal inspection.

Stepping outside, Capac walked over to Manco, the captain of the warrior escort, who was giving orders for camp to be set up and guards posted. Manco was responsible for Capac's swollen eye and broken lips as well as two cracked ribs and a festering sore caused by the heated tip of Manco's sword. It was with a mixture of fear and tightly controlled anger that Capac approached him now.

Manco was tall, a full head taller than any of the men under his command. Broad shouldered and heavily muscled, he was known for his almost freakish strength, great skill with any kind of weapon and a volcanic temper. His heavily pockmarked face, adorned with small, intense eyes that seemed too close together and an angry slash of a mouth that rarely smiled, was further marred by several long white scars that seemed almost to glow in contrast to his sun darkened skin. His head was clean-shaven and bore several scars as well, adding to the overall sense of menacing ugliness.

He was dressed in the warrior style; bare to the waist, his lower body covered by a knee length skirt and high, laced leggings that stopped just below his knees. Both the skirt and the leggings were made from the tough, dull grey hide of ripper cats, one of the fiercest of the many large, deadly predators found throughout the empire.

His sword hung in a scabbard that was tied around his neck and slung beneath the pit of his right arm so that it hung at a slight angle across his back, the sword's grip rising above his right shoulder for easy access. When night fell, bringing with it the bitter cold, he would drape a thick, full-length cloak of layered cloth over his shoulders. The cloak would fasten at the neck and was large enough to wrap fully around his body, protecting him from the cold while moving at night. His sword would of course be worn outside the cloak and kept at the ready.

He turned and smiled tauntingly as Capac approached. He disliked the Cuzco's personal servant. Not because he was a servant, a warrior after all was a servant in his own way, but because he was Lydacian. Why the Cuzco's trusted the strange servant priests he couldn't understand. They weren't Inchasa and would never be Inchasa. They were an odd, different people, a dying race that had been placed under Inchasa rule almost from the day his Inchasa ancestors had awakened in this place. He neither liked nor trusted them and had taken great pleasure in inflicting pain on Capac. The man had withstood far more than he had expected but, in the end, had told the Cuzco what he wanted to know.

"The Cuzco invites you to dine with him this evening," Capac said, avoiding the other man's eyes as he spoke.

"I would be honored, of course," Manco lied. He didn't like the new Cuzco, though he would give his own life to save the boy's without hesitation. He especially disliked being forced to spend his evenings retelling old stories of battles fought long ago. It was time to fight new battles. It had been too long and the men grew soft.

Turning away, Manco returned his attention to his men. They worked quickly and efficiently, having learned long ago that it was unwise to raise their commander's ire. He knew most of them hated him but he didn't care. Hate him or not, they would do what he told them to when he told them to and ask no questions. That was all he required of them.

And he in turn would do what the Cuzco told him to when he told him to. That was what he'd been trained for since his tenth year and he was too old to change now. Even if he had concerns about the boy, concerns he could never voice if he wanted to keep on living. But he couldn't turn a blind eye to what he saw either. He was one of the very few people who worked closely enough with the Cuzco to know that he was not a god as the people believed, but merely a man like any other. Or, in this case a boy like any other, with much to learn. Hopefully he would learn quickly. This inspection tour was a good beginning.

And it would be good to see Atahuallpa, he thought as he glanced out of the corner of his eye at the waiting Lydacian, knowing the man wouldn't dare leave until he gave him permission to do so. The recently completed Temple of the Sun was said to be truly magnificent, though he preferred to judge such things for himself. Unimpressed by beauty, he judged a structure based on the functionality of its design and the quality of the stone work. It was hard to imagine a temple more impressive than Pachacutec's.

He would also be inspecting the Atahuallpa garrison. They knew he was coming and he expected the captain there would have everything in order. He would find something to be displeased with anyway. Then he and the garrison commander, who just happened to be his brother, would move to the captain's quarters where the two of them would share a good meal and better drink. Leruk always had good drink.

His brother was a fool, one who believed that the men under his command would fight harder for a captain they liked and respected, a notion Manco found utterly absurd. But, besides having good food and excellent wine, Leruk had a well shaped river woman he'd captured several years earlier and he was always willing to share with his older brother.

And Manco had to admit that Leruk's warriors were always well trained and in good physical condition. Reports he'd received even suggested that the Atahuallpa garrison was being expanded in anticipation of more warriors being sent there as the city itself began to grow. There was wisdom in that. Not only because the garrison would indeed need to grow as the city did, but also because idle warriors soon became troublesome warriors. Better to keep them busy.

But no man would ever convince him that warriors would fight harder for a leader who showed them kindness. He knew beyond any doubt that his men would fight with all that was within them when the time came. Not because they liked or respected him, but because they were more afraid of him than they were of the enemy. That was leadership.

"How is your side?" he asked Capac with a taunting smile. He had enjoyed hearing the arrogant fool beg for mercy before finally giving up the deepest secrets of his people. He had needed to be put in his place for a long time but the previous Cuzco wouldn't allow it. The boy had been easily convinced, however.

"The wound is infected," Capac said in a flat voice.

"Of course it is," Manco said with another smile. "I dipped the tip of my sword in feces before cutting you that last time. You probably don't remember that, of course. I think you had already lost consciousness by then."

Capac said nothing, though his every thought was of hatred and revenge. They should have killed him. They would pay someday for what they'd done to him.

"I had heard of your book," Manco said. The book was supposed to be a Lydacian secret, though the Cuzco's had known of it's existence for years. "I had thought it was only a legend. I look forward to hearing what it has to say."

Again Capac said nothing. They had torn from him the knowledge of the book and of it's hiding place. And they had tortured him until he told them the secret of the herb. He would never be able to forgive himself for his weakness. He had betrayed his oath and his people.

There weren't many of them left, less than a thousand. His once proud, gentle people had been reduced to little more than a withering pocket of strangers in their own land, surviving only on the hope the sacred book gave them. And now even that would be lost. Because of him. Why did he have to be so weak?

"Next I will convince our young Cuzco that we no longer need you since we will have all of your secrets," Manco said with obvious relish. "I think I'll suggest that we kill all the males and use the females as whores. Before long you'll be only a faint memory. And then not even that."

Capac's limbs trembled as he struggled to control himself.

Manco laughed.

"Are you alright?" he asked with mock concern. "I hope I haven't upset you. I'm sure your mother and your sisters will be fine. They might even like being whores. You can never tell with women.

Now Capac lost control. Turning, he threw himself at the big warrior with fury and abandon, his eyes bulging with hate, his hands reaching desperately for the other man's throat. Manco knocked his arms aside and struck him savagely across his already bruised face. Capac fell to the ground with a groan. Laughing, Manco kicked him several times in the head and ribs before walking away, leaving Capac to lie on the cold ground, whimpering.

It was a long time before Capac was able to gather enough strength to drag himself to his knees and he was shivering with cold by the time he managed it. Pushing himself to his feet, he stood for a moment on unsteady legs then made his way carefully to the western edge of the steep roofed storage building beside the tambo. There he gathered his blankets and pack and moved away into the darkness to be alone.

He gathered some sticks from a nearby copse of trees and started a fire. Then he collected as much wood as he could lay his hands on and sat down to warm himself, sitting on one of his blankets and wrapping himself in the other two. It would be a long night, the bitter cold of the air exceeded only by the cold emptiness of his despair.

They had forced him to tell the Cuzco how to prepare the herb, how to moisten the leaves with the holy water until they gave off their dream giving smoke. He wondered if the boy was using the herb at that very moment. And if he was, did the herb have the same effect on Inchasa that it had on Lydacians? Would it give the boy the visions he sought? Or perhaps, he thought with a flicker of hope, would it cause the boy to have frightening dreams of pain and death? Or better yet, might it actually cause him sickness or death?

But no, he doubted that. Whether the herb would give the Cuzco true visions he couldn't say, but he hoped not. And even if it did, the boy had no training in the discerning of what he saw. It was not a simple thing to make sense of one's own vision. The Cuzco might need a Lydacian for that. It was something to hope for, at least. He needed all the hope he could get just then. So did his people.

Tomorrow they would arrive in Atahuallpa. He would have to risk making contact with some of his people there to tell them what had happened. It was too late to save the book, he could never get word to Pachacutec before the royal messenger arrived with the Cuzco's instructions for it's recovery, but there might still be a chance for some of his people to escape, especially women and children. Better to risk death while attempting escape than to submit to what the Inchasa had in mind.

Adding fuel to his small fire, he spread his blanket out on the ground and laid down gingerly. Whatever healing had taken place since his first beating had been undone by the second. It felt like every bone in his body was cracked or broken and he had trouble finding a position that would allow at least some small degree of comfort. Wrapping himself in his blankets and moving as close to the flames as he could without catching himself on fire, he drifted off to sleep.

He awoke hours later with a gasp, his eyes opening yet seeing nothing that was around him, his mind caught up in the vision that engulfed it. Some small corner of his mind told him it was impossible to have a vision without the aid of the herb. The rest soaked in every image, every sound, every sensation. After a moment even that small corner of his mind gave in to the wonder of the vision, not caring if it was a true vision or not, just so long as it eased some of the overwhelming sense of hopelessness, if only for a few moments.

The vision faded after a short time and he came back to himself. Throwing more wood on the fire, he sat up and tried to remember everything he'd seen. Could it be a true vision? Even without the herb? It felt just as powerful as any vision he'd ever had, just as vivid and real. But it was impossible. His mind must have been playing tricks on him, finding a familiar way to combat his guilt and fear, trying to give him some small reason to go on.

Lying back on his blanket, he looked up at the twin moons that filled the night sky, one slightly larger than the other, both giving off a reddish-white light that gave the sky around them a pinkish tinge. And then it happened. It passed so quickly that he feared his mind was playing tricks on him again. But no, he had seen it. He was sure of it.

It had been just like in the vision, a bright shaft of blue light streaking across the face of both moons like the powerful slash of a mighty sword of vengeance! It had cut across the top of the larger moon and the bottom of the smaller one, exactly as in his vision. It was a sign! It had to be!

He laughed out loud, the noise sounding so strange to his ears that he realized suddenly he hadn't laughed in years. Smiling, he covered himself tightly and moved closer to the fire again. It was a long time before he drifted off to sleep again, his excited mind trying to understand in a matter of minutes what would take several days of careful thought and consideration to interpret. He finally forced his mind to quiet down and drifted off to catch a few hours sleep before morning. He awoke at dawn, a new sense of hope in his breast, a new vitality coursing through his aching body.

Yes, he thought as he built up his fire and began to prepare a meager breakfast, he would definitely have to risk contacting the Lydacians in Atahuallpa. He had so much to tell them!

# CHAPTER 4

▼

# NEW BEGINNINGS

She was being followed. Wanchese was sure of it now. She could hear the small sounds they made as they moved carefully through the darkness. Her little ruse to send them in the wrong direction had failed. And they were getting closer. Taking her knife from its sheath at her waist, she turned to face them. She would not go back. She would die first.

He would be leading the chase, she knew. And he would be coming to kill her. Not right away. He would use her first. But once he had exacted the price of his warrior pride, Hunter Kane would kill her.

The others wouldn't know that. They would be searching for her out of concern for her safety. Certainly Secotan would be, and Geris. But even they couldn't help her now. She had defied their law and disobeyed Secotan's ruling. No one could help her now. So, she would die here in these strangely beautiful mountains. But she would die on her own terms, not Kane's.

Moving to the edge of a small clearing where the light of the twin moons would give her a little more visibility, she gripped her knife and waited for Kane to step from the darkness. These were dangerous mountains, especially at night. There was little doubt that when she sprang from the darkness and struck at Kane, at least one of the others would strike her down before realizing it was her and not a ripper cat or deathclaw. She would have to make the first strike a sure one. It was the only one she would get.

She could hear the sounds of their movements clearly now as they approached the clearing. Dropping into a crouch, she waited anxiously, coiled to strike. Almost too late she heard the voices. For a quick second her mind refused to believe what her ears were telling her. But there could be no mistake!

She stepped back quickly, deeper into the darkness, kneeling within some thick brush, her heart beating so loudly she thought surely they must hear it. Sitting down quietly, she placed her pack on the ground beside her and pulled her knees into her chest, trying to make herself as small as possible. Through the brush she watched the clearing.

The men who stepped from the darkness were the fierce men of her nightmares, the ones who had attacked her village so long ago. These were Inchasa. Not the tall, ugly one who had taken her parents from her, but his kind, his people.

Six of them stepped into the clearing and she could see their swords fastened outside their dark cloaks, the hilts rising above each man's right shoulder. This was the first time she'd seen an Inchasa since the day of her parent's death and she was filled with a confusing mixture of fear and hatred, feeling all at once an almost overwhelming desire to run away and find safety and an equally powerful urge to strike out at those who had taken so much from her. Wise enough not to let either emotion control her, she stayed where she was.

Then the men dropped their packs and began to unsling their weapons and she realized with horror that they were stopping to set up camp for the night. Now she had no choice but to move. They would want a fire. And a fire meant wood. They would almost surely find her if she stayed where she was.

Taking a deep breath, she stood soundlessly, knowing the darkness would keep her hidden as long as she made no noise. Then she lifted her pack and moved away through the forest, moving north as it seemed the Inchasa were heading south. She moved slowly. Only when the men began to move into the forest around the clearing in search of wood did she begin to move more quickly, hoping the sound of their movements would mask her own.

Soon she was far enough away to feel relatively safe. Sitting on a large stone, she rested until her heart and breathing returned to normal then moved off again, wanting to put more distance between herself and the Inchasa before stopping for the night. She wanted to have a good start on them if they noticed signs of her passing in the morning and came looking for her.

It was a long time later that she finally felt secure enough to stop. Finding a large sour tree surrounded by heavy brush, she crawled through the brush and sat, leaning her back against the tree's smooth skin, covering herself with her heavy sleeping robe and thick blankets. She would wait out the night here. The pungent smell of the sour tree would prevent predators from picking up her scent. And the best way to keep Kane or the Inchasa from noticing her in the darkness was to make no sound. And she was tired. More tired than she had ever been in her life.

The night was bitterly cold, even with her robe and blankets. She longed for a warm fire but told herself it wasn't worth the risk. Better to be cold than dead. Or captured. Wrapping herself tightly, she made herself as comfortable as she could and slowly drifted off to sleep; a restless sleep filled with dreams of pain and fear and loss.

She woke just as the first light of day was beginning to brighten the small patches of sky she could see through the dense forest around her. Standing, she took a short drink from her water bag then rolled her robe and blankets neatly and tied them to her pack. She ate a small illo gourd as she started off to the north, letting the sweet juices run down her throat, wishing she had more. There were only three of the small, yellow gourds left of the ten she had started out with. It would be good to set some snares and eat something more filling. But that would have to wait until she got higher into the mountains.

The cold of night quickly gave way to the warmth of day and her muscles soon felt loose and relaxed as she made her way higher and higher. She had spent a lot of time in the thin forest near the river as a girl, following her mother as she searched for roots and herbs or her father as he set snares for small game or hunted.

After her parents' death, Secotan had given her to an old woman whose children had all died of disease or warfare, hoping the two of them would help to sooth the other's loss. Instead, the woman had treated Wanchese more like a servant than a child, forcing her to take care of all the household chores, often calling her cruel names and telling her how ugly her scarred face was. The girl had taken to finishing her chores quickly then running off to the forest to set snares, gather herbs and remember her mother and father.

And as she'd wandered, she'd remembered all the things her parents had strived to teach her. She found she could remember her mother's voice pointing out which roots and herbs were good to eat or useful as medicines. And she heard again the patient voice of her father telling her how to move through the forest soundlessly, how to catch, skin and clean small game and how to read the signs the forest had to show those who would be still and look for them.

Though it was a hard life it had forced her to grow up quickly. And when the old woman died of fever, twelve year old Wanchese had refused to be taken in by anyone, insisting she was old enough to care for herself. She'd had no intention of being anyone else's servant. Secotan had allowed her to do as she wished, promising to watch over her as best he could. And he had. Until she'd needed him most.

Thinking of the village as she made her way along, she wondered if she and Dare Samuels might have become friends if she hadn't been forced to flee. Dare had begun coming to visit her fairly often over the last few months. It would have been good to have a friend. She couldn't remember ever having had one.

As full day broke, bringing with it a dry, powerful heat, she began to move west, rather than north, though she was still climbing higher. She was beginning to enjoy the physical effort more and more as she became more accustomed to it. It felt good to be moving, to be free, and she kept up a steady pace until her ragged, labored breathing signaled the approach of mid-day.

Then she stretched out beneath the shade of a low limbed tree and fell instantly asleep, confident in the knowledge that no one and no thing could move about in the overwhelming heat the next two hours would bring. They would have no more choice than she did herself. At mid-day you sought shelter or you died. It was just that simple.

She awoke just as the heat began to fade back down to a tolerable level and started off to the west once more. She moved steadily all through the rest of the day, though she was forced to move south for a short time to avoid what sounded like a deathclaw moving through the brush to the north. At nightfall she made a dry camp within a cluster of grey boulders that allowed several different avenues of escape should she be discovered, and spent another long, cold night huddled within her robe and blankets.

And that became the pattern of her life. For six days she climbed, stopping only at mid-day when the heat made travel impossible and at night when the forest made travel unwise. Her illo gourds were soon gone but she was able to gather other edible plants, roots and gourds as she traveled. By the third day she felt confident enough in her escape to start building a small fire at night, though she still took pains to keep it as well hidden as possible. The small flame brought her a measure of comfort and eased her mind more than she would have imagined.

The mountains began to change as she climbed, the forest beginning to thin slightly, different types of trees and vegetation taking the place of those that thrived at lower elevations. She was forced to cross and climb more ledges of rock as well. The only real constants were the heat of day and the cold of night. And the sounds of the forest.

She saw the tracks of deathclaws, ripper cats and two towed boars. These she gave a wide berth, especially if the tracks looked fresh. There were smaller animals though and she managed to kill a rooter, a small, six legged, longhaired forager. The hot meal renewed her strength and her confidence that she could survive out here on her own.

As the sun was descending toward the northern horizon, marking the close of her ninth day of freedom, she found a large spring surrounded by thick, dry brush and stopped to drink and fill her water bag. She spent the night beside the spring, knowing that nothing could get near her without first moving through the dry brush, nearly impossible to do quietly. She slept well and took the time to bathe and change into a fresh dress before starting off again in the morning.

Still moving west, she was momentarily forced to circle to the south around a large blackrock cliff that looked to her like a huge black finger thrust up out of the ground to accuse the sky of some unknown misdeed. On the southern edge of the cliff a wide, uneven shelf of blackrock opened up between the cliff and the tree line to the south and west.

She had gone only a few feet out onto the shelf when she sensed, more than heard, a rustling of movement behind her. Cursing herself for not being more careful, she pulled her knife from it's sheath and turned to face whomever it was who had found her, more determined than ever to die rather than let anyone make a servant of her. These few days of freedom had shown her what life could be and she was no longer willing to accept anything less.

She turned, clutching her knife tightly, hoping to find one of her pursuers within striking distance. But instead of finding herself facing Hunter Kane or an Inchasa, she turned to find herself looking straight into the powerfully muscled chest of a deathclaw!

She stood, momentarily frozen with fear, unable to will her legs to move. The beast was huge! It's sable coat glistened in the early morning sunlight as it stepped toward her on it's short hind legs, it's long, deadly fore legs free to rip and tear. It's coat blended in with the surrounding blackrock, making the yellow-whiteness of its teeth and claws seem even more menacing.

For a moment it just stood there, towering over her, seeming to look right past her as the seconds dragged by. Collecting herself, she decided she would die fighting, not running. The decision seemed to chase all the fear out of her and she stood tall, determined to die as bravely as her parents had. She dropped her pack and watched the beast, knowing it would strike once and then wait for her to turn and run. The seconds dragged by and still the beast didn't move. What was it waiting for?

# CHAPTER 5

▼

# TIDES OF DESTINY

Crawling to the edge of the shaded pool, Mitchell Harvey drank. He tried to drink slowly as he'd been told you were supposed to after a long thirst, but instead he gulped deeply, desperately, his tortured body pleading frantically for more. With an effort he finally forced himself to slow down, to breath to feel the wonderful paradox of the cool water running down his parched throat, causing a searing pain yet giving such overwhelming relief. Slowly the pain began to fade, leaving only the pleasure, the relief.

So, he was going to live. Lowering his naked, horribly sunburned body into the pool's inviting coolness, he wondered if that was a blessing or a curse. The way he felt, it was probably only delaying the inevitable. Still, at least now when he died it wouldn't be from choking on his own tongue.

Looking up at the strange, smooth skinned trees that surrounded the small pool of water, he was grateful for the shade they provided. He'd wandered for two full days, the huge merciless sun of this strange place beating down on his unprotected flesh. And for two nights he'd stumbled along, unable to stop moving, afraid the mind numbing cold would kill him if he did.

Toward the end of the second night he'd finally left behind the dry, shade-less plain of coarse brown grass on which he'd awakened into this nightmare, and started a slow ascent into these heavily wooded hills. He'd stumbled on the water purely by chance. And just in time. He doubted he could have made it through another night.

Looking down at his body, soaking beneath the gloriously cool water, he laughed bitterly. He'd been wanting to find the time to get out more, to get some sun and exercise. He was certainly getting all he could ever want of both now. And judging by the constant pain of want in his stomach he wasn't going to have any trouble losing those unwanted extra pounds either.

And funniest of all, here he was stumbling and crawling around this nightmare of a place, his skin feeling like it was on fire, his cracked and bleeding feet becoming more painful with every step, hunger knawing constantly at his empty belly, and what he felt most was alive, so very much alive! It had been a long time.

He wasn't even sure when he'd lost it, that boundless energy of childhood, the ability of a young mind to see excitement and possibility everywhere. But, lost it he had. Looking back over his adult life, especially the years since he'd left the military and started concentrating on building a successful business, it struck him suddenly that he hadn't been living at all. He'd been surviving.

Well, now that he was living, surviving was becoming something of a problem. Wherever this place was, and he had no idea where that might be, never mind how the hell he'd gotten there, it wasn't exactly friendly.

For what he guessed to be about two hours every afternoon the heat became so unbearable that the simple act of walking made his lungs feel like they were going to collapse and his heart as though it would burst. He'd thought he was going to die that first day until he stopped and covered himself with the long, coarse grass of the plain. It had given him just enough cover to keep breathing.

On top of that, combined with the bone freezing cold of night, any plants or grasses he'd tried to eat had only left him violently sick to his stomach. And worse, they'd left him even thirstier than he'd been before. He'd been lucky to find this water when he had and he knew it.

He also had no clothing to protect him from the heat of the day or the cold of night and no weapon to protect himself or hunt. All in all, he was pretty well screwed. So why did he find himself noticing how beautiful everything around him was? What made these trees different from the hundreds of others he'd seen? Or this sky? And why did he suddenly feel whole? Alton would say he had a few screws loose. And he might be right.

Grabbing hold of a protruding root, he pulled himself out of the deep pool. Breaking off some long, slim leaves from a nearby bush, he spread them on the ground beside the pool and laid down, hoping the leaves wouldn't give him a rash. He had enough problems.

He was tired. It felt good to just lie down, and to be in the shade, and to be able to breath. He needed some sleep. Resting his head on his arms, he struggled to slow his racing mind and breathing. Taking long, slow, deep breaths, he forced his mind to focus a little more each time he slowly exhaled. Within a matter of minutes he was focused and under control, his growling stomach the only part of his body that refused to be still. He drifted off to sleep wishing he could meditate himself up a hot meal. Or a cold meal for that matter.

Several hours later he awakened with a start. The day was coming to an end and there was the hint of a chill in the air. Wondering what it was that had awakened him, he bent over the edge of the pool and took a long drink then splashed his face with water.

Suddenly the peaceful quiet was rent in two by an anguished scream. It came from below the pool, back toward the bottom of the hills and the wide plain. Standing, he winced with pain. His feet hurt even more after the short rest.

Walking gingerly and moving carefully from tree to tree he made his way down the shallow slope toward the scream. He'd hobbled some two hundred yards when he heard male voices laughing and yelling in language he didn't recognize. Dropping into a crouch, he moved forward quietly.

Peering through some tall, wide leafed brush he saw them. There across a long, narrow clearing stood five dark skinned, smooth faced men. No clothing covered their dark, muscular upper bodies, revealing a wide array of intricate tattoos and piercings. Each had what looked like a sword strapped to his back and several of them carried wooden bows and quivers of arrows, others long spears. Below the waist they wore a knee length skirt made of grey animal hide and on their feet high laced moccasins of the same material.

At their feet laid the body of the woman who's screams had awakened him. A sixth man lay next to her, laughing and howling like an animal while he tried to get his skirt back in order. One look told Mitch there would be no more screams. The woman's eyes were open but there was no life in them.

One of the men, a short, deep chested young man with long, bloody scratches on his face and neck, took his spear, raised it high in his right hand and thrust it into the poor woman's lifeless body. The brutal violence of it shocked and enraged Mitch and he felt his body begin to tremble as he fought to control his emotions.

The men took off their weapons and dug into the large hide packs each of them carried, coming out with long, thick capes that they slipped around their shoulders and fastened at the neck before slinging their swords across their back again. That done they set out, moving downhill toward the plain below.

Mitch knew there was nothing he could do except to get himself killed too, but it still seemed wrong to just let them walk away. In the end, the hopelessness of confronting six armed men, especially in the shape he was in, forced its way through his rage and he stayed where he was, feeling frustrated and a little ashamed.

When he could no longer hear them descending through the forest below, he stood and stepped into the clearing. And nearly vomited. There at his feet, previously hidden from view, lay the horribly mutilated corpse of a man. His throat had been slashed and his torso cut open and pulled wide, his entrails spilling out onto the blood soaked ground around him. His face was badly beaten and bruised, his nose and mouth caked with dried blood.

It was several long minutes before Mitch was able to regain his composure. Then, taking a closer look at the man's face, he could see immediately that he was not at all like the men who had killed him. His hair was short and evenly cut and his battered face showed a short stubble, as if having gone unshaven for several days. His face and neck were sunburned and raw, the skin of his torso a pale white.

Hobbling over to the woman's limp form he gently turned her face toward him. Her hair looked well kept and evenly cut, though obviously uncombed. Her face and neck were sunburned as well as her arms and lower legs. Mitch had a feeling these two didn't belong there any more than he did.

Reaching out, he closed the woman's unseeing eyes and pulled her leather garment, bunched up around her belly by the men who had raped and killed her, down over her hips, past her thighs, covering her, giving her back what dignity he could. Then he picked her up and placed her beside the man. Having nothing to bury them with he covered their bodies with loose brush and stone. It wasn't enough but it was the best he could do.

He was tempted to take the woman's garment but after what had been done to her it just seemed too obscene to leave her there naked. The man's clothing was useless, having been cut and torn from his body, though Mitch did take his moccasins. They were a little too small but he was in no position to be picky. There was an empty pack lying to one side of the clearing and he rolled that up to take it with him.

He left the clearing just as full darkness fell. The cold moved in quickly, chilling him to the bone before he'd gone even half a mile up the steepening slope before him. It was tough going, stumbling through the thick brush and trees, all the time climbing higher.

Still, he kept moving. To stop was to freeze to death. Besides, he wanted to be as far away from that clearing as possible by morning. If those butchers came back they would see what he'd done and might come looking for him. And he was in no condition to face them. Not yet.

Struggling along, his mind slipping into that detached, meandering state that allows a man's body to endure extended physical labor and hardship without losing the will to go on, he climbed ever higher, all the while wondering about this place he had awakened to.

It was unlike any planet he'd ever seen before. The trees and rocks, even the soil itself, were of unusual textures and colors. He didn't recognize any of the animal life either. And he'd traveled widely, having visited over twenty different worlds in the course of his military and business life. Of course it was possible his perspective was somewhat skewed regarding this world. On those other planets he hadn't been stumbling around naked, wondering if you could eat tree bark.

Stopping to rest, he leaned against a thick, rough skinned tree, hugging his arms tightly around himself and clamping his hands within his armpits for warmth. He could hear the sounds of the forest and it's inhabitants and some of them sounded none too friendly. Hopefully they were as afraid of the clumsy oaf stumbling around in the dark as the clumsy oaf was of them. With a small smile at that thought, he set out again up the slope.

By sunrise he had reached the top of the slope he'd been climbing, crossed a low, rock-strewn ridge and started up an even higher peak. He'd been tempted to crawl down the ridge into a small, heavily wooded valley below, thinking there was a good chance he'd find water there. Some very loud, unmistakably unfriendly animals had changed his mind. If they looked anything like they sounded, up was definitely the way to go.

When the heat grew unbearable he stopped and rested in the shade of a wide limbed, yellow tree with thin, dry leaves that crumbled at his touch. He dozed off and on, dreaming of a cool drink and a long shower, then started off again when the heat subsided.

He climbed all that day and four more, soon moving high enough that there were fewer trees and more stones, a fact his aching feet found not the least bit to their liking. It wasn't long before his moccasins were torn and tattered and he was forced to go on barefoot. Coming to a wide shelf of black rock that led to a large, black cliff, he sat down to rest. He'd have to go around the cliff before he could go any further.

Just as he was gathering the strength to heave himself off the ground, a woman stepped from the trees directly opposite him and walked several steps out onto the shelf, looking around warily.

She was young, late teens or early twenties if he were to guess, with long, dark hair, parted in the middle that fell well below her shoulders. Her skin was smooth, tanned a deep brown. Her right eye was covered by a round patch and he could see where a scar continued down her cheek and behind her ear. She was dressed in a sleeveless, knee length dress of leather or hide and wore low, mouse-colored moccasins on her feet. She was a very shapely woman and beautiful despite the patch and scar.

He was still trying to decide whether he should call out to her or try to follow her secretly to wherever it was she lived, when a huge, black animal stepped from the forest behind her. Sensing the movement, the woman dropped the pack she carried in her left hand, drew a long knife from a sheath at her waist and turned to face the beast.

The thing was huge! Standing on its short hind legs it loomed over the woman, waving it's long, sharp clawed fore legs at her. Its body was thick and powerfully muscled, it's neck long and surprisingly thin. The head was large but narrow with an elongated snout filled with long, needle like teeth.

Pushing himself to his feet, Mitch stepped out onto the rock shelf. The thing lifted its gaze from the woman and looked right at him, its large, red rimmed, black eyes alive with bloodlust. Mitch froze where he stood, torn within himself. If he tried to help the woman he would die. There was no doubt about that. He really didn't want to die, not now. He was just starting to really live. Why did this have to happen now?

He'd always wondered what he'd do in a situation like this, when it was his life or someone else's. He'd always told himself he would have the courage to do what needed to be done, even to die well if necessary. Now he realized that no man could know for sure how he would react to a life and death situation until he faced one in reality. And this was his situation, his chance to see what kind of man he really was. He had to decide what he was going to do with it, and he had to decide right now.

# CHAPTER 6

▼

# TIDES OF CHANGE

Emerging from his longhouse, Secotan Samuels stood in the gathering darkness, gazing to the west and the Pemisipan Mountains. Hearing soft footsteps behind him, he knew it was Dare even before she slipped her arm around his waist and rested her head on his shoulder, wanting to share in his burden without intruding. He sometimes wished he could read his young wife's thoughts as easily as she seemed to read his.

"She will die out there alone," he said, giving voice to his fears. "She'll die and it will be my fault."

"If you want to blame someone, husband," Dare replied gently, "blame the fool who wanted to force her into his bed but wasn't willing to wed her. She ran away from him, not you."

"No," Secotan said sadly. "She ran away from all of us."

Wanchese had been gone for fourteen days now and Secotan hadn't slept a full night since, often finding himself rising at all hours of the night to walk quietly through the sleeping village. An old and almost forgotten tradition had been more important to him than one of his people and the burden of his decision weighed heavily on the Village Councillor.

"You made the only decision you could," Dare broke into his thoughts. "And so did she."

"You knew she would run?" he asked in surprise, turning to face her.

"No," Dare answered. "But I've done some thinking and I think I would have done the same in her place."

"Why?" he asked, wanting desperately to understand but not sure he could. If Wanchese was where he thought she was, the girl might as well have committed suicide.

"Because there are worse things than dying, husband."

The truth of that struck him like a blow. Yes, there were worse things than dying. That would explain the girl's refusal to submit to Kane. But what about the young warriors who had offered to take Wanchese as a wife?

"She could have accepted one of the other warriors," he said. "There would have been no shame in that."

Dare smiled. Her husband was a wonderful man, but he sometimes understood women little better than Kane did.

"A weaker woman might have been willing to accept that," she said. "But simply being a wife would never be enough for Wanchese. She wanted someone who truly cared about her, someone to share her life with, not just someone to be with."

"Couldn't a marriage to one of the young warriors have grown into that in time?"

"Possibly. But if it didn't she would have doomed herself to a life without love. Perhaps that wasn't enough for her."

Secotan nodded. Looking at it from that perspective he could see how unfair his decision must have seemed to Wanchese. But he couldn't look at it only from that one perspective. As Village Councillor he had to do what was best for the entire village. And he had a responsibility to the Councillor's of the other villages, just as they had a responsibility to him. And together they were charged with upholding the laws and traditions of their people. Even ancient, unused traditions born of another time, a time when their ancestors' survival had been by no means assured.

Would his decision have been any different if it had been one of his own daughters? But no, if the girl's father had been alive the problem never would have come up at all. He would have seen to it that Wanchese was wed by the lawful age. It might have cost him a little more than was customary, but he would have seen to it. Perhaps he should have made arrangements himself. He would have if he'd known what danger the girl was in. He simply hadn't seen the trouble coming.

Wanchese had been just a skinny little girl with a scar across her face and her soul. With her parents gone, she'd been disfigured, different and alone. After suf-

fering verbal abuse from some of the village children and cruelty at the hands of a
few witless adults, the girl had quickly grown sullen and withdrawn, spending
most of her time roaming the forest, speaking only when spoken to and sometimes not even then. No one had paid any attention when her sixteenth year
passed without her being wed. No one was interested anyway.

Then, seemingly overnight, her body had begun to blossom and she was no
longer just a skinny little girl. She very quickly became a not so skinny young
woman and the changes were both distinct and impossible to ignore. Men began
to notice her when she walked through the village and he had hoped the sudden
changes would encourage one of the young warriors to seek Wanchese as a wife.
To his way of thinking there were worse things than a wife who didn't like to
talk.

But Wanchese had resisted the advances of the young warriors. And Hunter
Kane had claimed the right of an ancient tradition, long unused and almost forgotten. A tradition born of a time when their ancestors were struggling desperately to survive in a strange and dangerous place, a time and place where
motherhood had been, of necessity, an obligation and a duty, not a choice.

Life was brutally hard and people were lost at a frightening rate to disease,
hunger and predators. Desperation can make men cruel as few things can and the
tradition was born that any young woman who reached her sixteenth year without being wed would be duty bound to give herself to any man who wanted her.
Any child born of the mating would become the responsibility of the man
believed to be the father. The woman would become a nursemaid to the child
and a household servant.

It was a thing no man would want for his child and fathers began to see to it
that their daughters were wed early, often paying for the privilege with crops, fish,
goods and even their own labor. As a result, the tradition hadn't been enforced in
over two hundred years when Kane made his demands of Wanchese, though its
memory was kept alive in the stories told around village campfires.

Tradition was a sacred thing among them, the sheltering cloak that had
brought them through the darkness and allowed them to survive and flourish.
There had been little he could have done for Wanchese without changing in a
matter of minutes the beliefs of over five hundred years. That the girl would run
was a thing he had never expected. Where could she go?

They had searched for her, of course. Finding tracks leading to the river, Kane
and some others ran to the steep bank where a small, thin warrior named Metan
Miller noticed that his dugout was missing. Reasoning that the girl would want
to travel as quickly as possible, Kane had decided to ignore the two villages sited

upstream and set out to search the two sited downstream. Secotan and four others had gone with him, afraid of what he might do to the girl when he found her. Geris Quick had gone upstream just to be sure.

Secotan had returned several days later with a heavy heart, Kane with a hot, lustful anger that bubbled just beneath the surface of his already raw temper. He had even privately accused Secotan of having helped the girl escape. How else could she have disappeared so completely?

To the east, across the river, were vast rock strewn, short grassed hills where nothing would grow and little could live. To the north lay a barren desert of stone inhabited by a strange, quiet people who built their homes among the cliffs, refusing to trade or even talk, wanting only to be left alone. To the west lay the cultivated lands of the five river villages. Beyond that a sparse forest and then, further west, the Pemisipan Mountains where even the bravest hunters preferred to travel in groups for fear of mountain predators.

Looking again to those far off mountains, Secotan felt deep within his heart that Wanchese was dead.

"I think she went up there," he said, pointing to the towering, wooded peaks.

Dare shivered at the thought, pulling herself closer to her husband.

"Then she is either very brave or very foolish," she said, thinking of the torn, withered bodies of hunters mauled by the talons of a deathclaw.

"She is likely just very dead," Secotan said quietly. "The brave die just as easily as the foolish in that place."

It struck him then that if keeping to his people's traditions brought him the pain he felt now thinking of Wanchese, it also brought him the comfort he felt now thinking of Dare. Though he had grown to love her more deeply than he would have ever dreamed possible, he had only married her out of respect for tradition.

He had saved her life during the same Inchasa raid in which Wanchese's parents had been killed. Dare had been kicking and screaming as an enemy warrior tried to drag her off. She had just bitten his arm and the warrior had apparently decided she wasn't worth the trouble. His sword had been raised and ready to strike when Secotan had come up behind him and killed the man with his hand axe. He'd sent Dare off to hide in the brush beside the river and returned to the battle, giving no more thought to her.

He'd been truly surprised when she had come and offered herself to him in the aftermath of the battle. This too was an old and seldom used tradition, that an unmarried woman of the proper age who owed her life to the bravery and skill of a warrior must offer herself to him as a wife in return for his kindness.

To refuse would have been an insult, both to Dare and to her father, and insult that would have resulted in a challenge to combat. Having no desire to kill a good man, a man he considered a friend, Secotan had accepted the girl's offering, thanking her father for the honor.

Three days later he'd stood in the presence of friends and family and pledged himself to a girl half his age, filled with doubts about his ability to be a good husband to someone so young and the fear that his other wives would never accept her. But Dare was no ordinary girl.

She'd proven herself a tireless worker, always willing to do her share and a little more. She had fit herself into the pattern of their life and added to the fullness of it, very quickly changing from a shy, quiet girl into a confident, capable young woman.

Over time he'd come to trust her judgment and to depend on her strength and good advice. He could tell her his dreams without fear of her thinking him foolish, and his fears without fear of her thinking him less of a man. He was fortunate to have such a woman. And he owed that good fortune to an old, seldom used tradition. How then could he simply disregard tradition when it wasn't to his liking?

"Come," he said, taking her by the hand. "It's getting cold."

Dare walked beside him to their longhouse, saddened that she didn't know what to say to help her husband. She had discussed it with Virginia and Manta in hopes that they might know what to do. They were older and had been with Secotan longer, but neither of them had been of any help. Manta said that the feelings of helplessness she was suffering were the price of being married to a good man, a man who cared about other people. Virginia thought it was the price of being married to the Village Councillor, a man with heavy responsibilities. Either way, they said, it was something Secotan would have to work out for himself.

Dare had a hard time accepting that. For the first time in a very long time she felt completely helpless. She had forgotten how terribly frustrating it could be. As they stepped through the doorway and into the longhouse she wished silently that it was her night to lie with Secotan. At least then she could hold him, and he could hold her.

# CHAPTER 7

▼

# ATAHUALLPA

The Temple of the Sun in Atahuallpa was indeed magnificent. It's exquisitely carved and perfectly fitted walls were built of a dull red stone not found in other parts of the empire. When contrasted against the beautifully crafted pillars of glistening blackrock that formed the Circle of Time at the very center of the temple, the dull red seemed to speak of indestructible strength and beauty.

The city that was just beginning to sprout up around the temple was also beautiful. The broad central avenue was formed of a grey stone that matched almost exactly that of the ripper cat's hide. The drainage ditch that ran along one side of the avenue was made from the plentiful blackrock, the sunken aqueduct on the opposite side formed of sparkling white silkstone. Even here the craftsmanship was without flaw, the stones fitting together so seamlessly that the tip of a sharp sword would not fit between them.

With the temple and central avenue completed, work had begun on the royal palace. When the palace was completed the mummy of the Cuzco's father would be brought to Atahuallpa and placed in the upper level. The lower levels would be occupied by the regional governor, his family and the palace servants. The red stone for this project was being quarried in a new location to the west of the city, the original quarry to the north having been exhausted.

After five days of inspection, the young Cuzco was very pleased and had marked the construction captain and regional governor as men who could be counted on. Obviously, all that could be done was being done, and done well.

"You have done well, Tupac," he told the governor.

"Thank you, my Cuzco," Tupac replied with a bow. "It has not been easy. We are dangerously short of slaves."

"Capture more then," the boy replied. "Go into the desert to the north if you must. There are plenty of people there."

"We have tried, my Cuzco," Tupac said, a hint of fear in his voice. The new Cuzco was said to be short tempered with those who disagreed with him. "But the people of the desert make poor slaves. The fact that their home is so near gives them hope and they never cease trying to escape."

"It is your job to see to it that they do *not* escape," the Cuzco said shortly. Had he misjudged this man?

"Yes, my Cuzco," the older man said. "And I will renew my efforts to that end. But I had hoped that in your wisdom you might consent to allow us to send the slaves we capture here deeper into the empire where escape would not be such an overwhelming temptation. Then the slaves they replace within the empire could be sent to work here."

There was a long moment of silence while the Cuzco considered that, a long moment of discomfort for the governor. If he had overstepped his bounds he would likely become a slave himself.

"There is wisdom in what you propose," the Cuzco said at last. "To send the slaves as far from their own home as possible would indeed discourage escape. I will consider it, Tupac. And you will have the slaves you need, even if I have to take them away from other projects."

"Thank you, my Cuzco," Tupac said with a bow, relief and pride washing over him at his emperor's words.

"And now I would like to retire for the night, Tupac. Please see to it that I am not disturbed until morning."

"Of course, my Cuzco."

Alone in his quarters prepared for him in the governor's temporary home, the Cuzco went through his belongings until he found a small, ornately carved, wooden box just slightly larger than his hand. From the box he took a large, reddish brown leaf wrapped tightly into a ball. Unwrapping the leaf, he uncovered a mound of smaller, darker leaves.

He crushed some of these smaller leaves between his fingers, letting the broken pieces fall into a large stone bowl. Returning to the small box he removed a very small, earthen jar and, pulling the wooden stopper from its neck, poured a small amount of thin, green liquid into the bowl. Replacing the stopper in the jar he carefully laid it back in the box.

He then swirled the contents of the bowl around until the leaf fragments absorbed the green liquid and small wisps of white smoke began to rise from them.

Finally, he placed a large, thickly woven cloth over his head and buried his face in the bowl, the cloth draped over the edges so none of the precious smoke would escape. Slowly the smoke began to fill the bowl and he breathed in deeply, taking the smoke deep within him, letting it fill him with its power, just as Capac had instructed him.

Within moments he began to feel the airy sense of detachment and freedom he'd come to crave more and more these past few days. He stayed in that position, breathing deeply, letting the smoke fill him, until his mind was bathed in the white light that always preceded his visions. Then he rose and laid down on his bed, the cloth draped over his face, his eyes closed, giving the spirits his undivided attention.

From the moment the vision began he knew that this one was to be different. Never before had his visions been so vivid, so real. The colors were so intense, the smells so overpoweringly real. And there were voices! There had never been voices before! He let his mind go, allowing it to run where it would, to show him what it was he needed to know.

He could see himself, magnificently garbed in a flowing purple robe and a breastplate of gold, standing before vast multitudes of cheering warriors. He saw himself raise his right hand and motion for the warriors to follow as he started across a wide plain, the warriors running after him, filling the air with their battle cries.

Suddenly, he was confronted by a large force of enemy warriors. Behind them was a wide river and across the river he could see women and children standing on a hill, watching. The enemy warriors raised their bows as one and fired, their arrows aimed directly at him. He saw himself throw his head back and laugh aloud as the cloud of arrows struck his body only to bounce harmlessly to the ground.

Then his own fierce warriors ran past him and leaped into the fray, slaying the enemy before them until those who had not yet been struck down threw their weapons away from them and begged for mercy. He saw himself raise his hand once more and his mighty warriors stayed their hands, coming and forming a protective line on either side of their beloved Cuzco as the enemy warriors came and bowed before him, begging his mercy and pledging their loyalty if only he would spare them.

At the sight of this the women and children crossed the river and came to bow down before him as well. His own warriors raised a loud victory cry and began to stamp the ground with their feet, calling his name again and again. Soon the very ground shook around him and a mighty pillar of blackrock burst forth before him, rising from out of the ground at his feet. Within the deep blackness of the pillar stood the image of his father, who quickly bowed before him as well.

"You have done well, my son," he said on bended knee. "Surely you will be the greatest of the Cuzcos for no weapon can harm you and you have won multitudes of slaves to build you many fine cities. Go forward and conquer, my son, for no man can stand before you."

With that his father's image disappeared and the pillar returned to the ground. His warriors grew silent and his slaves began to fade from his vision. The light too began to dim and the young Cuzco came back to himself, lying on his bed within the governor's house, his heart beating rapidly, his body quivering with excitement. He had seen his destiny.

\*     \*     \*     \*

Making his way to a crowded bazaar, Capac waited and watched the bustling crowd behind him. He was relatively sure no one had followed him. The Cuzco and Manco had shown little interest in him once he'd given them what they'd wanted. As long as he kept the Cuzco supplied with the herb he would be safe. At least until they forced him to show them where and how to find it themselves.

Stepping out into the flow of traffic once more, he made his way to a small armorer's shop. His knock was answered immediately by a young boy. Inside, a tall, thick middled man with dirty hands and an unpleasant odor tied a blindfold over Capac's eyes and led him toward the back of the shop.

"There is a ladder leading down directly at your feet," the grimy guide said. "Turn around and I'll help you get your footing."

Capac did as he was told and was soon climbing down a rickety ladder that shook disquietingly beneath his weight. When he reached the bottom, he stepped to one side and his guide followed him down and took his hand again. They walked a short distance from the ladder and the blindfold was taken off.

Capac opened his eyes to find himself standing in a torch lit room, face to face with Javet, the high priest of his people. A sense of unreality washed over him, as if what was happening couldn't possibly be real. Javet was said to be allergic to the sun's light and essentially a prisoner within his home in Pachacutec.

"Please forgive my cautiousness, Capac" the old priest said, his voice quiet and a bit raspy. "But my presence here must remain hidden. Please, sit."

He gestured to a crude wooden table with two long benches, one of which was already occupied by Kalil, the priest Capac had contacted upon arriving in Atahuallpa, and another man Capac didn't recognize. He sat on the empty bench and Javet joined him.

"Kalil you know," Javet said. "This is Duret, the man who will succeed me as high priest upon my death."

Duret looked at him appraisingly and Capac found himself unable to meet the man's gaze. What must these men think of him?

"How can you be here?" he asked weakly. "And what of the book?"

Javet and those closest to him were the keepers of their people's secrets. Had Javet somehow foreseen what was going to happen and escaped with the book? The journey from Pachacutec would have taken at least ten days. Had he been warned in a vision of what was to come?

"The book is safe," Javet said with a small smile.

"But….," Capac began.

"It is safe," Javet said, holding up a silencing hand. "The true hiding place of the book is known only to myself and Duret. You and all those who served the Cuzco's before you were never told its true hiding place, nor the greatest of its secrets. The book the Inchasa will find in Pachacutec is only a clever forgery. They will learn nothing from it."

"How could you know of the Cuzco's plans already?" Capac asked. "And how can you be here? It has only been three days since…"

"Those are questions for another time, Capac," Javet said kindly. "Please tell us what happened. We must know everything if we are to know what has to be done."

Capac sat stupidly, unsure where to begin. And what did Javet mean by "what has to be done?" What could they do?

"Please, Capac, we do not have a great deal of time."

"Yes, of course," Capac said, forcing his mind to focus.

"They beat me," he began, "and burned me."

"Who are they?" Duret asked, speaking for the first time.

"The Cuzco and Manco."

"Ah yes, Manco," Duret said. "He would be particularly well suited to the task. Please, go on."

"They forced me to tell them about the book, where it was hidden, what it contained, who knew of its existence."

"And you told them?" Duret asked.

"Yes," Capac said, head bowed.

"What else?" Javet asked.

"The herb," Capac said dejectedly. "I showed them how to prepare and use the herb."

Duret laughed lightly and the others smiled.

"Yes, the Cuzco has used it several times a day since, according to our sources."

"Sources?" Capac asked.

Duret smiled but said nothing.

"Has the Cuzco asked you to interpret his visions?" Javet asked.

"No, I don't even know if he's had any visions. Will the herb have the same effect on an Inchasa as on us?"

"A similar effect, yes," Javet answered. "Other Cuzco's have used the herb. The results have been mixed, but yes, the young Cuzco is likely capable of having a vision. How accurate those visions are we have no way of knowing. Or how accurate his interpretation of those visions."

"Other Cuzco's have used the herb?" Capac asked in disbelief.

"Yes," Javet told him, laying a comforting hand on his arm. "You are not alone in being forced to reveal secrets to the Inchasa, Capac. That is why our true secrets have never been fully revealed to all of our people, only enough to keep hope alive."

"Then, all is not lost?" Capac asked.

"No," Javet said with a smile. "But you already knew that."

"What?" Capac asked, confused.

"You have had a vision, have you not?" Javet asked. "A vision of what can be if we do our part?"

"How could you know?" Capac asked. He hadn't told anyone about his vision, having lost confidence in it by the time he'd reached Atahuallpa.

"That is not important," Javet said. "Tell us about it, please."

"But I didn't use the herb," Capac told him. "The vision can't be real."

Javet smiled and patted his arm again.

"I haven't used the herb in over twenty years, Capac," he said. "A very few of us are blessed with the gift strongly enough that they can learn to see without it. You, obviously, are one of those people."

"But...."

"Your vision, Capac, please."

Capac nodded tentatively, closed his eyes and tried to remember everything he'd seen.

"I saw a bright streak of light slice across the moons like a mighty sword," he began. "Then the two moons came together as one and dropped down onto the wide plain below the eastern mountains. They melted into the ground and the grass around them began to glow until it seemed it was on fire."

He hesitated here. This was where the vision began to turn very strange.

Javet motioned for him to continue.

"A strange beast rose up out of the grass, half man half huascar. His head and arms were those of a huascar, full of sharp teeth and poison claws, his torso and legs those of a man. He was attacked by huge numbers of Inchasa and he fought them. He killed an endless sea of them and the grass became drenched in blood."

"Then he turned and marched away to the east and a city sprang up from the blood soaked grass. A beautiful city. A Lydacian city. Our people came to the city, all of them, from all over the empire. And the children had no mark on their forehead, none. They were free. We were free. The Inchasa stayed in their own cities and left us alone, afraid the man-huascar would come back if they tried to attack us. Our city grew great. Our people grew great. Lydacia was reborn."

"A wonderful vision," Javet said. "Though the meaning of the man-huascar eludes me."

"It could symbolize the outsider mentioned in the book," Duret said.

"Perhaps," Javet agreed.

Just then the grimy armorer burst into the room.

"They come," he said breathlessly.

"Very well. Thank you, Shimek," Javet said with a nod. "We had best be on our way."

"Who is coming?" Capac asked fearfully. He knew what Manco would do to them if they found them here.

"The Inchasa, of course," Duret said calmly. "You had best come with us, Capac."

"You had best join us as well, Shimek," Javet told the armorer. "Our Inchasa friends won't let you live long if you stay. Is the entrance secured?"

"Yes," Shimek answered. "Take the torches and follow me." He had known this day would come and was ready.

Javet and Duret each took a torch from the wall and Capac fell in line between the two of them as they made their way down a long, narrow passageway, Kalil bringing up the rear. They moved as quickly as the cramped passage allowed and soon stepped into another torch lit room. Shimek doused the extra torches then led them into a somewhat wider passage.

"Almost there," he hissed a few moments later. "Keep quiet!"

The passageway took a sharp turn to the right and they stopped.

"Put out the torches," Shimek ordered. "And close your eyes."

They did as they were told and waited, the tunnel lost in total blackness. A moment later it was suddenly bathed in brilliant light and the men opened their eyes and waited for them to adjust to the light. When they could see again they found Shimek standing beside a thin stone door that swung out away from the tunnel to open onto a sunken jumble of stone and debris.

"Watch your step," he whispered as he turned and started out the door. He was leading them into the waste dump, just west of the city proper. He stepped out of the tunnel and silently picked his way across the dump, careful not to step on any stone that might start even a small slide. If they made no sound there would be no reason for anyone to look for them here. The others followed closely behind, each one giving the man in front of him several steps head start and then following directly in his footsteps.

Walking across the open space of the dump, Capac felt horribly vulnerable. A cold tingle ran up his spine and he had to fight the urge to turn around and look behind him to be sure no one was watching. The few minutes it took to make their way across the dump and into the small copse of trees at its western edge felt like an eternity to him and he slumped to the ground breathlessly when he reached the safety of the trees.

"There is no time for rest," Shimek whispered. "We have to keep moving."

Duret helped Capac to his feet and they fell in line behind the others, moving south and west, toward the thick forest that lined the western coast of the Inchasa empire. Shimek had no idea how long it would take the Inchasa to find the entrance to the underground tunnel but he had lived this long by never underestimating them. He saw no reason to change his thinking now.

He led them to a shallow canyon that cut across the broad plain between Atahuallpa and the forest to the west. They moved down into the canyon and made their way west at a comfortable but steady pace. Shimek kept a close watch on Javet to be sure the old priest wasn't being pushed too hard, but the old man showed no signs of distress. After an hours travel they came to a shallow pool within a basin of stone and stopped to drink and rest.

"How much further until we meet our friends, Shimek?" Javet asked as they rested. "It will be dark soon."

"They are not far," Shimek answered. "And they will have the cloaks you left with them as well as one for Capac, Kalil and myself. We'll have to keep moving through the night."

"Where are we going?" Capac asked.

Now that his fear had subsided a bit and he was able to think clearly, he found himself wondering what and where it was he was escaping to. There was nowhere he could go where Manco couldn't find him.

"Somewhere the Inchasa cannot follow," Javet answered, standing to his feet as he spoke. "And it is time we got back under way."

The others stood and Shimek led off down the canyon.

"And where might that be?" Capac asked doubtfully. Javet turned and smiled at him.

"You will see," Duret said from behind him. "You will see."

# CHAPTER 8

▼

# AWAKENINGS

Walking outside, Wanchese Hawkins stood at the entrance to the cave, inhaling deeply of the cool evening air, its scent rich with the odors of the forest around her, a gentle breeze caressing her smooth, sun darkened skin. This was her favorite time of day here in her new home, the sounds of the day at an end, the sounds of the night not yet begun. She let the silence wash over her, taking away for a time her cares, her worries and her doubts.

She had found the cave hidden in the folds of the blackrock cliff and thought it had likely belonged to the deathclaw. After a short, narrow entry the cave opened up to a space twenty feet wide by twelve feet deep with a ceiling of ten feet near the entrance, sloping down to a low point of three feet at the very back.

It was far from the neat, well kept longhouse she had sometimes daydreamed of but it was as good as she was likely to find for now. She couldn't have dragged the stranger much further anyway, even if there were something better nearby. She'd cleaned it as best she could. Hopefully the smell would go away soon.

And it somehow made a difference that she was there because she chose to be, not because she was forced to be. She had always felt trapped living in the village, confined. Being away these past few weeks she'd realized that. Not that she had ever really been a prisoner. But the opinions and expectations of others can trap a soul just as cruelly as any cage can trap a body. She wished now she had run away long ago.

If there was danger here in these rugged mountains, and there was, then there was beauty to match. She found the solitude refreshing rather than lonely. Being alone wasn't such a terrible thing as long as you liked the company. And in her time out here alone, with no one else's opinion to sway her judgment, she'd discovered that she liked Wanchese Hawkins just fine.

Of course, she wasn't really alone. The stranger was with her. He'd been unconscious since the day of his battle with the deathclaw, but he was there. She was still unsure why she hadn't just taken what deathclaw meat she could carry and left him to die. She hadn't asked for his help and he'd had no right to interfere. He was in for a surprise if he thought she was indebted to him. She didn't live by the laws of the village anymore. She owed him nothing.

After watching the last rays of New Roanoke's huge sun pass below the southern horizon, she turned and walked back into the cave to check on the stranger. He was pale and drawn, his body reduced to a pile of breathing skin and bone. She'd drawn out what she could of the deathclaw's poison before wrapping his shredded back and shoulders, but it had withered his body anyway, eating away at him with the passing days until she felt sure he would die. He was a stubborn one, though, this stranger. The deathclaw had learned that.

She'd been standing on the blackrock shelf waiting for the beast to attack when she had suddenly been thrown back, her knife torn from her hand. Then the stranger, his thick, fleshy body covered only by his pink, sunburned skin, stood between her and death. Turning, his eyes burning with bright intensity, he had spoken to her, his voice strangely calm.

"Go," was all he'd said before turning to face the deathclaw, her knife held blade up in his right hand.

For a moment the huge beast had seemed confuse by what had happened. But only for a moment. Then it had lashed out with its right fore leg, its poison laden claws ripping four ugly gashes down the man's left shoulder and arm as it let out a thunderous bellow. Then the beast had stood, its eyes alive with bloodlust, waiting for its prey to turn and run. But the man didn't run. And in the passing of a single second, the hunter had become the hunted, the predator the prey.

She had heard the cries of warriors in battle, when all that is within a man comes out of him in one terrible, glorious sound, but she had never heard as fierce a cry as the one that left the stranger's lips as he threw himself at the deathclaw, plunging the knife deep into its soft underbelly, ripping a great upwards gash.

Then the air had been filled with horrible cries of pain and fury, the beast ripping and tearing until the man's shoulders and back were a mass of raw, bloody flesh, the man ignoring the searing pain and driving in close to stab again and again. He'd stood there, still stabbing, even after the thing had moaned its mournful death song and fallen at his blood stained feet. It was as if he was unable to believe the thing was really dead. He had eventually collapsed on top of the bloody carcass, unconscious.

That had been seventeen days ago. There were healing plants in the surrounding forest and she'd done what she could for him. She expected him to die anyway, but her conscience would be clear.

In between caring for the stranger, collecting firewood, setting snares and doing all the needful things one has to do in the course of a day, she had gutted the deathclaw, saving most of the meat and smoking it in thin strips that could be stored in her pack. She had also scraped the thick black hide and stretched it out to dry. Taking it now from the back of the cave, she laid it over the stranger as he lay on a bed of dry leaves against the left hand wall of the cave.

A small, smokeless fire burned near the opposite wall, a round earthen pot warming on a flat stone at its edge. She broke some of the jerked meat into the bubbling pot and added some finger root and shallis, an herb that would help fight the stranger's fever.

Walking over to him, she didn't at first notice that his eyes were open. Then a weak moan escaped his lips and she bent to him quickly, surprised. Picking up a damp cloth she kept beside the bed, she wiped his face, neck and chest. His eyes were bright with fever and she knew that while they were open, they saw nothing. His body was awake but the fever still had his mind.

Filling a small, wooden bowl with warm broth, she fed it to him slowly. He finished most of the bowl before sleep took him again. A good sign, that. A very good sign. If he could get some of his strength back there just might be hope for him. She wiped his face and neck again, wondering what kind of man he was and where he might be from.

She had a feeling he was a newcomer, as the people of the villages called the strangers that came to them now and again, telling stories of strange, far off places out among the stars. This one spoke their language at least. Some of them came to them having to use hand motions to make themselves understood. They were more trouble than they were worth as far as she was concerned, though some of them had learned the ways of the village and been accepted into it.

But these were senseless musings, she decided as she slipped out of her dress and into her sleeping robe. If the man lived he would tell her where he was from and if he died, it wouldn't really matter where he'd been from. Putting it from her mind, she added some fuel to the fire and slipped beneath the thick hide beside the stranger and was quickly asleep.

She spent most of the following day splitting her time between spooning broth to the stranger, making a larger water bag from the deathclaw's innards and gathering wood for the fire. She was forced to range further into the forest to find good, dry wood that would give off little or no smoke. It was a problem she knew she would just have to live with. She would sleep in the cold rather than risk having someone see or smell smoke and find her hiding place.

As the day drew to a close, she went out and began to gather her snares. She picked up three, two to the north of the cave, one to the east, then set out to the south for the last one. One of the northern snares held a medium sized koiba, a small, hairless forager that left a good deal to be desired as a meal but whose tough skin was excellent for moccasin bottoms.

Examining her prize as she walked, and needing to move quickly if she was going to get back to the cave before dark, she almost walked right past the footprints. But, catching a glimpse of something out of place from the corner of her eye, she stopped and walked over to have a look.

What had disturbed her senses was an indentation in a group of burnt orange weeds at the base of a tall, thick sour tree. Moving on, she could see a large number of similar indentations. Footprints. But who's?

They led to the northwest so their route would take whoever had made them well wide of the cave, unless one of them found signs of her passing and decided to see who else was moving around these mountains. There seemed small chance of that, but she was still uneasy.

Breaking into a slow but steady run, she moved through the fading light, traveling north and east, back toward the cave. What would they do if they found the stranger there alone? And who were they? Kane and Secotan? Surely they would have given up their chase by now. Inchasa? She knew exactly what they would do if they found him. She ran faster.

Approaching the shelf, she slowed down and searched the area around the cave. She could see no signs of anyone's passage but it was growing dark quickly and getting harder to see. Deciding she could trust her ears if not her eyes, she slipped quietly from the forest and ran to the cave.

Inside, the stranger lay undisturbed. Taking the hide from the back of the cave, she covered him with it, causing him to stir slightly, shaking his head back and forth and moving his lips soundlessly. Returning to the back of the cave, she wrapped a blanket around her shoulders and went back outside, moving into the forest to the west of the cliff. The darkness would conceal her there and she could listen for sounds of someone approaching.

She waited beside a thick tree trunk, hearing nothing but the sound of her own heartbeat and the night music of the forest around her. She waited a long time, wanting to be absolutely sure no one was coming. She had just decided all was well and was turning to head back to the cave when the music stopped and everything went silent around her.

She listened intently, trying to stretch her awareness out into the darkness. But there was nothing. And then there was! It was a swooshing sound, like the limb of a tree had been bent forward out of the way and then released, something an animal wouldn't do. Looking toward the sound she saw movement and was able to make out a vague shape. Then came a hoarse whisper. Inchasa again! But these weren't moving through the forest unaware, intent only on finding a good place to spend the night. These were hunters, and they were hunting her.

She moved quickly and silently off to the north, making her way to the northern edge of the cliff and moving around it to the east. Within minutes she was at the eastern edge of the blackrock shelf wanting desperately to run for the cave, but holding back, not wanting to lead them to the defenseless stranger. She as least had a fighting chance. He would have none.

Watching and listening, she could hear them now as they called back and forth in hushed voices. She was reasonably sure they were still within the forest and not yet able to see the open shelf in front of the cliff. They would be there soon, however. If she was going to go, it had to be now.

$$*\qquad*\qquad*\qquad*$$

Shadows danced on the walls around him when Mitchell Harvey opened his eyes. To his right a small fire burned, the wood smell bringing back, unbidden, memories of other fires, other quiet awakenings. Those images faded quickly however as his hazy, shrouded mind fought through the dense fog of confusion that gripped it. This wasn't a weekend camping trip with Alton and Dad. It looked like he was in some kind of cave. And something was wrong. Very wrong.

Ignoring the rhythmic ache that pounded his skull with every beat of his heart, he fought to remember. Images and emotions flooded his mind. The woman. The bear. No, not a bear, but something big and nasty looking. Pain, terrible, searing pain. Fury. Rage, frightening, consuming rage.

He was still trying to decide if any of it had been real when the woman came running into the cave, the woman with the patch over one eye. She frantically kicked out the small fire, leaving him lost in blackness. Then the sound of her ragged breathing moved past him again, back the way she'd come.

It took four tries before he was able to sit up. Then, feeling for the wall beside him, he moved first to his knees and then carefully to his feet. His head began to swim and he had to steady himself against the wall until it settled down. His back hurt like hell and his head registered a throbbing complaint against his being up and about. He ignored both as best he could.

Picking up the thick, surprisingly heavy blanket that had been covering him, he wrapped it around his shoulders and slowly made his way in the direction the woman had gone. He took small, careful steps and stopped every two or three to steady himself against the wall. He felt like he was going to be sick.

His eyes began to adjust to the darkness and he could see where it was lighter up ahead. He moved toward the light, suddenly feeling an overwhelming need for fresh air. Then there was a soft gasp and the woman stepped from the darkness and placed her hand over his mouth. Her hand was trembling.

Then he heard the voices and understood her fear. It was the language of the men who had murdered the couple in the clearing. Had those butchers followed him after all? Pressing against the wall, he followed the woman as she carefully made her way nearer to the cave's entrance. As they approached it, she knelt close to the ground and motioned for him to do the same.

He could see them now. There were five or six of them, maybe more. Judging by the woman's reaction she wasn't on friendly terms with them. That spoke well for her as far as Mitch was concerned. What worried him was that he was in no condition to help her if trouble came. He wasn't even sure he was going to be able to stand up again.

The men were standing at the edge of the forest, where it joined the shelf of rock in front of the cave, arguing amongst themselves. The argument had reached a point where Mitch thought it might come to blows between two of them, when one of their number stepped from the forest to the east. Mitch didn't have to understand the words to recognize the voice of command. This man spoke and all argument ceased.

Pointing back the way he'd come, the man spoke sharply and stepped back into the forest. The others began moving off, following behind him. All but one. He held back for a minute, taking a long, slow look around, hesitating, not wanting to go. Then he spat what Mitch could only guess was an expletive and stepped off into the forest after the others.

"That one must have seen you," Mitch whispered.

The woman made no reply, only putting her hand over his mouth again. After several long minutes, she stood, moving closer to the opening, listening. Satisfied, she came back to where Mitch was trying to struggle back to his feet. He was far weaker than he ever would have dreamed possible. His head began to swim again and he felt himself starting to fall. The woman caught at him, grabbing him and helping him to his feet.

"Thanks," he managed, steadying himself against the wall. "Who are they?"

Grabbing him around his waist with her right arm and placing his left around her shoulder, the woman helped him back into the cave, making her way knowingly through the darkness and lowering him gently to the bed of dry leaves.

"They call themselves Inchasa," she said, her voice hard. "Some people sometimes call them Longwalkers. They are killers."

"I know," Mitch told her. "I came across some of them in the forest south of here. They had killed a man and a woman." The images from the clearing flashed in his mind. "They hurt them before they killed them," he added softly, feeling again the guilt of having let those murderers just walk away. The woman said nothing.

"I'm Mitchell," he said. "Mitchell Harvey."

"I am Wanchese Hawkins."

"Where are we?"

"The deathclaw's cave."

Deathclaw? Who or what is a deathclaw? He wondered. Then he thought again of the huge black beast, its long claws flashing at him, his flesh feeling like it had been seared by hot metal. Deathclaw. And this was its cave.

"It's dead?" he asked. Best be sure of that.

"Yes."

And I'm alive, he thought. What the hell do you know?

"How long have you been taking care of me?" he asked.

"Seventeen days," she answered.

"Seventeen days? That thing must have torn me up pretty good. Thank you."

"I don't need your thanks," Wanchese said, a little more harshly than she'd intended. "I did what I could for you because it was right, not because I cared whether you lived or died."

Not sure exactly what he was supposed to say to that, Mitch said nothing.

"I expected you to die anyway," Wanchese added after a moment of awkward silence. "Deathclaw poison is strong."

Poison? Mitch thought. That big son of bitch was poisonous? No wonder he felt like death. That would explain the name. The poison must be in the claws.

That seemed a little unfair. That thing was bad enough as it was, it didn't need poison. And what the hell had he said in his sleep to piss this first class bitch off?

"Well, thanks anyway," he said. Kill 'em with kindness, Mom used to say. Wanchese didn't answer.

"Do you live near here? Your people, I mean?" It seemed a pretty good guess that she wasn't one of those Inchasa cretins. Although she did seem to share their sunny disposition toward strangers.

"The village where I was born is far to the east, below these mountains," Wanchese answered. "There are no others living here."

"Those Inchasa don't live here?"

"No. They live below the mountains and to the west."

"What are they doing here, then?"

"I don't know," she answered. "They come here to hunt just as the warriors of the river villages do, but it's strange for them to be moving at night. No one hunts here at night."

Mitch could understand that. He wasn't sure he'd want to hunt up here in broad daylight with a laser rifle, never mind in the dark with a spear.

"Where are these river villages?" he asked. There had to be someone nearby who didn't pull out a man's intestines the first time they met him.

"To the east," Wanchese answered. "Along the Hope River. That is where I was born, where I came from."

And what are you running from, Wanchese Hawkins? Mitch thought with sudden insight. Whatever it was, it seemed to have made her more than a little angry with men. Or maybe that was just a natural reaction to him personally, a chemical thing. He'd heard that could happen. In fact, now that he thought about it, his lifetime experience with women seemed to prove that it could.

That made him think of Sandra and he wondered for the thousandth time since waking up in this nightmare if she had anything to do with all this. He had a feeling she did and was glad he'd made the arrangements he had with his lawyer before he left. Sandra was in for some unpleasant awakenings of her own.

Lying back on the bed of leaves, he pulled the heavy blanket over him and closed his eyes for a minute. His head had stopped throbbing and he found himself wondering if there was anything to eat. He hesitated to ask, thinking that food was probably in short supply if Wanchese had been stuck here in this cave with him for seventeen days. But he'd never been so hungry in his life. Hunger won.

"Is there anything to eat?" he asked hopefully.

"Yes," Wanchese answered. "I'll warm some broth."

Broth? Mitch thought, disappointed. Well, beggars can't be choosers. He could hear Wanchese moving around in the darkness. A few seconds later he heard two stones being struck together and a large spark leaped through the air. The spark caught and a small flame sprouted. Wanchese rearranged the stones around the flame, added sticks, and quickly had the earthen pot warming beside a small fire. Mitch noticed that the flames gave off no smoke. Wanchese knew what she was doing.

"It will take a few minutes," she said, handing him a long, thin strip of foul smelling meat. "Start with this."

Then she left, going to check out the area around the cave, he guessed. Taking a small, tentative bite, he was surprised to find that the meat actually tasted rather good. Gamy, but good. He'd eaten his own cooking enough over the years to have tasted far worse.

"Not bad," he said when Wanchese came back. "Tastes better than it smells."

She said nothing, only stirring the contents of the pot with a long wooden spoon. When the broth was warm, she dipped a wooden bowl into the pot and brought it to him. Sitting up, he spread the blanket over his lower body and then stopped, staring in disbelief at his withered body. It was a moment before he could speak.

"What happened?" he asked weakly. It seemed like some kind of awful dream. He'd been reduced to little more than a skeleton that still had its skin. He wouldn't have believed it was possible to look the way he did and still be alive.

"The deathclaw poison," Wanchese answered, placing the bowl on the floor beside him. "It eats away at the body from the inside."

"Will I get better?"

"I don't know. I think you will, at least partially, but I can't say for certain. I've never known anyone who survived a deathclaw mauling," she added with a helpless shrug when he looked at her questioningly. "You will have a better chance of recovering if you eat, that much I do know."

Nodding, he picked up the bowl and spoon. The broth smelled only slightly better than the jerked meat had but it too tasted surprisingly good and he ate two bowls. After that he felt better. Much better. And tired.

"Thank you," he said. "That's pretty good."

A curt nod of her head was Wanchese's only answer and he settled back onto his bed of leaves gently, careful not to put too much pressure on his back. He thought about turning over and lying on his stomach but just the thought of the effort required exhausted him.

"I have so many questions," he said. "So many things I need to know. But I think they'll have to wait until tomorrow. I'm exhausted."

In fact, now that his stomach was full, he was having trouble keeping his eyes open.

"Rest then," Wanchese told him. "It will be some time before you're strong enough to do much more than lay where you are. Your questions can wait."

Mitch was asleep before she finished talking.

# CHAPTER 9

▼

# UNPLEASANT SURPRISES

"Thank you for seeing me, Nathan," Sandra Harvey said as she took a seat in one of the two chairs that sat facing Nathan Squire's desk. "I know it was short notice."

"Not at all, Sandra," Squires said politely, his quick glance taking in the woman's long, shapely legs, thin waist and full breasts that swelled her blouse just enough to make it impossible not to notice them. Her skirt was short yet business like, giving a pleasing flash of thigh as she sat down and crossed her legs. She was a stunning woman. "What can I do for you?"

"Well, I didn't know who else to turn to, and you've been such a good friend." She smiled sweetly at the thick, balding little lawyer. "I tried to transfer some funds from one of our accounts and found that the access codes have been changed. Mitch apparently forgot to give me the new codes before her left."

"Yes, I'm aware of the changes," Squires said.

"Oh good," Sandra said happily. "Then you *can* help me. I was so afraid I'd have to bother Mitch with this and I hate to interrupt him while he's away on business."

"Actually," Squires said, aware that it gave him more than a little satisfaction to do so, "I don't think I can help you, Sandra. Only Mitch has those new codes."

That was a lie, of course. He had the access codes to all of Mitch Harvey's accounts stored in his secure database, along with a new will and a revised life insurance policy that weren't going to make Sandra Harvey very happy.

"I'm afraid you'll have to get in touch with Mitch after all," he added. Let Mitch have the satisfaction of telling her she no longer had access to any of his funds. He'd left the greedy bitch more than enough to live well while he was away.

"I really hate to do that," Sandra said, a hint of desperation in her voice. "Doesn't Mitch give you all his access codes?"

"I'm afraid I'm not at liberty to discuss that kind of client information, Sandra."

"What are you talking about, Nathan? I'm his wife! Surely you can discuss my husband's business with me!"

"I'm afraid not, Sandra. You'll just have to get in touch with Mitch on Rittenmere."

"Well, that's asinine!" Sandra exploded. "I know damn well you have those codes, Nathan. And I have every right to have them. Now, are you going to give them to me or do I have to take other measures? You're not the only lawyer in town, you know."

Her face turned first red and then white as Nathan Squires sat smiling at her.

"Hire any lawyer you want, Sandra," he said. "It won't do you any good. Besides, Mitch left you more than enough to live on while he's gone."

He let that sink in for a minute. Yes, that's right, I know exactly how much your husband left you.

"I'm terribly sorry, Nathan," Sandra said, the sweetness returning to her voice. "Really, I am." She shifted her body in the chair so that more of her thighs were exposed beneath her skirt. "I don't know what gets into me sometimes."

Squires said nothing, though he did glance appreciatively at her legs. It really was too bad she was such a bitch. He could see how Mitch could have convinced himself she was something other than the greedy leech that she was.

"And you're right, of course," she continued, "Mitch did leave me with a reasonable amount of money. It's just that I'm afraid I was tricked into a bad investment, taken advantage of really, and I hate to tell Mitch about it while he's away. He has so much on his mind already. You can understand that, can't you, Nathan?" She smiled at him.

"I'm sorry to hear that, Sandra," he said nervously. Damn, she could make it hard to think straight! There was something in her eyes that gave just the right hint of desire. "If you could give me some information maybe I could look into the matter for you."

"On, no, no, that won't be necessary. I've already retained an attorney to check into it for me. All I need is a small transfer of funds to tide me over until Mitch gets back."

"I'm sorry, I really can't help, Sandra. I'm afraid you're just going to have to talk to Mitch."

"I really don't see why that's necessary, Nathan," she said. "It would be so much more...enjoyable if we handled things just between the two us."

"I...ah...I'm sorry," Squires said weakly.

"Please, Nathan," Sandra pleaded. She had to have that money. Even if she had to sleep with this overstuffed rat to get it. She'd have to try another angle. Her eyes quickly filled with tears.

"Mitch went to Rittenmere with another woman," she wailed. "He's got someone new and he's abandoned me, Nathan!" She buried her face in her hands and sobbed.

Squires was uncomfortable. It was possible Mitch had someone else. He wouldn't really blame him if he did. But even if he did, Sandra was far from abandoned. Where was this desperation coming from?

"I need money to live on, Nathan," Sandra said through her tears as she stood and bent over the front of the desk, taking his hand in hers. "Please, I need your help. I feel so alone."

Well, I'll be damned, Squires thought, recognizing her words as the invitation they were. She's more desperate than I thought. He could feel his erection pushing against the top drawer of his desk.

"I'm sorry, Sandra," he said, almost wishing he were the kind of man who could screw a friend's wife and still look himself in the eye in the morning. Sandra could probably be a real wild one in bed when she wanted something. And she definitely wanted something now. He just couldn't figure out why.

"Are you sure you can't help me, Nathan? I'd be so very grateful if you did."

"No, I'm sorry, I can't," he said, forcing himself to look away. Yes, he could definitely see how Mitch could have been taken in.

The Invitation in Sandra Harvey's eyes turned to hot hatred as she released his hand and stormed to the door. Squires let her see her self out. It would have been very embarrassing for him to stand just then.

*     *     *     *

The Temple of the Sun was filled to overflowing as a new day dawned on Atahuallpa. A day of rest had been called so that all of his subjects could hear the Cuzco's proclamation. Grateful laborers mingled with warriors, artisans and stone masons, waiting to hear what their young ruler had to say.

The Cuzco stood at the very center of the temple, within the circle of shimmering blackrock pillars, lifted high upon a wooden platform by his bearers. As the first rays of the new day's light fell across his face, he raised his right hand high, calling for silence. The throng grew quiet and waited. For many of them this was their first chance to see their new king, to take his measure and form an opinion of him based on something more than rumor and hearsay.

"This is a great day, my people," the Cuzco began, and those who knew him well were struck by the change in his voice, in his manner and bearing. He was confident, self-assured. He no longer seemed like a boy trying to convince himself and those around him that he was a man.

"This day we begin a new and glorious age in the history of our great people. No longer will we be served by others of our own kind. No more will our young men be forced to labor within the mines and quarries. No more will they spend their vital energies building our magnificent cities. They are far too valuable for that. *You* are far too valuable for that. The ways of our fathers must be no more!"

There was a rustling within the crowd as people turned and looked at one another, the Cuzco's energy beginning to build within them, though none of them was really sure what he was trying to tell them.

"I have seen a vision!" the Cuzco announced. "A vision of what we are to become, a vision of conquest, a vision of glory, a vision of victory!" He stopped to smile down on his people as an excited muttering made its way through the temple.

"You have all heard the stories of how our people lived before we came to this place; how we conquered all before us, defeated any who dared oppose us, ruled over any who were not of our blood. It is time to return to the old ways. It is time for us to take our rightful place as rulers and conquerors. Only then can we truly begin to achieve the greatness that is our destiny.

"No more will you toil in the fields like dull animals, no more will you labor to erect our magnificent temples and glorious cities. You were not meant for such things. Were you born to be beasts of burden? Is it your destiny to spend your lives struggling merely to survive? Were you meant to be lowly servants and laborers?

"I tell you, you were not! That is not your destiny! I tell you, you were not meant for such things. I was not meant for such things. I am a conqueror! I am master of all my eyes behold! I am the Cuzco! And you are my people! Who can stand against us?"

The crowd erupted into a joyous chorus of exulting voices as a sense of excitement and purpose flowed through them. The Cuzco stood on his platform, his hands on his hips, a glowing smile on his face, a new sense of power radiating from his slender frame.

Suddenly Manco pushed his way to the front of the crowd, his heart filled with joy at finally hearing the words he had so longed to hear. Dropping to his knees before the raised platform, he lifted his face to his emperor, tears rolling down his scarred and battered face.

"I am Manco, my Cuzco," he cried, "and none shall stand before you. You will rule over all that your eyes behold. On my life, I pledge it will be so!"

Other warriors in the temple began to cheer and cry out as they too pledged their lives to the realization of the Cuzco's vision. Soon everyone within the temple was caught up in the new spirit of their coming conquest, their coming greatness. The air was filled with a deafening chorus of voices shouting the praises of their Cuzco, celebrating his strength and his wisdom. Truly he was a god!

Looking up at the Cuzco now, Manco knew in his heart that this was not the same boy who had arrived in Atahuallpa four days earlier. The frightened, insecure boy had become a confident, spirited leader of men, with a sure path for his people. This day he had truly become a Cuzco.

Did it matter that the Lydacian herb was at least partly responsible for the change, or that the Cuzco seemed more and more drawn to it with each passing day? Not to him. All that mattered was that he would finally know battle once more. And he would know glory. His had not been idle words. He would know victory or he would know death.

The bearers lowered the Cuzco to the ground and the young emperor made his way through the crowd, letting them touch him, letting them feel the strength of his presence. Manco walked at his side, watching the crowd, ready to step in should anyone become too exuberant.

Making their way out of the temple, they moved quickly down the avenue to the governor's house where the Cuzco gave one last wave to his subjects before moving inside, motioning for Manco to follow.

"Come," he ordered then walked to his quarters, Manco close on his heels.

"You have seen much of the territory controlled by our enemies, have you not, Manco?" he asked when he was seated in a comfortable, high backed chair.

"Yes, my Cuzco. More than most."

"Good. Tell me then, the people of the river, is one of their villages bordered by both the river and the wide plain to the east?"

"Yes, my Cuzco. The southernmost of their villages borders the plain."

"I had thought as much," the Cuzco said thoughtfully. "And how may people would you say live in that village?"

"People or warriors, my Cuzco?"

"People."

Manco thought back to the reports he'd received over the last several months.

"A rough estimate from the last raiding party would be in the area of twelve to fifteen hundred, my Cuzco."

"So few?"

"Yes, my Cuzco. There are four other villages of approximately the same size as well."

"And warriors?"

"Five hundred in the southernmost village, the same in the others, more or less. A more accurate estimate will be possible when the latest raiding party returns."

"You have fought against these people, Manco. What kind of adversary are they? Will they stand against us?"

"They are warriors, my Cuzco, I will give them that. Yes, they would fight if we came against them. But they would not stand a chance of defeating us if we face them with equal numbers. We are Inchasa."

"Yes," the young Cuzco said, "we are Inchasa, Manco. And I think it is time our enemies learned just what that means. How long would it take you to prepare a force of five thousand warriors to move against the river villages?"

"Five *thousand*, my Cuzco?"

"Five thousand."

Manco was quiet for several minutes. Five thousand? The very thought of what a force that size would be capable of made his heart race.

"It would take several months, at least, my Cuzco. It is a ten day march from Pachacutec to the river. Supplies would have to be stored at one day intervals along the route of march. That means large storage shelters would have to be built and then stocked with food and water. As for the training of the men, several months would be enough time to choose and prepare those you deem worthy, my Cuzco."

"What about weapons? Are our men properly armed for such a battle?"

"No, my Cuzco," Manco had to admit. His men were, and Leruk's, but few others. "We would have to arm many of our warriors with new weapons. And everyone would need a much larger supply of arrows. But these things could be seen to while the men are trained."

"Then you have no doubt we could be armed, supplied, and prepared for a sustained offensive by the celebration of the Inti Raymi?"

"None, my Cuzco," Manco answered confidently. The Festival of the Sun was nearly five months away, more than enough time.

"Good. Thank you, Manco," the Cuzco said with a smile. "I name you Chief Warrior of the Empire. I will see to it that a proclamation is prepared and read throughout the empire to that effect. From this point on you will be responsible for the preparation of my army for battle. All garrison commanders will report directly to you. If you find any of them unsatisfactory, you have my permission to replace them. I want my men ready for battle, Manco. That means they are to be as well trained and as well equipped as it is within my power to make them. Do you understand?"

"Yes, my Cuzco," Manco answered, dropping to one knee.

"What of Capac?" the Cuzco asked. "Have you made any progress?"

"No, my Cuzco. He must have left the city, along with the armorer, Shimek."

"Why would an Inchasa help a Lydacian escape us?"

"I don't know, my Cuzco, but I will find out."

"No. Your duty is to prepare my army. I will have someone else look into Capac's disappearance. Is that understood?"

"Yes, my Cuzco."

The boy nodded his satisfaction.

"Choose the best of the Atahuallpa garrison to come back to Pachacutec with us," he said. "The rest will stay behind to guard the city. And prepare the slaves working here to come with us. Replacements are already on their way. Questions?"

"None, my Cuzco."

"Good. That will be all."

# CHAPTER 10

▼

# NEW LIFE

Mitchell Harvey sat quietly on a large, flat stone at the foot of the tall black cliff, enjoying his first breath of fresh air in twenty-one days. He slowly unwrapped the thin cloth that had been wrapped around his chest and back as a bandage. His wounds were healing and the itching was driving him crazy. Still, the warmth of the sun on his skin felt good.

He was having some trouble adjusting to the sight of his own body. It still seemed impossible that he could look the way he did and be alive. He was pretty sure he could see every bone in his body. The fact that Wanchese couldn't reassure him about his chances for a full recovery didn't make him feel any better.

His appetite had certainly returned, which he hoped was a good sign. He'd been a little uneasy at first when he'd learned that the surprisingly tasty meat he'd been eating was deathclaw. But, after thinking about it, he'd decided it was perfectly logical. The big bastard would sure as hell have eaten him if things had turned out the other way around.

And Wanchese found all kinds of exotic tasting roots and herbs to season the stew that constituted the bulk of their diet. There were several different kinds of gourds that could be baked and eaten as well, though he found most of them sharply bitter.

He was still sitting outside when Wanchese came back from gathering wood for the fire. He thought she looked angry, probably because he was outside, but it was hard to tell with her. He got the feeling she had liked him better when he was unconscious.

"You shouldn't be out here," she said, confirming his suspicions.

"I needed some fresh air."

"If you fall you will break something. There is nothing to protect your bones."

Mitch shrugged. She was right, but he was going stir crazy sitting in the cave.

"And you should not remove your bandages," Wanchese continued. "If your wounds become infected you won't have the strength to fight it."

Mitch still said nothing. To think he'd lived through days and nights of hellish wandering through the forest and a battle with a huge, poisonous animal, only to be nagged to death.

Wanchese brought the wood into the cave then came back out and went into the forest to the west. She came back a few minutes later with the cured hide of a small animal she'd had staked out to dry in a clearing on the north side of the cliff.

"What's that?" Mitch asked.

"Koiba," she answered as she walked to him.

Placing the hide flat on the ground in front of him, she wordlessly placed his feet on it and traced their outline with a small, flaky red stone. When she was finished, she removed his feet, picked up the hide and went back inside.

Mitch watched her go. Obviously she was going to make him some new moccasins. She'd given him what she called a breechcloth the day before. It was just a long piece of cloth cut the width of his body and a woven belt. The belt was tied around his waist, the woven cloth run underneath the belt in front of him, through is legs and underneath the belt in back of him, the two ends hanging down as far as his knees in both front and back. It was actually pretty comfortable. Certainly better than running around bare ass.

He stood up carefully. Wanchese was right about what would happen if he fell. And he couldn't afford any broken bones. He made his way slowly to the cave, stopping to rest every few steps. He was still weak but the fresh air had been a good idea. He felt much better.

Inside, Wanchese was using a long thorn as an awl to bore holes in the koiba hide. She looked up when he came in but didn't say anything.

"Why do you use koiba hide?" he asked, taking his usual seat on the bed of leaves.

"Because it's thick and strong and doesn't wear out as fast as other hides."

Mitch nodded. He'd thought as much.

"You didn't seem surprised this morning when I told you I was from a place far from here," he said.

"Others have told us of the places among the stars," she said, not looking up from her work.

Mitch looked at her in surprise. He'd spent the better part of the morning trying to figure out how he was going to explain that to her.

"Your own people told you this?"

"No, other newcomers. They come with their stories of having been brought here from far off places. My own people were brought here from another place long ago."

"Do these newcomers live in the villages by the river?"

"Some do. Most of them don't live long."

"I think it was other newcomers I found," Mitch said, thinking aloud, "the ones the Inchasa killed."

"It is possible. Inchasa enjoy killing, though they sometimes use newcomers as slaves."

Mitch wondered what would be worse, having your insides yanked out while you watched or being forced to live as a slave to those sadistic bastards. Neither option seemed very pleasant.

"What do your people do with newcomers?"

"They are taught to work the fields. As long as they do their share they're allowed to stay. In time they learn how to take care of themselves and become part of the village."

"Is that what you're going to do with me? Show me how to take care of myself and then send me on my way?"

"I have some doubt you'll ever be able to take care of yourself," Wanchese answered, just the slightest hint of a smile on her lips.

Mitch laughed. She just might be right.

"If you live long enough to regain some of your strength, I'll try to show you what you need to know," she continued. "For now, just watch what I do and try not to hurt yourself."

"Yes maam," Mitch said, bringing his right hand to his forehead and saluting. Wanchese just shook her head while he laughed.

He watched her as she worked, knowing that he would likely have to make some moccasins himself if he lived long enough to wear this pair out. Which reminded him.

"I've been thinking," he said then smiled when she looked up skeptically. "I know," he added, "it's hard to believe, but it's true. Those Inchasa that we saw will be coming back this way. Maybe we should do without a fire except for cooking."

"I know they will be coming back," she said. "That's why I don't want you going outside. You'll have no chance if they find you out there."

"That's true," he said. "I hadn't really thought about that. I'll stick close to the entrance until I'm getting around better. But what about the fire?"

"It will be cold. I'm not sure you're well enough yet."

"I'll be fine. That deathclaw hide is more than warm enough."

"There is little to worry about once full dark falls," she said. "But we could avoid it as often as possible while the sun is out."

"O.K, then," Mitch said. "Are we actually agreeing about something?" he asked with mock surprise.

"You finally said something intelligent," she shot back.

Mitch laughed and Wanchese smiled despite herself, encouraged that his spirits were so high. Where the spirit led, the body often followed.

"There is a chance they won't even come back this way," she told him. "They are likely a raiding party heading for the river villages. A hunting party wouldn't have come so far into the mountains."

"There weren't very many of them. How could they raid a village with only six men?"

"They won't raid the villages themselves, not with so few warriors. They'll watch the fields and try to capture women and children working there."

"For slaves?"

"Yes. They especially like to capture young women."

I bet they do, Mitch thought. All the more reason not to take any chances. He could live without a fire.

"Can I ask you something?" he asked hesitantly.

Wanchese nodded. She had wondered when he would ask.

"What happened to your eye?"

"An Inchasa cut me with a knife," she said, her voice devoid of emotion. She preferred not to talk about herself, especially about what had happened that day.

"A long time ago?" Mitch asked.

"Eight years," Wanchese answered. She had explained to him that there were fifteen months in a year, each lasting thirty-one days.

"How old were you?"

"Eight."

Mitch did the math. Sixteen of her years at fifteen months per year would make her about......twenty one by his way of reckoning, or there abouts. That would make her around ten when she lost her eye. That must have been tough. He decided to change the subject.

"Do you think you could show me what you're doing?" he asked. "I'll have to make some myself sooner or later, I expect."

✳     ✳     ✳     ✳

"Come," the soft, raspy voice of Mother Shaw called.

"Thank you for seeing me, Mother," Secotan Samuels said after taking a seat opposite the frail looking elder.

"I am always pleased to see you, Secotan," the old woman said. "What can I do for you?"

Secotan was uneasy. He started to speak several times, stopping at the last second each time.

"Just say it, son," Mother Shaw said gently. "When you've lived as long as I have, there is little you haven't heard before. Out with it."

Secotan smiled. That was likely true. Mother Shaw's stooped shoulders, thin grey hair and spotted, wrinkled skin bore witness to her seventy-nine years of life. Her knowing, intelligent, often mischievous eyes bore witness to a spirit that was far from tired. She was something of an advisor to many of the villagers, one who never broke a trust and who would never do or say anything in someone's absence that she wasn't willing to do or say in their presence. While not everyone liked her, nearly everyone respected her, and Secotan had often sought her advice as Village Councillor. He was afraid that what he was about to say was going to leave her very disappointed in him.

"I am going to resign as Village Councillor," he said, trying to sound confident in his decision. Mother Shaw wasn't fooled.

"Because of Wanchese Hawkins?" she asked.

"That's part of it," he admitted.

Mother Shaw nodded her understanding and waited for him to continue. She knew there was more and was willing to be patient. He would come to it in his own time.

"That girl deserved more from life that what it gave her," he said. "More than what I gave her."

"Yes," the old woman agreed. "I would have liked to have spoken with you before you made your decision."

She met his eyes when he looked at her.

"In her place, I would have run too," she continued. "Even death would be better than what that young fool had in mind for her."

Secotan nodded.

"Dare said the same thing," he told her.

Mother Shaw smiled.

"She is wise beyond her years, that one," she said. "I knew you would be happy together."

Secotan smiled again. Mother Shaw said much the same thing to most of the married villagers, the happy ones anyway. What she said to the unhappy ones he could only guess.

"I had some doubts at the time, myself," he admitted. "I was so much older."

"Age is nothing," the old woman said with a dismissive wave of her hand. "Such things do not decide happiness. You were well suited to one another, that is what matters."

"Actually, my happiness with Dare is part of what I've been struggling with, Mother," Secotan said, then hesitated, wondering if what he was about to say would change the elder's opinion of him. "If I were to speak the truth of what I feel about many of our old traditions, I would have to tell our people that I think many of them are no longer needed. Yet I owe much of my own happiness to one of them."

Mother Shaw shook her head. She knew Secotan thought the only reason Dare had become his wife was because he had saved her life and she had felt she owed him a debt. That was nonsense.

"You are wrong, Secotan," she said. "Dare would have offered herself to you regardless. You were the man for her and she was wise enough to know it. Your saving her changed only the timing of her offer, not the substance of it. You owe your happiness to the kind of man you are and the kind of life you live, not tradition."

"Possibly," Secotan said doubtfully. Dare had in fact told him much the same thing on several occasions, but he had trouble believing it.

"And none of what you've told me explains why you wish to resign," Mother Shaw said. "Tell me."

"What do you mean?" Secotan asked. "How can a man who no longer believes in our traditions be Village Councillor? What is a Councillor's duty if not to protect and enforce his people's laws and traditions?"

"To protect his *people*," the elder answered firmly. "And you well know it. That is why you struggle within yourself. You let tradition become more important to you than a young girl, and now you can't live with the guilt your decision causes you. So, you will resign and let someone else make those decisions from now on. I had not thought you a coward, Secotan."

Secotan was speechless. He could feel his face grow hot as he struggled to control his anger.

"Well?" Mother Shaw prodded.

"Well what?" he snapped back.

"Well, are you a coward? Or are you the kind of man who can admit his mistakes and learn from them, even use them to make himself a better man, a better Councillor?"

"I did what I thought was best for my people," Secotan said stiffly.

"Did you?" the elder asked. "Or did you do what you thought was expected of you? What you thought would please the other Councillors?"

Secotan said nothing, but all the anger drained out of him, leaving him feeling weak and sick to his stomach. Was that what he'd done?

"Do you know why you were chosen as Village Councillor, Secotan? At such a young age?"

He remained silent, refusing even to raise his head.

"Look at me!" the elder snapped and he raised his eyes to meet hers.

"You were chosen because the people of this village trusted you, because they were confident you would do what you felt was right even when it was not easy to do so. We didn't choose you because we thought you would care for our laws and traditions. We chose you because we trusted you to care for us, each and every one of us."

"Then I've failed even more miserably than I thought," Secotan said dejectedly. Mother Shaw laughed, surprising him.

"And now it's time for you to crawl into a hole and lick your wounds, is that it?" she asked. "If you cannot be without fault, you cannot be worthy of being Councillor, is that what you're thinking?"

"Yes, that is exactly what I'm thinking," Secotan shot back angrily. "A girl is dead and it's my fault. How is it I'm supposed to feel about that?"

"You don't know Wanchese is dead," Mother Shaw told him. She had a feeling that girl wouldn't die easily. "And if she is then, yes, part of the responsibility is yours. But not all. And how you are supposed to feel about it is sorry that you didn't do what your heart told you was right."

Reaching out, she lifted his chin until she could look into his eyes again.

"You will never know peace unless you follow your heart," she said. "If you have truly done what you believe is right, even when you make mistakes you'll be able to live with them. You cannot be true to your people until you are true to yourself."

"If I'm true to myself, my people won't want me as their Councillor anymore."

"Perhaps. What of it?"

He looked at her, confused. Did she think the village would be better off if he was replaced?

"You aren't listening to what I'm saying," Mother Shaw said, sensing his confusion. "You were chosen as Councillor because of who you are, because of what we believed was in your heart. If we were wrong, then that is our mistake and we will make it right. But how can we know, if you refuse to show us what is truly in your heart?"

Leaning over, she gently took his hand into hers and patted it reassuringly.

"Be who you are, Secotan. Let us decide whether or not that is good enough to be our Councillor. Better you be rejected for who you really are than accepted for who you pretend to be."

Secotan nodded his understanding, if not his acceptance.

"The question then becomes," the old woman concluded, mischief brightening her eyes, "do you have the courage to show your people what is truly in your heart?"

# CHAPTER 11

▼

# QUESTIONS

"What's with the long face, Slim?" Alton Harvey asked his long time friend on the VML monitor.

"I may be overreacting, Alton," Nathan Squires said. "God, I hope I am. But Sandra came to see me two days ago. She was in an uproar because Mitch had changed the access codes to his accounts and she needed money. I told her I couldn't help her. When she left, I tried to get in touch with Mitch on Rittenmere and the hotel said he never checked in. I called Confederation Headquarters and they said he never showed up on Rittenmere at all. They've left messages both at his house and at the office and he hasn't gotten back to them."

"Hold on, Nate," Alton broke in. "The Confederation doesn't know where he is? And neither does Sandra? What about the military?"

"Same story," Squires said. "That's why I'm worried. Mitch doesn't blow off clients, especially big ones. I've tried to get back in touch with Sandra but she doesn't return my calls. I stopped by the house this morning but she didn't answer the door."

"Alright," Alton said, "go back to Sandra's visit. What was her problem?"

"O.K," Squires said, taking a deep breath and letting it out slowly. "Mitch and I were going to go over all this with you when he got back. He finally was able to admit the truth about Sandra to himself. He came to me a little over three weeks ago and changed all the access codes to his personal and business accounts to keep her from getting her hands on his funds while he was gone. He transferred a good sized sum to her account to tide her over until he got back. He also cut her out of his will, leaving everything to you and your folks. Same thing with the life insurance policy. He's going to file for divorce, Alton. I have the data pads in my safe."

Alton was quiet for several minutes while he thought things through. He didn't want to overreact. He also didn't want to waste time if his brother was in trouble. The fact that Mitch hadn't called as he'd promised he would once he got settled on Rittenmere hadn't really worried him. He knew how easy it was to get busy and forget to stay in touch. But his brother took his business seriously. He wouldn't just not show up.

"Do you think Sandra got wind of his plans somehow?" he asked.

"I don't know, Alton. All I know is she was pretty desperate to get her hands on those access codes. She even tried to make me believe Mitch had run off with another woman and abandoned her."

"Well that's definitely bullshit, Nate. Even if there was another woman, he would have just brought her with him."

"What about your parents, have they heard from him?"

"No. I talked to my mom this morning and she complained about not hearing from him. He was supposed to call me, too. I figured he was just busy."

"So what do we do if nobody knows where he is, Alton? Should I get in touch with the police?"

"Yes," Alton said after thinking about it for a second. "Go file a missing persons report, at least. It'll be kind of embarrassing if Mitch *is* just out getting laid, but I can't believe he wouldn't have told one of us where he was going."

"No," Squires agreed, "me either. And he definitely would have told someone from the Confederation if he was going to be late showing up on Rittenmere."

"True," Alton said. "I'll be there in two days, Nate. Set me up in the Ambassador, will you? And keep trying to get in touch with Sandra."

"Of course," Squires replied, visibly relieved. Alton was taking this seriously, too. Between the two of them there was very little they couldn't accomplish if they set their minds to it. "I'll keep asking questions in the meantime."

"I'll get in touch with some people I know, too. See you in a couple of days."

"Alright, Alton, I'll see you then. I wish it were under different circumstances."

"Me too, Slim. And Nate, thanks. I owe you one."

"Just get here, Alton. I have a bad feeling about this."

"You and me both, Slim. You and me both."

The screen went blank.

Nathan Squires stood and walked out of his office, stopping only long enough to tell his assistant that he was going out and didn't know when he'd be back. He took the elevator to the fifth floor and caught a shuttle cab, ordering the autopilot to take him to the police station. It wasn't far and ten minutes later he was standing in front of a reception desk encased in laser proof glass.

"What can I do for ya?" a bored looking young officer asked.

"I'd like to file a missing persons report," Squires told him.

"Have a seat," the officer ordered, pointing to a row of battered, grimy looking chairs against one wall of the entryway. Squires chose the least offensive of the chairs and sat down to wait.

He was still sitting there fifteen minutes later when a door to the left of the enclosed desk opened and Sandra Harvey came walking out, followed closely by a tall, muscular man in a cheap suit. Sandra's eyes were anything but friendly when she saw Squires.

"Hello, Nathan," she said. "What are you doing here?"

"I came to file a missing persons report. Mitch isn't on Rittenmere."

"Mrs. Harvey has already filed a report," the tall detective said, reaching into his breast pocket and pulling out a data recorder. "Who might you be?"

"My name is Nathan Squires. I'm Mr. Harvey's attorney."

"I see," the detective said. "And when did you last see Mr. Harvey?"

"A little more than three weeks ago. I had lunch with him the day before he was scheduled to leave for Rittenmere."

The detective nodded.

"Any special reason?" he asked.

"I was just wishing him a good trip. Mitch isn't just a client. He's also one of my closest friends."

"Nothing that might be related to his disappearance, then? Nothing about a new woman friend, perhaps?"

"No," Squires answered. Obviously Sandra had told the detective the same story she'd told him. "Mitch only had eyes for Sandra. And who could blame him?" he added with a smile. "In any case, Mitch had business on Rittenmere. If there were another woman he would have just brought her along, wouldn't he?"

"That's why I'm so worried," Sandra put in, her face the picture of pained innocence. "I'm afraid Mitch might have gotten himself involved with someone who wasn't being honest with him, someone who might have wanted to take advantage of him, maybe even hurt him."

"Yes, I've been thinking the same thing," Squires said, staring hard at Sandra.

Her face never changed. She was playing the worried wife to the hilt. Squires was suddenly very sure that Sandra Harvey was involved somehow in Mitch's disappearance. He was also very sure that the tall detective was looking at her as if she were the Virgin Mary. Sandra had beaten him to the punch.

"Well," he said, deciding he was wasting his time here, "if Sandra has already filed the report I guess I don't need to bother you any further, Detective....I'm sorry, I don't think I caught your name."

"Madden," the man provided.

"Nice to meet you, Detective Madden. Could you let me know what you find out, please?" He handed the detective a business card. "Feel free to call me anytime, day or night."

"Of course," Madden said, glancing quickly at the card.

"Thank you," Squires said. "Nice to see you again, Sandra. Please call me if you need anything."

With that he turned and left. But he didn't head back to the office. There was a very good private detective he used on a regular basis and he seemed like just the man for this job. Sandra was smart, but if she was involved in this, there would be a clue out there somewhere. If there was, his friend would find it. He needed some kind of proof that Mitch had disappeared and that Sandra was involved. Otherwise, talking to the police was going to be a waste of breath.

"I'm not sure I trust that man," Sandra Harvey said when Squires had walked away. "He's always made me nervous. I tried to get Mitch to switch attorneys more than once but he wouldn't even talk about it. It was almost like Mr. Squires had some kind of hold over him. Do you know what I mean?"

"Yes," Detective Madden said sympathetically. He'd have to check this Squires out. "Don't worry, Mrs. Harvey, I'll get right on this. I'll call you as soon as I come up with anything."

"Thank you so much, Detective," Sandra said, squeezing the man's hand. She'd already been sure to flash him some cleavage when she leaned over his desk to write down her address for him. She had a feeling he'd be calling sooner rather than later.

"Glad to be of help," Madden said with a smile.

I'll bet you are, Sandra thought as she gave the big idiot one last smile before turning and walking out of the station.

Well, she thought with satisfaction as she strolled down Main Street, that should get the ball rolling. Once Mitch was officially declared missing, she'd have to wait exactly one year before she could file to have him declared dead and collect the life insurance money. Until then, she was going to go see a lawyer about getting those access codes released to her. She knew damn well Squires had them. Maybe she could find someone to steal them for her. It was something to think about anyway.

Hailing a cab, she got in, gave the auto pilot her address and leaned back against the seat, trying to think of a suitable man to put the hook into. Or a suitable woman for that matter. She didn't really care. As long as they had plenty of money and a weakness for blondes. But they had to have a lot of money. She'd grown accustomed to a luxurious lifestyle since getting married and she had no intentions of settling for less ever again.

She wasn't worried about Squires or Madden. She'd used the people she had precisely because they were the kind of people who didn't talk, not even to cops. In their business, if you talked, you died. She expected Madden would make a few perfunctory inquiries and then decide she was right, that Mitch had run off with somebody. Then, if she read him right, he'd offer to comfort her and help her through this difficult time. A police detective didn't make enough money to suit her, though. She needed someone else. But who? She'd have to do some research on the net, see who made the real money. There was always somebody. You just had to know where to look.

$$* \qquad * \qquad * \qquad *$$

The Central Longhouse, a high ceilinged structure some one hundred fifty feet long and seventy feet wide, with a round roof of thick thatch, was filled to overflowing. Nearly everyone had come to hear Secotan Samuels speak, having heard rumors that he was going to take another look at some of the old traditions, a closer look. He hadn't disappointed them.

He had just told them that it was time for each one of them to decide for themselves whether or not the old unwritten traditions were still relevant and to live their lives accordingly. It was a message that both shocked and surprised his people, many of whom were unsure they wanted the responsibility of making those choices for themselves. There was a certain comfort for them in having no choice but to live as their parents and grandparents had lived before them.

Hunter Kane sat smiling to himself as Secotan finished speaking and sat down, thinking that the Councillor had just slit his own throat. The people of the village would never stand for this. He would wait and let others denounce this foolishness before adding his own weight to their contempt. He wanted it to be very clear that his personal animosity toward Secotan had nothing to do with his views. The fool had brought this on himself.

Geris Quick was the first to stand. His rebuke would be a gentle one, Kane thought, in deference to a lifetime of friendship. But others would not be so kind.

"I speak as a man and as a father," Quick began, "not as a friend of Secotan Samuels."

Kane was pleased. Even Quick wasn't going to hold back.

"And as a man of this village," Quick continued, "I must agree with our Councillor."

Kane grew even more pleased. Let both of the old fools destroy themselves. It would save him the effort later.

"We have all heard the stories of the enormous struggles our ancestors faced trying to survive here in this place," Geris went on. "I honor their courage and offer thanks to their memory that our people are still here. Because they did what needed to be done, we have survived.

"But we no longer struggle on the edge of extinction. We no longer need every female to bear children as soon as she is able. Our people will not cease to exist if we allow our daughters to marry when they choose to do so, whether it be in their fourteenth year or their thirtieth. As a father, I would like to give my daughters this choice. I stand with Secotan."

Next to stand was Nathaniel Whyte, a slight, pinch faced young man respected for his wisdom despite his sometimes comic ineptitude as a hunter and warrior. A gifted healer and known as a distiller of fine drink, he was well liked among the villagers.

"I also agree with Secotan," he began, struggling to make his voice heard throughout the longhouse despite his soft, measured tone. "Men and women of wisdom can no longer support old, no longer relevant traditions simply because that is how they have always lived. True wisdom allows for necessary change."

Finished, he took his seat and people smiled. You could always count on Nathaniel to keep his comments brief.

Kane was starting to get angry with the direction things were taking when Dasemun Wing, a short, barrel-chested man of twenty-four who was just beginning to grow thick around the middle, stood to speak. Wing could be counted on to disagree with almost anything Secotan Samuels said. Kane was one of the few who knew the reason for Wing's antagonism; a long standing infatuation with Dare Samuels. Wing had harbored secret hopes of wooing the girl before Samuels had stolen her away.

"I must disagree," Wing began. "The reason we no longer struggle for survival, for our very existence, is our adherence to these sacred traditions some of you would so easily cast off. If we do as Secotan suggests, I believe we will find ourselves once again on the edge of extinction within a generation. These traditions have served our people for more than five hundred years. We would be foolish to disregard the wisdom of those who came before us. I beg you to reconsider, Secotan, before all we have worked to become is lost."

Wing took his seat and Hunter Kane stood.

"Dasemun Wing speaks with wisdom," he began levelly, trying to impress on those who heard his voice that his too were words of wisdom, not emotion. "This place is no less dangerous now than it was in our ancestor's time. The only thing that has changed is that there are now more of us to share the burden of survival. That would quickly change if we abandoned our sacred traditions. Our ancestors were indeed wise. And they understood what was necessary if we were to survive and grow strong. If they were here today, I believe they would council us to follow their example. I beg you to continue to heed their wisdom."

A great many more people spoke, divided more or less equally on the issue. It was far from the overwhelming rebuke Kane had expected, but there was enough discord that he would be able to undermine the people's trust in Samuels. It would take time, but it could be done.

Then Mother Shaw stood to speak.

"Quiet please," she said to silence the whispered arguments taking place after the words of the previous speaker. The longhouse quickly grew silent and all eyes turned to the elder. Only then did she continue, her soft but firm voice filling the silence.

"I cannot speak as to what our ancestors would say were they here among us. Nor do I think it matters. They are gone. We are here. We must decide for ourselves what is best for us, just as they decided what was best for them. All Secotan has done is give each of us the power to decide for ourselves what is best. There can be no harm in that."

She paused a moment to let that thought take hold.

"Ten years ago we made Secotan Samuels our Coucillor. I don't know why each of you did so, but I chose him because I trust him and believe in his wisdom and judgment. If he says it is time to look anew at the old and long unused traditions, I say we do.

"This will not change the written law of our people. What is written in the Book of Law cannot be changed without the calling of a Grand Council, and Secotan has not called for that. He speaks only of the old traditions passed down to us through the generations by word of mouth."

The Grand Council was the name given to a meeting of the five Village Councillors. It met three times each year and could also be called together in times of emergency by any of the five.

"Wanchese Hawkins is no longer among us because of one of our ancient traditions. She may well be dead. I cannot help but feel that any tradition that harms even one among us, harms us all. Wanchese left because she would rather risk death than submit herself to a tradition that in our present circumstances would have turned her into little more than a village whore. I can no longer support such a tradition. As I said, what harms one among us, harms us all."

The old woman took her seat and all eyes turned to Hunter Kane, who sat red faced with anger. It had been his demands that had caused Wanchese to flee and Mother Shaw's words were a rebuke. A gentle, indirect rebuke to be sure, but a rebuke none the less. The entire longhouse seemed to hold its breath as Kane stood to speak.

"I was within my rights, old woman," he spat angrily. "You must forgive me if I don't hold my people's sacred beliefs in such low regard as you. I won't soil the memory of my ancestors that way. As for Wanchese Hawkins, she was nothing more than a leech upon this village. She ate our food, drank our water, and what did she give in return? Tell me, old woman, what did she give other than a surly attitude and open disdain for all of us? I gave her a chance to serve at least some small purpose. Better she be a whore than a leech, sucking out our life's blood while giving nothing in return."

There were murmurs of surprise and disapproval at that. That was going too far, even for Kane. Wanchese's attitude hadn't been completely without reason. Many of those within the longhouse had looked back over their own treatment of the girl with more than a twinge of guilt. They had earned her disdain.

"You speak bravely," Kane went on, oblivious to the disapproval of those around him, "knowing that my honor as a warrior prevents me from taking any revenge against an old, dried up hag like you. I only wish you had a living son so I could kill him right in front of you. But that's impossible because a woman like you is incapable of having any but sick, weakly made children who die at the first sign of struggle!"

"That is enough!" Secotan cried, unable to control himself any longer. Mother Shaw had already endured the pain of outliving her three sons and one daughter. He would not see her endure Kane's cruelty.

Kane spun to face him, his fists clenched, fighting down the urge to hurl himself at the man he had come to hate and strike him down. He had no fear of Secotan, only what the others might do if he killed the old fool here in the Central Longhouse.

"I will decide what is enough," he exploded. "It is my honor she has questioned and I will deal with her as I see fit!"

A cold menace came into Secotan's eyes as he stepped forward to stand face to face with Kane. Then the room became deathly still, and when Secotan spoke, his voice raised the hair on the skin of every warrior who heard it.

"You will speak to the elder with proper respect, Hunter Kane, or you will deal with me outside."

Anyone who had forgotten that a warrior dwelt beneath the normally kind and gentle spirit of their Councillor was immediately reminded of the fact. There was unmistakable danger beneath his calmly spoken words. Before Kane had time to accept the challenge, Geris Quick stood and spoke.

"You will deal with me as well," he said. "The elder spoke no ill of you, Kane." That wasn't strictly true, but it was true enough. "You have no call to speak ill of her. I won't stand for it."

Neither will I," a young warrior named Roland Dile said, standing as he spoke. Before long, nearly every warrior in the longhouse was on his feet, adding their support to Mother Shaw.

Hunter Kane was in a difficult position. He couldn't stand against the entire village, yet to back down would cause him to lose face. In the end, he knew he had very little choice. His anger had gotten the better of him.

"I apologize, Mother Shaw," he said through clenched teeth. "I let my anger get the better of me. This talk of discarding our sacred traditions weighs heavy on my heart. I'm sorry, elder."

Mother Shaw said nothing, not trusting herself to speak, only looking at Kane with undisguised contempt. Secotan, understanding there would be no apology to him, decided to let things lie. He would have to deal with Hunter Kane one day, but this was not the day. He said nothing as Kane turned and walked out of the longhouse.

Mother Shaw walked over to him.

"Thank you, Councillor," she said, standing on the tips of her toes and kissing his cheek. "It is cowardly to speak so of the dead." She had born four good children. That they had died was through no fault of their own.

"I know you are wise enough, Mother Shaw," Secotan said loudly enough for everyone to hear him, "to know that you have a village full of sons and daughters who would be lost without your wisdom."

Nodding her head and squeezing his hand tightly, she said "Thank you," her voice breaking with emotion. There were tears running down her cheeks as she too walked from the longhouse. Dasemun Wing turned and followed, knowing that Samuels had won again.

# CHAPTER 12

▼

# LIVING HOPE

Wanchese Hawkins stood watching Mitchell Harvey as he made his way gingerly through the forest. She shook her head as he nearly lost his footing and grabbed hold of a tree limb to steady himself, dropping the small bundle of sticks he'd spent the last twenty minutes collecting. She watched as he carefully bent down and gathered the fallen sticks and started on his way again. Then she circled to the south and hurried back to the cave so he wouldn't know she'd been keeping an eye on him.

A few minutes later he came out of the forest, dropped his bundle on the ground and sat down on the flat stone he often used as a seat when outside. He was breathing heavily and she saw that his arms and legs were shaking. He was pushing himself too hard but she had given up trying to tell him so. It was easier just to keep an eye on him from a distance. And she understood that he was really only trying to help, to make at least some small contribution. She would have preferred he wait a few more weeks.

"Whew!" he said. "I think I might have overdone it a little today."

"You?" she asked sarcastically.

Mitch laughed.

She had to admire his spirit. She had watched him struggle to walk a little further each day, doggedly pushing himself to his feet each time he fell or collapsed from weakness. She might question his intelligence occasionally, but not his courage.

"What animal makes those thick, three toed tracks?" he asked.

"I don't know," she answered.

She'd seen the tracks, too. And she'd seen the animal that made them. But she had no idea what it was called. It seemed harmless but she wouldn't take any chances with one until she knew for sure. That was another reason she didn't like Mitchell roaming around in the forest. There was just too much she didn't know about this place.

"Oh, right," he said. "Sometimes I forget you're new around here too. Where were you headed when we ran into each other anyway?"

Wanchese shrugged.

"Up," she said. "Higher into the mountains."

"Why?"

"That's none of your concern. I go where I want to go."

"I know that. I was just making conversation."

"You are always making conversation," she said, "and always about me. I'm tired of all your questions. You know all you need to know about me."

"Sorry," Mitch said, then gathered his bundle and went into the cave. Wanchese watched him go, feeling a little guilty about having snapped at him. But he asked about things that were simply none of his business. She didn't have to tell him anything she didn't want to. She wasn't his woman. She owed him nothing. Turning away, she stepped into the forest to go check on her snares.

*      *      *      *

Capac stood in the doorway of his large, second story room, looking out in wonder at the small city that spread out before him. Tears stung his eyes as he watched a procession of priests make their way down the narrow street below him, moving toward the temple where they would offer prayers for the next ten hours, just as other priests had in the time before the Inchasa. His people were alive. Truly alive. That was the greatest of the secrets that had been revealed to him over the last five days.

The wondrous revelations had started when he and the others had reached the end of the canyon leading away from Atahuallpa. There they'd been met by twenty warriors; Lydacian warriors armed with Lydacian weapons. Warriors with full heads of hair, their brows free of what Capac now saw as the shameful tattoo of servanthood.

Then he'd learned as they made their way through the forest toward the sea that Shimek, the grimy armorer, was Lydacian, one of seventy spirited away at their birth to be schooled in the Inchasa way and speech before being sent back to pose as Inchasa and supply Javet with information. Some of them had even become Inchasa warriors!

And when they reached the sea beyond the forest they were met by a Lydacian ship, an ocean going ship, something he'd heard and read about but never dreamed he'd see with his own eyes. This ship was long and wide with a weighted keel that acted to right the ship when the huge waves of the stormy sea did their best to capsize it. Two tall masts held huge black sails that sometimes touched the sea as wave after wave buffeted the ship, rolling it nearly onto it's high walled sides.

The crew were small, hard muscled men with shaven heads and strong, calloused hands. They wore shoes and short pants in daylight and added shirts and treated slickers when night fell. The captain, older and slightly taller than most of his men, had placed each passenger into a high backed wooden seat set in a long row along the ship's center line and made them fast with thick hide straps at their waist and chest. It was far from comfortable. Fortunately, the trip had lasted only three hours.

He knew he would never forget the feeling of awed disbelief he'd felt as the ship had approached the large island, sailed around a wooded point and made its way into the smooth waters of a well protected harbor, behind which sat a city; an unmistakably Lydacian city with high walls of stone painted a sparkling white and squared watchtowers placed at regular intervals. Above the wall rose the domed roofs topped with the tall, thin spires that his grandfather had told him his people once built. At the top of each spire was a small crystal that reflected the sun's light, giving the city the appearance of a glittering jewel. He had wept openly at the sight.

"It's lovely, isn't it?" a woman's voice asked from beside him as he gazed out at the city.

"Yes," Capac answered, turning to see a lovely young woman standing in front of the door beside his. "I'm still having a little trouble believing it's real."

"And I have trouble believing there is anything else that is real," the woman said with a smile, walking the few steps across the shared balcony that separated her door from Capac's. "I've lived here all my life. I've never seen anything else."

"You're lucky then," Capac said. "Living among the Inchasa is an experience you can do without, take my word for it."

"I will," the woman said. "But I'd like to hear about it. I can't help being curious."

"And what is your name, curious one?" Capac asked with a smile. The young woman's earnest innocence was wonderful to see. There was little time for innocence among the Inchasa.

"I am Sahil. Would you mind telling me about life over there?" she asked, making a vague gesture toward the sea and the land beyond it. "I'll understand if you'd rather not."

"I think I'd like that, actually," Capac said. "And it's nice to meet you, Sahil. My name is Capac."

"I know," Sahil said. "And it's nice to meet you, too. Would you have breakfast with me? We could talk while we eat."

"I wish I could," Capac answered honestly. "But I have to meet Javet and some others at the civic building. I'll be free this evening, though."

"Tonight then," Sahil said brightly. "I'll make something special, something uniquely Lydacian. I know just the thing."

"I'll look forward to it," Capac said with a respectful bow. "Until tonight, then."

Sahil went back inside and Capac returned to his own room, where he grabbed a sweet tasting palenta fruit to eat while he walked and set out for the civic building.

The sight of so many of his own people walking freely upon the streets of their own city, many of them with unshaven, unmarked foreheads, still made his chest tight with inexpressible joy. He found himself walking slowly through the crowded streets and bazaars grinning happily and exchanging greetings with those he met, his ears still thrilling to the sound of his own language spoken aloud all around him. He was the last to arrive at the civic building but Javet and the others seemed unconcerned.

"I take it you like Lydacia City, Capac?" Javet asked with a sad smile, his eyes filled with sorrow.

"Yes," Capac answered, wondering what news had caused Javet this new pain. He hoped he hadn't done anything to cause it. "It's the most beautiful city I've ever seen. And to hear our language spoken so feely!"

"Yes," Javet said with a knowing nod. "It is a balm to the soul, isn't it? I love to just wander the markets and listen."

"That's why I'm late, actually," Capac told him. "I was doing just that."

"Good," Javet said, laying a friendly hand on Capac's shoulder. "And now it is time for us to decide how we are going to make it possible for all our people to know that very same feeling. We have news. Please, sit."

Capac took a seat at the long stone table that filled the main room of the two story civic building. The men joining him around the table were the most influential among his people, many of whom he had believed dead. Finding them all here had been another exciting surprise.

"Please share your news with everyone, Duret," Javet said when he too was seated at the table.

"The young Cuzco has had a vision," Duret said. "He has seen his people winning a glorious battle, defeating the people of the river to the east. He has issued orders for an army of five thousand warriors to be raised, equipped and trained."

The number caused an excited stir to ripple around the table. Duret waited until it grew quiet again before going on.

"Our sources tell us that the main goal of this attack is the capture of large numbers of slaves. They plan to move out after they celebrate their Inti Raymi sun festival."

"This could be bad for us," one of the elder priests said. "The Inchasa army will be even stronger than before."

"True," Duret said. "But that army will be more than ten days march to the east and busy waging a war against the river people. If our people flee the Inchasa lands at that moment, who will be left to stop them? We could move all of our people to safety."

"And what happens when the Inchasa army returns?" a young priest named Milek asked.

"They will find us gone," Duret answered. "But they will have thousands of new slaves to put to work. They won't need us anymore. In fact, we're told that Manco has already counseled the Cuzco to kill our people once we are no longer needed. Our men, anyway. What they want to do with our women you can guess for yourself. We *must* bring them to safety."

"The Inchasa will follow," Milek argued.

"They cannot follow," Duret replied. "Their reed boats would be sent to the bottom of the sea long before they ever sighted this island."

"What do you think, Capac?" Javet asked. "Will the Inchasa pursue us if we bring our people here?"

"No," Capac answered, thinking of the Cuzco's open disdain for him and his people. "Once they enslave the river people, I expect they'll be only too happy to be rid of us. But Duret is right about what the Cuzco will do to anyone left behind."

"I agree," Javet said. "And while it pains me to know that another people will be forced into bondage in our place, I think we can only do what is best for us and our people. Here Lydacia will live and grow strong again."

"What of Capac's vision?" Milek asked. "What of the city on the plain? Perhaps we are meant to follow and join forces with the river people to defeat the Inchasa. What if we are the man-beast of the vision? We could defeat the Inchasa, completely wipe them out."

"I must confess, the man-beast continues to puzzle me," Javet said. "But I still believe our best hope to be the plan we discussed. Whether the city be here or on the plain, what matters is that our people will be free."

"What does the book say?" Capac asked hesitantly. He didn't want to question Javet, but his vision had been of a city on the plain.

Javet stood and left the room. When he returned, he carried in his hands the sacred book, which he placed gently on the table. He leafed through the pages knowingly until he found the passage he was looking for.

"And our people will be raised up to new glory," he read. "New cities will spring up from the ground, the old ways will be as new and peace shall reign over the land for generations. The streets will be filled with gladness and the singing of children will meet the ears of those who walk the lands of our rebirth.

"As for the oppressor, a sign shall light the night sky. The sword of a mighty avenger will slice the very heavens in two. On this night will come one who will walk where our enemies have walked, who will see with new eyes and know the blackness of their hearts. And they will not know him as their destruction, for he will not seem as one who should be feared. But fear him they will, when at last their eyes are opened, and they behold the warrior within."

Javet gently closed the book and looked at Capac.

"What do you say, Capac? How would you interpret this? Should we build our city on the plain?"

"No," Capac answered after thinking about it. "The book says there will be a time of peace for our people. If we build our city on the plain, we'll have to defend it to keep it. The Inchasa would never leave us alone."

"That was our thinking as well. What of the rest of it? Do you believe we are to be the avenger the prophecy speaks of?"

"I don't know. The Inchasa certainly don't think of us as a danger. And they would be very surprised to find so many capable warriors among us."

The Inchasa had come upon the Lydacians after a prolonged period of peace, a time that found them with few trained warriors and in no condition to resist an armed invasion. To the Inchasa, they would always be helpless and inferior. At least until proven otherwise.

"Yes, that's true," Javet admitted. "Still, I believe the prophecy points to an outsider. It would be more specific if we were meant to rise up against the Inchasa in force. Taking this opportunity to bring all our people to safety seems the wiser path."

"Then that is what we should do," Capac said. He could trust Javet with the lives and hopes of his people far more easily than he could his own interpretation of his vision.

"Where will everyone live?" Milek asked. "The city is over crowded as it is. We'll have to expand, and that means tearing down a wall."

"No," Javet told him proudly. "We will build a new city, one just as beautiful as this one. We have room to grow here, Milek, and grow we shall. There is no need for us to feel crowded ever again."

He and the High Priest before him had been secretly moving their people to the island in small numbers for over fifty years. As they had hoped, the Inchasa had assumed the race was simply dying out and taken little notice. Now there were over seven thousand Lydacians on the Island. But that still left nearly a thousand living among the Inchasa.

"I still don't like the idea of the Inchasa having more men trained and available to attack us," Milek argued. "If we can build ships strong enough to sail to this island, so can they."

"What else troubles you, Milek?" Javet asked. He had lived long enough to know he could not always think of everything. Perhaps Milek had some legitimate concerns.

Milek hesitated then decided to speak his mind.

"I'm afraid we may be risking all we've worked so hard to build," he said. "The Inchasa are not fools. They will discover where we've gone and they will follow us. Their pride will demand it, whether they need us anymore or not. They will never rest until we are destroyed."

"What would you have us do?" Javet asked. "Leave the other's behind?"

"No, of course not," Milek said, though that was precisely what he thought they should do. As far as he was concerned, the survival of the Lydacian way of life was more important than eight or nine hundred people, most of whom were old and of little use anyway. "But we don't have to lead the Inchasa to us by bringing them here. We could help them escape to the mountains. They could make a new life for themselves there."

"I see," Javet said, disappointed. Milek had been such a promising pupil. Perhaps he would outgrow his selfishness in time. "I understand your concerns, Milek, but I would rather risk leading the Inchasa here than abandon my own people. If they stay within the reach of the Inchasa, they will be hunted down and killed. We will bring them here and deal with what comes."

"Even if it brings our own destruction?" Milek asked angrily. "The destruction of all we've worked to regain?"

"Yes," Javet answered softly. He would trust in the prophecy and the strength of his people to overcome any mistakes he and the others may have made in interpreting it. If fear for their own safety and comfort was more important to the men around this table than helping the rest of their people reach safety, theirs was not a society worth saving.

"Unless others among you agree with Milek," he added with a questioning glance around the table.

"No," Tilac, the elder priest who had spoken earlier said. "Either all of our people are free or none of us will ever be, not truly."

Heads nodded in agreement around the table. Javet smiled with relief.

"Good," he said. Then he turned and looked at Capac.

"There is something else. The Cuzco has announced that if you are not waiting for him when he reaches Pachacutec ten days from now, he will kill one Lydacian every day until you return."

"I see," Capac said, his spirit crashing to the depths of despair. "I will have to meet him then, won't I?"

"No!" Milek said angrily. "He knows too much to go back."

"I will die before I tell them anything," Capac said, looking into Javet's sad, knowing eyes. "I swear it."

"I know you will," Javet said, putting a comforting hand on Capac's arm. "I wish there was something we could do, my friend."

"So do I," Capac said. "When do I leave?"

"You will return to Pachacutec with Duret and myself," Javet told him. "We leave tomorrow morning."

"Will you be safe there?" Capac asked.

"I believe we will. No one saw us in Atahuallpa and we will do our best to stay out of sight and draw as little attention to ourselves as possible. That is all we can do."

"Yes," Capac said sadly, "I suppose it is. Thank you, Javet. Thank you for bringing me here, for letting me see all of this. I thought you had given up on us, that we had all given up on ourselves."

"That was what we wanted you to think, Capac. And what we needed the Inchasa to think. But we have never stopped believing. Our people live again, my friend. Do not lose faith."

"I won't," Capac said, determined to redeem himself, whatever the cost. Manco would have to kill him. He would not betray his people's hopes again.

"And what will the Inchasa do when you can stand the pain no longer and you tell them about this island, Capac?" Milek asked nastily. "What will they do then?"

Capac looked up at the young priest, his heart too heavy with sadness for him to become angry.

"If they were to learn of this island," he said softly, "they would kill every last one of our people remaining within their empire, and likely try to find a way to reach out and destroy this place. But they will not learn of it, not from me. I expect the Cuzco wants to make and example of me, to show our people that no one can escape him. He will force me to show him how to find and gather the herb and then he will kill me, probably in a public ceremony of some kind so that everyone can see what happens to Lydacians who defy him."

"You speak bravely of death now," Milek said, "when words come easily. But will you still have courage when a knife is at your throat and every part of your body cries with pain?"

"I will," Capac answered, a new determination lighting his eyes. "Because I know this place exists, I will. They will kill me whether I tell them what they want to know or not. My silence will at least give my death some meaning. I will not betray our people again."

"I know you won't," Javet said, glaring Milek into silence and trying desperately to believe what he was saying. "I know you won't."

# CHAPTER 13

▼

# CONSEQUENCES

"You are certain?" Secotan Samuels asked the tall, slender young woman sitting beside him with downcast eyes. Rela Rivers had just told him that she no longer wished to become the wife of the young warrior with whom her father had made arrangements. He had known something like this would happen but had hoped it wouldn't happen so quickly.

"Yes," Rela answered. "I'm certain."

Also sitting with Secotan were Rela's father, Saul Rivers, and the young man in question, Jon Cloud.

"And you?" Secotan asked the young warrior.

"I no longer want her for a wife," Jon Cloud answered stiffly, trying not to show the pain and embarrassment Rela's words brought him. He had thought they were getting along well. What had he done wrong?

"It's not that I don't like you, Jon," Rela said softly, seeming to understand what he was thinking. "You've been very kind and I know you are a good man and will be a good husband. It's just that I…. I don't want to marry until I'm in love. I'm sorry."

"I understand," Jon Cloud lied. He wasn't even sure he knew what love was. And right now he really didn't care. He just wanted this meeting to be over so he could get out of the village and be alone.

"Then what is the difficulty?" Secotan asked.

"*I* am the difficulty," Saul Rivers said angrily. "You said that every man would be free to choose for himself how he wished to live, whether he would follow the old ways or not. Well, I choose to do exactly that. And anyone living in my long-house will do the same."

"I see," Secotan said, rubbing his temples to relieve a sudden ache in his head.

"Then I will live somewhere else," Rela said defiantly.

"You will sit there and be quiet!" Saul snapped back.

"Please," Secotan said, holding up his hand to quiet them. "There are several questions here and none of them will be answered unless we discuss them with our emotions under control."

He looked around the tiny circle until everyone was looking at him. Satisfied, he continued.

"What I actually said, Saul, was that each *person* would be free to decide for themselves whether or not they choose to live by the old ways, not each man."

Saul grunted his opinion of that. Since when did women have a voice in such things?

"And," Secotan went on, "it is written in our law that a child passes into adult-hood with the coming of their fourteenth year." Rela looked up hopefully at that. She was fourteen and a half. "As an adult, Rela has a right to make decisions for herself."

"Then a man no longer has the right to decide how his longhouse will behave?" Saul asked angrily. "That is not what you told us, Secotan."

"No, that is not what I told you and that is not what I'm saying now. Of course a man has the right to choose how his longhouse will behave. But, as an adult, Rela does indeed have the right to go and live somewhere else if she dis-agrees with you. Is that what you want?"

"Of course not," Saul said.

"Then you will have to allow her the freedom to make these choices for her-self," Secotan told him.

"It is not right to take away a man's authority over his children this way, Seco-tan," Saul said. "It will bring us great trouble, I think."

"Taking away a man's authority is not my intention, Saul. I only want to give each adult the freedom to choose for themselves. And Rela has become an adult. Just as my Elinor will become an adult five months from now. And I will have to allow her the freedom to make her own choices. I only hope I've taught her well enough that her mistakes will not be too many or too great." Please God, let them not be too many or too great.

"But Rela is my daughter, not yours. I have the right to raise her according to the old ways if I choose to. You cannot take that right away from me."

"No, I can't. And I don't want to. You have every right to demand that Rela live according to your wishes as long as she remains under your roof. All I'm saying is that Rela has the right to leave rather than obey those demands. I would hate to see that happen. Enjoy her while you can, Saul. She'll be gone from your longhouse soon enough."

"You would leave your family over this?" Saul asked Rela. "You would do that to your mother?"

"Yes," the girl answered. "If you force me to."

"Very well," Saul said sadly. "I don't want to lose you, Rela, or force you from our home. I only seek what I believe is best. Jon Cloud is a good young man."

"I know, father," Rela answered. "And he will find a wife who will love him, as he deserves."

"Yes, I'm sure he will," Secotan said. "In fact, I believe my Elinor was less than happy to hear of Jon's impending marriage."

Jon Cloud smiled shyly at that, though his eyes still betrayed the pain he was feeling. Secotan put a friendly hand on the boy's shoulder. Elinor could do far worse than Jon Cloud. Far worse.

"What of the betrothal agreement?" Saul asked. "I gave this young man my arm in solemn agreement, my word. What will the village think of a man who breaks his solemn oath?"

"You haven't broken your oath," Jon said, wishing Saul would stop arguing and let them get this over with. "I know that. We can tell the village that Rela and I came to this decision together. There would be less shame in that for all of us."

People would still wonder, Jon knew, and some would guess the truth, but there was nothing he could do about that. He only hoped his father never found out the truth.

"You would do that?" Saul asked, grateful for the young man's offer. He wondered if he would be so gracious in Jon's place. Why couldn't Rela see what a fine young man she was turning her back on?

"Yes, if Rela agrees."

"Of course," Rela said, knowing that what Jon proposed would be better for everyone, including him. He didn't really deserve what was happening to him. But she was afraid she would regret it the rest of her life if she wasn't honest with herself now. She had to do this.

Jon Cloud nodded, hoping the meeting would at last be over.

"What of the betrothal gift?" Secotan asked, crushing Jon's hopes.

"I'll repay everything Saul gave me," he said quickly. Would this never end?

"No," Saul said. "I paid only a few baskets of fish and crops. I'd be honored if you would consider it a gift among friends, Jon."

"Thank you," Jon said, looking up for the first time. It was a kind offer. One that would ease some of his shame and showed a measure of respect between them. "The honor is mine."

"It is decided then?" Secotan asked.

"It is," Saul said and Rela and Jon nodded their heads in agreement.

"But I tell you plain, Secotan Samuels," Saul added, "I will never forgive you for this, or forget. You've taken away more than you've given us by allowing our people to question the old ways. I no longer trust you and I will do everything I can to see you removed as Councillor of this village."

Secotan nodded. There were plenty of other people who felt the same way. At least Saul had said so to his face.

*     *     *     *

Mitchell Harvey sat outside the cave busily putting the finishing touches on a staff he had carved for himself from a stout tree limb. He'd gotten tired of dragging his ass off of the ground and hoped walking with the staff would help his balance and strength. He'd carved it to a length of six feet and a width of one and one half inches and had spent the last two days tirelessly smoothing it with stones and loose sand.

Finished smoothing the last of the rough spots, he threw the handful of sand he'd been using to the ground and stood to his feet, hefting the staff in his hands, liking the feel of its weight and balance and the smooth feel of the wood in his hands. Not bad for an amateur, he thought. Not bad at all.

"It is finished?" Wanchese asked.

She was amused at the time and effort he had put into the walking stick, thinking that the rough tree limb would have served the same purpose. But, it had given the stubborn fool something to do that kept him busy and out of harms way so she hadn't said anything.

"Yeah, I think so. What do you think?"

"It will serve the purpose. And desa wood is strong."

"Good," Mitch said, looking the staff up and down with satisfaction. He'd chosen the limb he had because it had been close to the length and weight he was looking for. If it was a strong wood so much the better. It could be used for more than just walking. He knew how to use it as a weapon and having it made him feel a little less defenseless. Not that it would be much good against a deathclaw or one of the big grey cats Wanchese had shown him, but it was better than nothing.

"Have you seen any sign of those Inchasa coming back this way?" he asked, moving the staff through a few basic block and strike movements and wondering if he was kidding himself. He wouldn't last thirty seconds against one of those Inchasa swords. No wood was that strong. Still, it was something.

"No," Wanchese answered. "It's too soon. They were heading toward the northern villages. I really doubt they'll come back this way."

"I hope you're right," Mitch said. "I like to be prepared for the worst, though."

Wanchese nodded. She felt the same way. If she'd been able to find any kind of good, secure shelter further north, she would move. The cave was snug and relatively comfortable, but there would be no escape for them if they were discovered while they were inside.

"They'll keep moving south from one village to the next until they find some stragglers or a poorly guarded group working in the fields," she told him. "If they don't find anyone, they'll just watch each village for a short time to gather information and then return home."

"That's why you don't think they'll come back this way, because they'll be returning from further south?"

"Yes. Coming back here would be out of their way."

"You're probably right," Mitch said, though he couldn't shake the feeling that those men would be back for another look. Maybe he was just being paranoid.

"I'd like to test this thing out," he said, holding up the staff. "Could I go with you when you head out to check one of your snares?"

"Alright," she answered. At least if he was with her she could keep an eye on him. "We can go now if you like."

"Sounds good to me."

Wanchese put aside the dress she'd been mending and got to her feet, grabbed her pack and stepped off into the forest to the east without another word. Mitch chuckled, thinking that this was the first interpersonal relationship he could ever remember having where he was the talkative one, and stepped into the forest after her.

"Have your people ever been friendly with the Inchasa?" he asked as he followed along behind Wanchese, who he knew was keeping a slow pace for his benefit.

"They are no longer my people," she answered sharply. "But no, the people of the river have never been friendly with them. They didn't even know the Inchasa existed until they came out of the night and attacked."

"How long ago was that?"

"A long time ago, when there was only one village."

"The river people never talked with them at all? Or traded?"

"The Inchasa never asked to talk or trade. They just attacked. That is how it has always been."

Well, Mitch thought, I can believe that. He'd seen the way the Inchasa reacted to strangers. Not exactly a friendly "Hello, welcome to the neighborhood."

"Have the river people ever attacked them?" he asked.

"No. The Inchasa village is very large, with many warriors, and is surrounded by a wall of stone. Besides, they have nothing the river people want."

"I just thought the men from the river might have tried to rescue some of the people the Inchasa captured," Mitch said. What kind of man would just let someone steal his wife and children without trying to get them back?

"It has been done," Wanchese told him as she stepped under a fallen tree that was leaning against a large black boulder. "But the Inchasa guard their slaves heavily when they're outside the wall. They have more warriors than the people of the river do."

"The river people have tried then?"

"Yes," Wanchese answered. "Many have died and only a few come back alive. My father came back," she said with obvious pride.

"He rescued someone?"

"Yes, his sister. He went to the Inchasa village and brought her back himself."

"He must have been a very brave man," Mitch said, thinking of what kind of balls it took to go into enemy territory alone, never mind getting close enough to rescue a prisoner.

"He was," Wanchese said as she reached the small seep where she had placed her snare. "He feared no one. My mother sometimes got angry with him because he had no fear. She was very angry when he came back from the Inchasa village."

Mitch smiled, thinking of similar exchanges between his own parents. His father had an unhealthy fascination with poisonous reptiles and often took what his mother considered foolish and unnecessary risks to capture and study them.

"Sounds like my father," he said as Wanchese reset the empty snare, some lucky critter having somehow triggered it without getting caught. "My mother's always telling him he was born with too much courage and not enough brains."

"Then you are definitely your father's son," Wanchese said, but there was no malice in her voice and Mitch could see that she was fighting back a smile.

"Yeah," he said with a grin, "my mother's always saying that too."

"Your walking stick seems to help," Wanchese said when she'd finished resetting the snare. "You're walking much better."

"I feel a lot more steady," Mitch admitted. "I was getting pretty tired of falling on my face."

"Sit still then. You're fortunate not to have broken any bones yet."

Mitch shrugged. He didn't know how to explain why he had to be doing something, helping in at least some small way. Stupid male pride, probably.

"I felt guilty sitting around while you did all the work," he said.

"I'm used to work. It would be better if you let your body heal," Wanchese retorted, but she didn't seem to be as angry as usual.

"I know. But I'm alright now that I have this," he said, hefting his staff. He really was walking a lot better. Wanchese looked unconvinced.

"Do you need to rest before we start back?" she asked.

He shook his head and she stepped past him, leading the way.

"Do the Inchasa always travel in groups of six?" he asked. "I've seen them twice now and both times there were six of them."

"No, not always. They send six men on small raids and to gather information. But they have attacked river villages with as many as one hundred men, though that hasn't happened in years."

"Why not?"

"Because they lost too many warriors the last time they did. Twenty seven, I think. My father killed five of them himself before he died."

"How many men did the village lose?"

"Thirty one warriors were killed, as well as five women and one child. Three other women were carried off."

That would explain why the Inchasa didn't attack entire villages anymore, Mitch reasoned. Losing thirty men to save your village from destruction was an acceptable loss. Losing twenty-seven to capture three women wasn't.

"I'm sorry about your parents," he said, wishing he'd never brought the subject up. He'd had no idea that the last major Inchasa attack had been the one Wanchese's mother and father had died in.

"What are you sorry for?" Wanchese snapped. "You didn't kill them."

"No, I just meant…." he started to say, but Wanchese had increased her pace and was quickly moving away from him.

"Never mind," he muttered, knowing that he couldn't keep up and Wanchese wasn't interested in hearing what he had to say anyway. He'd pissed her off yet again. He seemed to have a natural talent for it.

"Damn," he said, swinging his staff against a thick tree with a thud. When would he learn to keep his big mouth shut?

# CHAPTER 14

▼

# SMALL VICTORIES

Standing outside Pachacutec's northern gate, Capac was struck by the sudden realization that this could well be the last day of his life. He trembled despite the heat of the late afternoon sun as he watched Manco marching at the front of the Cuzco's party. Behind him were the men of his detachment, the royal litter, a large group of the dark skinned slaves from the northern desert, and rank after rank of warriors from the Atahuallpa garrison, as well as men gathered from tambos along the way. The smile that lit Manco's face as he came close enough to recognize who it was standing beside the gate did nothing to ease Capac's fear. He knew the smile of the hunter.

"You cost me a bottle of wine, you filthy Lydacian," Manco said as he approached the gate. "I bet my brother you would be too much of a coward to show yourself again, no matter how many people the Cuzco killed." Then he walked up and slammed Capac to the ground with a vicious backhand.

"The fact that I don't know how to fight doesn't make me a coward," Capac retorted from where he lay on the dusty ground. He wiped the blood from his broken lips with his hand and got back to his feet, suddenly eager to get things over with. Manco could hit him, cut him, burn him and even kill him, but he would never again defeat him.

"Brave words," Manco said, a taunting smile on his face. "But before I'm done with you we will see just how much courage you have, Lydacian. I promise you that."

"Yes," Capac said, "you're very good at hurting people who can't defend themselves."

He saw the anger he was hoping to raise light Manco's eyes briefly, but then the warrior visibly relaxed and smiled knowingly.

"Take him to the palace," he ordered one of the warriors under his command. "Lock him in one of the basement rooms. And don't let him goad you into killing him. The Cuzco wants him alive. For now."

The warrior nodded and pushed Capac roughly through the gate into the city.

Inchasa hurled insults at him as he walked through the crowded streets, but he paid no attention. Instead, he took comfort in the sympathy in the eyes of the occasional Lydacian who crossed his path. One woman even risked reaching out to touch his arm.

"Thank you," she said emotionally when he turned to look at her then was gone before he had a chance to reply. Word of the Cuzco's ultimatum had spread quickly and many within the Lydacian community had believed Capac would not come back, that they and their families would die to buy his freedom. His return had been met with a combination of relief and grudging respect.

Inchasa women laughed at him as a tear rolled down his cheek and onto his broken lips. There was no way they could know that his were tears of joy, of redemption, and of pride. In each Lydacian face he passed he saw gratitude, sympathy and respect, things he thought he'd forfeited forever when he gave in to weakness and betrayed his people's secrets. The contempt and laughter of all the Inchasa in the kingdom was nothing when compared with that. He walked the rest of the way to the palace with his head held high.

The warrior locked him in a cold, dank cell, which was lost in total darkness with the closing of the heavy wooden door. Arranging his robe beneath him, Capac sat on the cold stone floor and closed his eyes, scrolling through in his mind's eye all of the vivid images of Lydacia City, of Javet and Duret, of Sahil and the wonderful meal he had shared with her his last night in the city.

The memories eased his mind, though he still felt a shiver of fear when the heavy door swung open a long while later and a warrior ordered him to stand. He was led out of his cell and up onto the main level of the palace, where Manco was waiting for him.

"The Cuzco would like to speak to you," he said with a grin.

Capac followed him to the Cuzco's quarters, quickly running through his mind all the information Javet had told him he could give the Cuzco without endangering their plans. Javet still help out hope Capac could live through this ordeal. Capac had no such delusions.

"Your wayward servant, my Cuzco," Manco said as they walked into the Cuzco's chambers.

"Where have you been?" the young king asked sternly. "And I strongly recommend you tell me the truth."

"I ran away to the forest by the sea," Capac answered.

"Why did you run?"

"Because I thought you were going to kill me."

The Cuzco smiled at that.

"Then perhaps you are not as stupid as Manco thinks," he said. "Why did you come back?"

"I heard about your decree," Capac answered simply.

"You heard about my decree in the forest?"

"No. I heard about your decree when I went to a tambo to steal food."

"What do you think, Manco? Is he telling me the truth?"

"I think he is far more truthful when he is bleeding and in pain, my Cuzco."

"You may be right," the boy said with a bored smile. "See to it."

Before Capac had a chance to react, Manco had stepped forward and struck him hard across the face, knocking him to the floor. He tried to protect his face and head but Manco rained blows on him, stopping only to kick him in the stomach and groin when his arms got tired. The taste of blood in his mouth and nauseating pain became Capac's world until he could stand no more and slipped into unconsciousness.

He woke up back in his dark cell, stripped naked and lying on the cold floor. His entire body ached and it was painful to breathe. He had tried to prepare himself for the pain, to set his mind to ignore it and think of the triumph to come. But now that he was here, with his body broken and bleeding, he wondered if Milek had been right. Maybe he wasn't strong enough.

Pushing himself off the floor, he struggled to his feet and took hesitant, unsteady steps around the room, trying to get some warmth back into his body. He was just starting to fell the slightest bit alive when the door swung open. His guard seemed surprised to see him awake. He hesitated a moment then shrugged his shoulders and threw a bucket of cold water over Capac's head and chest. He laughed when Capac couldn't suppress a surprised yelp. Then he led him back up to the main level where Manco stood waiting again.

"He was awake," the guard reported.

"Really?" Manco asked, obviously surprised. "I'll have to pay closer attention to my work this time."

He turned and walked toward the Cuzco's chambers again, the guard pushing Capac along behind him, moving slowly as Capac was limping noticeably. The Cuzco watched him walk in, gave a quick nod to Manco and watched as the big warrior started in on Capac's battered face and body again.

After a short but spirited beating, Manco started in with is knife, slicing the bottom of Capac's feet and between his toes and fingers. When he grew bored with that, he heated his knife in the hearth and seared the still sensitive wound from the last beating. Capac heard himself cry out, but it seemed as though it was someone else's voice, someone far away who was obviously in terrible pain. He felt himself slipping toward unconsciousness again and hoped it would come quickly. Then he heard the Cuzco say, "That will do for now," and cold water was thrown over his face again.

"Are you ready to be truthful with me?" the Cuzco asked.

"Yes," Capac whispered. "Anything, anything at all. But please, no more."

"That's better. Now, where did you go when you ran?"

"To the forest by the sea. That's the truth, I swear it."

"And how did you get out of Atahuallpa?"

This was one of the questions Javet had told him to answer truthfully as there was a good chance they had found the tunnel.

"An armorer named Shimek helped me," he answered.

"Why would an Inchasa help the likes of you?"

"He…he has a fondness for young boys," Capac lied. "A priest in Atahuallpa found out about it and threatened to turn him in if he didn't help us."

"I see," the Cuzco said, thinking the story could be true but not sure he believed it. "But how did you get out of the city?"

"There is a tunnel underneath Shimek's shop. It leads to the waste dump on the western edge of the city. He led us there and then down the canyon to the forest."

"That much at least is true," the Cuzco said and Capac knew that Javet had been right. They had found the tunnel.

"How many men escaped with you and who were the others?"

"There were five," Capac answered, his voice weak because he was having trouble breathing. "Shimek, two of his friends, the Lydacian priest who knew Shimek's secret and me."

"Where are this Shimek and his friends now?" the Cuzco asked, thinking it likely Capac was telling the truth now. His scouts had told him they had tracked five men down the canyon before losing the trail in the forest.

"I don't know. Truly I don't. They left us at the edge of the forest and said they'd kill us if we tried to follow them."

"I'm not sure I believe that," the Cuzco said. "Do you think you could persuade him to be a little more forthcoming, Manco?"

"It would be a pleasure, my Cuzco," Manco replied, placing his knife back into the flame of the hearth.

"No, please," Capac pleaded, "I swear I'm telling you the truth!"

The Cuzco ignored him and Manco smiled cruelly as he pulled his knife out of the fire and walked to where Capac lay huddled on the floor.

"Your oaths mean nothing," he said. "Everyone knows Lydacians can't be trusted."

Then he thrust the hot knife into Capac's chest, between his second and third rib, and left it there, laughing at the smell of seared flesh and Capac's cries of agony.

"Are you feeling more truthful yet?" the Cuzco asked. He knew he was likely being told the truth but he desperately wanted to find this Shimek and have him torn to pieces in front of the entire city. He couldn't have Inchasa helping Lydacians, no matter what the reason.

"I'm telling you the truth," Capac sobbed. "I'm telling you the truth!"

"Again please, Manco," the Cuzco ordered, and Manco held his knife in the fire again before searing the other side of Capac's chest. At the Cuzco's direction, he repeated the process several times until Capac's chest was filled with sores and the room with the smell of burnt human flesh.

"Enough," the Cuzco said finally. He looked at Manco questioningly and the big warrior shrugged.

"I don't think he knows where the traitor is," he said. "He would have told us."

"Agreed," the Cuzco said with a nod. "Have him brought back to his cell. Put straw down on the floor and give him blankets and clothing. See to it that he is attended to by one of their healers. I don't want him dead yet."

"Yes, my Cuzco," Manco answered with a bow of his head.

Then he walked out of the room and called for two warriors to carry Capac back to his cell. If they noticed the tears flowing down the Lydacian's cheeks they understood them no better than the Inchasa women on the streets of Pachacutec. They had no way of knowing they were tears of relief and triumph, that the half conscious shell of a man they carried was filled with more joy and pride than either of them had ever known.

"I told you, Milek," he whispered in his own tongue. "I told you."
His face was too battered for the Inchasa to recognize his smile.

✳     ✳     ✳     ✳

Two weeks of tireless effort had gained Alton Harvey and Nathan Squires nothing but dead ends and wasted time. Nathan's private detective had come up empty, too. No one was willing to talk to them no matter how much money was waved in their face. Desperate and growing more convinced every day that Mitch was in serious trouble, Nate Squires had called in a favor he had promised himself he would never call in. He hoped it was worth it.

"Nathan, my old friend," Simon Bellotti said, gripping Squire's hand tightly. "It's been too long."

"And you must be Alton Harvey," he said, turning to offer his hand to Alton. "I've heard great things about your new resort."

"Thank you for seeing us," Alton said.

"Yes, I'm very grateful for your time, Mr. Bellotti," Nate Squires added.

"Simon, Nathan, Simon. My friends call me Simon."

Nathan Squires was a little uncomfortable with that. Simon Bellotti ruled the largest black market operation in the entire Traegus Sector, and he did so with an iron fist. He was not the kind of man a respected attorney was expected to be on a first name basis with.

But, when he'd been fresh out of law school, Nate had been assigned to defend a young Simon Bellotti of perhaps the only offense he had ever been accused of, of which he was innocent. He'd gotten the charges dismissed and Bellotti, just another young tough at the time, had told him that if he ever needed anything, all he had to do was call. That had been thirteen years ago. But when Squires had called, Bellotti had cleared his schedule for the day and insisted they come to his home.

Bellotti was a big man, both tall and broad. He wore his hair cropped short now just as he had when Nate had last seen him. His sharp blue eyes lent a certain handsomeness to a rough, crooked nosed face that bore the scars of a hard fought journey to the top of a harsh profession.

"Can I offer you gentleman a drink?" he asked, walking over to a large bar at the far end of his surprisingly small, though nicely accommodated, office.

"Yes, thank you," Nate and Alton said at the same time.

"Scotch alright?"

"That will be fine," Alton said.

"With a splash of water for me," Nate added.

When they had their drinks and Simon Bellotti was seated behind his large, highly polished desk, he opened a humidor and offered his guests a cigar. Both men politely declined and Bellotti decided to do the same as a courtesy.

"Now, what can I do for you, Nathan?" he asked.

"Well, Mr...., Simon," Nate began uncomfortably, "I don't want to offend you and I hope you won't take offense at our coming to you in a matter like this. We simply didn't know where else to turn."

Bellotti made a "go on" gesture with his hand.

"Alton's brother, Mitchell, is missing. He's not the kind of man to just run off unannounced, especially not when he has business commitments going unmet. We wondered if you might have sources of information that could be of use to us in tracking him down."

Bellotti was quiet for a moment, his chin resting on his steepled fingers as he thought.

"How long has he been missing?" he asked.

"At least five weeks, we think," Nate answered.

"Would he have any enemies to speak of? Serious enemies, I mean. Ones who might want him out of the way?"

Nate and Alton looked at each other, a silent question passing between them. Was that possible? Would Sandra resort to such extreme measures? They'd argued the point back and forth almost daily and Alton had grown desperate enough to admit it was at least possible. He nodded and Nate turned back to Bellotti.

"That is a possibility."

Bellotti thought that over for another minute then took a deep breath and released it slowly through is nose.

"I can make inquiries," he said, then turned and looked at each man in turn. "If you will give me your word of honor that you won't seek to harm the man I'm going to call, you're welcome to stay while I speak to him. If not, I'm afraid I'll have to ask you to wait outside."

"You think this man might be involved in my brother's disappearance?" Alton asked.

"Possibly. But if he was, it's only because someone paid him to be, and paid him well."

"That's who we'd want to get at if that were the case," Alton said. "I give you my word, Mr. Bellotti, I won't look to hurt your source."

Bellotti nodded and turned to Nate Squires.

"Agreed," Squires said. "I'm not looking to hurt anyone. I just want to find my friend."

"Good, good," Bellotti said, turning his chair to face the VML console to the right of his desk.

"Activate," he said.

The screen began to hum.

"Demetrius Nestor," he instructed and the VML made the connection.

"Demetrius, how are you?" Bellotti asked the somewhat worried looking face that appeared on the screen a few minutes later.

"I'm well, thank you, Mr. Bellotti. How can I be of service?"

"I need an honest answer to a question, Demetrius," Simon Bellotti said with a cold smile. "I would be very disturbed if I were ever to learn that you hadn't been completely honest with me. Do you take my meaning, Demetrius?"

"Yes, sir," Nestor said, his mouth suddenly very dry. People who crossed Simon Bellotti usually ended up taking a one way cruise on Demetrius Nestor's ship. What would happen if he himself crossed the man he didn't want to know.

"Normally I wouldn't think of interfering in your business dealings, Demetrius, I hope you know that. But this concerns a man to whom I owe a debt of honor and I'm afraid I must, just this once, ask you to indulge me."

"Anything, Mr. Bellotti. Anything at all."

"Good man. To the point then. Have you had occasion to make a man by the name of Mitchell Harvey disappear recently?"

Oh shit! Nestor thought. He didn't like the sound of this at all.

"Yes, sir, I believe that name is familiar to me," he said.

"And would the name of the person for whom you performed this service also be familiar to you?"

"Yes, that name would be familiar to me also."

"Good, Demetrius, good. What happened to Mr. Harvey?"

"He was relocated to one of the planets in my possession, Mr. Bellotti," Captain Nestor answered, feeling sick to his stomach. What the hell had that Harvey woman gotten him into?

"What was Mr. Harvey's physical status when you last saw him, Demetrius?"

"He was alive when I last saw him, sir. But I'd be very surprised if he stayed that way for long."

"And the name of your client?"

"It was his wife, sir, Sandra Harvey."

"Thank you, Demetrius. I appreciate your candor. You may consider me in your debt. If there is ever anything I can do for you, all you need to do is ask."

"Thank you, Mr. Bellotti," Nestor said numbly. This call had suddenly turned from disaster into good fortune.

Simon Bellotti switched off his monitor.

"I can have more information for you in a few days," he said. "I'll find out where he was brought and when he got there. But you need to understand that Captain Nestor is right. You're brother is most likely already dead. I'm sorry."

"That's more than we could have ever found out without your help, Mr. Bellotti," Alton said. "I appreciate it."

"It was my pleasure, and the least I could do for Nathan. I'll be in touch when I know more."

# CHAPTER 15

▼

# GATHERING STORMCLOUDS

Captain Leruk led his small force of Inchasa warriors and the large slave detail they guarded into the forest at the edge of the wide plain to the east of the Inchasa lands. He had been charged with locating and constructing the crude supply shelters that would feed the Inchasa army as it made its way along the planned route of march. There would be twelve shelters in all, one at the eastern edge of the Inchasa lands, nine sited at one day intervals and two at the final stop, one day's march from the enemy village. The structures didn't have to be ascetic or even very well made, but they had to be large enough to supply five thousand hungry, thirsty warriors. He had his work cut out for him.

"There's a spring a little way into the forest, Leruk," a tall, angular warrior with a well done tattoo of a dagger running across his left cheek said as Leruk approached.

"Thank you, Girak. See that everyone drinks."

Girak nodded and set off to see that the slaves were allowed to drink and that a meal was prepared. With so much work ahead of them, the slaves had to be kept strong.

When he had gone, Leruk looked the area over carefully. They would build the first shelter here. They would build just within the edge of the forest until they started getting close to the area the river villages traveled. Then they'd build deeper into the forest and take the time to hide the structures well.

It was quickly growing dark as Leruk made his way up through the thick trees and brush, but he thought he could see several promising locations within easy walking distance of the spring. Satisfied, he made his way toward the spring for some water.

One of his men had just dropped to his knees to drink when there was a sudden shrill screech followed by screams of pain and surprise. Running quickly toward the sound, Leruk leaped across the small pool of water to find his man writhing desperately on the ground, a vilarca clinging tightly to his throat. Drawing his sword, he struck the long, thin creature at the point where it's slim three foot long body joined its wide, flat head.

His sword sliced easily through the animal's scaled skin, severing the head, the body dropping to the ground, convulsing and flopping about. The head remained clamped to the dying warrior's throat, its powerful jaws refusing to release their grip even in death. Taking his knife, Leruk pried the jaws open, careful not to touch the poison filled fangs.

There was nothing more he could do. Kneeling, he took the man's hand and looked into his panic stricken eyes.

"I'm sorry, my friend," he said. "There's nothing I can do."

"What?" the warrior whispered, and it was a moment before Leruk realized that the man wasn't asking him to repeat what he'd said, but rather, what it was that had bitten him.

"A vilarca," Leruk told him and the warrior nodded his understanding. Leruk stayed with him the few minutes it took him to die.

Looking up, he was angered to see all of his warriors gathered around him and their fallen comrade.

"Who's guarding the slaves?" he snapped.

Fear suddenly making their hearts pound, his men ran back down to the plain, where they'd left the slaves to prepare a meal. Girak came back a few minutes later.

"One slave is missing, Leruk," he said, his head bowed in shame.

"Only one?" Leruk asked, surprised at his good fortune. He wouldn't have been surprised to find half of them gone.

"Yes," Girak answered. "The stupid one, the one who's always claiming to be sick."

Leruk knew immediately which slave Girak was talking about. He'd thought more than once about killing the lazy fool just to be rid of him. He nodded acknowledgment to Girak.

"Have our men bring the body down to the plain," he ordered. "Prepare a funeral pyre and gather everyone around it. Call me when everything is ready."

"Yes, Leruk," Girak answered, his head still hung in shame. He turned to go then stopped short.

"I'm sorry, Leruk," he said contritely. "I should have known better than to leave them unattended."

"Yes, you should have, Girak. But what's done is done. See that it doesn't happen again. Now, go."

When Girak was gone, Leruk uttered a muffled curse. He didn't have time to send a search party after the escaped slave. The Cuzco had given him two months to complete the shelters. He needed every available hand if he was going to meet that schedule. Still, if he had to lose a slave, at least he'd lost the most useless of the lot. It wouldn't slow their work and might even make things move more quickly. He'd have his men spread the rumor that the slave who ran had been captured, tortured and killed. That should keep the others from trying to run.

Things here had gotten off to a bad start, but he knew and had faith in the overall plan, a plan that depended on those under his command completing these shelters on schedule. Once that was done, they would be filled with the supplies that would give the Inchasa army strength as it moved toward the southernmost river village. When that village was defeated they would move north to the next and continue that way until all five villages had been destroyed and their people conquered and enslaved.

It was a good plan. By attacking each village separately, they would be assured numerical superiority. Estimates put the number of warriors in each river village at between five and seven hundred. They'd have no chance against the five thousand men the Cuzco was sending against them.

Of course, the Cuzco hadn't liked the plan at first, insisting that his vision had been of two large forces doing battle, not one large force and five smaller ones. Manco had finally convinced him by assuring him that this method of attack would allow them to capture more of the enemy alive, thereby giving them more slaves to bring home to the empire.

But none of that could happen until the supply shelters were completed. He would work his slaves and his men hard, and even pitch in himself. Unlike many other warrior captains, he didn't think his rank precluded him from performing physical labor.

"Set up a guard rotation, Girak," he ordered as his second in command led four male slaves up to the spring to move the dead man's body. "I want no man to stand more than five hours. There is a lot of work to be done and we'll need every man rested and ready to do his part."

"I will see to it," Girak said as the slaves lifted the body and he and Leruk fell in behind them as they made their way down toward the plain.

"Good," Leruk said quietly. "And have the men spread the word in the morning that we've caught and killed the fool who ran. After torturing him, of course. I want the rest of these slaves thinking only of the work in front of them, not whether or not they might be able to escape too."

"Of course," Girak said just as quietly. "We're not going after him?"

"We can't spare the time or the men. He won't live long out here alone anyway."

"I'm sorry, Leruk. I heard the screams and thought you were under attack. I should have known better."

"Consider it forgotten, Girak. I know you won't make the same mistake again. And there was no real harm done. I should have killed the useless fool days ago anyway. Now someone, or something, will do it for me."

"Thank you," Girak said, fully aware that many another captain would have had him beaten for his lapse in judgment.

"See to the preparation of the pyre," Leruk ordered as they stepped from the forest and out onto the plain, slave and warrior alike pausing to watch as the body was carried past. "It's time to send our brother on his next journey."

*　　　*　　　*　　　*

Dare Samuels worked quickly and efficiently to clean and bandage Michael Wolf's bruised and beaten body while Nathaniel Whyte crushed and mixed some herbs in a stone bowl. Hunter Kane had beaten the man nearly to death and Dare was more than a little afraid for him.

"Will he live?" Secotan asked quietly.

"I don't know," Dare answered. "We'll know more when the swelling goes down. What happened?"

"Kane was looking for a way to remind everyone that he's still a man to be feared, despite what happened with Mother Shaw. Michael was too young and too proud to walk away when Kane insulted him."

"Oh no," Dawn Wolf moaned as she ran into the room and looked down at the unrecognizable face of her husband. "No, Michael, no." She dropped to her knees beside Dare and wept.

"I told him to stay away from Kane," she sobbed. "I told him."

"Every wife and mother in the village told their men the same thing, Dawn," Dare told her as she worked. "Kane may not have given Michael a choice."

"Will he be alright?"

"Yes," Dare answered, hoping she was telling the truth. "But he's hurt badly. It will take time."

"What will happen to Kane?" Dawn asked, looking up at Secotan angrily. "Will he be punished?"

"No," Secotan answered quietly. "He has three men who swear Michael struck the first blow. I can't punish Kane for defending himself."

"This wasn't defending himself," Dawn said, running her hand gently over her husband's swollen cheek.

"No," Secotan had to admit, "it wasn't. But no one else who saw what happened is willing to argue with Kane's version of events. His three friends all say Michael kept getting up and coming after Kane again and again and that Kane had no choice but to defend himself."

"And you believe them?" Dawn asked angrily. "Everyone knows Kane was angry and looking for a fight!"

"I know, Dawn, and I'm sorry. But I can't accuse him of something without more proof than that."

"Forget about Kane," Dare advised sternly, "and put your energies into helping Michael get well."

Dawn settled down with that and took her husband's hand in hers just as the blanket in the doorway was thrown aside and Michael's second wife, Pemi, burst into the room. She said nothing, only covering her mouth with her hands and dropping to her knees beside Michael, on the side opposite Dare and Dawn. She was young and had only been married for two months. She didn't know what to do or say so she did nothing and stared down silently at the man she was just beginning to know.

"He'll be alright," Dawn said comfortingly. She liked Pemi very much.

Pemi nodded absently, still looking down at Michael.

"I have to go," Secotan said. "I'll come back when I can. You'll call me if there are any changes?" he asked, exchanging a knowing glance with Dare, who nodded.

Leaving Wolf's longhouse, Secotan made his way through the village to Kane's. Kane and some of his friends were sitting outside drinking and laughing together as he walked up. Secotan was saddened to see that Saul Rivers was one of them.

"Well, if it isn't our esteemed Councillor," Kane said sarcastically when he saw Secotan. "I'd offer you a drink, but I only drink with men I like."

The other men turned to see Secotan's reaction to that as Kane laughed.

"That's alright, Kane," Secotan said calmly. "I only drink with men I respect."

Kane's laughter stopped short and he stood up slowly, his eyes locked with Secotan's.

"Watch your tongue, Samuels," he said threateningly, "or your wife will be taking care of you, too."

"I think you're the one who should watch his tongue, Hunter," Geris Quick said, stepping from the shadows beside Kane's longhouse.

"Here to protect your friend again, are you, Geris?" Kane asked. "Don't you get tired of watching over him?"

"Secotan doesn't need my protection," Geris said with a thin smile, his eyes sweeping the faces of the other men sitting around Kane's fire. "I won't interfere if anything happens between the two of you. I just want to make sure there is someone other than your friends here to tell who started it."

Several of the men around the fire looked uncomfortable and turned their eyes away when Geris looked at them. Kane only smiled.

"How is poor Michael Wolf, anyway?" he asked.

"Not well," Secotan answered. "And you'd best hope he recovers. If he dies I'll call for a formal inquiry. Something tells me the sight of his grieving widows and two fatherless children might cause some villagers to suddenly remember just exactly what they saw happen between the two of you."

"Don't be too sure, Samuels," Kane said. "Only the Village Councillor can call for an inquiry, and from what I've been hearing, you may not be Councillor much longer."

"Perhaps not," Secotan said. "But I am Councillor now. And as long as I am, I'll do what I have to, to protect the people of this village."

Kane laughed.

"Is that a threat?" he asked.

"Just a warning," Secotan said, surprised he was able to stay so calm. "Any more incidents like this one will be investigated fully. Not everyone is afraid of you, Kane. You'd best remember that."

"That's what Michael Wolf said," Saul Rivers said slyly. "I wonder if he still feels that way?"

Kane and the others laughed and Saul looked up at Secotan, smiling.

"Enjoy your title while you have it, Councillor," Kane called as Geris took Secotan by the arm and led him away from the fire. "You won't have it long."

"He's probably right," Secotan said when they were out of earshot of Kane and the others. "Half the village isn't even speaking to me anymore."

"A lot of spineless fools," Geris said, spitting on the ground as he walked. "Most of them are just afraid of having to make up their own minds about something. They'd rather you tell them what to do."

"You're honestly not upset about what I did?" Secotan asked.

"No," Geris answered. "I meant what I said at the meeting. I married two of my daughter to men they would never have chosen for themselves. Neither of them is truly happy now and it pains me every time I see them."

"But Sara is very happy," Secotan said. "You arranged her marriage, too."

"Yes, that's true. Still, what kind of man could be happy with that, one out of three? Not me."

"There is no guarantee they would have chosen any better for themselves, though, Geris. They may even have chosen worse. Their men don't beat them and they're well provided for, at least."

"Are you trying to talk me out of supporting you?" Geris asked with a laugh.

"No," Secotan said with a grin. "I'm just giving you the same arguments I've been giving myself lately. Maybe I over reacted to what happened because life had been so unfair to Wanchese."

"No, Secotan," Geris said as they reached the Wolf longhouse and stood outside the door. "You just had the courage to say what more than a few of us had been thinking for some time."

Secotan laughed.

"Only after Mother Shaw called me a coward," he said.

Geris smiled. That sounded like Mother. Then his face turned serious.

"I think you did the right thing, Secotan," he said. "And there are more of us than you think who will put up a fight if they try to have you removed. We'll stand by you, my friend. But watch out for Kane. He'll have it out for you now, and he'll wait until he thinks he has an advantage to take you on. It's his way."

"I know," Secotan said. "And thank you. I just hope Michael doesn't die. I meant what I said about conducting a full inquiry. I don't care what it costs me personally. That boy didn't deserve a beating like that."

"Who ever gets what they deserve from this life?" Geris asked.

"That's true," Secotan said. "If we did, a dirty old man like you would probably be unable to get hard at night."

"This from a man married to a woman half his age!" Geris shot back, and the two of them laughed heartily.

Dare stuck her head out the door and shushed them testily. Her appearance only made the men laugh even harder and she went back inside shaking her head and wondering what could be so funny.

# CHAPTER 16

▼

# NEW DIRECTIONS

"All settled?" Alton Harvey asked Nathan Squires as he walked into the galley.

"Yes," Nate answered. "Are we ready to go?"

"Finally," Alton answered. "Just got our exit clearance. As soon as Mr. Bellotti's man delivers the package, we're off."

They were aboard Alton's personal ship, a brand new luxury transport into which he'd had installed some bulked up shielding and two hide away laser canon. If Simon Bellotti didn't come through on his promise to set them up with an identification code to get past the armed ships guarding Triton, they were going to need both.

"He already came," Nate said, sliding a data pad across the table. "Mr. Bellotti sends his regards."

"Great," Alton said, grabbing the data pad and heading for the bridge. The sooner they got going the sooner they could be there. Triton was just a little further out than the middle of nowhere.

He got them under way and through the first jump-gate, then turned the ship over to his pilot, Tommy Blanchard, and headed back to the galley. Finding Nate gone, he moved to the guest cabin his friend was berthed in for the trip. He'd been a little surprised that Nate had wanted to come along, but he hadn't had the heart to tell him no. He'd never have been able to find out what had happened to Mitch without Nate's help. He owed him.

"You're not doing anything indecent to yourself in there, are you?" he called into the intercom outside the cabin door. The door slid open and he walked in to find Squires sitting at a small table, shaking his head and smiling.

"No," he said. "I found where you hide the booze on this tub and I'm helping myself." He rattled ice in his now near empty glass. "Are we there yet?"

"No," Alton answered with a laugh, "not yet."

They were quiet for a minute and Alton sat down across from his friend.

"Damn, Nate," Alton said, "I hope he's still alive."

"Me too. Have you given any more thought to how we're going to locate him?"

"No," Alton answered honestly. "But between the three of us we'll come up with something. Now pass the booze. Tommy's driving this tub for now and I am at liberty to indulge myself."

"What did you tell your mom and dad?" Nate asked as he passed the bottle across the table.

"Not much," Alton answered as he poured. "No sense worrying them. There'll be plenty of time to give them the bad news later if he's dead."

"Or the good news if he's alive," Nate said, trying to be positive.

"Yeah, that too," Alton said. Then he looked up and his eyes were hard.

"I'll kill her if he's dead, Nate. I'll kill her with my bare hands."

"Let's cross that bridge if we come to it," Nate Squires said, shocked at himself for not trying to talk his friend out of such a notion, even more shocked at the realization that if it came to that, he wasn't really sure he'd try to stop it. Sandra deserved whatever she got.

"Remember the time that gorgeous redhead hit on Mitch in the bar on Sylvas?" he asked to get his mind off the subject of Sandra and what she deserved.

"Yeah," Alton said with a grin. "She barely got 'Hello' out of her mouth before he was yelling, 'I'm married.' I thought he was gonna' shit his pants when she put her hand on his thigh and said 'Are you sure?'"

They laughed at the memory.

"He finally managed to tell her was sure, though," Nate said. "It took him a minute to get it out, but he told her. I'm not sure I could have done the same."

"She was something," Alton said. "But Mitch was always kind of old fashioned like that. He deserved better than Sandra, that's for sure."

"I know," Nate said. "And I deserved that redhead. I spent a weeks pay trying to get her room number."

"She couldn't give it to you," Alton said with a wicked grin. "She'd already given it to me."

"You bastard!" Squires bellowed. "The least you could have done was tell me so I wouldn't keep spending my credits on her!"

"You looked like you were having a good time," Alton said. "I didn't want to ruin it for you."

"Bullshit! You just didn't want to spend your own money on her. You really are a cheap prick!"

Alton laughed and refilled their glasses as Nate tried to keep a straight face.

"I should have known," he said finally, giving up and letting a grin spread across his face as Alton laughed again. "Now put Mr. Bellotti's crystal in that terminal and let's see what we're up against. I can't wait to find Mitch and tell him about the redhead."

Alton laughed and slid the crystal into the terminal. A geographical overlay of Triton came up on the wall screen and the two of them looked at the daunting task that confronted them.

"That's a lot of area to cover," Nate said as the overlay cycled through a pre-arranged presentation that brought the land mass they were interested in into sharper focus, enlarging it repeatedly until it filled the screen.

"Yeah," Alton agreed distractedly. "That red dot down near the bottom is where they dropped Mitch. Let me bring up the topography."

He punched a command and the map focused even further, enlarging the area around the red dot and bringing up the detail of the large, flat plain of grass where Mitch had been left.

"That's a long walk with no water," Nate said. "No matter which direction he decided to go." To the north of the dot were uninhabited mountains, to the south the sea, with populated areas to the east and northwest.

Alton nodded his agreement. Captain Nestor might not have killed Mitch directly, but he sure as hell didn't do him any favors. Or them. They were going to have to search a huge area now. There was no way of knowing which way Mitch had gone.

"Which way would you go?" he asked. "You wake up in the middle of a huge field of grass, it's dark, you're freezing your ass off, nothing familiar in the night sky and no distinguishing features in the land around you, which way do you go?"

"I don't know," Nate said dejectedly. "We've got our work cut out for us, Alton."

"I know. This might take longer than we thought, Nate. Are you sure you want to stay?"

"More so than ever. I want Sandra punished, and we can't prove a damn thing unless we bring Mitch back with us. I'll stay as long as it takes."

"O.K," Alton said. "And thanks. I don't know how I'll ever be able to thank you for all you've done, Nate."

"How about giving me that redhead's number?" Squires asked with a grin. "That would be a good start."

"You got it, Slim," Alton said with a laugh. "You got it."

*     *     *     *

Wanchese was relieved to see Mitchell step from the forest. He'd left more than an hour earlier to go fill the water bags and gather some wood. She was getting worried and had been on the verge of going out to look for him when she heard him making his way through the woods to the east of the cave. As his body grew stronger, he was becoming more active. She would have preferred he stay close to the cave for a while longer.

The water bags were slung over his bare shoulder and in his hands he carried a bundle of broken branches and the walking stick he'd carved for himself. He carried the stick with him everywhere, despite the fact that he seldom needed it anymore. His balance had improved dramatically over the last several days, though he was still thin and unhealthy looking.

"I think I found some of that worm root," he said with a smile, pulling some of the soft, pulpy roots from where he'd had them beneath his arm. He brought the water bags and wood into the cave and came back out to where she was sitting.

"Is this it?" he asked, holding several of the long, dirt encrusted roots out for her inspection.

She nodded that they were indeed worm root, deciding it would be pointless to remind him yet again that he was still far from well and shouldn't be going off by himself. She knew she'd be wasting her breath.

"I did a little exploring over to the east," he said with that childlike excitement that annoyed her so. "I was feeling pretty good today."

Again, Wanchese said nothing. She couldn't deny that he was recovering well. His ribs were no longer visible and his arms and legs no longer looked skeletal. His eyes and cheeks were less sunken and hollow and his shredded back and shoulders had healed into a solid mass of mottled flesh. His skin had turned from pink to brown and while he still didn't look healthy, he no longer looked like he should be dead.

"You should have washed the worm root," she said, aware that she was being ill tempered again. This man seemed to bring that out in her.

"I wanted to bring the wood back first. I'll head over to the spring and wash it now."

She watched him step back into the forest, unsure what enraged her more, when he snapped back at her sharp remarks or when he simply ignored her ill temper and continued with whatever he was doing as if the two of them were the best of friends. She disliked being snapped at. She also disliked being ignored. Especially when he did it with that small, half concealed smile of his.

He had not as yet made any mention of her being in his debt and she now thought it unlikely he would. His people seemed to have no such tradition. He'd also made no mention of his battle with the deathclaw since the first night he woke. She wondered if he understood just how unusual a thing it was for a man to survive such an encounter. She had difficulty understanding what he was thinking.

She'd seen the way he watched her as she moved around the cave and the area surrounding it. He seemed to find her pleasing to look at and she'd expected to have trouble with him during the long, cold nights huddled beneath the deathclaw hide. There had been no such trouble though and she sometimes wondered if he liked women. But if that were true, why did he watch her the way he did?

He came walking back to the cave, the clean roots in his hand, glancing at her as he walked past and into the cave. He came out again a minute later after having added the worm root to the simmering pot beside the fire.

"I saw some footprints today," he said as he sat down nearby.

"Where?" Wanchese demanded, standing to her feet.

"Over by the big spring," Mitch answered. There were two springs in the vicinity of the cave. They used the smaller, closer one to fill the water bags and clean utensils. The larger, more distant spring fed into a shallow basin and they used that one for bathing and rinsing their clothes. This spring was some twenty minutes walk from the cave.

"How many?" Wanchese asked, hoping he had taken the time to check. There was still so much he didn't understand.

"Not many," he told her. "It looked like only one or two people. I thought they were yours at first, but they were too big, I think."

"You should have come and told me right away," Wanchese snapped. "I'll go and look. You stay here."

"Why don't I go with you? Then I can show you right where they are."

"No. I'll move faster alone."

"I know," he said with a smirk. "I just thought you might like some company." His sarcasm was lost on Wanchese.

"No," she repeated. "I'll go alone."

It really is too bad she's such a bitch, Mitch thought as he watched her go. She was one very well made woman. As Alton was fond of saying, "God sure knew what he was doing when he put her together."

There were still a few hours before dark and he didn't feel like sitting around watching stew boil so he picked up his staff and headed off into the forest to the west. He changed his mind a minute later and turned north. He hadn't seen what was up that way yet.

He walked slowly. He was still weak and one hard fall would almost certainly mean at least one broken bone. And an endless amount of grief from Wanchese. He could live without either.

After walking for what he guessed to be twenty-five or thirty minutes, he came to a small spring and dropped to one knee to drink. As he lifted his head after drinking, he caught sight of something strange out of the corner of his eye. Standing, he walked over to investigate.

At the base of a tall, thick shrub covered with large round leaves of dark purple was a puddle of thick black liquid that bubbled periodically. It was a small puddle, no more than a foot square. He could feel heat radiating from the liquid when he stretched his hand out toward it. There was no odor that he could detect.

Picking up a long, narrow stick, he dipped several inches of hit into the puddle. When he pulled the stick out, the thick ooze began to hiss and within a matter of thirty or forty seconds had hardened, forming a thick, dull black shell around the tip of the stick. Reaching out, he touched it, ready to pull his hand back at the first hint of pain. But there was none. The ooze had formed a smooth shell over the stick that was warm but cooling quickly.

Walking over to an outcropping of white rock, Mitch swung the stick so the tip covered with the black shell would strike it, curious to see how much force it would take to crack the shell. But when the stick struck the stone, it wasn't the shell that cracked. Instead, a small section of rock shattered and flew off into the air, leaving behind only a small indentation and some dust.

Surprised, Mitch switched the stick around and struck the rock with the uncovered end. This time it was the stick that shattered. Switching the stick once more, he swung the hardened tip as hard as he could. There was a loud crack and his face was stung by flying slivers of stone. Turning his head, he wiped his closed, watering eyes and hoped he hadn't done himself any permanent damage.

When his vision cleared and he was reasonably sure he hadn't blinded himself with his stupidity, he looked around to find a thick section of stone three inches long and five inches around lying on the ground. He smiled.

Walking over to the bubbling pool of ooze, he pushed the branches of the shrub aside and dipped his staff into the puddle, pushing three quarters of its length down into the ooze. Then he pulled it out, waited for it to cool and dry, and dipped the other end. When that end dried, he repeated the process.

He dipped the entire length of the staff a third and fourth time before walking over to the rock outcropping again. He raised the staff over his head in a two handed grip, his hands spread out evenly over the staff so that an equal distance showed on each end, turned his head to the side and brought the staff crashing down on the stone outcropping.

More rock splinters stung his bare chest and arms and he jumped back in surprise as a large chunk of rock broke off and fell near his feet, coming to rest painfully against his shins. Looking down, he was shocked. A solid two-foot by three-foot section of stone lay at his feet. And the hardened shell of the staff wasn't so much as scratched when he wiped the dust off of it!

Smiling, he broke the hardened tip from the small stick he'd first dipped into the ooze and buried it at the base of a low-limbed tree. Then he picked up his new weapon and started back to the cave. It would be dark soon and he didn't want to get lost and have to listen to Wanchese's wise-ass remarks.

He found his way back and was standing outside the cave, practicing with his staff, when he heard the sound of movement through the brush to the east. It was Wanchese. That he had expected. The thin, dirty looking man with her was a surprise.

The man walked ahead of Wanchese, his hands tied behind his back, Wanchese following behind, with her knife in her hand, watching him very closely as they stepped from the trees and walked across the shelf to the cave.

"Sit," Wanchese ordered.

"Well," Mitch said with a smile, "I see you've brought home a pet."

Wanchese gave him a look of mingled disgust and impatience. His sense of humor seemed to escape her.

"He says he escaped from the Inchasa," she said. "I haven't decided yet whether or not I believe him."

Mitch looked at the man with new interest. He didn't look like he could escape from a motivated bunch of ten year olds, let alone Inchasa. Something about him screamed of weakness. Still, you couldn't judge a man by his looks.

"What's your name?" he asked.

"Royal Simms," the man answered tersely.

"A Danurian," Mitch said, recognizing the accent. The man said nothing and Mitch got the feeling Simms disliked him already. He was also pretty sure the feeling was going to be mutual. Something about the slimy bastard made him think of a used shuttle salesman.

"How long were you a prisoner?" he asked.

"Seven or eight months, I think. It's hard to say. All I did was work and sleep. You lose track of time."

That had a ring of truth to it, Mitch thought. And the man was obviously a newcomer. But that didn't mean he wasn't now a card carrying Inchasa who happened to get separated from his friend.

"You escaped from their city over to the west?" he asked.

"No. I was part of a labor party sent to build storage buildings down by the plain to the south. The Inchasa are storing up supplies to attack some river village over to the east."

Mitch looked over at Wanchese, who was looking hard at Royal Simms.

"Why would they need to store supplies?" she asked. "They've always lived off the land as they moved."

"That was when they moved in small groups," Simms said. He wanted to be as helpful as possible to the woman. Damn! He hadn't seen a body like that in a long, long time. It was disappointing to find a man with her. "This time they're talking about bringing every able bodied man they've got. I heard some people say as many as five thousand warriors."

Wanchese was quiet. That was an impossible number and she didn't believe it for a second. But a large-scale attack was possible. Not that she really cared what happened to those fools in the river villages. But the thought of other children seeing their mothers and fathers killed right before their eyes bothered her.

"Get up," she ordered. "We'll eat. Then you'll tell me more."

She gestured with her knife for Royal Simms to stand and precede her into the cave. Simms did as he was told and he and Wanchese walked into the cave. Mitch stood and followed, wishing he'd never said anything about those damn footprints.

# CHAPTER 17

▼

# OLD WOUNDS
# REOPENED

Noref, the tall, plain faced, big boned healer sent to see to Capac's wounds was drying his feet after having soaked them in a healing solution of warm water and crushed kalas herb. This was the most trying of her duties, as the mixture caused Capac a great deal of pain. It was necessary if he was ever going to walk again, however, so she forced herself to ignore his cries of pain and his pleas for her to stop.

She was thinking that he would thank her some day, when the cell door was thrown open and the Cuzco marched in. Noref stopped what she was doing and bowed her head in feigned respect. She'd had more than ample opportunity to see what happened to those who angered the young king and she had no intention of ending up like poor Capac.

"Is he well enough to return to his duties yet?" the Cuzco demanded gruffly.

"He's still not well," Noref answered, glancing at Capac who, she was surprised to see, showed no fear at the Cuzco's sudden appearance. She really shouldn't have been surprised. Capac had proven to be completely different from what she'd been told to expect. Perhaps what had happened to him had changed him.

"He looks well enough to me," the Cuzco said.

"His body has healed well," Noref said timidly, "but his feet have not. It will be some time before he'll be able to walk again."

"What I have in mind for him he can do lying or sitting," the Cuzco said. "I will have some men bring him on a litter."

"And what might that be?" Capac asked in a tone Noref feared would earn him another beating. He wouldn't survive the next one, she knew. But the Cuzco only smiled.

"You are going to keep a record of the new era of greatness the Inchasa people are about to enter," he said. "You will write down all that has happened and all that will happen as we conquer and enslave our enemies. It will be the Inchasa sacred book, except ours will be based on fact, not impossible dreams and childish fantasies like yours."

"Why me?" Capac asked. "Why not one of your own people?"

"A Cuzco does not explain himself to slaves. You will do what you're told and do it well or your people will suffer the consequences. I'm inclined to let your people simply die out over time rather than kill them all as Manco has suggested, but that could change. Understood?"

"Yes," Capac said wearily. It always came down to that with this stubborn, spoiled boy. Do what he says or others will suffer. Capac wished they'd just kill him. Which was probably why they didn't.

"Good. I will send some men to bring you to your old room. Your healer will stay as long as she's needed. You will be provided with all the medicines and food you require and a supply of paper and ink as well. Manco will bring you to my chambers this evening and I will tell you of my great vision so you can write it in the book. Any questions?"

"No," Capac answered. "But Noref will need her own room. I don't need constant care anymore."

"I will decide when you no longer need constant care. She'll stay with you."

With that, the Cuzco turned and left the cell, leaving the door open behind him.

"Don't push him," Noref said in Lydacian. "You won't survive another beating."

"I don't really care if I survive," Capac told her. "But I won't let our people suffer for my sake. I'll try to behave."

"You shouldn't be in such a hurry to die," Noref said and Capac looked up at the plain faced, broad shouldered woman and smiled. Did she know about the island and Lydacia City? Was that what gave her hope? But he would never see the island again and he knew it.

"I said I would behave," he said.

"No," Noref answered with a smile that made her face warm if not beautiful, "you said you would try. That's not good enough."

"Alright," Capac said with a laugh, "I'll behave."

"Better. Javet sends his regards."

"You spoke with him?"

"I did. He knows what you've been through and that you kept your word. He asks that you take as much care for yourself as you do for our people."

"I'll try, Noref. Tell him I'll try. But they'll kill me sooner or later. No one can change that, not even Javet. And now I have to spend my last days writing down the actions of this spoiled child and making them seem regal and heroic!"

"I know," Noref said. "But your suffering buys our people precious time, Capac, time that brings us ever closer to freedom. Javet himself has said so."

"Then I will suffer gladly, Noref. I will suffer gladly and die a happy man."

"Remember you said that when I soak your feet tomorrow," she said.

"I'll try," he said with a laugh. "But I said suffer gladly, not suffer quietly." Noref smiled.

"I'll take what I can get," she said. "Now sit up and let me change those bandages before they come to bring you upstairs."

\*         \*         \*         \*

"How goes the work, Leruk?" Hador asked as he stabbed a diloc gourd and pulled it from the fire.

"It goes well," Leruk answered, taking a gourd for himself and removing it from the thick hallas leaves it had been baked in. "The first shelter is finished and tomorrow we move on to the second site. What about you? What are you and your detail up to?"

"We're headed for the northern river village," Hador answered. He was in charge of a six man scouting detail. "My orders are to observe each village for several days and get a precise picture of their numbers; how many warriors, how many women, how many children, and so on. The Cuzco wants exact figures."

"Didn't a detail just come back from the river?" Leruk asked.

"Yes," Hador answered, taking a long drink of rew from his wine bag before passing it to Leruk. "And we were there not long ago ourselves. We were really only interested in capturing women and children, though. I wasn't confident in our information on the villages and offered to go back."

"You offered?" Leruk asked with a skeptical look. He'd known Hador long enough to know he didn't volunteer for anything.

"Yes," Hador said with a laugh. "Honestly, I offered. We had some good hunting on our last trip. My men are anxious to get back to the mountains."

"Good hunting meaning you found a woman?" Leruk asked. "What was she doing in the mountains?"

"How would I know?" Hador asked with a grin. "All I can tell you is she had skin as smooth as nurak milk and a wild, strong willed spirit. I'm hoping there are more where she came from. So are my men."

"Only you would volunteer for a mission just to find a woman, Hador," Leruk said, laughing. "You'll never change. How long will you be gone?"

"The Cuzco himself gave me my instructions," Hador said, suddenly completely serious. "I don't intend to disappoint him. We'll spend at least five days observing each village. Add the travel time to that and I expect we'll probably run into you again not long before you finish with the shelters."

Leruk nodded his acceptance of Hador's estimate. It was good that he was taking his mission seriously and not thinking only of women. They would need his information to plan the attack.

"It will be good to go into battle again," he said, passing the bag back to Hador. "Drill and hard work are all well and good, but a warrior loses his edge if he goes too long without real combat."

"True," Hador said with a nod. "And I have a score to settle with the river warriors. I was with Manco the last time we attacked. It still makes my blood boil to think we lost so many for so little. I intend to get even."

"So does Manco," Leruk said. "What happened, Hador? How could we lose so many men?" It was a question that had troubled him for a long time, but it wasn't the kind of thing he could ask his brother.

"I don't know," Hador answered quietly. "We attacked exactly as planned and the men fought bravely. But the river warriors fought like animals, refusing to stop fighting even after they'd been wounded. The women, too. They put up such a fight that we killed more of them than we dragged off. Before we knew it the surprise had worn off and the alert had been spread. We suddenly found ourselves outnumbered and had to withdraw. We didn't even have time to gather our dead and wounded."

"It will be different this time, Hador," Leruk said. "They'll be the ones who are outnumbered and you will have your revenge, my friend."

"Yes, I know," Hador said with a nod. "But don't let your men underestimate these river warriors, Leruk. They are not the blundering idiots so many of our men think they are. They can fight. Make sure your men are ready."

"I will. And so will Manco. My brother is no fool. He remembers that defeat with the same anger and pain you do, Hador. The army will be ready when the time comes to avenge our fallen friends. Manco will see to that. The enemy will have no chance."

"I'll drink to that," Hador said with a grin, hefting the wine bag in his hand. "Here's to victory, vengeance and smooth skinned river women!"

✳     ✳     ✳     ✳

"SeaVista One, you are cleared for atmospheric entry," their contact on board the armed escort vessel said over the audio link. "Please tell Mr. Bellotti I'm glad I could be of service."

"Affirmative, Lewiston," Alton called back. "We'll pass that along."

"Well, Simon came through," Nathan Squires said with relief. "Now all we have to do is find Mitch down there."

"You have the coordinates for that plain, Tommy?" Alton asked for the third time. Simon Bellotti had come through in spades, even giving them the coordinates of Mitch's exact drop point.

"Yeah, I still got 'em, boss," Tommy answered patiently. "You sure you don't want to drive?"

"Yes, I'm sure I don't want to drive, wiseass," Alton said with a grin. He really needed to calm down. Tommy was a better pilot than he'd ever be.

"Alright," he continued as they descended through Triton's atmosphere and headed for the drop coordinates, "here's how we play it. We start at the drop point. If we don't find anything there, we move to the southeastern edge of the plain and make a low level, instruments only pass over the southern edge, moving east to west. We'll scan for life form readings and human remains. We'll have to search the entire plain that way. There's a lot of area to search and I want to be thorough so this could take a while. Questions?"

Nate and Tommy both shook their heads.

"Alright," Alton continued. "If we don't find Mitch on the plain, we'll move on to the mountains, the lower elevations anyway. I don't think he'd climb too high if he made it that far. After that we'll have to make some high level passes over the populated areas. We're going to have to figure out some way of picking

Mitch out among the crowd so keep that in mind as we work and let me know if you have any thoughts."

"Sounds like a plan, boss," Tommy said. "We're coming up on the drop point. You want me to set her down?"

"No life form readings?" Alton asked.

"Not a one."

"Alright, set her down and we'll have a look."

"Is it day or night down there?" Nate asked.

"Day," Tommy answered as he gently lowered the ship to the ground. "About two hours of daylight left, if our information is correct."

"Do you have the med-kit to check DNA results if we find anything?" Nate asked Alton.

"Yeah, it's in my back pack. I could live without having to use it though."

"It's the only way we can be sure, Alton."

"I know. I'm just saying I wouldn't mind not finding any dead bodies, that's all."

"Amen to that," Tommy said as he stood up from his seat and stretched. "You boys ready for a first hand look at this paradise?"

"Absolutely," Alton said, gesturing toward the door. "Lead on, oh intrepid one."

Tommy smiled and left the bridge, Alton and Nate on his heels. Tommy lowered the entry/exit ramp on the starboard side and the three of them were struck almost instantly by a wave of hot, heavy air that had them sweating before they reached the end of the ramp.

"Son of a bitch," Tommy said. "This place is an oven."

"This is late afternoon?" Nate asked.

"According to our information," Alton answered before walking out away from the ship for a long, slow look around.

What he saw was not encouraging. Nothing but grass and more grass, unless you counted the shimmering heat waves. Mitch was left here with no food, no clothing and no water? Could he possibly have survived?

"He can't possibly be alive," he said when Nate walked up beside him.

"Don't underestimate him," Nate replied. "He wouldn't die easily. Don't forget how stubborn he can be."

"I know, Nate, but look at this place. Could anyone survive this with no water?"

"I don't know," Nate had to admit. "What do you say we have a quick look around?"

"Alright," Alton said, and the three of them separated and moved in an ever widening circle search pattern around the ship. They found nothing but grass.

"O.K," Alton called to the others. "Let's get back to the ship. If he did get dropped here he didn't stick around long. Let's start our instrument scan."

Tommy and Nate looked as hot and uncomfortable as he felt when he met them at the ship.

"Paradise, my ass," Nate said as they trudged back up the ramp.

Alton led the way straight to the galley and the three of them drank a tall glass of ice cold water, a luxury they knew Mitch wouldn't have had. Their faces were grim as they made their way silently to the bridge. Tommy lifted off and they headed southeast to start the instrument scan.

"Alright," he said when they reached the starting point, "can one of you guys watch the scan readouts for me so I can concentrate on driving?"

"I got it, Tommy," Alton volunteered.

They scanned slowly down the southern edge of the plain as night fell. Five hours into the scan they found human remains recent enough to fall within the time frame they were looking at. Tommy set down long enough for Alton to get a DNA sample. It wasn't Mitch.

They continued the low level scan for another six hours, Tommy and Alton switching off the driving duties to keep everyone fresh. Further west they found the remains of a small group of people, but they were all too old to have been Mitch. When they reached the western edge of the plain, they set down to grab a quick bite to eat and get some sleep.

"This is going to be slow going," Tommy said as they sat wearily around the table in the galley. "Even slower than we thought. At this rate it'll take us ten or twelve days just to check the plain."

"I know," Alton agreed. "But what other options do we have? I won't leave without knowing what happened to my brother. I don't care how long it takes, I'm going to bring him home."

"Agreed," Tommy said. "I just wish there was a faster way."

"Me too. Don't be afraid to speak up if you think of something to speed things up. You know a hell of a lot more about this sort of thing than I do."

"Will do," Tommy said. "But right now I need some sleep. I'll set the scanners to raise an alarm if anything comes within visual range of the ship. See you guys in five or six hours."

"Make it eight," Alton said. "I think we could all use it. You too, Nate. Eight hours."

"O.K," Nate said wearily. "See you tomorrow, Tommy."

Tommy headed off to bed and the two old friends sat together silently, each wondering if the other felt as hopeless as he did. There was no way they were going to find Mitch alive. The best they could hope for now was to bring his body home so his parents could bury him. And the cops could convict Sandra. There was that.

"Why the hell did Captain Nestor leave him here in the middle of nowhere?" Nate asked. "Why not near people, or at least near water?"

"Mr. Bellotti's information is that Mitch killed one of Nestor's men when they went to grab him. I find that a little hard to believe, but that's what Bellotti's source claims. Nestor sure as hell did everything he could to make sure he had no chance. I hope Mitch did get one of the bastards."

"Killed him how?" Nate asked. "Mitch didn't keep any guns that I know of."

"Didn't say," Alton answered. "The report just said that Mitch killed the guy and Nestor was pissed about it so he left him to die. I guess part of his agreement with Sandra was that he couldn't kill him, so he did the next best thing."

Nate just shook his head. Sandra had probably done that so she'd pass the life insurance polygraph. She had a big surprise coming on that score, though. He wished now that he'd made Mitch tell her about the changes he'd made. She might not have done this if she'd known she had nothing to gain.

"We better get some sleep, Alton," he said. "We've got another long day ahead of us tomorrow."

Alton nodded and stood to his feet.

"You go ahead," he said. "I'm going to go out for a little air first."

Nate went off to bed and Alton lowered the ramp and walked out into the cold night air. Within seconds he was shivering from head to toe and his teeth were chattering noisily. He tucked his hands underneath his arms and stood looking up at the clear night sky. Turning, he went back inside and closed the hatch, knowing within his heart that there was no way his brother could have survived out there without clothes or water.

"But I'll find you, Mitch" he whispered. "I'll find you and I'll bring you home. I promise you, I'll bring you home."

# CHAPTER 18

▼

# A SECOND CHANCE

Royal Simms had always been something of a ladies man. In fact, he was reasonably sure that the reason he'd ended up where he had was his romantic success with the daughter of a very powerful man. And she'd been just one of many.

So it had come as a painful blow to his ego when Wanchese Hawkins had not only refused his advances, but gone so far as to threaten to slit his throat if he ever touched her again. When she'd accepted his offer to go with her when she traveled higher into the mountains to the west in search of a secure place a little further from the Inchasa routes of travel, he'd assumed that she wanted to be alone with him as much as he wanted to be alone with her. He'd been wrong.

So he'd spent the last five days trying to convince her that it had been an honest mistake, that he'd thought she was as attracted to him as he was to her. They'd been getting along so well and she seemed to enjoy his company. What was he supposed to think?

It was pretty clear she didn't belong to Harvey. In the three days he'd spent with them there hadn't been so much as a hint of romance between them, not even at night when they shared a bed. And during the day, Wanchese spent most of her time snapping at the stupid bastard and getting even more pissed when all he did was smile. The closest thing to friendship he'd seen pass between them was when the woman told Harvey not to get lost while she was gone. Harvey had gotten a good laugh out of that.

And Harvey himself made him more than a little uncomfortable. It had been immediately evident that it was Wanchese who made the decisions between the two of them. And any man who would sit quietly by and let a woman tell him what to do was lacking in the balls department as far as he was concerned. So it had both surprised and disquieted him when he'd answered one of Harvey's seemingly endless questions with sarcastic rudeness and Harvey had responded by locking eyes with him, saying nothing yet refusing to look away. Something in the man's eyes had left him feeling cold all over, even after he'd given in and looked away.

And then Wanchese had announced that she was going to go west to look for a better place, a place a little further out of the way, and he'd volunteered to go along, desperate to be alone with her and wondering idly if her body would look as good naked as he imagined. All he'd gotten for his trouble was six cold nights of shivering beside a small fire and six hot days of sweat and sore feet. But now they were finally almost back.

Once they got back to the cave, he'd steal some food and move on. There were other people on this lousy rock and they were bound to be more hospitable than Wanchese. He half expected she'd meant it when she threatened to slit his throat.

"I told you to stop that," she snapped now, shaking him loose from his thoughts.

"Sorry," he said, not meaning it.

He'd shaved a point onto a stick about three feet long and one inch thick and had been swatting some of the forest vegetation as he walked. Every time he did it, Wanchese acted like he'd just kicked her. The girl was way too uptight for her own good.

They had made their way east and were now just a little south of the cave. Wanchese turned north at a large boulder she used as a landmark and picked up her pace. He moved to catch up. Almost there.

They'd walked another fifty feet or so and he was just about to swat another thin, reed like plant when Wanchese spun around, looked behind him then grabbed him and threw him to the ground. He fought her furiously, afraid she was going to make good on her promise to slit his throat.

"Quiet!" she hissed into his ear, clamping her hand over his mouth. It was another second before he heard the Inchasa.

His heart beat heavily in his chest as they moved toward the boulder he and Wanchese had turned at. When it looked like they were going to go right by and he had just let himself start breathing again, he heard one of them order a halt.

"What's this?" he asked.

Lifting his head, Simms could see the broken shrub branch the man held in his hand. He could feel Wanchese's accusing glare on him but refused to look at her. How could he have known?

"Spread out, ten paces apart," the Inchasa warrior ordered. "Let's see who else is out there."

"Like a river woman!" another of them crowed.

They spread out and started moving toward him and it was more than Royal Simms could stand. He couldn't let them catch him again. If they wanted the girl, they could have her. Throwing Wanchese away from him, he lurched to his feet and set out running for all he was worth. His mind raced as quickly as his heart as he crashed through the trees toward the cave. If they weren't satisfied with Wanchese, maybe they'd settle for Harvey. Either way, he was getting away. He couldn't be a slave again.

He could hear them crashing through the forest behind him as he broke from the trees and ran past Harvey, who was standing out on the open shelf in front of the cave with his stupid walking stick. A lot of good that thing was going to do him now. Simms ran right past him, across the shelf and back into the forest to the west of the cave, running west and north before moving into some thick brush and throwing himself to the ground. If he stayed there and didn't make any noise, they'd never find him.

*     *     *     *

Mitch was more than a little surprised when Royal Simms came bursting through the trees, across the shelf and back into the forest. There was a look of sheer terror on the slimy little weasel's face, though, so he wasn't at all surprised when Wanchese burst through the trees and screamed, "Inchasa!"

"How many?" he asked, wondering why he felt so calm. He really should have been scared senseless, but he wasn't. Somewhere in the back of his mind, he'd known this day would come, though he would have preferred to wait a bit longer. Still, it was here and he knew what he had to do. His death would have meaning.

"Six," Wanchese answered, looking at him like he was more than a little crazy. What did it matter how many? Why wasn't he running?

"Run," he told her. "I'll hold them as long as I can."

Then he turned away as the first of the Inchasa came crashing through the trees right in front of him. For a long second Mitch just looked at the wild eyed face that confronted him. He saw the cold, soulless eyes, the freshly healed over scratches on his face and neck and, for just a split second, the vision of a woman's tortured, lifeless eyes.

And then, even as he heard the sound of the others crashing through the last of the trees and into the clearing, he brought his staff up over his head in the smooth, flowing, two handed motion he'd practiced hundreds of times a day since Wanchese had been gone, and swept it down with all his might.

The sound of the man's head splitting was sickening, but Mitch had no time to think about it. There were five more Inchasa standing in the clearing and they were looking at him with surprised anger. There was no time to think or even feel. He attacked.

Two of them had come out on his right, three to his left. The two to the right were closest so he attacked them first, the nearest one moving away just as he brought his staff crashing down. The Inchasa screamed with agony as the blow meant for his head fell wide and crushed his left collarbone and shoulder.

The other warrior on his right had hurriedly drawn his sword and was stepping forward just as Mitch stepped toward him with his right foot and swung the sleek black weapon horizontally across his body, swinging left to right at chest height, instantly crushing the stunned Inchasa's ribs. He dropped his sword and Mitch struck him a glancing blow to the head before turning to face the other three.

One of them was a tall, thickly built warrior who stood with his sword drawn and at the ready. A second, somewhat smaller man stood beside him, his sword drawn but held with less confidence. The third was only a boy. His sword was drawn and in his hand, but he was frozen with fear. He looked like he was going to either cry or vomit, or maybe both.

Mitch caught sight of Wanchese out of the corner of his eye and wondered why she hadn't run yet. He wasn't sure how much longer he was going to be able to keep this up. His arms and legs were starting to feel heavy and his chest was heaving like he'd just run a marathon.

Then the tall, thick warrior spoke to the man beside him and the two of them advanced on Mitch together. Deciding that being aggressive had served him well so far he stepped forward and attempted a repeat of the overhead strike he'd used earlier. But his strike wasn't as powerful as before and this man was a more dangerous adversary. The big man blocked the strike with his sword and then quickly ran his blade inside the staff and flicked it forward, catching Mitch in the upper chest, leaving a long, shallow gash up to his left shoulder. Surprised and angry, Mitch stepped back to regroup.

But before he could even get his feet set, the two Inchasa charged at him. Throwing his staff up over his head horizontally, he managed to block the big warrior's downward sword stroke. At the moment of impact, when he was certain he'd blocked the strike, he lifted his left knee high and kicked downward at the smaller man. The kick landed solidly, breaking the man's right knee with a terrible crack, just as he'd been about to run Mitch through.

He fell with an anguished scream, smashing into Mitch, knocking him off balance for just the briefest fraction of an instant. But that was all the big Inchasa needed. Instantly sensing what had happened, he pushed hard with his sword, sending Mitch tumbling backward to the ground. Smiling, the big warrior raised his sword for the killing blow.

Mitch knew he was dead. It was only a matter of time now. But he wanted to give Wanchese a fighting chance to escape. So he quickly rolled at the man, trying to get close enough to make a powerful sword stroke more difficult. As he finished his roll, he swung a feeble blow at the man's legs, hoping to at least slow him down. The solid black shell struck cleanly on his right ankle, not doing any real damage, but causing the man to jump back with a surprised yelp. Before he could recover, Mitch had scrambled back to his feet.

Now it was Mitch's turn to smile. And when the Inchasa smiled back, Mitch couldn't help but laugh. This man was a real warrior, one who had already known what Mitch was just now discovering; that these half thrilling, half terrifying moments when a man held his life squarely in his own hands were the moments he was most alive.

Standing with his staff at the ready, his fatigue suddenly forgotten in the rush of adrenaline, he met the Inchasa's eyes and gave a short nod of respect. To his surprise, the Inchasa returned the gesture. Then the two of them circled warily, Mitch moving to his right, putting the big warrior between himself and the only other enemy still on his feet. The boy still seemed frozen with fear, but that was a real sword he was holding and Mitch would have felt uncomfortable with his back towards him.

Suddenly, the big man's sword flashed forward with amazing quickness and Mitch felt hot blood running down his right arm. The sword leaped at him again, before he even had tome to recover from the first strike, this time slicing his left shoulder, just missing his neck. Moving to his left and back a step, Mitch watched his enemy pursue him.

Then, knowing that if he was wrong he was dead, he waited until he sensed the big Inchasa tensing for another strike and stepped in quickly, knocking the sword to the side and bringing a vicious blow down on the man's unprotected hands. As the sword fell to the ground, the Inchasa briefly met Mitch's eyes and gave a final nod of respect as the killing blow fell.

Turning quickly, aware that the feelings surging through him were at once thrilling and more than a little frightening, Mitch faced the last remaining Inchasa. The boy stood wide-eyed with fear, looking at the bloody scene around him. Then he dropped his sword and ran across the shelf and into the forest to the west. Mitch let him go. He had no desire to kill a child.

Only then did he see that the warrior with the shattered knee had drawn his bow and notched an arrow while he'd been busy fighting the other warrior. The bow was still clutched in his hands as he lay in a pool of his own blood, his throat slit from end to end. Wanchese stood behind him, her bloody knife still in her hand. A handy woman to have around, Mitch decided. As long as she was on your side.

"Thank you," he said, briefly meeting her eye before walking over to check on the two injured Inchasa. He didn't know what to do. It didn't seem right to kill them now when they were defenseless, but he didn't want to nurse them back to health until they were well enough to try and kill him again, either.

Then there was a high-pitched, agonized scream off to the west and he turned his head and looked that way. As he turned back, he saw with horror that the Inchasa with the crushed shoulder held a knife in his good hand and was drawing it back to throw it at him.

Realizing there was no way he could reach the man in time, Mitch jumped to his right, dropped to one knee and ducked his head to the ground. The knife sailed past, only inches from his head. Leaping back to his feet, he jumped forward and crushed the man's skull even as he tried desperately to scramble away into the forest.

The other warrior, the one Mitch thought would have only a few broken ribs and a sore head, was in fact dead. The glancing blow to his skull had left the right side of his head a gruesome mix of blood, bone and grey matter that made Mitch quickly turn away.

As he stood looking at the terrible scene around him, realizing that it was over and he was still alive, he could feel himself starting to shake, his body not quite knowing what to do with all the adrenaline still coursing through it. He forced himself to take several deep breaths and tried to regain his composure. His emotions were running wild, jumping from the joy of being alive to the guilt of having taken human lives to a nagging fear that some small part of him had enjoyed it.

As he regained control of his emotions and the adrenaline started to subside, he suddenly felt very weak. He sank to one knee, his elbow braced against his thigh, his head in his hand, and said a quick prayer of thanks.

Wanchese came to him.

"Are you hurt badly?" she asked.

"I'll live," he said wearily. "I know a good healer."

"A good thing for you that you do," she replied with a small smile.

"I do seem to get into my fair share of trouble, don't I?" he asked.

Wanchese just shrugged.

"Come, I'll clean your wounds," she said.

"No, not yet," he told her. "We should get these bodies away from here. There could be more of them running around out there. No sense making ourselves easy to find."

Wanchese nodded. That was reasonable.

"I hope that was Royal Simms I heard scream out there," she said, nodding to the west. "I hope the sniveling coward ran straight into the den of an angry deathclaw."

Mitch laughed.

"And I thought you two were getting along so well."

"So did he," Wanchese said dryly.

Mitch smiled.

"Tried to get a little too friendly, did he?" he asked as he bent down and tossed the largest of the Inchasa over his shoulder.

"Yes," she replied simply. Then she threw the smallest of the Inchasa over her shoulder and followed behind unsteadily as Mitch made his way into the trees to the east.

"Can I ask what happened?" he asked when they stopped to rest.

"He tried to make me his woman," she answered quietly. "Put his hands on me, tried to kiss me. I discouraged him with my knife."

"I bet you did," Mitch said with a smile. "He behaved himself after that?"

"He sulked like a spoiled child after that. But I told him I'd slit his throat if he ever touched me again. I didn't have any more trouble with him."

Mitch smiled, wishing he could have seen the look on Simms' face. Then he shouldered his burden again and headed deeper into the forest.

It was nearly dark by the time they finished removing the bodies and returned to the cave. Mitch was completely exhausted and shaking with fatigue when he finally sat down and took a drink of cold water. Wanchese built a fire, heated some water and cleaned his wounds. Then she covered them with a healing salve and wrapped them tightly. That done, she put the stew pot on the fire.

"I've never seen a walking stick used as a weapon before," she said.

"It's something I learned from a friend," Mitch told her, not sure what else to say. "He was a good teacher."

"So it would seem," she said.

Mitch started to say something then stopped himself before reconsidering and plunging ahead.

"I've never killed anyone before," he said.

Wanchese looked surprised but said nothing.

"There was a man," Mitch went on, "one of the men who brought me here, I think, that I hurt badly. He may have died, but I don't know for sure."

"You weren't a warrior where you come from?"

Mitch chuckled. If she only knew.

"No, I wasn't a warrior."

"You fight well. I would have thought you a warrior from birth."

Mitch was quiet for a long moment, surprised by the depth of pleasure the compliment evoked within him.

"Thank you," he said. "You're pretty handy to have around yourself."

Wanchese looked thoughtful at that.

"I've never killed before either," she said.

"Well, I'm glad you did. That's twice you've saved my life now."

"And twice you've saved mine."

"Yeah, I suppose so," Mitch said. "I hadn't really looked at it that way."

Wanchese looked at him for a long time then seemed to come to a decision.

"I owe you an apology," she said. "I've been harsh with you when you gave me no real reason to be. I was afraid you'd think I was your woman because you saved me from the deathclaw. Also because you sometimes behave like a complete fool," she added with a smile, "but mainly because I didn't want you to think I belonged to you. In the village where I was born it is tradition that when a man saves a woman from death, she is honor bound to offer herself to him as a wife."

Mitch looked at her in surprise. Was she serious?

"Well, as far as I'm concerned, you saved my life just as many times as I saved yours. I think we can call it even."

"Good," Wanchese said with relief. She was getting tired of always having to be hard and disapproving. Sometimes Mitchell wasn't completely unpleasant to have around. Not often, but sometimes.

"What happens if a woman saves a man's life?" he asked.

After thinking about it for a minute, Wanchese smiled.

"I don't know. That's a very good question."

Mitch had a feeling there were some people she would like to ask that very good question. She rarely talked about her old village but it seemed pretty clear that she'd left as much out of necessity as by choice. He hesitated to ask her about it, not wanting to ruin what seemed to be at least a temporary truce between them.

"What happens if a man doesn't want to marry the woman he saved?" he asked instead.

"To refuse is a great insult, not only to the woman but to her whole family. It would mean a fight to the death with one of the men of her family."

"That's a bit drastic, isn't it?"

"It is their way," she answered with a shrug.

"Is that the only way people can get married?"

"Of course not. A man can ask a woman to be his wife anytime after her fourteenth year and a woman can offer herself to a man once she reaches that age as well. But there is no insult in refusing someone then. Most often, a woman's father will arrange a marriage for her, though not always."

"What if a man who's already married saves a woman's life?"

"Then he takes another wife," Wanchese answered, looking at him like he was none too bright.

"Oh, I see," Mitch said. It wasn't really all that uncommon. "Where I come from you can only have one wife. Can a woman have more than one husband?"

"No," Wanchese laughed. "Not unless the first husband dies."

Mitch nodded his understanding. Obviously a male dominated society. He could see where that could be hard on an independent woman like Wanchese. There were always ways around that, though. Strong women had been subtly influencing their supposedly dominant men since the day Adam got his first good look at Eve.

"You're not married?" he asked, thinking she may have been widowed at an early age. That might explain some of her attitudes toward men. Maybe she didn't wan to get close to someone only to lose them.

"No," she answered simply, seeming slightly embarrassed at the admission.

Well, so much for that theory, Mitch thought.

"I'm surprised," he said.

"Why?" she asked cautiously.

"Because you're a beautiful woman," he answered with a shrug. "Not to mention a good cook and handy in a fight," he added with a smile.

Wanchese studied his face for a long time before deciding that he was sincere. No one had ever called her beautiful. Not since her parents had died, anyway.

"No one in the village thought I was beautiful."

It must be a village full of blind men and idiots, Mitch thought then changed the subject.

"I had a wife back where I lived. She wasn't much of a wife, though. I finally figured out just before I ended up here that she didn't really care about me. She only wanted to be my wife because I could take care of her well."

"What's wrong with that?" Wanchese asked. What good was a husband who couldn't take care of you?

"What I mean is, she didn't really care about me, didn't love me. I wanted her to love me."

"Oh," Wanchese said. She knew what love was. Her parents had loved each other.

"I guess that sounds a little foolish out here, doesn't it?" Mitch asked.

"No," Wanchese answered after thinking about it for a minute. "Not to me. I've seen women who offer themselves to a man they have no feelings for just because he is a brave warrior and a good hunter. They end up with bellies that are full and hearts that are empty."

Yeah, Mitch thought, I can relate to that. There was more to this woman than he'd first given her credit for. There was a calm assuredness about her. She seemed to know who she was. He felt like he was just now starting to figure that out for himself.

"I've been to places where a man can have more than one wife," he said, changing the subject again. "And places where a woman can have more than one husband. I even went to one place where a man isn't allowed to speak to a woman without permission."

Wanchese looked at him to judge if he was serious and then asked with a grin, "Is this place far?"

Mitch laughed.

"I'm afraid so."

They were quiet for a few minutes while Wanchese dished up stew for the two of them.

"How are your wounds?" she asked when she was settled again.

"Fine, thank you."

"Good," Wanchese said. "I have to go to a river village. If you feel strong enough, I'd like you to come with me."

"I feel fine," Mitch lied. "You're going to warn them?"

"Yes, then they can at least get the children out of harms way. I doubt the Inchasa are really sending as many men as Simms claims, but they're definitely up to something. There shouldn't be so many of them moving back and forth across these mountains."

Yes, Mitch thought, moving the children out of harms way would be important to her.

"I'd like that very much," he said. "When do we leave?"

"There is still time. We'll let your wounds heal."

"You're sure there's time?"

"Yes. If the Inchasa are building the storage shelters as Simms claims, there is. The shelters will have to be filled with supplies before they can move and that will take time."

"O.K," Mitch said. That made sense, and he really could use a few days rest. "That'll give me time to practice with these," he said, picking up the bows he'd taken from the dead Inchasa. It would also give him time to dip some of the arrowheads in the black ooze. Maybe he'd even have time to work a little with a sword. From what he'd seen of this place so far, there was no such thing as too many weapons.

# CHAPTER 19

▼

# FRUITLESS EFFORTS

Secotan Samuels was standing outside their longhouse staring up at the Pemisi-
pans again when Dare found him. She threw his cloak over his broad shoulders,
fastened it at his neck for him and then slid inside its warmth with him, wrapping
her arms around his waist and resting her head on his chest. They stood together
in silence as the last of the afternoon's warmth was forced into a hasty retreat by
the cold march of coming night.

Secotan looked out at the now barely visible peaks to the west and thought
once again of Wanchese Hawkins, of his decision and what it had cost her, and
what the lesson he'd learned from it was likely about the cost him. But his loss
would be minor compared to Wanchese's. He would only be losing his title and
the responsibilities that went with it. She had lost her life. And with it, any
chance she might have had to find the happiness she deserved. He had nothing to
complain about.

And Mother Shaw had been right. Knowing he'd done what he believed was
right did make all the difference. He was at peace with his decision to let his people choose for themselves how they would live, and he was at peace with the fact
that it might cost him his position. He would have to remember to thank her. It
had been a painful lesson, but one worth learning.

"You're going to have to kill Hunter Kane someday, aren't you?" Dare asked
into the silence, bringing a surprised grin to Secotan's face. The depth of Dare's
insight still sometimes caught him off guard.

"If I'm still Councillor after tonight then yes, I expect I will, sooner or later. He's not a very good loser."

"And if he and his friends succeed?" Dare asked.

"It will depend on who gets voted in as my successor. If Kane or one of his men takes over we'll leave this village. I won't have my family's future decided by men like them. If Geris or Nathaniel or someone like them is elected we'll stay, though there might still be trouble with Kane. He's not a very good winner, either."

"Mother Shaw says you'll win. I think she's right. The people of the village aren't as easily fooled as Kane thinks."

"No, but some of them are no happier with my decision than he is. Belief in the old traditions is strong. They might not be willing to vote Kane in as Councillor, but I think a lot of them are willing to vote me out."

"We'll see," Dare said, giving him a squeeze. "I think you're in for a surprise. I've noticed a difference in a lot of the people who were against your decision at first. They're not as distant or as cold as they were. I think they've had time to get used to making some decisions for themselves and aren't so afraid of the idea any more."

"Perhaps. We'll know soon enough."

"What did the other Councillors say?" Dare asked. She knew Secotan had sent messengers to the other members of the Grand Council telling them of his decision and the intentions of those who opposed it. His messengers had returned earlier in the day but he'd been closed mouthed about what they'd had to say.

"They still support me as Councillor, though Elan White did say he disagrees with my decision and thinks it unwise."

"Why haven't you said anything? The people should know that the Council still supports you."

"No," Secotan said firmly. "I want them to decide for themselves. It's better if they don't know where the Council stands."

"I think you're wrong, Secotan. I think they have a right to know what the Council thinks."

"You may be right," Secotan said, lowering his face and kissing the top of Dare's head lightly. "You usually are. But I've made my decision."

"Stubborn," Dare said, but there was no anger in her voice. She knew she was one of the few women in any of the river villages who could tell her husband she thought he was wrong about something without him becoming hurt or angry. That was one of the reasons she truly believed her husband was the best man for the job of Councillor. He was secure enough in himself to listen to the opinions of others without feeling threatened if they were different from his own.

"I've been called worse," Secotan said with a smile.

Dare laughed.

"I can imagine," she said. The first weeks after Secotan's decision had been tense ones, with people they had considered friends suddenly finding reasons to avoid them. She could imagine the things he had been called.

But things had changed now. She had noticed a difference in the people of the village. The friendliness had returned to their eyes and they had stopped avoiding her. Everyone except Kane and his friends, that is. And she didn't mind having them avoid her.

"I should go," Secotan said. "It's almost time."

"Alright," Dare said. "I should go see that the children are ready for bed. I'll see you there."

She gave him a quick kiss and was gone.

Secotan made his way through the village to the Central Longhouse, where many of the villagers had already gathered. Most of them greeted him with a nod or a wave of their hand. Hunter Kane was there, standing at the front of the building, looking anxious to get things started. He ignored Seoctan completely.

"Where have you been hiding all day?" Geris Quick asked as he came and stood beside Secotan. "What did the Council have to say? I've been trying to get Raleigh to talk all afternoon but he won't budge."

"Not everyone is as fond of gossip as you are," Secotan said with a smile. He hoped the other messengers had been as dutiful as Raleigh.

"Just answer the question," Geris said, but his eyes laughed.

"Which one? Where I've been hiding or what the Council said?"

"Both, you pain in my backside!"

Secotan laughed.

"I haven't been hiding. I've been out walking in the forest. I needed some time to myself. And the Council still supports me as Councillor. I ask you to keep that between the two of us for now, though, old friend. I want these people making up their own minds."

Geris looked at his friend, meeting his gaze for a long minute.

"Are you sure that's best?" he asked. He sometimes wondered if Secotan really wanted to win this fight. Not that he'd blame him if he didn't. Being Councillor was a time consuming job with little real reward other than the title. Still, Secotan was the best man for the job. The village needed him, whether these people knew it or not.

"I am," Secotan answered. "If I'm going to be Councillor, I want it to be because the people want me to be, not because the Council wants me to be."

"Alright," Geris said grudgingly. "I'll keep it to myself. Unless it looks like Kane is going to be elected. If that happens, I'll do whatever I have to do to stop it."

"Fair enough," Secotan said as he scanned the faces in front of him until he found Dare and his other wives at the back of the room. They must have left Elinor in charge of the children so they could all be there for him. Good women, his wives. He was a fortunate man.

"Why don't you take your seat, Geris, and we'll get started."

"Good luck, my friend," Geris said, gripping Secotan's right forearm with his right hand before turning and going to his seat. Secotan waited until Geris was seated and then raised his hands high over his head to get the crowd's attention.

"Thank you all for coming," he said. "If you could please settle down now we'll get this meeting under way."

The crowd quieted.

"Thank you. I think you all know why we're here and where I stand on the issue so I won't waste your time restating my views. We're here because some of you have a different view and we need to decide which view, and which Councillor, this village will follow. Hunter Kane is the leader of the group that disagrees with me and wants to have me replaced. Please listen to what he has to say and make your own decision."

Secotan nodded to Kane and went and stood against the wall to his right. Kane seemed a little surprised at having the floor so soon and looked unsure of himself, as if he'd expected to have more time to get his thoughts in order.

"I…ah…I wouldn't say I'm the leader of the group that opposes Secotan," he began, "just a concerned member of this village who happens to share the opinion of many other people here. I believe it is a mistake to abandon the old ways, and I believe it is a mistake to allow ourselves to be led by a man who would do so. I call for a vote to renounce Secotan Samuels as our Councillor.

"I also call for a vote to nominate Saul Rivers as our new Councillor. He is a man of wisdom and peace, a man who would serve this village well. That is all I have to say. I think you all know what has to be done here tonight."

Kane moved off to the side and Secotan returned to the front of the room.

"If anyone else would like to speak, you may do so now," he said. "You may also nominate someone else for Councillor in the event I am renounced."

Nathaniel Whyte stood.

"I nominate Geris Quick," he said, "though I will vote against your renounce-ment, Secotan."

"Thank you," Secotan said.

"I nominate Hunter Kane," Dasemun Wing stood and said. "And I plan to vote for your renouncement, Secotan."

"Of course, Dasemun," Secotan said. "Anyone else?"

A tall, middle-aged man named Rolf Gardiner stood to speak and all eyes turned to him. Rolf was a quiet man and had never spoken at a meeting that any-one could remember.

"I have something to say," he began, his speech slow and measured, as was his way. "When Secotan announced his decision to allow us to choose for ourselves whether or not we would follow the old ways, I was against it. I told myself I was against it because I was a man who respected tradition, and because I wanted my children and my grandchildren to be raised the same way I was. But that wasn't true.

"The real reason I was against Secotan's plan was that I was afraid of it, afraid of what might happen if we were allowed to make choices for ourselves, if I was allowed to make choices for myself and my family. I have since remembered that I am not a man who allows fear to govern his thoughts or his life. I have changed my mind, just as I think a great many of you here tonight have changed yours, and I will vote to keep Secotan as our Councillor. I can think of no one more worthy of the position."

"Thank you, Rolf," Secotan said. "Anyone else? No? Alright then, let's get on with the vote. The first order of business is to vote on whether or not you choose to renounce me as your Councillor. A vote of 'aye' is a vote to remove me, a vote of 'nay' is a vote to retain me. Any questions?"

There were none.

"Very well, let's vote. When I ask you to, all those in favor of removing me please say 'aye' and stand to your feet. I'd like Geris Quick and Dasemun Wing to please come to the front here and count those who stand so we can be sure of an accurate count."

Geris and Wing stood and went to the front of the room.

"All those in favor of renouncement, please stand and say 'aye'."

Approximately one third of the room stood with a staggered chorus of 'ayes'. Hunter Kane stepped forward and glared at people who remained seated, his fiery gaze taking in the entire room. People looked away, not wanting to make eye contact. I could be a dangerous thing to openly defy Kane.

"What are you waiting for?" he spat. "On your feet! I know some of you agree with me. You, Riker, I spoke to you just last week and you told me you would vote for renouncement. On your feet, man!"

"I've changed my mind," Riker Ash said uneasily, not making any eye contact.

"Do we have a count?" Secotan asked.

"I count two hundred and eighty seven, counting Dasemun and Kane," Geris said.

"Dasemun?"

"Agreed," Wing said dejectedly. How could things have gone so wrong?

"Thank you. You people can be seated. All those in favor of keeping me as your Councillor, please stand and say 'nay'."

The majority of the rest of the room stood, though some chose to abstain completely.

"Geris?"

"I count five hundred and eighty one, counting myself."

"Dasemun?"

"Close enough," Wing said. "I stopped at three hundred."

"Very well," Secotan said with relief. "I thank you all for coming and for your support. As for those who voted against me, please know that I hold no animosity toward you. You have every right to your opinion and I won't hold it against you. I give you my word on that. Thank you and good night."

Geris came over and gave Secotan a boisterous hug.

"I knew it!" he exclaimed.

Secotan shook his head and laughed. Then others began coming to congratulate him and he exchanged a word of thanks with each of them, extending his arm in friendship to Rolf Gardiner as the quiet man approached him. They gripped forearms and Gardiner nodded when Secotan thanked him.

The time went quickly, as people exchanged greetings and went back to their homes. At the end, only Secotan, Geris and Kane were left, though Saul Rivers and Dasemun Wing lingered outside in case trouble started.

"You've won nothing," Kane said when they were alone. "The Council will never stand for this. I'll send a messenger to each of them tonight and have you removed before the week is out."

"The Council supports me, Kane," Secotan said. "I sent messengers out myself and all of the members of the Grand Council support me, though not all of them agree with my decision. You can send as many messengers as you like. It won't change anything."

"We'll see about that," Kane said coldly, walking up and standing nose to nose with Secotan. "And even if you're right, there are other ways of removing you."

He smiled.

"More enjoyable ways," he said. "The time will come when your office can no longer protect you, Samuels. And when that time comes, I'm going to be there waiting."

"I'll look forward to it," Secotan said, meaning it.

Kane grinned and walked away, picking up his cloak and walking out into the cold darkness.

"Remember what I told you," Geris said. "Watch yourself. He'll pick a time when he thinks he has an advantage."

"I know, Geris, I know. I'll be careful."

"Warn your family, too," Geris said gravely. "He's not above hurting women and children, either."

Secotan looked at him a long time before speaking.

"I will," he said finally. "And thank you. I owe you."

"Oh, I know. I keep a running tally."

Secotan laughed and they slung their cloaks over their shoulders and walked out into the night, each knowing that trouble was coming and that they would be in the middle of it when it came.

"Come to my longhouse," Secotan said. "I traded a basket of fish for some of Nathaniel's brew."

"Ah, now that's an offer I can't refuse!" Geris said happily.

"Somehow I had a feeling you'd say that," Secotan said.

They both laughed and walked on into the night.

\*       \*       \*       \*

"Turning on exterior guidance," Tommy announced as Alton reached the bridge. Their scan of the plain had provided no clues and they were beginning a night scan of the lower mountain elevations. The exterior guidance system would allow them to scan safely without worrying about running into a cliff or clipping an especially tall tree.

They were scanning at night to avoid being seen by some human life forms moving along the edge of the plain and the lower elevations of the mountains. The guidance beam would allow them to scan at close range.

"I've got something," Alton called slightly more than an hour into the scan.

"I see it," Tommy said. "I can't put down anywhere near by, though. You can either go down by cable or hike up from the plain. Your choice."

"We'll use the cables," Alton said. "Come on, Nate, I think I'll need your help on this one."

"Right."

Tommy hovered just over the top of the small clearing where the remains were as Alton and Nate were lowered to the ground by cable and winch. They found what was left of the two bodies almost immediately, but it was a long time before they could bring themselves to move close enough to get samples. The putrefying remains had been desecrated by scavengers and the elements. Alton finally managed to gather a sample from each corpse, and they were hauled back up to the ship.

"Scans are negative," Alton said into the intercom when he was through vomiting. "Keep going, Tommy. We'll be up in a minute."

"You got it, boss," the pilot said.

"You alright, Nate?" Alton asked when Nathan Squires came out of the bathroom.

"Not really," he replied. "You?"

"I've been better."

Ten minutes later they were back on the bridge, a little peaked and not very talkative, but back at their stations as they continued the scan. The rest of the night proved as fruitless as the previous ten and they moved to a spot at the southernmost point of the plain, where it bordered the sea, and set down for the day.

The three of them headed off to get some sleep, the automated controls set to alert them to any approach by human life forms. Not finding Mitch's corpse near the original drop point could be a good sign. Or it might just mean he had died somewhere else. It was hard to say. Tonight they would start scanning the populated areas to the west. Maybe they'd have more luck there.

The morning found Alton and Nate tired and untalkative. Tommy on the other hand, was alive with energy and had breakfast ready for them when they shuffled into the galley.

"I've been thinking," he said excitedly as he poured a cup of coffee. "I read an article a couple of months back about amecyclezene. It's a preservative used in just about every kind of food in the whole Traegus Sector. The FFADA was whining about how long the stuff stays in the system and calling for tests on the long-term effects. They said it remains in traceable amounts for as long as six months!"

"Six months!" Alton said. "Son of a bitch! Can we program the instruments to scan for it?" he asked excitedly, suddenly no longer tired. "Can they be that specific?"

"Yeah, no problem," Tommy told him. "I'll look up the chemical composition and program the computer. Shouldn't take more than fifteen or twenty minutes."

"Will it work with a high level scan or will we have to wait for nightfall?" Nate asked.

"High level should work fine."

"If you weren't so ugly I could kiss you, you little shit!" Alton exclaimed.

"Well, for once I'm glad I'm ugly, then," Tommy said with a grin. Then he hightailed it to the bridge to get started.

"Whatever you're paying him, it's not enough," Nate said when he was gone.

"You just might be right," Alton said with a smile. Suddenly things looked a lot brighter.

"You got any cards?" Nate asked.

"Sure. What'd you have in mind?"

"Feel like a little cribbage? Say, a credit a point?"

"You're on," Alton said with a grin. "I hope you have some money saved, Nate. I'm suddenly feeling very lucky."

# CHAPTER 20

▼

# SETTING A NEW COURSE

Mitchell Harvey awoke with a start to the sound of someone moving around inside the cave. Wanchese's foot had moved during the night and was touching his so he knew it wasn't her. A figure moved from the back of the cave and stepped into the pale circle of light surrounding the small fire just as Mitch set his hands firmly on the ground, ready to push himself up as quickly and quietly as possible. He stopped in mid-motion. Royal Simms. He should have known. Simms moved to a spot near the fire, hesitated for a second then spread a blanket and laid down.

"I should get up and slit your throat," Mitch said softly.

"I thought of it first," Wanchese said into the darkness, surprising him. He'd been sure she was asleep.

Simms said nothing, correctly assuming that whatever he said would be the wrong thing. They didn't understand, they couldn't. They couldn't know what he'd been through with the Inchasa.

And what the hell were they doing here anyway? They should have been either dead or taken prisoner. He'd come to the cave to take whatever food and clothing had been left behind. But, on seeing them here, alive, he hadn't been able to bring himself to leave. He didn't want to be alone. He had to make them understand.

"You're no longer welcome here," Wanchese said coldly.

"You don't understand," Simms said pleadingly. "I...I...I couldn't get caught again. I just couldn't. That's why I ran. I'm no coward. I killed one of them, out there in the woods. I can show you!"

The boy, Mitch thought, remembering the scream he'd heard during his fight with the Inchasa. Simms must have killed the boy. A defenseless child scared out of his mind. He hadn't thought he could dislike Royal Simms any more than he already did. He was wrong.

"Is that why you came back?" he asked angrily. "To tell us about your glorious battle to the death with an unarmed boy?"

"He had a bow!" Simms protested. "And a knife!"

"Hmph!" Mitch snorted. "Why'd you come back? And no bullshit!"

It had been three days since the fight with the Inchasa, but even Simms couldn't be stupid enough to think they would welcome him back after what he'd done. Or had he come back expecting to find them gone, dead or taken prisoner? That seemed more likely.

"I needed food," Simms answered honestly. "I thought you two would be...gone."

"Sorry to disappoint you," Mitch said.

"Since you're here," Simms went on, ignoring Mitch's sarcasm, "maybe Wanchese could tell me how to get to one of those river villages?"

"Why?" Wanchese asked.

"Because I have to go somewhere," Simms said. "Somewhere where there's people. I don't like being alone. And I don't want to live in a friggin' cave!"

Mitch doubted Wanchese was feeling very sympathetic to Simms' wants and needs, but he had an idea.

"We're going to one of them ourselves in a few days," he said. "If we let you come along, and I'm leaving that entirely up to Wanchese, will you teach me how to speak Inchasa along the way?"

"Why do you want to know?" Simms asked.

"Does it matter?" Mitch shot back.

"No," Simms admitted. "I don't suppose it does. Alright then, yes, I'll teach you what I know."

"Wanchese?" Mitch asked.

"It is important?"

"I don't really know. I think it could be."

"Very well, then," she said, obviously not liking the idea. "If you think it's important, he can come."

"Thank you," Mitch said, aware that this was the first time she had deferred to his judgment on something important. "And, since you did think of it first, you can have the pleasure of slitting his throat if he misbehaves."

"Thank you," Wanchese said with a laugh.

Predictably, Royal Simms failed to see the humor in the situation.

"It will be light soon enough," Wanchese said, sliding out from under the warm hide and standing. "I'll make something to eat."

As she got their breakfast ready, Mitch went to the forest for a load of wood. It was a constant need for them and he had begun to form the habit of gathering two or three arm loads a day, whether they needed them or not. It all got used eventually.

After they'd eaten, Wanchese changed the dressings on Mitch's wounds, adding some of the healing salve. She was silently amazed at the transformation his body had undergone in the three short days since the battle. His once frighteningly thin limbs were beginning to thicken and his chest and shoulders were starting to fill out, growing deeper and broader with each passing day. It was as if the deathclaw poison had finally been chased completely from his system and his body was making up for lost time. Even his once sallow skin was turning a deep bronze.

"How did you two manage to escape?" Simms asked as she finished securing the last of the bandages. The wounds surprised him. He had assumed the two of them had eluded capture the same way he had, by running for their lives. How could Harvey have gotten hurt? "And where'd you get those cuts?"

Mitch just ignored him but Wanchese looked at him with undisguised disgust.

"How do you think he got them?" she asked. "Not all men run from battle like frightened children," she added bitingly.

"What are you saying? Are you trying to tell me he fought those Inchasa? Don't make me laugh," Simms said. He'd seen Inchasa warriors in action and he doubted there was any one man alive who could fight six of the brutal bastards and live to tell about it. And what would Harvey have fought them with, that stupid walking stick?

"Mitchell fought them," Wanchese said angrily. "While you were running away like a frightened child and likely soiling yourself in fear, he stood like a man and fought them!"

"Fought them with what?" Simms asked.

"Wanchese fought them, too," Mitch said quietly, not really wanting to talk about it. "I'd be dead if not for her."

"I did little," Wanchese said, but there was pride in her voice and in the way she held herself. "You had already wounded the man I killed."

"You killed one of them?" Simms asked, looking from one to the other of them. "What about the other four?"

"They are all dead," Wanchese answered.

"All of them?" Simms asked in disbelief. "How?"

"Mitchell fought them, they are dead," Wanchese said simply.

"That's a story I'd like to hear," Simms said, suddenly very glad he hadn't pushed Harvey any further than he had in the days he'd spent with him.

"No one is especially interested in what you'd like," Mitch said shortly. He'd done what needed to be done. He knew that. But he had no desire to talk about it, especially not with Royal Simms.

"I was just curious," Simms said defensively. If this was how he was going to be treated, maybe he'd be better off trying to find one of the river villages on his own. But, even as he thought it, he knew he would stay. The three days he'd spent slinking through the woods alone had been the most terrifying days of his life. Worse even than his servitude.

"I'm going to go check the snares," Mitch said, suddenly needing some fresh air.

"I'll go with you," Wanchese said and stood to her feet. "I'll just need a minute to get dressed."

Mitch nodded and Wanchese took her dress and stepped into the darkness at the back of the cave. When she was ready, they set out to the west, leaving Simms to himself.

Mitch brought along a bow and quiver of arrows in addition to his staff and stopped occasionally to fire at a large tree or some small game. He didn't his anything but he thought he might be able to get a feel for the thing with some practice. Wanchese gave him some pointers and he could see immediately that she knew what she was doing.

When all the snares were checked and the catch secured, Wanchese put down her ever-present pack and gave him some serious instruction. She was a better teacher than he was a student, however, and he could see he'd need a lot of practice before he could use the bow with any confidence.

They practiced the better part of the morning and then passed the mid-day heat in the shade of a tall, wide limbed tree that reminded Mitch of the pine trees he'd seen on his grandfather's plot of land back on Earth. Except instead of green or brown pine needles, this tree sprouted thick leaves shaped like palms and colored a deep blue.

When the heat subsided enough to travel, they started on again.

"I would like to bathe," Wanchese said as they set off. "It's not far to the large spring. Would you keep watch for me?"

"Sure. I could use a good wash myself when you're done."

While Wanchese bathed, Mitch worked with his staff, practicing various types of blocks and strikes and paying particular attention to the way his balance shifted as he moved. He never wanted to find himself flat on his back in the middle of a fight again. He'd been lucky and he knew it.

When it was his turn to bathe, Wanchese handed him the brown lump of soap she carried in her pack. He didn't know what she made it from, but he was going to have to find out. It looked foul but it actually smelled pretty good. Kind of fresh and outdoorsy.

Taking the soap, he disrobed, removed his bandages and stepped into the cool water, congratulating himself for having resisted the temptation to sneak a look while Wanchese was dressing. And he had been tempted. But he didn't want her to catch him sneaking a peak like some sex starved boy. Though he had to admit, as he regained some of his strength, he was starting to feel a little sex starved. He assumed it was a good sign.

As he washed his face, he marveled again that he still had no beard, not so much as a rough stubble. He'd asked Wanchese about it the first time he'd bathed and she'd told him about the mixture of herbs and illo juices she called locaram that kept hair from growing for months at a time. She could have made a fortune with the stuff back on Sylvas.

When he was finished bathing, he scrubbed and rinsed his breechcloth and belt, put them back on and rejoined Wanchese, his soiled bandages thrown over his shoulder. Wanchese took the bandages and put them in her pack.

"I've been thinking," she said as she ran a long, thin-toothed comb through her hair. "If we're going to be traveling, you'll need a cloak. I could make one from the deathclaw hide if you don't mind the weight." Deathclaw hide, while extremely warm, was also extremely heavy. For that reason, it was seldom used as clothing.

"That sounds fine," Mitch said. "Will it still be long enough to use as a blanket, though? That thing really keeps out the cold."

"Yes, it should still be fine," Wanchese told him.

"I'd like that, then. Thank you."

"It's nothing," Wanchese said uncomfortably.

"I've been doing some thinking, too," Mitch said. "I've been feeling a lot better the last couple of days and I think I could be ready to travel tomorrow or the next day. Maybe we should leave as soon as possible and take the time to head south and see if we can't find one of the storage shelters Simms has been talking about. It might make it easier for the people on the river to take us seriously if we've actually seen them for ourselves."

"That might be a good idea," Wanchese said thoughtfully. "We would have to head south and west to avoid running into the labor party he escaped from. That would add time to the journey and put us at risk. There seem to be a lot of Inchasa roaming these mountains."

"You'll get no argument from me there," Mitch said. "It was just a thought. If you think it's too risky, we can skip it."

"No," Wanchese said. "I think we should do as you say. We'll just have to be careful."

"O.K," Mitch said. "Whatever you think best. You know a hell of a lot more about this place than I do."

Replacing the comb in her pack, Wanchese swung the pack to her shoulder and started back toward the cave, thinking about the odd man walking behind her. It seemed strange to her that a man who was so fierce in battle could be so different at other times. When she tried to put into words his manner toward her since they'd come to an understanding about her having saved his life as many times as he'd saved hers, the word she came back to most often was, gentle.

He spoke to her with respect and seemed to give weight to her words. It was sometimes difficult to believe that the quiet, affable man offering to carry her pack or go out in search of firewood in her place, was the same man who had attacked the deathclaw so viciously and had fought the Inchasa with an almost frightening passion for battle burning in his eyes.

And yet, thinking back to her childhood, her father had been a respected hunter and a feared warrior, and he was a gentle father and husband. She had always associated gentleness with weakness. Perhaps she'd been wrong. Perhaps a man could be both gentle and strong. Perhaps a woman could, too.

Suddenly, Mitch grabbed her from behind.

"Quiet!" he whispered into her ear, his breath hot on her skin.

"What do you think you're...." she started to say, but stopped short as Mitch pointed off to the south and she saw a deathclaw moving away from them, lumbering slowly to the east.

They stood together silently as the beast stopped and stood on its hind legs, sniffing the air. Wanchese felt the breeze against her face and was glad. They were upwind. After a few curious sniffs, the deathclaw dropped back down to all fours and started off again.

"Sorry I grabbed you like that," Mitch said when it seemed safe to talk again. "I saw the thing and I guess I sort of panicked. Sorry."

"Don't be," Wanchese said. "I'd much rather you grab me than the death-claw."

"That's the first one we've seen since...before," Mitch said.

Wanchese nodded.

"We may be leaving just in time," she said. "As the scent of the dealthclaw you killed fades, new ones will start exploring its former territory. So will ripper cats."

"We'll see more of them as we travel, then?"

"I'm afraid so. We will have to be very careful."

"Great," Mitch said, shaking his head in resignation. "I've never seen a place where so many things want to kill you."

Wanchese smiled.

"Really?" she asked innocently, looking back at him as she started walking again. "I would have thought with your personality you would have run into that problem everywhere."

"Shut up," Mitch said, but he laughed and threw a stick at her. Wanchese smiled and kept walking.

"Actually," she said, "you're not nearly as annoying now that you've stopped asking so many question. I thought I was going to go out of my mind those first few days after you wok up."

"Sorry," Mitch said. "There's just so much I don't know about this place, and I hated being a burden. I wanted to be able to do some things for myself. I didn't mean to be such a pain in the ass."

"Pain in the ass?" Wanchese asked.

"It's just an expression," Mitch said with a smile. "Another way of saying annoying."

"Oh," Wanchese said.

The fact of the matter was, she had noticed a change in Mitchell as he began to understand what needed to be done and how he could help do it. He was quieter now, though not sullen. Just quiet. He seemed more content to learn by watching now rather than asking questions. She hoped it wasn't because she had snapped at him. She understood now that he was only trying to learn things he needed to know.

"I don't mind the questions so much now," she said a little uncomfortably.

Mitch looked at her with gratitude. Her words were as good an offer of friendship as he was likely to get from this stubbornly self-sufficient woman and he admired her for saying them. They had probably been hard for her to say.

"I appreciate everything you've taught me," he said as they stepped from the forest and out onto the open shelf. "I know it hasn't always been easy."

Wanchese turned to say something to him but was interrupted by Royal Simms.

"Where the hell have you two been all day?" he asked. "I was starting to think you'd gone off and left me."

Mitch looked at Wanchese and they smiled at each other.

"I thought of it," she said, "but you said you wanted to learn Inchasa."

"I'm glad you didn't mention it," Mitch replied with a grin. "It would have been awfully tempting."

"Very funny," Simms said, then walked into the cave to sulk.

"I have to go somewhere for a little while," Mitch said to Wanchese. "Up to the north of the cave. It'll only take an hour or so."

"Alright," she said, understanding that he didn't want her to go with him and wondering why. "I'll clean the catch and get the hides stretched out."

Mitch sensed her disappointment and immediately felt guilty. What the hell was he so worried about? If he asked Wanchese not to tell anyone about the black ooze, she'd keep quiet.

"Actually, there's something up there I'd like to show you," he said. "If you're not too busy."

"You are sure?" she asked.

"Yeah, I'm sure."

She nodded and Mitch went into the cave to tell Simms they'd be back in a little more than an hour, then they set off to the west and turned north toward the cliff Mitch was reasonably sure was the one near the ooze.

"Have you ever seen anything made like my staff?" he asked. It was possible Wanchese's people knew all about the ooze and he was worrying for nothing.

"What do you mean?" she asked.

"With this," Mitch answered, tapping that hard black shell with his knuckle.

"No," Wanchese said with a shake of her head. "I've wondered what kind of pitch you used."

"It's not pitch. It's something I found while I was out walking. It's very hard, harder even than iron, I think."

"You found it up here?" Wanchese asked.

Mitch nodded.

"I'd like to keep it just between us," he said. "If no one else knows about it, it gives me kind of an edge."

"That's why you wanted to come by yourself?"

"Yes, but I trust you. If you tell me you won't tell anyone, I know you'll keep your word."

"Thank you," Wanchese said, surprised how deeply moved she was at his trust. "I give you my word."

"Thanks," Mitch said. "It's just a little further."

A few minutes later they came to the cliff and followed it around to the east until they came to the spot where the large section of stone had been broken off. Mitch stepped over to the shrub that hid the puddle and moved the branches aside. Wanchese watched curiously as he dipped five arrows deeply into the bubbling black liquid.

He handed her one of the arrows and she ran her hand along the smooth black shaft.

"This will make it stronger?" she asked.

"It should. If it works as well on the arrow as it did on my staff, you might even be able to kill something as big as a deathclaw with just one arrow. If you hit it in the right place, anyway. These arrows should penetrate deeper."

Wanchese nodded but he could see she was skeptical.

"Stand back," he told her, "and turn your head to the side. You might even want to close your eyes."

She stepped back and turned her head a little to the side but watched him as he stepped up to the outcropping of rock.

"Here goes," he said. "Cover your eyes. There'll be rock flying all over the place."

Then he raised his staff and bought it crashing down on the stone, squeezing his eyes shut and wincing as tiny slivers of rock pelted his face and chest.

He turned to find Wanchese staring in amazement at the large piece of rock broken off from the cliff. She turned and looked at his staff. He walked over and showed it to her.

"Not so much as a scratch," he said with a smile.

She reached out her hand and touched it, shaking her head, not sure she believed what she'd just seen.

"How?" she asked.

"I have no idea," Mitch answered. "I stumbled on it completely by accident."

Wanchese nodded her acceptance of that. She expected that was how many things people used every day had been discovered.

"Can you dip some arrows for me?"

"Absolutely. How may?"

"How many did you do?"

"Five."

"I'll take five as well, then."

Mitch took out five more arrows and dipped them in the ooze then handed them to Wanchese, who put them in her pack.

"You're wise to keep this a secret," she said as they started back toward the cave. "I wouldn't want the Inchasa to know about this."

"No, me either," Mitch agreed.

"And I thank you for your trust," she said seriously. She understood now why Mitchell didn't want anyone else to know what he'd found. She doubted she would have trusted him with such a secret.

"You've earned it," Mitch said, which made her feel a little guilty about her last thought. He had earned her trust, too. Trust came hard to her, though. She couldn't change that.

"When do you think we'll leave?" he asked, wondering how well Simms was going to take the news that they were going to go check on what the Inchasa were doing before heading to the river villages.

"Two days should be enough to make our cloaks," she answered. "If you think you're ready."

"I'm ready," Mitch said. "I feel a little better every day."

"Alright," Wanchese said, wondering again why she was bothering to warn the people of the river. She shook her head at her own weakness. She should just move higher into the mountains and forget them. Let them deal with their own problems like they had always let her deal with hers.

She would go, though, because somewhere deep inside she knew she would never forgive herself if she didn't. What a fool she was. She was a fool for risking her own life for people who cared nothing for her and she was an even bigger fool to let Mitchell risk his for people he'd never even met.

"Are you sure you want to go?" she asked. "There's a good chance we'll run into more Inchasa. We might run into more than we can fight."

"I'm sure," Mitch said. "Thanks for asking, though."

They walked on in silence until they were almost to the cave then Mitch stopped and turned to face her.

"There's something you should know before we go," he said, looking her in the eye as he spoke. "If we do run into more than we can fight, I'll die fighting before I'll let them take me prisoner. And I'm not real good at running away, either, so you just do what you have to do to get the hell out of there and don't worry about me, O.K?"

Wanchese was tempted to tell him that she wasn't very good at running away either, that she was just as brave as he was. But she knew he wasn't questioning her courage.

"I understand," she said instead. "We'll just have to be careful and make sure we don't run into any."

Mitch nodded and they started walking again.

Wanchese watched him as he made his way into the clearing and nodded to herself. She would be proud to die fighting beside this man.

# CHAPTER 21

▼

# THE GRIND

Capac hobbled slowly up the steps that led to the top of the city wall at the east end of the palace, his face a grim mask of determination and total concentration. He was breathing heavily by the time he reached the top and leaned against the waist high wall. He felt Noref's arm brush his as she moved up to stand beside him. He moved slightly so that his arm rested against hers.

He wasn't sure how they had become lovers. It had just happened one night, and then the next and again, until it became a normal part of their relationship. For his part, he was filled with a confusing rush of emotions each time they touched, one part of him hungrily relishing the physical and emotional intimacy, the other feeling foolish and ashamed for having allowed himself to place Noref in such danger.

There was little doubt that the Cuzco knew of the change in their relationship. They were watched carefully day and night. The Cuzco would know. And if Capac ever tried to defy him in even the smallest way, Noref would be made to suffer. Thinking of what they would do to her in order to hurt him made him sick to his stomach.

"It's a little frightening, isn't it?" Noref asked, indicating the plain below with a jut of her chin.

"More than a little," Capac answered both her question and his own thoughts. As far as they eye could see, stretched across the plain to the east, were groups of

Inchasa warriors. Each group was being instructed in the use of a particular weapon, here the sword, there the lance, sling or bow.

The sight of so many armed Inchasa was very disconcerting. They lived with the constant fear that the Cuzco would catch wind of the Lydacian plan to escape and turn those soldiers on their own people before heading off to conquer the river villages.

"I thought it was idle boasting when the Cuzco said he would raise and army of five thousand," he said sadly. "But, there it is. I feel sorry for the river people. They'll have no chance, no chance at all."

"I know," Noref said, looking out at a small knot of men using slings to hurl stones at wooden targets. "But try not to think about it. There's nothing we can do to help them. We can only help ourselves."

"I suppose that's true."

"Try to think of Lydacia City, Capac" she whispered in Lydacian. "Soon you will see it again, and when you do, all of this will have been worth it."

He smiled and nodded, not having the heart to tell her the truth. Better she live with the happiness of a lie than the sorrow of the truth. He would never see Lydacia City again.

He was the writer of the Inchasa book. For whatever reason, the Cuzco wanted him and only him, to author the story. He would have to go with them when they marched on the river villages. To refuse, or try to flee, would only result in search parties being sent to find him, search parties that might stumble onto evidence of the planned exodus of his people. That was something he couldn't risk.

They stood together quietly then, looking to the east where the warriors trained, and to the north where smoke from the fires of a hundred forges rose unceasingly into the copper sky. The Cuzco was sparing no expense. His men would go into battle superbly armed.

"How go the preparations?" he asked after several minutes, leaning close, his voice the softest of whispers.

"Very well," Noref whispered in return. "Small numbers have begun drifting already."

"Already?" Capac asked nervously. "Is that wise?" Why would Javet take such a risk so soon?

"It is, for the old and infirm," Noref said.

Capac nodded, understanding. They were quietly moving those who wouldn't be able to travel quickly. When the time came to go, they would have no time to waste. Another reason he would never see Lydacia City again. He could barely hobble on his scarred, swollen feet. He would only slow the escape.

"Javet asked me to tell you not to be frightened by your dreams," Noref whispered.

"What?" Capac stammered. "How could he...? But...?"

"He is Javet," Noref answered with a shrug, as if that somehow explained how the old priest could know about the dreams, dreams he'd spoken of to no one, not even Noref.

And the dreams were frightening. They always ended with him standing in the middle of a brutal battlefield with broken, bloodied bodies strewn all around him, and him standing face to face with the red eyed man-huascar of his earlier vision. They always ended before he got to see what the beast was going to do to him, but it was hard to imagine it being anything good.

"Tell him I'll try," he said. "I just wish I knew what they meant."

"Tell me about them," Noref said, and he told her.

"And Javet doesn't know what the man-beast represents, either?" she asked when he was through.

"No."

"Well, if it kills Inchasa, it can't be all bad."

Capac had to smile at that. He hadn't thought of it that way.

"I suppose that's true," he said, turning to look at her with a smile.

"Of course it's true. And Javet wouldn't deceive you. If he says not to worry about it then you don't have to worry about it. There are enough things to worry about here without adding your dreams to them," she concluded, motioning toward a circle of men near the base of the wall where Manco had just stripped a warrior of his sword and thrown him to the ground as if he were a child. The others all laughed and cheered as Manco held his own blade to the fallen man's throat.

"Besides," she concluded, "you'll be in Lydacia City by the time the Inchasa reach the river. The man-beast won't be able to hurt you there."

Capac looked away, not sure what to say. Letting her think he was going to escape with the others was one thing, intentionally deceiving her was something he didn't want to do.

Noref sensed his unease and was suddenly worried.

"Capac?" she asked.

He turned to face her, his face telling her all she needed to know.

"Why would you go with them?" she asked, suddenly very frightened.

"Because I have to. If I try to escape with you and the others, the Cuzco will send men after me. I can't risk that."

"Why, because of the book? He can get someone else to finish it, Capac. Why does he need you?"

"I don't know, Noref. But I think you know as well as I do that he gets some perverse sort of pleasure from the fact that I'm the one writing it. I can't go with you."

"Then I won't go either," she said angrily. She refused to let the Inchasa and their petty little king deny her what little happiness she'd found in life.

"No!" Capac said quickly, taking her hands in his and squeezing them. "You can't, Noref. Your life would be in danger. They'll use you to force me to do what they want. I won't see you hurt."

"If they hurt me, they hurt me. But I will not leave you, Capac. I will not give up this small bit of happiness out of fear. I won't let them do that to me."

"I don't want to lose our happiness either," he said softly. Neither of them had ever voiced their feelings before and even this small admission was hard for him. "But I couldn't bear to see you suffer, Noref. Please, tell me you'll go? Please!"

"I'll go when you go," she answered, "and not before. Besides, you'll need me. Your feet are in no shape to be marching for ten minutes, let alone ten days."

"No, they're not. And I don't want you to end up the same way or worse, Noref. You can't stay."

"Well, I'm staying and there is nothing you can do about it," Noref said, then turned and started for the stairs, Capac's hand in hers.

"Come along," she said with a smile, pulling him along behind her. "Now that I know I bring you happiness too, I think I'd like to make love with you when I can see your face."

"What?" Capac asked, thinking he must have heard her wrong. But when she didn't answer, he quickly hobbled along after her, just in case he'd heard her right.

\*     \*     \*     \*

"How are the men progressing?" the Cuzco asked Manco as they sat down to a meal of baked skyva fish.

"Better, my Cuzco. The work is beginning to show results now. And the new weapons we've been receiving are excellent."

"Good," the boy said with a satisfied nod. "Now I want you to choose thirty of your best men, men you know will be ready when the time comes for the battle, and send them to the mountains to hunt. We need more meat, both to feed the men while they train and to fill the supply shelters. Send slaves with them to smoke and wrap the meat. Choose them tonight and send them out tomorrow."

"I will see to it, my Cuzco," Manco said, pleased with his king's foresight. And he knew just the men to send out.

"I also want ten men sent to help my fisherman," the Cuzco added. "And slaves to smoke the extra fish they bring in. The produce harvest is already set and we will have sacks of grain, gourds and roots ready for travel in five days time. Take as many slaves as you need to transport them."

"Yes, my Cuzco."

"I received word from Leruk this morning and the first three shelters are ready. I want them stocked with all the necessary supplies as quickly as possible. There are springs nearby so send a work crew with empty barrels that can be filled with water and stored. Choose your men wisely, Manco. These supplies are just as important as those new weapons you and your men are so proud of."

Manco nodded his understanding.

"And see to it that Capac is given full details of our preparations. I want all this written down so that future generations of Inchasa will see the work it took for us to ascend to greatness."

"Of course, my Cuzco."

"And have that ugly woman of his sent to me. I have a chore for her."

"When would you like to see her, my Cuzco?" Manco asked, knowing that the task her wanted Noref for was to gather more herb for Capac to prepare for him.

"As soon as I'm done eating. And don't bother having her watched anymore. Now that the two of them are lovers, she won't risk running off. She knows what would happen to him if she did."

Manco smiled and nodded.

"Any further word on the traitor?" the Cuzco asked. Thoughts of the man who had helped Capac escape from Atahuallpa were never far from his mind.

"None, my Cuzco. I have the armorer's shops being watched just in case he tries to find work."

"Don't bother," the Cuzco said. "And call off the search for now. We'll deal with him later. Right now I want every available man getting ready for the coming conquest."

"Very well, my Cuzco."

"And take it easy on the men, Manco," the boy said with a sudden smile. "You make them look like children. Are they that poor or are you that good?"

"Both, my Cuzco," Manco answered with a smile of his own. "And I have to be hard on them to make them better."

"I suppose so. But try not to injure them, will you? Sometimes I'm afraid you're actually going to kill one of them."

"I will try to restrain myself, my Cuzco," Manco said and the two of them laughed together.

"Thank you," the Cuzco said lightly. "Now, have some more wine and tell me again about the last time we battled the people of the river. Tell me everything, Manco, and then you and I will decide how best to avenge ourselves."

"Yes, my Cuzco," Manco said with lustful excitement in his eyes. He'd been waiting for this day. He knew every mistake they'd made and how to correct it. And the main one had been bringing too few men for the task. The Cuzco had already corrected that problem. With five thousand men no one could stand against them. He looked forward to reaching the third enemy village, the village that had defeated them so long ago. His heart would know no real peace until he'd seen it burned to the ground.

*     *     *     *

"Anything?" Nathan Squires asked as he made his way onto the bridge.

"Not a thing, Nate," Alton responded wearily.

They had scanned the small western city for three days before making their way north, scanning all the small roadside settlements along the way. They'd even made their way to the northern city still under construction and scanned it and all the construction and quarry work sites around it.

Next they would scan the small city Tommy had found hidden away on a little island ten miles off the coast. Nate was growing tired and frustrated while Alton considered the fact that they hadn't found Mitch's remains a good sign. Tommy was totally absorbed in the problem and seemed to take comfort in treating the search as an exercise, a puzzle to be solved.

"What's Tommy up to?" Alton asked.

"Making dinner," Nate answered as he plopped into the co-pilot's seat beside Alton.

"He said it's up to you whether you want to scan that desert to the north or not."

"No, we probably shouldn't have bothered coming this far north. I just wanted to be sure. We'll check out that island next, though I can't really see Mitch letting anyone talk him into crossing that ocean in those storms."

"He might not have had a choice."

"My thoughts exactly. So, we'll check that next. I'll go park us for the night."

"Tommy's working on some kind of map overlay that will show the patterns of movement for the areas we've scanned so far. I don't really see the point, but it gives him something to do."

"You sound jealous."

"I am. There are only so many card games I can take your money at. I need new challenges."

"I'll try to do better," Alton said with a laugh. "Seriously, though, how are you holding up?"

"I'm fine, Alton. I'm just worried about Mitch. This is taking too damn long."

"I won't argue with you there," Alton said seriously. "But what else can we do?"

"Nothing. And that's the frustrating part. Forget I said anything. How are things on Teluride?"

"Fine. Jenna runs the place better than I do."

"That's because everyone's afraid of her," Nate said only half jokingly.

Alton laughed.

"Don't I know it," he said. "She's worth every penny I had to fork over to get her to leave the military. How about you? Did you check in with Darlene?"

"Yeah. Somebody wasted a lot of time and money trying to break into my secure data base, but other than that, nothing new. Some of my clients are getting antsy but I referred all of them to Hale Michaels. He's as good as they come."

"But not as good as you," Alton said, "or they'd be his clients and not yours."

"He runs a very close second," Nate said with a grin.

"Is that data base thing what I think it is?" Alton asked with a raised eyebrow.

"I hope so," Nate answered with a smile. "And I hope Sandra paid them a ton of money to try it, too."

"To try what?" Tommy asked as he walked onto the bridge.

"To break into my data base," Nate answered. "She wants Mitch's financial access codes."

"What a girl," Tommy said with a shake of his head. "Why is it all the good ones are already married?"

"Something tells me that one's going to be available again," Alton said with a laugh, "if you want to try your luck."

"I'll pass," Tommy said. "Now, where are we headed, the desert or the sea?"

"The sea. I wasted enough of our time coming up this far."

"It wasn't a waste," Tommy said seriously. "It's one more place we can check off as scanned. I know you, boss, and we're not leaving this rock until we've either found him or searched every square inch of this place. At least now we know where he isn't. We're making progress."

"Damn slow progress," Nate said. "But thanks for the pep talk. You're one of those glass half full kind of guys, aren't you?"

"Well, a man's outlook on life brightens considerably when he gets laid once in a while, Nate. You really ought to try it."

"Up yours, Tommy," Squires said with a laugh. "Now, did you come up here for a reason or are you just getting some exercise?"

"I just wanted to make sure Alton knew how to get back to the parking garage."

"Up yours again, Tommy," Alton said with a grin.

"And, once I've seen to it that he lands without bending anything," Tommy continued, "I thought I'd lay out the search pattern I've been working on while you two stuff your faces with my lasagna."

"You've been a busy boy," Alton said.

"Well, I've been thinking. We're basing our search pattern on the assumption that Mitch has reached a point of safety, safety in this case meaning a place where he can survive another day, and then stayed put.

"What if that's not what he did? What if he survived long enough to find someone willing to help him survive, then moved on, trying to find out where the hell he is and if there's any way off this rock? What if he's seen the contrails of the mining ships moving through the atmosphere? What if he's not content to just sit and hope somebody comes to rescue him?"

"Hold on a minute, Tommy," Alton said. "Now you're making me feel even worse than I did before. If he's moving around it's going to take us even longer to find him, unless we just stumble across him, and I don't think any of us want to bet on that."

"No, we don't," Tommy admitted. "All I'm saying is it doesn't do us any good to lock into one way of looking at this. That's why I'm working on the map overlay. If we can figure out the more heavily traveled routes down there, we can concentrate our search there. If he is moving, and I'm not saying he is, he'll be moving along regularly traveled routes, routes where he knows he can find water. No man who fought his way across that plain with no water is going to take a chance on going through that again."

"O.K," Alton said, "that makes sense. And it will narrow our search area a little. But we still need to remember, we don't know if he's alive, Tommy. He might have wandered into the worst place he could possibly go. We just don't know."

"True," Nate said. "But if that's true then it doesn't really matter how long it takes us to find him, right? I think Tommy makes sense. We figure out the high travel areas and scan them first, along with the populated areas, just in case Mitch did make it to safety and stay put."

"Alright," Alton said after a minute. "What do you need from me, Tommy?"

"Just a few high level probes."

"I thought you said they weren't sensitive enough to detect the amacyclezene?"

"They're not. But they are sensitive enough to track life form readings and relay the patterns of movement. And they can cover the whole landmass continuously instead of just one small area at a time like we can."

"Fine," Alton said. "Launch as many as you need. How many do we have?"

"We've got ten and I only need four. I'll get 'em up and running right after we eat."

"Sounds good," Alton said. "Thanks, Tommy. Have I mentioned lately that sometimes that warped little mind of yours is handy to have around?"

"Yeah. You also mentioned a raise."

"Oh, I must have been drunk. I don't remember saying anything like that. Do you remember me saying anything like that, Nate?"

"As a matter of fact, I do," Nate answered.

"Hey, you're supposed to be on my side," Alton complained.

"Sorry, Alton," Nate said with a shrug. "But he does most of the cooking and my daddy taught me a long time ago never to cross the person who prepares your food."

"Yeah," Alton said, "and you've been eating ever since."

"Up yours, Alton."

# CHAPTER 22

▼

# ALLIANCES

Wanchese had decided it would be best to approach Philip Granganimeo's village with their warning. He and Secotan were the only Councillors she thought likely to listen to what they had to say. Philip's village was the southernmost and therefore the closest, but the real reasons she chose it were fear that personal animosity towards her might prevent Secotan's people from listening to her and the fact that Philip's village would likely be the first to be attacked. She hoped that fact alone would force him to listen to her.

She had also decided it would be best to approach the village in daylight, so they were making camp a little more than an hour away, still well within the sparse forest to the west of the village's cultivated land. They would spend the night there and approach the village at first light.

She watched as Mitch gathered stones and wood and set up a place for a fire. His body had continued its transformation as they traveled and he was now broad shouldered and thickly muscled, with only his horribly scarred back and shoulders left as a reminder of how close he'd come to death.

Each morning he would go off by himself to meditate and work with his weapons. She sometimes followed him and watched from a distance, not fully understanding what it was he was doing, but sensing that this too somehow made him stronger.

They also spent time learning the Inchasa language from Simms, the only real purpose he served on the trip other than showing them where to find the storage shelters. She had difficulty remembering much of what she learned but Mitchell seemed to need to hear something only once or twice before he understood. Sometimes he would work with her to help her keep up.

In return, she took time as they traveled to point out which roots, herbs and plants were useful as food or medicine and taught him how to move through the forest with as little sound as possible. By the time they reached the third shelter, he had learned how to stalk game while going unnoticed and downed his first meat.

They'd moved higher into the mountains again after looking over the third shelter and headed straight for Philip's village. She'd seen enough to make her believe Simms was telling the truth. Whether Philip would believe them she didn't know, but she would try anyway. Then her conscience would be clear.

Mitch got a fire going and Wanchese roasted some meat. When they'd finished eating, it was nearly dark and Royal Simms rolled up in his blanket and quickly dropped off to sleep, an event both Mitch and Wanchese welcomed with great relief. It was the only time the man ever seemed to stop talking.

Wanchese came and sat across the fire from Mitch, wrapping her blanket tightly around her shoulders, as it had already grown uncomfortably cold.

"Hi," Mitch said. "I'm not tired if you want to catch some sleep. I'll keep watch for a while."

"I'm not tired either, thank you," she lied. She had to do this before she lost her nerve. If she slept on it she'd probably change her mind. She took a nervous breath.

"I have a favor to ask of you, Mitchell," she said and Mitch stopped fiddling with the fire and gave her his full attention. It was the first time he could remember her calling him by name and he sensed that what she had to ask him was important.

"Shoot," he said.

"These are marriage bands," Wanchese said, pulling two dark pieces of cured hide from beneath her blanket.

Mitch could see that one of them was short and wide while the other was long and thin and that each had several thongs hanging from them. It was too dark for him to see more than that, though.

"This is a marriage headband," she continued, indicating the longer, thinner one. "They are worn by women. This is a marriage armband, worn by men. They are decorated with matching colors and designs to identify the wearers as husband and wife."

Mitch nodded his understanding, though he had no idea why she was telling him all this now.

"I would offer you this armband," Wanchese said quickly, nervously. "My difficulties with my village stemmed from the fact that I am not yet married. If you and I were to wear the marriage bands, I couldn't be bothered anymore."

"Well, sure," Mitch said, "if it'll help you out. But won't they know we aren't really married? Don't you need a priest or a holy man or something for it to be legal?"

"No," Wanchese explained. "All that's necessary is for each of us to accept the band from the other. By accepting it, you pledge yourself to the one who offers it."

"Then we'd really be married?" Mitch asked.

"Yes, but we would be man and wife in appearance only. Once we left the village and returned to the mountains you would be free to remove the armband. I wouldn't hold you to your pledge."

"Oh," Mitch said, surprised that he was actually a little disappointed. But hell, who could blame her. What good was a husband who didn't know the first thing about providing for a wife in this place. He was more of a burden than a help.

"You don't want to," Wanchese said, misinterpreting his reluctant reply. "I understand. Please forget I mentioned it. It's too much to ask."

"No," Mitch said quickly. "It isn't too much at all. I'd be happy to wear the armband for you."

"You are certain?" she asked.

"Absolutely. You just took me by surprise, that's all. I've never been proposed to before," he added with a grin.

Wanchese nodded then stood and moved around the fire to kneel beside him.

"You should kneel also," she said, "or we should both stand."

Mitch lifted himself off the ground and tucked his legs underneath him so that he was on his knees, facing Wanchese.

"I, Wanchese Hawkins, offer you this marriage band," she said solemnly, holding the armband out to him. He reached out to take it and she shook her head.

"No," she said. "Just hold out your right arm."

Mitch did as he was told and she tied the band tightly around his right forearm. It reached from his wrist almost to his elbow, with the thongs being tied so they hung from the back of his arm.

"Now you offer me the headband and tie it around my head," Wanchese instructed and Mitch took the band from her.

"I, Mitchell Harvey, offer you this marriage band," he said assuming he was supposed to mimic her actions. Wanchese bowed her head and lifted her long black hair high over her head. Mitch tied the band tightly in place and sat back onto his feet while she adjusted it to a more comfortable position.

Looking at the bands, he could see that they matched exactly and that they were very well done. They were made of a deep black hide and embroidered with a skillfully rendered scene of a spring flowing out of a jumble of rocks and into a large pool. Beside the pool were four brilliantly white claws, curved slightly at the bottom and each dripping a small crimson drop of blood.

"They're beautiful," he said as Wanchese drew her knife and cut the extra length from the thongs hanging off his band.

"They belonged to my parents," she told him. "They met for the first time at a spring like that. I added the claws to symbolize our first meeting."

"Is that what you were doing when you went off by yourself these past few nights?" he asked.

Wanchese nodded.

"I also made you this," she said, handing him a thong threaded through small holes drilled into the dull end of the eight deathclaw claws. "It's a necklace."

"Thank you," Mitch said. He slipped off his cloak and started to tie it around his neck then stopped, looking at her.

"The poison?" he asked.

"It's gone," She answered with a smile. "I boiled them to remove all traces of it."

Mitch finished tying it around his neck and draped his cloak over his shoulders again.

"I wish I had something to give you," he said self-consciously.

"Doing me this favor is gift enough," Wanchese replied seriously. Now she could enter the river village on her own terms.

"I think I will get some sleep now," she said after an awkward silence.

"Here, take this," Mitch said, unfastening his cloak and slipping it off again. "I'll be warm enough here by the fire with just your blanket."

"Thank you," she said, slipping her blanket off and quickly exchanging it for the deathclaw cloak. She laid down on the bed of leaves she'd prepared earlier and was quickly asleep.

Mitch sat beside the fire with his own thoughts, wondering if anyone knew he was missing yet, if Alton or his parents had any idea of what had happened to him. It was unlikely. He just hoped Sandra hadn't been able to get her hands on any of his money. He didn't really care about the money itself, he just didn't want her profiting from what she'd done.

After several hours, when he felt confident they were in no danger, he banked the fire like Wanchese had shown him so that it would still be there in the morning, and rolled up in her blanket for some sleep. He spent a long, cold night slipping in and out of sleep until the first grey of dawn started to lighten the blanket of darkness around them. Then he got up and added fuel to the fire.

When full dawn arrived, he woke Wanchese with a gentle nudge and Simms with a kick in the ass. They ate a quick breakfast and put the fire out carefully before starting for Philip Granganimeo's village.

They entered the village just as its people were preparing their morning meal. There were curious looks and whispers as they made their way through the village. They were a strange looking group; a one eyed girl they had all been told was dead, a broad shouldered warrior wrapped in a deathclaw hide and a smaller, dirtier man dressed in Inchasa grey. Someone had run ahead to tell Philip they were coming and the Councillor was waiting for them outside his longhouse.

He looked at them long and hard, especially Royal Simms. He'd lost one of his daughters to an Inchasa raid and he still thought of her often. He'd even secretly gone to the Inchasa city several times but he never saw her. The men who had taken her from him were never far from his thoughts and just the sight of the grey clothing brought back the pain and anger.

"Welcome," he said finally, deciding to hear them out before making any judgments. "Please, sit." He motioned to where two of his wives were spreading a large, brightly colored blanket on the ground. "You will share our morning meal with us."

"Thank you," Mitch said when he realized Wanchese was waiting for him to answer for them.

"It's good to see you, Wanchese," Philip said. "We had thought you dead. I'm pleased to see we were wrong."

Wanchese was tempted to say something sarcastic. She doubted anyone in any of the river villages had lost any sleep over her. She decided this wasn't the time.

"This is my husband," she said instead, "Mitchell Harvey. He is a newcomer but a brave and fearsome warrior. That is Royal Simms, also a newcomer and recently escaped from Inchasa slavery."

"Escaped, you say?" Philip asked, turning to Royal Simms and looking at him doubtfully.

"Yes," Simms told him hesitantly, looking back and forth between Wanchese and Harvey in confusion over the "This is my husband," remark. "I escaped and ran into Wanchese in the mountains."

"Ah," Philip said, turning back to Wanchese, his handsome black face breaking into a broad grin. "So that's where you went." He nodded appreciatively. She was a brave one.

"Yes," Wanchese said. "We've come to bring you important news, Philip."

"Well," Philip said, "please sit down and you can tell me your news while we eat."

They all sat on the large blanket and Philip's wives served a simple meal of shredded fish and thick, round bread, while Royal Simms told Philip what he'd heard while he was a slave. Philip listened quietly and asked several questions.

"You believe this?" he asked Wanchese doubtfully when Simms was done.

"I do," she answered. "We've seen the storage shelters they're building to supply their army. If you send some men west along the edge of the plain, they'll find them. But send a strong party. They'll also find Inchasa."

Philip was thoughtful for a moment. He found the story difficult to believe. Five thousand warriors? That was foolishness. Still, even if a smaller attack was coming, it would be helpful to know before hand.

"Thomas!" he called, and one of his young sons came running. "Go find Virgil for me and ask him to join me here." The boy ran off through the growing crowd of curious onlookers who were trying to hear what Philip and his unusual guests were saying.

He returned a few minutes later followed by a tall, thin, hawk-faced warrior whose entire body seemed to be decorated with intricate black tattoos of various shapes and sizes. His voice was deep and sonorous when he spoke.

"You sent for me, Philip," he asked, glancing curiously at Wanchese and the others.

"Tell Virgil what you've just told me, please," Philip said and first Simms and then Wanchese told him what they'd told Philip, with Wanchese adding that there were a lot of Inchasa moving across the mountains and that they could well be anywhere.

"Take ten good men, Virgil," Philip said when they were finished. "Find these shelters and see whether there is any other reason the Inchasa might be building them. Then come back here as quickly as possible. And be careful, Virgil."

"Of course," Virgil replied with a curt nod before turning and making his way through the crowd.

"Please forgive me for not taking you at your word," Philip said to his guests. "I don't doubt that you believe what you say, only that what you say can possibly be true."

"I understand," Mitch said. He wasn't completely sure they weren't over-reacting himself. But those shelters were there, right where Simms had said they'd be and they had certainly seen a lot of Inchasa moving back and forth across the mountains.

"That's an interesting cloak," Philip said to Mitch, who was unfastening and removing it.

"Yes, it is," Mitch replied with a smile. "Wanchese made it for me. She does nice work."

"Mitchell killed the deathclaw it's made from himself," Wanchese broke in, knowing what Philip was really asking and that Mitchell wasn't likely to tell him. "With this," she added, pulling her knife from its sheath at her waist.

Philip said nothing, but his doubts about the truth of what she'd said showed plainly on his face.

"Show him your back, Mitchell," Wanchese said quietly.

Mitch looked at her but she was still looking at Philip, anger burning in her eye. He realized that Philip thought she was lying. He turned his back to Philip.

The wounds had healed into a sold mass of mottled, discolored flesh and white scar tissue. There could be no doubt that something had torn into him with ferocious abandon. Philip had seen what a deathclaw's talons could do. He'd just never seen anyone who had survived it.

"I apologize," he said softy. "You must be a brave warrior indeed."

Mitch didn't answer, only turning and sitting facing Philip again, his face turning red as he heard the crowd muttering about what they'd just heard.

He wasn't really all that sure about how brave he was. He knew that he'd done what he had because death seemed an easier fate than living with the knowledge that he was a coward. He wasn't at all sure that that counted as bravery.

"If what you say is true," Philip said thoughtfully, "we'll need to call a Grand Council. And I know Secotan will be thrilled to learn that you're alive, Wanchese. I'll send a messenger to the other villages and ask for a Council. It can't hurt to have everyone on their guard."

He stood.

"I'll be back shortly," he told them, leaving his guests to share an uncomfortable silence with his family and the curious onlookers.

Finally, after several minutes that seemed like hours in the heavy silence, one of Philip's daughters came and sat beside Wanchese. Her name was Anna and she had recently celebrated her fourteenth year. She was tall and lithe and moved with fluid gracefulness. Her face was plain yet wholesome looking with open features dominated by large, dark eyes that matched her creamy brown skin.

"I'm Anna," she said shyly.

"Hello, Anna. I am Wanchese."

"Yes, I know," the girl said. "I…well, we heard about you. They said you were dead, but I hoped you weren't."

"What did you hear?" Wanchese asked, wondering what kind of tale Kane had spread.

"That you ran away rather than…do…what Hunter Kane wanted you to do," Anna said awkwardly.

Wanchese didn't know what to say. She had expected anything but the truth.

"That's true," she finally managed.

Anna smiled at her.

"I would have run, too," she said then continued in a rush. "Did you really threaten him with a knife?"

Mitch laughed out loud and Wanchese tried to look at him sternly but found herself unable to keep a small smile from her lips. She knew Mitchell was laughing because of what she'd told him about Royal Simms' advances and her solution to them.

"Yes, I did," she said to Anna.

"My father says that Councillor Secotan has changed the tradition in his village and that each person is free to decide for themselves whether they want to live by the old ways or not."

"That can't be!" Wanchese exclaimed.

"It's true," Anna insisted. "My father is thinking of making the same changes here. And Councillor Ananias already has."

Wanchese looked at the girl in stunned silence. Could it be true?

Anna grew uncomfortable, afraid she might have said something she shouldn't have. She was still learning the rules of adulthood and meant no offense.

"So a woman is free to decide for herself when she will wed?" Wanchese asked when she found her voice.

"Yes," Anna said. "In those villages they are. I think my father will do the same here."

"You think you father will do what the same here?" Philip asked, stepping through the crowd and catching only the end of the conversation.

"Change the old traditions, father," Anna said sheepishly, suddenly looking far less certain of her father's intentions.

"I haven't decided yet," Philip told her. "Besides," he went on mischievously, "I've seen the way you look at young Raven Howe. I doubt I'll have to worry about you not being wed by your sixteenth year."

"Father!" Anna yelped in embarrassment.

Philip laughed and pulled his daughter into a playful embrace. He often wondered how much longer he'd have this beautiful one in his longhouse. The years went so quickly.

"I've sent messengers to the other villages," he told Mitch and Wanchese. "A Grand Council will be held in five days in Secotan's village. Virgil will be sent there to tell us what he's found when he returns. We'll decide then how serious a threat we face."

"That sounds smart," Mitch said. "It can't hurt to start getting yourselves prepared."

"No, it can't," Philip agreed. "I leave in two days. You're welcome to travel with me and my party if you wish."

"Travel where?" Wanchese asked.

"To Secotan's village," Philip answered. "The others need to hear what I've heard, and from you." A sweeping gesture of his right arm took in all three of his visitors.

Wanchese said nothing. She was hesitant to return to her old village. Regardless of what Anna had told her, there were sure to be some who would still resent her. All the more so if her running away had brought about the changes Anna said it had.

"If what you tell me is true," Philip said reasonably, "the others must be convinced to act. I'll need your help to convince them."

"Yes, of course," Wanchese said, thinking of Anna and what her life would be like as an Inchasa slave. "I'll be ready to travel when you are. If my husband agrees," she added hastily, having forgotten that she was now a wife.

"Whatever you think best," Mitch said, causing a few raised eyebrows among those listening. They weren't used to hearing a warrior deferring to his wife so openly. "You know these people, I don't. I trust your judgment."

"We will go, then," Wanchese told Philip, amused at the surprised mutterings of the crowd.

"Very well," Philip said. "You're welcome to share my longhouse while you're here. Now, if you'll excuse me, I have arrangements to make." With a nod, he turned and walked away.

"I'd like to hear about those old traditions sometime," Mitch said to Wanchese.

"Later," she said in return. "Right now all I want to do is bathe and maybe get a little more sleep."

"I'll show you where we bathe," Anna said brightly. "It's not far, just down the river."

"Thank you," Wanchese said. She liked this girl. There was an innocence about her yet a hint of shrewdness, too. Standing, she picked up her pack and followed the girl through the dispersing crowd.

"I think I'll skip right to the sleep part, myself," Mitch said to no one in particular.

Gathering up his cloak and his weapons, he set off in search of a quiet, shaded spot for himself, preferably one with a nice little breeze. He found what he was looking for beneath a wide limbed tree beside the river, rinsed off and laid down. He was asleep by the time Wanchese found him and spread a blanket of her own.

# CHAPTER 23

▼

# FIRST BLOOD

The last storage shelter was complete ahead of schedule, a turn of events that would normally have made Leruk extremely happy. Instead, he was worried. Hador and his scouting party should have met them days ago, on their way back to Pachacutec. It was possible they had simply taken another route back, but Leruk doubted it. Something had happened. He was torn between a desire to go look for his friend and his orders to report immediately upon completion of the final shelter. There was really only one choice.

"Girak!" he called to his second in command.

"Yes, Leruk?" Girak asked as he came jogging up to join his captain.

"You'll return to Pachacutec with the slaves and two warriors. The others will stay here with me, waiting for the scouting party."

"As you wish," Girak answered. He would have preferred to stay behind himself and let Leruk bring the report back to the Cuzco. He was a warrior, not an administrator. But, if Leruk wanted to stay behind himself, there was a good reason for it.

"You can choose who goes with you," Leruk continued. "Be ready to move out after you've eaten."

"I will see to it."

That decision made, Leruk turned his mind to another question. How long should he wait? And if Hador and his men didn't come, should he and his remaining men try to gather information themselves? He would only have two warriors with him, not really enough to venture into enemy territory. Still, they needed that information.

His thoughts were interrupted when Girak trotted up to him with an excited report.

"A labor party is coming, Leruk," he said with a smile. "They've been sent to fill water barrels for this sight and the two after it. Other parties are on their way to do the same for the others."

"They are accompanied by a full warrior guard?" Leruk asked.

"Yes."

"Good, good," Leruk said with relief. "Then you'll travel to Pachacutec alone, Girak. Our slaves can join this labor party and I'll keep the rest of our warriors with me."

This was a real stroke of good fortune. With two more warriors free to go with him he would have a strong enough force to chance entering enemy territory. He could at least gather information on the first village they would attack.

"Perhaps one of the others could travel to Pachacutec?" Girak ventured. He knew what Leruk was thinking and wanted to go along.

"No, Girak," Leruk said with a smile. "I need you to go. I'm sorry."

And he was. He understood that Girak would much rather go with him than return to Pachacutec to repeat the same report over and over again until everyone was satisfied.

"You're the best man I have for giving a complete, accurate report," he explained. "And it's important, Girak."

"Of course, Leruk. I apologize…"

"Not necessary," Leruk cut him off. "I would have been disappointed in you if you hadn't tried."

"Thank you," Girak said. "And be careful, Leruk."

"I will. Tell Manco and the Cuzco the scouting party hasn't come back and I'm going to go gather what information I can on the first village. I'll come back as soon as I can."

Girak nodded and trotted off to gather his equipment, eat a quick meal and set off for the royal city. Leruk set to work transferring his slaves into the care of the labor party. When he was finished, he and his men ate and then set off to the east.

After five days of hard travel, as they were approaching the area where the plain, the sparse forest and the cultivated land of the river village came together, his lead scout came to Leruk at a run and reported a party of enemy warriors moving his way.

Leruk moved his men a good distance into the forest and watched as the enemy force passed them by some fifty feet away. The men noticed their tracks and stopped momentarily to investigate, then decided to move on.

Leruk was tempted to attack. They were outnumbered but surprise would be on their side. In the end, he decided against it. If even one of the enemy managed to escape and get back to the village, the Inchasa presence here would be discovered.

Of course, there was a chance it would be discovered anyway, especially if this was a work party headed to the forest for timber. But he hadn't seen any tools to indicate that was the case. He decided to let them pass and see to his duty. He and his men could take a different route on the way back to avoid running into them again.

Arriving at the edge of the forest, at the far edge of the river village's cultivated land, they passed the day watching the villagers toil in the fields. That in itself told him something. People expecting an attack do not send their women and children out into the fields so lightly guarded. If Hador and his men had been caught, they hadn't talked.

As the day drew to a close and the sun began fading from the sky, the people returned to the village for their evening meal. When full darkness fell, Leruk and his men made their way through the fields and closer to the village. They stayed at the edge of the fields until the village grew quiet and only a very few people were still out and about.

Leruk estimated the village had five hundred or so able bodied warriors, some of which would be young and inexperienced. Another percentage would be older men, passed their prime physically, but still capable. No match for the force the Cuzco was bringing.

He was about to dispatch his men to circle the village and get an exact layout of the buildings in it when one of his men nudged him sharply and pointed to a spot on the other side of the village. There, sitting beside a fire talking with a river woman, was the escaped slave! His rough, soiled slaved cloak was unmistakable. Besides, Leruk recognized the lazy bastard's face.

He could hear his men cursing quietly as each one saw what it was their captain was looking at. This was not good. Surely the fool would have told the villagers what he knew. The question was, how much was that? Leruk had a sick, hollow feeling in his stomach.

"Telis," he whispered to the warrior who had first seen the slave, "tell the others to move back to the forest and wait for us there. Then rejoin me here."

Telis crawled away silently to pass along the instructions. He was back a moment later and he and Leruk waited until they could be sure their companions were safely back across the fields and into the forest.

Then the two of them moved swiftly and silently into the village, concealing themselves in the shadow of one of the long, round roofed houses the river people built, not fifty feet from where the slave sat. Drawing two arrows, Leruk notched one in his bow and placed the second close to hand. Telis did the same.

Pointing first to the woman and then to Telis, Leruk indicated that he wanted him to kill the woman while he himself dealt with the slave. Then he pointed to the arrow notched in Telis' bow and then to his own throat to show where he wanted the first arrow put. Then, pointing to the second arrow, he indicated that he wanted that one put into the center of the chest. Telis nodded and the two of them stood.

The first arrows did as they were intended to and kept the slave and the woman from crying out. The second arrows struck home seconds later. Leruk and Telis were already half way across the fields when the bodies were discovered and the alarm raised. Rejoining the others on the opposite edge of the field, they set out quickly across the sparse forest and into the mountains. They were long gone before any pursuit could be organized.

\*        \*        \*        \*

Three days later, Wanchese felt a momentary shudder of misgiving as Secotan's village came into view. She tried to force it from her mind, telling herself that she was the one who'd been wronged. If the people here would not accept her as a guest, she would simply leave. She took more comfort that she cared to admit in the knowledge that Mitchell would go with her. She had never spoken of it with him, but she knew he would.

Unaware that she was doing it, she moved closer to him as they entered the village. A few people called out greetings to Philip and the others from his village. She and Mitch received only curious stares. The onlookers had seen the marriage bands. Looking at their faces she was glad she had decided to keep them on despite what Anna had told her. She held her chin up and moved closer to Mitchell.

Secotan Samuels was waiting for them in front of the Central Longhouse. He greeted Philip warmly and then surprised both himself and Wanchese by wrapping his arms around her and squeezing her tightly. He was so relieved to see her alive that he was hugging her before he knew what he was doing. Hearing she was alive was one thing, seeing it with his own eyes was another.

"Welcome, Wanchese," he said after letting go of her and regaining control of his emotions. "Welcome!"

Only then did the marriage band register in his mind.

"You are wed!" he exclaimed, looking from Wanchese to the well set up stranger with her.

"Yes," Wanchese said, uncomfortable with his emotional display. She had prepared herself for cold rejection, not a warm welcome. She wasn't really sure what to say or do.

Secotan smiled at her briefly before stepping back and calling out loudly to all those gathered around to witness Wanchese's return.

"I want all of you to hear me," he said loudly, his face set with grim determination. "I am not the only one who needs to say these words to this woman."

He looked at Wanchese again.

"I'm sorry, Wanchese Hawkins," he said loudly enough for everyone to hear. "I failed you, both as a Councillor and a man and I am truly sorry. I hope you can forgive me."

Wanchese was dumbstruck. Fighting back tears, she nodded her acceptance of his apology and managed to croak, "Of course."

"Thank you," Secotan said. "Though I've failed you, I have also learned from my mistakes."

"So I've heard," Wanchese said with a small smile.

Secotan laughed out loud. It had been so long since he'd seen her smile.

"Marriage seems to agree with you," he said. "I don't believe I've ever met your husband before, have I?"

"Oh, no, forgive me," Wanchese answered, "Secotan Samuels, this is my husband, Mitchell Harvey."

"It's a pleasure to meet you," Secotan said.

"And you," Mitch replied, having already decided he was going to like this man. It had taken real balls to do what he'd just done.

Secotan smiled and rested a friendly hand on Mitch's shoulder as he turned to Philip and the others.

"You're all welcome to come to my longhouse," he said. "But I'll understand if some of you have friends or family you would rather see."

"Thank you," Philip answered for everyone in his party and they all followed Secotan as he started for home. Most of those with Philip broke away as they moved off and made their way to the meet friends or loved ones. Philip, Wanchese and Mitch followed after Secotan.

Wanchese received a few timid greetings as she made her may through the village. Hunter Kane glared at her murderously as she passed his longhouse. Glancing at Mitchell, she saw the fire of battle flicker in his eyes as he met Kane's glare with one of his own. She thought she could feel the very air grow cold around him.

There would be trouble between the two, she knew. And not only because of her. Mitchell was everything Kane was not and the two seemed to sense in each other a born enemy.

As they left Kane behind and stepped into Secotan's longhouse, they were greeted warmly by his three wives and his three remaining unmarried children. Seeing the marriage band on Wanchese's head, Dare quickly pulled her aside and started excitedly asking questions. The men made themselves comfortable on blankets spread around the unlit hearth that occupied the center of the longhouse.

"None of the others have arrived yet," Secotan said when they were all seated. "Would you rather wait until everyone is here, or can you tell me why you've called the Grand Council? You bring important news, I'm told."

"We do," Philip said. "The escaped Inchasa slave who brought it to us is dead, however."

"What happened?" Secotan asked.

"As near as we can tell," Philip explained, "a group of Inchasa were watching our village. They must have recognized the slave. He was sitting beside a fire with Jikan Werts when they were both struck by two arrows, one to the throat, the other to the chest."

Secotan looked at him, his eyes silently asking about Jikan. Philip shook his head sadly.

"Roger and Hattie?" Secotan asked.

"Jikan was their first born," Philip said with a shrug. "They are as you would expect."

"The enemy warriors?"

"Gone before we could organize a search."

"You heard the slaves story before he was killed?"

"Yes. Mitchell and Wanchese have heard it as well."

Secotan nodded.

"What can you tell me, Mitchell?" he asked.

"Well," Mitch began, "Royal Simms claimed that the Inchasa have a new king, a young one, and that he plans to attack your villages here along the river. They plan to start with Philip's village and work their way north until they've conquered all of you."

"Why?" Secotan asked. "Why now? We've lived in peace for more than eight years."

"According to the slave," Philip answered, "their new king needs more slaves to build new cities and work their fields."

"You believe this?" Secotan asked Philip.

"I'm not really sure," Philip answered honestly. "I sent Virgil to see what he can find and he sent a messenger back to tell me to prepare for an attack. The fact that enemy warriors were watching my village concerns me."

"They may have merely been looking for the escaped slave," Secotan said.

"True," Philip agreed. "As I said, I'm not sure. Virgil will bring us more information when he comes back."

"What exactly did the messenger say they found?"

"A storage shelter one day's travel from our village. A shelter large enough to supply a large scale attack."

"Large scale?" Secotan asked.

"If the slave is to believed, five thousand men. Virgil estimates closer to two thousand."

"Two thousand!" Secotan exclaimed. "That's impossible!"

"So one would think," Philip said. "I'll feel better when I can speak to Virgil directly. He should arrive here in two or three days."

"Can I ask a question?" Mitch asked hesitantly.

"Please," Philip answered.

"Well, I'm a newcomer here and I don't profess to have experience in matters like this, but if your goal was not just to defeat your enemy but rather to overrun him quickly and decisively enough to ensure yourself of capturing a lot of slaves, wouldn't you want to use overwhelming force?"

Secotan and Philip looked first at one another and then at Mitch.

"There may well be wisdom in that," Philip said thoughtfully. "Wanchese told me I should listen to this one," he added, indicating Mitch with a nod of his head.

"She may be right," Secotan said. "And, speaking of Wanchese, I'd love to hear how you two came to be together, Mitchell."

"We saved each other's lives, I guess you could say," Mitch told him with a smile. "I kept her from being killed by a deathclaw and she returned the favor."

"That's a story I'd like to hear," Secotan said, real interest on his face.

Mitch wasn't really comfortable talking about what had happened, at least not his part in it. But he liked these men and didn't want them to think him aloof or rude.

"I came across Wanchese at exactly the same time a deathclaw did," he told them. "She was facing the thing with her knife in her hand and probably didn't really need my help. That's one though little lady."

Secotan and Philip laughed, nodding in agreement.

"But," Mitch went on, "not knowing her, I rushed to help her. I was able to kill the deathclaw but it almost killed me at the same time. Wanchese dragged me to a nearby cave and nursed me back to health."

"You killed a deathclaw?" Secotan asked. "With that?" He pointed to the sword Mitch had taken off one of the dead Inchasa.

"No," Mitch answered. "I didn't have the sword then. I used Wanchese's knife."

Secotan looked doubtfully at Philip, who silently nodded that he indeed believed the story. Secotan turned back to Mitch, looking at him carefully. There was obviously a good deal more to this man than met the eye. Not that what met the eye was unimpressive. He was broad shouldered, heavily muscled and carried himself well. But to kill a deathclaw with nothing more than a hunting knife? And live to tell about it? That was extraordinary!

"His back bears the scars of the battle," Philip said. "Show him, Mitchell."

Mitch turned his back toward Secotan. He was getting tired of this. But, if it would help establish his honesty, he'd bite his tongue and bear it. These men didn't know him and what he was telling them was apparently an uncommon thing.

"What I did was the easy part," he said when he'd turned to face Secotan again. "Wanchese spent weeks taking care of me. I'd be dead without her."

Just then there was a sharp rap at the door of the longhouse.

"Enter!" Secotan called loudly, and two men stepped into the room, calling a greeting as they did so. Philip and Secotan stood to meet them and Mitch followed their lead.

"Elan, Manteo," Secotan said, "it's good to see you."

Elan White and Manteo Hatarask were the Councillors of the two villages sited north of Sectoan's.

"And you, Secotan," Elan White said. "Philip, my friend, how are you?"

"I'm well, Elan," Philip answered as the two reached out their right arms and grasped each other's forearm. Then Philip released Elan and did the same with Manteo Hatarask.

"This is Mitchell Harvey," Secotan said and the two men nodded Mitch's way. "Mitchell, this is Elan White and over there is Manteo Hatarask."

"Nice to meet you," Mitch said, and they all took a seat.

"You're the man who brings us news?" Manteo asked when they were all seated.

"Myself and Wanchese," Mitch answered.

Manteo nodded.

"Ananias isn't here yet?" Elan White asked.

"No," Philip said with a smile. "He'll be here for the evening meal. I stopped by his village on my way here, but he wasn't ready to travel."

"As expected," Manteo said and the three Councillors laughed, giving Mitch the impression that this Ananias fellow was usually the last to arrive when these men came together.

"Well," Elan said, "perhaps Manteo and I could hear what you have to say while we wait?"

"Of course," Mitch said. "I'll get Wanchese."

"Interesting scars," Manteo said, looking at Mitch's back as he walked away.

"More interesting than you think," Secotan said. "Ask me about it later."

"I'll do that," Manteo said, his interest aroused.

Mitch came back with Wanchese and the two of them went over everything Simms had told them plus what they'd seen for themselves. They were still answering questions when Ananias Dare knocked and was given permission to enter.

"Uncle!" Dare Samuels called as he entered, running to him and throwing her arms around his neck.

"Ah, my little flower," Ananias said, squeezing her tightly. Then he stepped back and looked at her. "You are not with child?" he asked in mock surprise. "Has Secotan grown too old to give you more children?"

"Uncle!" Dare chided, slapping his arm playfully.

Laughing, Ananias walked over and embraced Secotan. Introductions were made and Wanchese and Mitch told their story again while the evening meal was served. When they were finished, the faces of the five Councillors were grave.

"When do you expect Virgil here?" Elan asked Philip.

"Knowing Virgil, he'll move quickly. I expect he'll be here in three to four days. Most likely three."

"If he doesn't run into trouble," Secotan said. "If there are as many Inchasa roaming the area as Wanchese tells us, there's a good chance he and his men will run across some."

"Even if they did," Philip said, "Virgil would send a man back to my village while he and the others fought the Inchasa."

"Yes, that's true," Elan said. "Virgil is uncommonly shrewd. Still, I think I'll send a messenger back to my village to have my warriors begin preparing for the possibility of attack."

"I was thinking the same thing," Manteo said. "There is nothing to be gained by waiting and much to be lost by being unprepared."

"I'll do the same," Ananias said. "And thank you for coming to us, Wanchese. Many another in your place would have left us to our fate." He reached over and squeezed her hand.

The others echoed his thanks, making Wanchese more than a little uncomfortable, then went their separate ways to begin making preparations each of them hoped would be unnecessary. If what they'd been told was true, their very existence as a people was in jeopardy. And they had not fought and struggled to provide a better life for their children and grandchildren only to see them forced to spend the rest of their lives as Inchasa slaves.

"At least they seem to be taking this seriously," Mitch said to Wanchese after the others had left.

"Yes," she agreed. "Thank you for your help, Mitchell. It's easier for them to believe another warrior than to believe me alone."

"I'm not really sure I qualify as a warrior," Mitch replied, "but you're welcome. And I think those men would have listened to you whether I was here or not. They respect you more than you think."

"You still don't understand, do you?" Wanchese said, shaking her head. "You are more of a warrior than any of those men. It burns deep within you in a way I've never seen before. And if these men respect me, it is because you have treated me with respect in front of them."

"If you say so," Mitch said. He didn't think of himself as a warrior. And the reason these men respected Wanchese was because she was a strong, intelligent woman. He didn't feel like arguing the point, though.

"I'm tired," he said. "We've done more than our share of walking these past couple of weeks."

"Yes, we have. Would you like to rest for a day or two before we leave?"

"You think we should leave?" he asked in surprise.

"We've done what we came here to do," Wanchese answered. "I thought you would want to leave."

"I'll go if you want to," Mitch said. "I hadn't really thought about it, I guess. Whatever you think best."

"I'll stay if that's what you want," she told him, thinking she would like to stay for a day or two and spend some time with Dare.

"Alright," Mitch said. "We'll stay and see what they're going to do."

He didn't want to admit it, but the thought of leaving knowing that these people would soon be fighting for their very lives didn't sit very well with him. He wondered how Wanchese would react to that?

"We might even be able to be of some help," he added tentatively.

"Yes," Wanchese said, turning away to hide a small smile. "I think we might."

Mitchell couldn't walk away from this fight, she suddenly realized, but didn't want to tell her so. She should have known as much, really. He wasn't the kind of man to run away from someone in need of help. She of all people should have understood that.

# CHAPTER 24

▼

# CONFIRMATION

Sweat streamed down his slender body as the Cuzco stood from his bed and made his way across his bedchamber to a low stone table. There he poured cool water from an ornately decorated pitcher into a matching basin and bent low to wash the perspiration from his face. The cool water was refreshing and he felt the calm assuredness that always came after his visions wash over him as he dried his skin and made his way to the main chamber and sat in his high backed chair.

This vision had been slightly different than those he'd had the previous two nights, more intense, more revealing. His visions had followed that pattern of late, coming in groups of three with each night bringing a clearer, more intense version of the same vision. Then he would go several nights with no visions at all no matter how much herb he used. Then the cycle would begin again.

He had had visions regarding how best to defeat the river people, how and when he should then move against the arrogant strangers to the southeast, how best to prepare his army for what was to come, which building projects he should undertake first after securing the slave force he needed, how to ensure large enough harvests that he would be able to feed his own people as well as the increased slave population and when and where he should take a wife.

He had put into action each and every vision he had seen and the results had been unerringly successful. The new land he had ordered cultivated had proven rich and fertile, his people had wholly embraced his plans for their future, his army had grown strong and eager and the slaves already under his control had accepted their fate and done whatever was asked of them. Even the Lydacians seemed to have come to understand and accept Inchasa superiority.

So he knew that his victory over the river people would come to pass exactly as he'd seen it, with his army overwhelming the river people as a whole and not in several small battles as Manco planned. He had no idea how it would come to be so, but he knew without a doubt that it would.

He also knew that once that battle had been won, no one would ever doubt his visions again. Manco and the other warriors who went along with his plans only because they lusted for battle and smugly trusted in their own ability to bring them victory, would see that he had been right, that everything had happened exactly as he'd said it would. And they would never doubt him again.

Then he would send one thousand men back to Pachacutec with the river women and children. He would bring the river warriors with him as he crossed the river and moved against the slit-eyed farmers to the southeast. The river warriors would fight for him, he knew, because they would know that to refuse would mean death for their woman and children. He would march south with more than seven thousand men and crush the people there before turning back to Pachacutec. He would return a legend, with more than five thousand slaves to build his kingdom.

He was still in his chair, letting his thoughts flow from victory to victory, when there was a sharp rap on the door to his chambers.

"Come," he ordered, and the door opened to admit Manco and his brother, Leruk.

"This one brings news, my Cuzco," Manco said with barely restrained anger.

The Cuzco let his gaze run appraisingly up and down Leruk's dirty, sweat stained form. His news was obviously important or Manco would have ordered him to bathe before bringing him before his king.

"Your messenger brought word that the storage shelters are complete, Leruk," he said, "and that the scouting party never returned. You went to scout the first village?"

"I did, my Cuzco," Leruk said, dropping onto bended knee as he spoke.

"What did you find?" the Cuzco asked, curious at the look of undisguised disgust Manco shot his brother at his question.

"I found there a slave that had escaped from my labor party, my Cuzco," Leruk answered calmly. He had already accepted his fate. He deserved to die the death.

"I see," the Cuzco said, running his right hand thoughtfully over his chin. "And you're afraid this slave has told the river village of our intentions?"

"Yes, my Cuzco."

The Cuzco laughed and Manco looked at him in surprise while Leruk remained on bended knee, confused by the laughter but not daring to look up.

"Stand up, Leruk," the Cuzco said.

Leruk did as he was told, but still averted his gaze.

"There is nothing you could have done to prevent what has happened, Leruk," the Cuzco said with an assured smile. "It was necessary in order for my vision to become reality. Now we will face the enemy man against man and fulfill our destiny as has been foretold, as I knew we would."

"We don't know for sure that the enemy is alerted to our plans, my Cuzco," Manco interjected, still glaring at his brother. "The slave may have known very little of our language."

The Cuzco laughed again and there was a far away look in his eyes when Manco looked at him.

"You may not know it, Manco," he said, "but I do. I have seen what the future holds. You need not fight it."

"Of course, my Cuzco," Manco said, wishing he could force his mind to accept what his king told him. Everything the boy had ordered done had proven the right thing to do and others had complete faith in his every word and decision. He wondered if he simply lacked the ability to believe in another man as much as he did himself or if he was in some other way deficient. He wished with all his heart that he could push the doubts from his mind.

"You may go," the Cuzco told him. "I want to speak with Leruk for a moment."

Manco bowed and left.

"Tell me about the enemy village," the Cuzco said when he was gone.

"What would you like to know, my Cuzco?"

"The area around it, is it as Manco and the others have told me, the plain and the river come together there?"

"It is, my Cuzco."

"And is there a high bank beyond the river where the women and children can witness our victory?"

"There is, my Cuzco."

"Excellent," the boy said with a satisfied nod. "And how many warriors did you count?"

"I would estimate a little more than five hundred, my Cuzco."

The boy broke out in a wolfish grin. Everything was exactly as he'd seen in his vision. They would face a force of at least twenty-five hundred, he was sure. The other villages along the river would come to the aid of the village he planned to attack. It would be a glorious battle, one worthy of him.

"Thank you, Leruk," he said. "You may go. Send Manco back in."

Leruk bowed and quickly took his leave, thrilled to be leaving with his head still attached to his body.

Manco returned a moment later.

"My advisors are gathered in the great hall?" the Cuzco asked.

"They are, my Cuzco."

"Good. Let's go see what they have to say," the Cuzco said. Then he stood and walked from the room, Manco close on his heels.

"Have you spoken with the smith and the armorer?" the boy asked as they walked.

"Yes, my Cuzco. Your sword and your armor are completed and await only your approval."

"I'll look at them after this meeting, then," the Cuzco said as he entered the great hall. "Have them sent for."

Manco nodded and left to see to it.

"Is everyone here?" the Cuzco asked as he took his seat at the long table of polished white stone that filled the north end of the great hall.

"Yes, my Cuzco," the others around the table answered in unison.

"Good. There are several matters of importance to discuss. First, how are the supply parties progressing?"

"We are ahead of schedule, my Cuzco," the advisor in charge of supplies answered. "The fifth and sixth shelters have been supplied and a warrior guard posted. The rest will be completely stocked within the next ten to twelve days."

"Very well," the Cuzco said. "And my army?"

"They also progress well, my Cuzco," the administrator charged with the organization and training of the army said. "I've seen to it that Manco has gotten everything he's asked for. He assures me that the men will be trained, equipped and ready to move well ahead of schedule."

The Cuzco nodded his acceptance of that. Manco had already told him much the same thing.

"Very well. I want the men marched to the Apus within the sacred valley three weeks from today, then. We will celebrate the Inti Rami there together before marching on the enemy."

The Apus, believed to be the sacred dwelling place of the spirits, was an open walled temple set in the middle of the lush green valley beside Lake Paccaritambo, four days march to the east. There the Cuzco would spend the eight days of the yearly Inti Raymi Sun Festival joined in body and spirit with his men.

"It will be done, my Cuzco," his advisors answered as one.

The young king smiled. There were no questions about why his army would spend the festival in the sacred valley. His advisors were learning to trust that he knew best. That was a start.

✶    ✶    ✶    ✶

"Virgil has returned, Mitchell," Wanchese called from the riverbank. "Philip thought we might want to hear what he has to say."

"O.K," Mitch called. "Be right with you."

Ringing out his breechcloth one final time, he walked out of the river and got dressed. Then he picked up his staff and walked to where Wanchese was waiting for him, her back turned to give him privacy.

"We already know what he's going to say," he told her as they started toward the village, "but I guess we should listen anyway."

"I think Philip would like your help in deciding what to do now that they know we're telling them the truth."

My help? Mitch thought, running his fingers through his now long, wavy hair. What the hell do I know about this kind of thing?

"You have any brilliant suggestions I could throw out and pretend are my own?" he asked with a smile.

"No," Wanchese answered seriously. If the Inchasa were really bringing five thousand men, she wasn't sure there was any good way to prepare for what was coming.

Everyone was already at the Central Longhouse by the time Mitch and Wanchese arrived. Everyone except Ananias, that is. He came in a minute later to the good natured ribbing of his fellow Councillors.

"Well," Secotan said when everyone was seated, "what do you have to tell us, Virgil?"

"It is as the woman says," Virgil responded. "There are storage shelters within the forest. I traveled far enough to look at three of them and they are all large, suggesting that there will be a large party."

"Could these shelters be intended for a different purpose?" Manteo Hatarask asked. "Storing smoked meat while the hunters return to the mountains for more, perhaps?"

"I don't think so," Virgil answered. "They wouldn't need such large shelters for that, or so many. Also, there are a lot of tracks and signs of much coming and going all along the edge of the plain. Some were very recent. I chose not to investigate, thinking it was more important to bring you my report."

"A wise choice, Virgil," Philip said. "Now, I ask you to speak plainly. What do you believe is happening?"

"The Inchasa prepare to strike," Virgil answered without hesitation. "Either at us or the yellow skinned farmers to the southeast. I believe they will attack us."

"How long?" Secotan asked.

"Several weeks, at least, I would think. The storage shelters I saw hold no supplies yet. I suggest we have the nearest shelter watched. When it is ready, the Inchasa will be ready."

"An excellent idea," Philip said. "I'll see to it."

"You think the attack will be against your village, Philip?" Elan White asked. "I do."

"The men I sent out form my village found tracks as well," Manteo said. "How can we be sure our villages won't be attacked at the same time?"

"Yes," Elan said. "I would hate to return from defending your village, Philip, only to find my own family killed or taken prisoner."

"We could bring our families with us," Ananias suggested. "Then we'd be able to protect them no matter which direction the attack comes from."

"True," Manteo said. "But what if the battle goes badly for us? We will have delivered our families into the hands of the Inchasa."

There was silence at that. These men had no illusions. The battle could very well go against them. For themselves, they could accept that. For their families, they could not.

"I'll bring my family with me," Secotan said, making his decision. "And I'll fight all the harder because they're there. I don't think I could keep my mind on the battle at hand unless I knew they were safe."

"I'll do the same," Ananias said.

"I'm afraid I can't do that," Elan said. "I'll send my people into hiding away from our village and tell them not to come back until they're sent for."

"Who will know where to send for them, Elan?" Ananias asked. "The enemy has ways of making even the bravest man tell them what they want to know. If we lose, your people will still be in danger."

"That's true," Elan said thoughtfully. "Still, that is my decision. I'll limit as much as possible the number of people who know where they're hiding."

"I'll leave my women and children where they are," Manteo announced. "My warriors and I will gladly fight by your side, Philip, but I won't put our women and children at risk." His village was the furthest north of all the river villages. He thought his people would be safe there, despite the tracks his scouts had found.

"Thank you," Philip said. "All of you."

"Could I ask a question?" Mitch asked timidly, not wanting to get in the way but eager to help.

"Please," Philip said. He liked this Mitchell Harvey. There was something about the quiet man that made him instinctively trust him. There were very few men he could say that about.

"The farmers Virgil spoke of," Mitch asked, "would they be willing to help?"

"Why would they?" Secotan replied.

"Because if the Inchasa defeat us here," Mitch answered, and Wanchese noticed that he said 'us', not 'you', "I doubt they'll stop there. Those farmers would likely be next on their list. Maybe we can convince them that by helping us they're really helping themselves."

"You know them best, Philip," Manteo said. "What do you think?"

Philip's people had begun trading with the people to the southeast and were the only village that came into direct contact with them.

"I doubt they'd be willing to help," Philip answered. "They're a peaceful people, Mitchell, who prefer to tend to their own affairs. I don't think they would want to become involved."

"If I were willing to go and talk to them," Mitch asked, "could you provide me with someone who knows the language?"

"Roger Werts, the man who lost his daughter when Royal Simms was killed, has had the most contact with them," Philip said. "He may be able to help."

"Would it be alright with all of you if I tried?" Mitch asked.

"You couldn't make any promises in our name," Elan White said immediately. He liked this Mitchell Harvey too, but some men became very free with their promises when they involved someone else's property and rights.

"I understand," Mitch said. "Can I tell them that if they help us, we'll help them if the Inchasa attack them rather than Philip's village?"

The five Councillors thought that over.

"You can tell them that for me," Philip said. "I'll pledge myself and my warriors to their defense if they'll help us." It was his village that was most threatened. He couldn't afford to be as stubborn as the others.

"I'll pledge my men also," Ananias said. "But only if the chinamen take an active part in the battle."

"I'll do the same," Secotan said.

"Chinamen?" Mitch asked.

"That's what the farmers to the southeast are called by our ancestors in the book of our history," Secotan explained.

A book of their history? Mitch thought. Would I love to get my hands on that! It would have to wait, though.

"I can't agree," Elan White said. "I'll gladly pledge my warriors to Philip's defense, but I know nothing of these farmers."

"I'm afraid I'm inclined to agree," Manteo said. "If the Inchasa don't attack Philip's village, I'll give a feast of thanksgiving and then order my warriors back to their own homes."

"Alright," Mitch said, "that's something to bargain with, anyway. I'll go talk to them."

"When will you leave," Philip asked.

"In the morning. Can I count on your man to go with me?"

"I'll send a messenger to ask him," Philip said, "but it will be Roger's decision whether or not he goes."

"That's all I can ask for," Mitch said.

"Very well," Secotan said. "I think it's time to set our people in motion. The sooner we gather at Philip's village the better our defense will be."

Everyone stood and each man set off to put in motion the necessary preparations. Mitch and Wanchese walked out of the village to stand beside the river.

"Will you come with me?" he asked. "It would really help me out." Not to mention keep her away from Hunter Kane while he wasn't around. He couldn't tell her that, though, or she might think he was getting it into his head that she was his woman and therefore his to protect. He couldn't have that.

"I'd be glad to come," Wanchese answered, glad that Mitchell would be leaving the village. She wanted to keep him away from Hunter Kane as much as possible. It was only a matter of time before there was trouble between the two of them.

"Good," Mitch said with a smile. "Is tomorrow morning alright?"

"The morning will be fine," Wanchese answered. "I'll get everything packed and ready tonight."

"Great. Thanks. I appreciate your help."

"You're welcome," Wanchese said, then smiled slyly. "Besides, you'd probably starve without me. Not to mention getting lost and dying of thirst."

She was still laughing when Mitch finally managed to throw her in the river.

# CHAPTER 25

▼

# TWISTS OF FATE

Captain Demetrius Nestor looked admiringly at the ceiling high tapestry that graced the west wall of Simon Bellotti's entryway. The priceless, old world embroidery revealed an exquisite mural of the important events in the legend of King Arthur, from birth to the pulling of Excalibur from the stone, to the acceptance of his broken body by the Lady of the Lake. Nestor had a replica of the tapestry in the dining room of his house in Sylvas City. He knew he was now looking at the original. Simon Bellotti would never own a replica.

"Beautiful, isn't it?" Bellotti asked as he entered the room through an arched doorway. "It cost me more than I care to admit, but I couldn't help myself."

"I can imagine," Nestor said. "I know what a replica cost me."

"Well, it shows you have good taste, anyway, Demetrius," Bellotti said with a smile. "Thank you for coming on such short notice. Why don't we go out to the garden?" he added, waving Nestor through the archway.

"Would you like a drink?" Bellotti asked when they reached the enclosed garden, where they were met by a bodyguard masquerading as a butler. Bellotti took a drink from the tray the man held out to him.

"Yes, thank you," Nestor answered. "Whatever you're having, Mr. Bellotti."

Bellotti handed him a drink and the two of them sat down in opposing chairs. Nestor waited, nervously sipping his drink while Simon Bellotti composed his thoughts.

"Something has recently come to my attention that concerns me a great deal," he said after a long silence, causing Nestor to break out in a cold sweat. He tried desperately to think of what he could have done to piss Bellotti off and came up with a long list.

"I'm going to require your relocation services again," Bellotti went on, his words causing Nestor to unconsciously breath a loud sigh of relief. Bellotti smiled at the sound.

"As there are some special circumstances involved," he continued, "I will pay you twice the normal rate."

"That's really not necessary, Mr. Bellotti," Nestor said quickly, though he automatically calculated the net profit of the proposed fee in his mind.

"I insist," Bellotti said, then waited until Nestor nodded his agreement.

"I had dinner with my brother last night. I believe you know Steven, don't you, Demetrius?"

"Yes, sir," Nestor answered.

Steven Bellotti was a big brute of a man with more money than brains. He lived a lifestyle fully as extravagant as Simon Bellotti's was reserved, and was known to throw his money and his weight around with abandon.

"Steven had a dinner companion," Bellotti went on. "A very beautiful young woman as a matter of fact. Normally, that would be of little concern to me. Steven has had many attractive young women to dinner before. This one, however, he tells me is 'the one' and I'm afraid I can't have that, not with what I know about the young lady."

"I see, sir," Nestor said, now truly at ease. Steven Bellotti had obviously fallen in love with some high priced hooker. "You'd like me to make the young lady disappear?"

"Yes, but as I said, there are some special conditions. I don't want the woman killed. I want her delivered alive to that secluded little planet you sometimes use, Demetrius. I also want her supplied with enough essential supplies that she'll be able to survive if she so chooses."

"That can be easily arranged, Mr. Bellotti."

"Good. But I'm not finished. I also want the woman's identity known to only the two of us, no one else. Not your crew, not your woman, not your priest, not your mother. Disguise her, make her wear a veil or a mask, do whatever you have to do, Demetrius, but no one else is to know who she is. Do we understand each other?"

"Yes, sir, I understand."

"Good. Because if word of what happened to his lady friend ever gets back to my brother, I'll have only you to hold responsible, Demetruis. Understood?"

"Yes, sir," Nestor answered, turning his eyes away from Bellotti's icy glare.

"Steven has taken the young lady off planet for a little romantic getaway. They're due back on Thursday. I'd like the woman gone by Friday morning. The funds will be transferred to the usual account by midnight tonight."

"Yes, sir. I'll take care of it as soon as they get back. All I need is a name, Mr. Bellotti."

Bellotti met Nestor's eyes and smiled coldly.

"The young woman's name is Sandra Harvey, Demetrius. I believe you already know where to find her."

*       *       *       *

Searching the small island had turned into more work than Alton and the others had expected, with not only the island itself having to be scanned, but two ships at sea and a slow but steady stream of people making their way west from the stone city on the mainland in groups of one and two. It was hard to overcome the feeling that they were wasting precious time on dead end after dead end.

Still, the mood remained positive as they set down on the plain for the night and gathered for dinner. After all, they hadn't found a body, as each man had privately feared they would sooner or later. In this case, no news truly was good news.

"Well, we know he's not on this side of the plain, anyway," Alton said.

"True," Tommy agreed. The more areas he could fill in as searched on his map overlay the better he felt. He knew they'd find Mitch sooner or later. Every day brought them closer.

"I still think we should have searched higher into the mountains," Nate Squires said. "With those slave drivers moving back and forth along the edge of the plain like they are, he probably figured it was better to head into the mountains than let them catch him."

"But that assumes he didn't just head east to one of the areas we haven't searched yet, Nate," Alton said.

"Yeah," Nate argued, "but the only water in the area is in those mountains. As far as we know, he didn't have anything to carry water in, right? So he'd have to stay near the water as he traveled."

"Our first scan of the mountains took all those water holes into consideration, though," Tommy chimed in. "We followed them from west to east and back again. Either he went higher into the mountains or he had already reached one of the settlements along the river before we started looking for him. I think we're better off searching the populated areas first."

"Maybe," Nate said wearily.

"Can I make a suggestion without anyone threatening to throw me off the ship?" Tommy asked with a grin.

"I make no promises," Alton said, smiling back, "but go ahead."

"I think we need a day off, Alton. We've been going at this hot and heavy for weeks now. I think we need a break."

"Oddly enough, I've been thinking the same thing myself. I was afraid you two would mutiny if I suggested it, though."

"I don't have the energy," Nate said. "A day off sounds like a good idea."

"O.K.," Alton said. "We'll take tomorrow off and then start scanning those villages on the river. Sound good?"

"Aye, aye, skipper," Tommy said. "And since I'm not going to be flying tomorrow, you think maybe I could have some of that booze you two have been hiding?"

"I don't know," Nate said. "I've heard about you pilots. You're not going to get drunk and try to take advantage of me, are you?"

Tommy laughed.

"There's not enough booze in the whole sector to get me that drunk!" he said.

"Well, in that case, I suppose we can let you have a little taste," Alton said. "But remember, we're only taking one day off. Try not to over do it."

"I'll do my best," Tommy said with an impish grin before asking, "Anybody for strip poker?"

"I knew you couldn't be trusted!" Nate bellowed then made a show of modestly buttoning his shirt all the way to his neck.

"Mother warned me about men like you," he added, crossing his legs and flitting his eyelashes coyly.

Alton and Tommy laughed and Alton went to one of the storage compartments in the galley and pressed his right thumb to the lock. The door hissed open and he reached in and removed a half empty bottle of scotch. Then he took three glasses from a wall unit and went back to his seat, poured two inches into each glass and sat down.

"Aaaah," Tommy said after taking a slow sip and letting the warmth run down his throat and into his belly. "That's good stuff. No wonder you've been hiding it."

"Hey, at least I didn't confiscate your private stash," Alton said with a wink at Nate Squires.

"I have no idea what you're talking about," Tommy said innocently. Truth was, he did have a bottle hidden in his stateroom. He hadn't been sure if Alton knew about it or not.

Alton just smiled and let it go. He trusted Tommy completely. He just didn't want him thinking he could put one over on the boss.

"There's something else I've been thinking about," Tommy said to change the subject.

"I'm almost afraid to ask," Nate said, "but what might that be?"

"Well, I don't mean to be a defeatist here, but have you two considered the possibility that Mitch is dead and someone either buried or burned his body? There may not be any remains for us to identify."

"I've considered that possibility," Alton said soberly.

"I figured you had," Tommy said. "And I know that's something we'd worry about only after we've exhausted all other options. I just wanted to make sure you were aware of the possibility, that's all."

Alton nodded.

"We've got a lot of area left to search before I'll start worrying about that, though, Tommy," he said.

"I know, boss. The thought just struck me when we saw that funeral pyre outside the city yesterday."

"Yeah," Alton said, "me too."

*    *    *    *

Roger Werts was waiting for them when Mitch and Wanchese reached Philip's village. Anxious to be of some use and needing something to occupy his mind, he hoped accompanying the stranger and his woman would be a means to that end. He just wished he could find an escape for his wife. She was taking Jikan's death even harder than he was.

As the three of them traveled southward, Roger taught Mitch what he knew of the farmer's complex language. Fortunately, Chinese, along with English and Spanish, was one of the three languages taught at every school in the Traegus Sector and Mitch had a basic knowledge to build on. Most of what Roger knew had to do with trade and trade goods, but from that Mitch was able to glean similarities between the Chinese he'd learned in school and the particular version the people here spoke. It was something to work with anyway.

On the third day out from Philip's village, they arrived at the walled gate of a timber fortress. A sentry saw them coming and called out to someone below. Another man climbed up to stand beside the lookout and examined the three travelers carefully. After a minute, he called down to the men manning the gate and it swung open slowly. Two soldiers walked out to meet them and they were ushered inside, the gate closing after them.

This was an outpost garrison, Roger explained, a first line of defense against attack. Most of its inhabitants were soldiers, though there were several women in sight when Mitch and the others were brought in. Roger knew the commanding officer and many of the men. This was where he came twice a year to meet with merchants from the interior who were interested in trade.

"I greet you, Warlord Zeng-de," Roger said to the slight Asian man who climbed down from the watchtower to meet them.

"And I you, Roger Werts," Zeng-de replied, a question in his dark, unlined face. "It is not yet time for us to meet."

"No, it isn't," Werts agreed. "But there is important news and I asked this warrior to share it with my friends and partners in trade."

Zeng-de looked at Mitch appraisingly. Reaching out, he touched the smooth black of the staff in Mitch's right hand, a question in his eyes. Sensing what he wanted, Mitch held it out to him.

Zeng-de stepped back and hefted the weapon knowingly. Then he slowly moved through a series of blocking and striking movements. His motion was smooth, his balance even and unfaltering. The weapon instantly became an extension of his body and it was immediately evident to Mitch that this man was a master.

"What is this wood?" he asked when he handed the staff back to Mitch.

"He asks what kind of wood that is," Roger Werts translated.

"Tell him I found the wood high up in the mountains to the west," Mitch said. Explaining the truth would have been difficult and time consuming. Roger translated his reply.

"You use this as a weapon?" Zeng-de asked.

"Yes," Mitch answered, having caught the word for weapon and guessing what he was being asked.

Zeng-de spoke to one of his men and pointed to one of the buildings within the fortress. The man went inside and returned with what Mitch guessed was Zeng-de's personal weapon, a long, rounded staff six feet long and one inch thick. Taking it, the warlord stepped back and motioned for Mitch to follow.

"We will test on another?" he asked. Werts translated.

"It would be an honor," Mitch answered. Roger translated and the two men began to circle warily.

Zeng-de was quick and surprisingly strong for such a thin man. His movements were sure and powerful and it took all of Mitch's skill to block a series of attacks. What was worse, Mitch had a feeling the man was going easy on him, holding back as a courtesy. Zeng-de had obviously grown up with a weapon in his hands and it showed in every line of movement, every transfer of balance, every darting strike and parry.

The two of them were soon sweating and Mitch thought he could feel Zeng-de growing less cautious, pressing a little harder. At one of his overhead strikes, Mitch instinctively thrust his staff up horizontally over his head. In his haste to make a good showing against a more skilled opponent, he momentarily forgot his staff's special construction and threw the block up full force. Zeng-de's weapon splintered at the point of contact, a two foot section snapping off and dropping to the ground.

There were murmurs of surprise from the watching men, who saw this as an indication of the stranger's strength and power. Zeng-de looked at his weapon in stunned silence. Made of the strongest wood known to his people and treated with a special ointment to harden it further, this staff had been passed down from his grandfather to his father and finally to him. He had planned on passing it on to his own son one day.

He picked up the broken shaft and examined both pieces closely. There were no structural weaknesses he could see. It had simply snapped.

"I must have some of this wood," he said, pointing to Mitch's staff. "I'll bring you some," Mitch said when Roger Werts had translated for him. "When I'm able. I don't know when that will be, but I give you my word as a warrior, if I survive the coming battle, I'll bring you a weapon like this." He gestured with his staff.

"Coming battle?" Zeng-de asked when Roger had translated.

"Yes, Warlord," Roger answered. "That is what this warrior has come to talk with you about."

Zeng-de nodded.

"Come," he said. Then he turned and walked into his quarters, his visitors following behind.

When they were inside and seated at a long wooden table, Zeng-de's wife came and offered them cool water, which they drank gratefully. Then Mitch and Zeng-de began their negotiations, Roger Werts translating.

"What is this battle you speak of?" Zeng-de asked.

"The people from the west prepare an attack," Mitch answered. "They bring five thousand warriors. We don't know if they will attack the village on the river or you. We've come to propose and alliance."

"My scouts have told me what the evil ones do along the edge of the forest. It is odd, what they do. But how can you be sure they will attack?"

Well, Mitch though, the fact that he called the Inchasa 'the evil ones' seemed like a good sign.

"One of our people escaped from them," Mitch said, knowing it wasn't exactly the truth but again not wanting to get into any long explanations. "He was a slave among them and knew their language better than they thought he did. He ran away and came to warn us."

Zeng-de considered that, his dark eyes moving from Mitch to Roger and back again. Werts he knew to be a fair man and from this he decided it was reasonable to assume him an honest man. The big warrior was another matter entirely. He would have to spend some time with him before judging his honesty, though he could see no advantage in their lying to him.

"What is it you want from us and what do you offer in return?"

"We ask that you fight with us if we are attacked. In return, we'll fight with you if you are attacked."

"All of your warriors will fight with us?" Zeng-de asked skeptically.

"No," Mitch answered honestly. "Only three of the river villages will send their men to fight beside you. A total of fifteen hundred men, or there abouts."

His answer gained Mitch respect in the warlord's eyes. It would have been an easy thing for him to lie about, but the muscular warrior had chosen to answer honestly.

"It is unlikely the evil ones will attack us," he said. "The line of march they prepare leads to you, not us. Why should my people risk raising their wrath against us by helping you?"

"Because if we're defeated, you'll be next. I think you know that. I think that's why this fortress is here, why strong warriors like you are here. Your people know the evil ones will come sooner or later. Fight with us now and we'll fight with you then."

Zeng-de smiled. This was a shrewd one. His people did indeed live with the knowledge that sooner or later the evil ones would try to conquer them again. They had tried in his grandfather's time and in his father's time and he had no doubt that they would try in his time. His people had both patience and a long memory.

"I will send a messenger to Hongzhi," he said, "and see what the elders have to say. They will decide whether or not the Emperor should hear of your offer."

"I understand," Mitch said.

"Will you do me the honor of dining with me?" Zeng-de asked. "We seldom have visitors here and my wife would never forgive me if I didn't ask you into our home."

"Yes, thank you," Mitch answered, glad for the opportunity to spend some time with this man. "The honor will be ours."

# CHAPTER 26

▼

# REALIZATION

"You should get some rest," Alton told Tommy when he found him on the bridge studying his map overlays. They had spent the past four days scanning the river villages and the surrounding areas and come up with nothing again. They were all tired, frustrated and dejected.

"I will, boss," Tommy said as he punched a button on his console and looked at the new information on his screen. "I just want to add the latest data from the probes to the overlays."

"Alright," Alton said, "but don't overdo it. Get some rest."

"I will," Tommy said. "I just want to check one more thing."

Confused by the population stats, he called up a map of the entire area and over laid the stats onto it. On a hunch, he did the same with the population centers to the west and then blended them both into one large map.

"Son of a bitch!" he exclaimed, suddenly recognizing what it was he was looking at.

"What?" Alton asked.

"We're walking right into a war here!" Tommy said excitedly.

"What the hell are you talking about?" Alton asked.

"Look at these map overlays, Alton," Tommy said. "You put in your three," he added, referring to the mandatory three year hitch required of all Confederation citizens. "You must recognize what's going on here."

"I put in my three running an officers mess, Tommy," Alton said. "I don't have a friggin' clue what I'm looking at."

"Alright then, let's start with the population centers to the west," Tommy said, switching back to that overlay. "Here to the north is what looks like a fairly large scale construction project, but our scans show hardly anyone there to do the work. Then here, all along this road leading south are these evenly spaced shelters, each with only one man."

"And here, at this small city to the south, our scans show no more than half the population we expected. But over here, in the middle of nowhere," he moved his finger to a secluded valley at the eastern edge of the area that met the mountains and the wide plain, "we find a shitload of people gathering around a lake with no structures to speak of for miles around."

Tommy stopped for a moment as Nate Squires came walking onto the bridge.

"Take a seat, Slim," Alton said. "Tommy thinks he's onto something."

Squires nodded wearily and took a seat.

"O.K," Tommy continued, turning back to the view screen. "Here, moving east along the edge of the plain, we find large groups moving back and forth between the small city and these large, evenly spaced structures all along here." He ran a finger along the boundary between the mountains and the wide plain, tracing a line eastward.

"Now, let's look at the villages we just scanned," he said, punching a button and calling up the second overlay. "Here, all the way to the north, we find a good sized village with half as many people as we expect. The next village has even fewer and those that are there seem to be moving west toward the mountains in groups of ten and twenty."

"The middle village and the one south of it are completely empty, while the southernmost village is swamped with a hell of a lot more people than it could possibly support. With me so far?"

Alton nodded and Nate shrugged his shoulders and waved for Tommy to go on. He'd catch up later. Tommy punched another button and the two maps were merged into one.

"Now," he said, "we've got these people to the west gathering here," he pointed again to the secluded valley, "and moving supplies along here." He traced the route east toward the river villages. "And these people along the river are gathering down here in this village, the point these western people are pointing toward."

"What we have here," he concluded, turning to look at Alton, "is what we in the Advanced Intel Assessment Corps used to call a convergence point. These people are getting ready to go at it."

Alton and Nate looked at the map in silence for a moment.

"Couldn't they just be getting together for a celebration or a harvest or something?" Nate asked. "They could all be part of the same culture for all we know."

"No," Alton said, catching on to what Tommy was saying. "These people build with stone, even putting in aqueducts and stone roadways within their cities. The people along the river build with wood, mud and reeds. I think Tommy might be right. The question is, does it help us or hurt us?"

"I don't know," Tommy said. "But since we know those people to the west would have either killed Mitch or made him a slave, these people to the east seem like our best bet. I think it's time we start asking some questions."

Alton sighed heavily. He really didn't want to put his friends in any more danger than he already had. Making contact was a risk. But Tommy was right. It was time to start asking some questions, even if they had to use sign language and draw pictures in the dirt to do it.

"Alright," he said, "we'll ask some questions. But let's get some sleep first."

Tommy and Nate nodded their agreement and the three of them went back to their rooms. They all dropped off to sleep quickly and slept well into the afternoon. Tommy was the first one awake and he quickly got the others up and moving. They ate a good meal then Alton and Nate put together some warm clothing and threw some blankets in a pack in case they ended up spending the night outdoors.

"Where to?" Tommy asked when everything was ready.

"Over where the action is," Alton answered. "Put us down a mile or two away from this last village, the one everyone seems to be moving toward."

"You got it," Tommy said, lifting the ship off the ground as he spoke. He had them at the drop point in a matter of minutes.

"Good luck," he said as Alton and Nate left the bridge. "And be careful."

It took less than an hour to walk the two miles to the village. They approached it from the plain so they would be visible well before making contact. They didn't want anyone thinking they were trying to sneak up on them.

As they came closer, they could see that the villagers were hastily building a wall of timber and earth across the open section of plain just before the village. As Alton and Nate approached, feeling horribly naked and unprotected, the work stopped and all eyes turned toward them. By the time they reached the wall, a small group of men had moved out to meet them.

"Hello," Alton said with a wave of his hand, feeling stupid but not knowing what else to say now that he was there.

"Hello," a powerfully built black man answered, looking at their clothing curiously. "You are newcomers?"

"Yes," Alton said in surprise. They spoke English!

"I am Philip Granganimeo, Councillor of this village. Welcome."

"Thank you," Alton said. The men gathering around them were all dressed in only a cloth that covered their sex organs and little else. Some also wore wide, colorfully decorated bands on their right arms, though not all. Most bore at least one tattoo and some wore many. There were a variety of hairstyles, ranging from cleanly shaven heads to hair reaching down to their buttocks. All of them were dark skinned and well muscled.

"I'm Alton Harvey. This is my friend, Nathan Squires. We're looking for my brother, Mitchell Harvey, another newcomer."

"Ah," Philip said, looking again at the tall, handsome man in the strange clothing and wondering how he could wear so much and still bear the heat. "Mitchell has gone to ask the chinamen to the south to join us in our battle against the Inchasa. He'll be back in five or six days, I expect."

"He's alive then?" Alton asked. "You've seen him?"

"Yes, he's alive," Philip said. "You had thought him dead?"

"We didn't know for sure," Alton answered, smiling and clapping Nate on the shoulder with relief. "We only knew he'd been brought here and left to die."

"He would be a difficult man to kill, I think," Philip said with a smile. "You're welcome to wait for him here, but as you can see, we're rather busy. I'll ask one of my wives to see to your needs."

"No, no, thank you," Alton said. "If Mitch has gone south, we'll start heading that way and meet him on his way back."

"Are you certain?" Philip asked. "The nights here are very bitter."

"Yes, I'm sure," Alton said, "but thank you."

"Very well," Philip said. "I wish you a safe journey."

Alton and Nate turned away and headed back the way they'd come. Philip and the others went back to work.

"Tommy," Alton called into his audio link once they were out of sight of the village.

"What's up, boss?"

"We're coming back to the ship. Meet us at the drop point."

"Any luck?"

"We'll see," Alton answered. It was possible the man the people at the village said had traveled south was his brother. It was also possible that it wasn't. He'd feel a lot better after they scanned the area.

"We've got a good lead, anyway," he added. "Somewhere we can scan tonight."

"Great," Tommy said. "See you at the drop point."

It was dark by the time they met up with the ship. They took off immediately and headed for the first population center to the southeast. It was a medium sized settlement, a thousand people or so, but it was the first place someone would have come to as they traveled southeast.

The computer filled out the structural image before moving on to the life form scan. A tall wooden wall surrounded the entire area, the settlement within its protective walls consisting of ten large wooden, one story buildings with thatch roofs as well a twenty-five smaller buildings of the same materials. The life form reading began to fill once the structure was fully outlined.

"Stop!" Alton said as the scan passed over one of the smaller buildings. "Go back to that last one."

Tommy did as he was told, a broad smile spreading across his face. The second set of readings matched the first. Amecyclezene. There were only trace elements left after all this time, but it was enough.

"Go break out the booze, Slim," Alton said, turning to Nate Squires and gesturing to the view screen, his eyes tearing up despite his best efforts to prevent it. "I think we've found our man."

$$* \qquad * \qquad * \qquad *$$

The Sacred Valley was a rich expanse of lush green hidden between two lines of mountains. At its center was Lake Paccaritambo, beside which sat the small open air temple with its raised alter of white stone. The Inchasa had offered sacrifices of jenar rams and hinnok bulls upon that alter since the day their ancestors had first awakened to their strange new life.

This was the Apus, the place where the spirits lived, those who had come before and those who had always been. It was here that Inchasa warriors had come for hundreds of years to seek the council of the spirits and prepare themselves for battle. But never had so large a force gathered within the valley as the five thousand warriors now gathered around the sacred temple.

It was a sight that soothed Manco's troubled mind and questioning spirit. Even with an inexperienced boy commanding these men, they would achieve their victory. Perhaps not the quick, overpowering victory they had originally hoped for, but victory just the same. He had begun to have reservations about their ability to control large numbers of male slaves anyway. Better to kill the warriors and enslave the women and children. They were easier to control.

In that respect, Leruk had done them a favor with his inept handling of his small slave force. Now that the enemy knew they were coming, they would mass their forces and the Cuzco would have to accept the need for all out destruction. They would annihilate the male population and see to it that the river people all but ceased to exist. The way war should be, as far as he was concerned.

And if the Inti Raymi's eight days of feasting and celebration caused his troops to lose some of their hard earned conditioning and discipline, the ten day march to the enemy village would restore them. They'd be ready when the time came. If only the Cuzco would let some of his more experienced advisors prepare the battle plan.

But, that was not to be and Manco and others like him would see to it that the Cuzco's orders were strictly obeyed and that victory was won despite them. It would be their blood that would bring the boy the glory he sought and their deaths that would raise him up to the greatness he dreamed of. But, that was the way of things. He was of royal blood and they were simple warriors.

A flaming arrow arched high into the air, seemed to hang there for a long second then plunged into the waters of lake Paccaritambo. It was time to begin.

"It is time!" he cried loudly from his place beside the stone alter and the crush of warriors at the rear of the temple parted.

The Cuzco strode regally through their midst, into the temple and up the stone stairway to the alter. He was dressed in a helmet of polished silver, a deep purple cloak that fell the length of his body, a golden breastplate and matching golden guards on his arms and legs. Around his neck was a long silver chain from which hung a golden representation of the sun. He looked like a king, a Cuzco and Manco had to admit there was a sense of power about the boy.

"It is indeed time," the Cuzco said loudly when he reached the alter, "time to celebrate the Inti Raymi, time to make our sacrifices to the spirits who will guide us to victory, time to prepare ourselves for the coming battle."

There were cheers all around the valley as his words were relayed to those too far away to hear him.

"It will not be an easy victory. Our enemy knows we are coming and will have made ready to meet us. Some among us will give their lives for our victory. We will return here when the battle is won and honor those brave warriors with offerings and tales of their deeds in battle. Others of us will be wounded striving for our victory. We will honor those brave warriors every day of their lives by providing for them whatever their hearts desire for as long as they live among us!"

Now a thunderous eruption of cheers erupted from the men gathered around the temple. After a moment, the Cuzco held his hands high to quiet them.

"And some of us will perform feats of bravery in battle so great that they will one day be sung of in songs by our children."

He paused now, letting his words be filtered back to the farthest reaches of the crowd. Then he turned around slowly, his gaze taking in each and every man within his vision, and cried out in a voice full of strength and power.

"Those few we will honor by building them cities that will bear their name for all time!"

Manco felt the hair on the back of his neck rise and his skin begin to tingle with excitement. A city bearing his name for all time? Now that would be greatness! And looking at the smiles on the faces of the cheering men around him, he could see that they were thinking the same thing. Perhaps the Cuzco was wiser than any of them knew.

"And now," the Cuzco cried, holding his hands up to quiet his cheering army, "and now it is time to make our first sacrifice."

He held out his arm and the throng of warriors behind him parted again. A royal servant came forward, pushing along in front of him a young river woman dressed in a long white gown, her hands tied in front of her, a cloth stuffed into her mouth.

There were whispers of surprise as the woman was led up the stairs and laid on the alter then tied in place with stout ropes as wood was piled below and around the alter. They had never seen anything other than animal sacrifices.

"Accept this sacrifice, great spirits," the Cuzco cried as he drew a long knife from beneath his cloak, "and grant us our fervent wish for victory over our enemies!"

Stepping forward, he took the woman by the hair and pulled her head back so that her throat was fully exposed.

"And grant us the courage and strength to slay all those who oppose us, just as we now slay this seed of our enemy!"

The knife sliced smoothly into the woman's neck, cutting the large main artery on the side opposite the Cuzco and spilling her blood out onto the alter, a dark stream spouting from her neck with every beat of her heart, it's thick, flowing red standing starkly against the pure white stone.

"We have spilled our enemy's blood," the Cuzco roared as his men suddenly forgot their surprise and began to yell and scream in lustful exultation as they watched the woman's blood stream down the stone. "Now let us burn them within the fire of our wrath!"

Manco stepped forward on cue and with a lighted torch and touched it to the wood below the alter. The fire caught and smoldered for a moment as he walked around the alter and touched the torch to all sides. Then the flames leaped up and the alter quickly became engulfed in fire.

"Such will be the fate of all who stand against us," The Cuzco cried as the fire poured over the woman's body and his men cheered him, reaffirming in his mind his decision to repeat the ritual each evening throughout the eight days of the Inti Raymi. It had come to him in a vision that such a momentous occasion called for a new, more glorious sacrifice. He could see now that spilling the enemy's blood was a fitting way to ask the spirits favor.

"Now," he said with a triumphant smile, "let us begin the feasting and celebration!"

# CHAPTER 27

▼

# A TIME TO LEARN

Warlord Zeng-de's wife, Nang-de, was happily showing Wanchese how to make the flat, hard crusted bread that both she and Mitch had developed a liking for. The language barrier seemed to have no effect on them and Mitch was glad to see that the two of them had become fast friends. For the first time since he'd met her, Wanchese seemed genuinely happy.

He and Zeng-de had developed a mutual respect that had quickly turned to friendship as well. It had started the first morning after their arrival, when Zeng-de had come upon Mitch while he was meditating. Both surprised and impressed, he had taken a seat a short distance away and begun to seek perfect balance himself. It had been a morning ritual for the five days since.

As had the afternoon teaching sessions in Which Zeng-de worked tirelessly with Mitch to improve his fighting stance and balance. And Mitch often sat at the rough plank table as he was doing now, drinking cool water and watching the women clean up after the evening meal.

He liked to watch the way Wanchese moved. She was a graceful woman, pleasing to look at because of both her physical beauty and her competence. There was no wasted movement once she understood what needed to be done and the best way of going about it. There was a kind of beauty in that, too.

The elder, Chin-Tsong, had come and listened to what Mitch had to say, but was less than enthusiastic. He said he would present the proposed alliance to the Council of Elders and the Emperor at Hongzhi, but that he doubted they would

risk becoming involved in someone else's fight. He openly admitted that he
thought it was a bad idea and would do his best to prevent it when he got back.
He was scheduled to leave the next morning, as were Mitch, Wanchese and
Roger Werts.

Mitch was thinking that he was going to miss the peacefulness of this place
when there was a loud cheer from outside. He smiled, knowing Zeng-de must
have pitted two groups of his men against each other in the completion of some
task. It was a good way to build an atmosphere of camaraderie as well as relieve
some of the monotony of the soldier's lives. Zeng-de was an intelligent commander.

And the men under his command were good men. Mitch was impressed with
their skill and discipline as well as the courtesy they showed Wanchese, who was
rarely allowed to perform any type of labor outside the walls of Zeng-de's quarters without one of them asking if "the warrior's lady" would be kind enough to
let them carry that wood or bucket of water for her. Wanchese was made uncomfortable by such things and Mitch sometimes thought she was confused by kindness.

Zeng-de came through the door and motioned for Mitch to follow him outside. Mitch stood, grabbed his cloak and followed. They walked to the main gate
and Zeng-de ordered it opened. The two of them walked out away from the fortress until they came to a large, flat boulder at the eastern edge of the camp's tilled
ground. Zeng-de sat on the boulder and dug in his pocket for his pipe. Lighting
it, he inhaled deeply then passed the pipe to Mitch, who took it and sat down
beside him.

The two of them sat like that until the tobacco was gone. Then Zeng-de
banged the pipe on the boulder and set it aside to cool.

"You fight with the river men?" he asked. Mitch had told him the truth of his
situation over the last few days, no longer comfortable with lying to his friend.

"Yes."

"Why?"

"I don't know," Mitch answered honestly. "They're my wife's people, or at
least they were. And I like many of them. That and I'm afraid of what I'd feel if I
just walked away, knowing they need all the help they can get."

The same reason he couldn't walk away from Wanchese when she faced the
deathclaw, really. He was afraid he wouldn't be able to live with himself if he did.
He was probably a fool for feeling that way, but he did.

"It will be bad," Zeng-de said.

"Yes," Mitch agreed, knowing his friend was trying to prepare him for what was coming. If only there were more time. There was so much he could learn from this man.

"I want you to have this," Zeng-de said, pulling a cloth wrapped package from beneath his heavy coat. "It is a dagger, very sharp and very strong. It was a gift to me from an old friend. I think you would like him."

"Thank you," Mitch said, reaching out and accepting the dagger, wishing he had something to give in return.

"It is a weapon worthy of a warrior," Zeng-de said. "I pray it brings you victory."

"If it does," Mitch said, "I'll bring you a staff like mine."

"I will look forward to it," Zeng-de said.

Then they sat together in silence for a long time, simply enjoying the company of another warrior and a friend. It was very late when Mitch finally draped his cloak over Wanchese and slipped into bed.

Wanchese woke several hours later to find herself wrapped tightly in Mitch's arms. She was frightened for a moment, thinking that he was trying to take her in her sleep. Then she realized he was asleep himself and unaware of what he was doing. She was ashamed of having thought him capable of such a thing. Telling herself that she didn't want to wake him, she stayed where she was and quickly fell back to sleep.

When next she awakened, the smell of roasting meat and brewing tea told her that Nang-de was up and preparing the morning meal. She slipped quietly from bed, changed out of her sleeping robe into a dress and went to help.

Soon everyone was up and about and Mitch and Zeng-de went off to their morning meditation. When they came back, the meal was served. Then Wanchese insisted on helping Nang-de clean up. She would be leaving her friend soon and wanted to spend her last moments at the fortress with her.

Mitch loaded Wanchese's pack and placed it and the one he used to carry his cloak outside beside the gate. Zeng-de followed with a pack of his own.

"What's this?" Mitch asked.

"I travel to Hongzhi with the elder," Zeng-de answered.

"Oh," Mitch said, disappointed. He'd hoped his friend was going to travel a ways with them.

"I send ten of my best men to escort you to the village," Zeng-de said. "They will see that you arrive safely."

"Thank you," Mitch said. "That's very kind of you."

"It is nothing," Zeng-de said.

Roger Werts came and stood beside them, his pack in his hand, and goodbyes were exchanged. Roger had grown quiet and withdrawn in the time they'd spent at the fortress and Mitch hoped he had found some sense of peace for himself. He was a good man.

Wanchese came out, carrying two freshly filled water bags, one of which she handed to Mitch.

"Open the gate," Zeng-de ordered. Ten of his men came forward and took up positions in front of the group, many of the others calling out a farewell and good wishes. When the gate was open, the ten soldiers walked out of the fortress and waited for those they were to protect.

"I hope to see you soon, my friend," Zeng-de said, clasping Mitch's right hand in his.

"Me too," Mitch said. "You've taught me so much, Zeng-de. I don't know how I'll ever be able to thank you."

"Keep yourself alive," Zeng-de said with a small grin, "and bring me the weapon you promised."

"I'll do my best," Mitch said with a laugh.

Then he and the others turned to go. But as they started through the gate, Nang-de broke from her place beside her husband and ran to Wanchese, gathering her in a tight embrace. Wanchese's eye grew moist with emotion as she put her arms around the first real friend she had ever known. Nang-de let her go, kissed her cheek and went back to stand beside Zeng-de. Wanchese turned and walked out the gate, Mitch and Roger following close behind.

"They're damn good people," Mitch said as they walked away from the closing gate.

"Yes," Wanchese agreed. "Zeng-de wishes he could help, I think."

The ten soldiers encircled them as they walked, placing three to the front, three to the rear and two to each side. Mitch wondered if Zeng-de knew something he didn't or if his men just took their job very seriously.

"You were happy there," he said, hoping Wanchese would be willing to open up a little.

"Yes," she said. "It was good to have a friend."

"You could go back and stay with them until after the fight," Mitch said hopefully. He was worried about what would happen to her if he was killed.

"I will go back when you do," Wanchese replied, thinking that there was no reason for Mitchell to involve himself in the coming battle. He had done all that he could. But, he was a warrior and he wouldn't leave Philip and the others to fight alone. It was not in his nature.

It was the reply Mitch had expected and they walked on in silence as the sun quickly turned the cool morning into a furnace of shimmering heat. They followed a narrow dirt path that wound through grassy hills and knolls. It was hot but pleasant and several hours passed very quickly.

Then, just as they reached the crest of a shallow incline, Mitch saw the three lead soldiers suddenly break into a run, over the crest and out of sight. He and the others ran to the top of the hill and found the three soldiers holding two men flat on the ground, each with a sword at his throat.

Mitch broke into a run and arrived on the scene just as one of the prostrate figures said, "Hey, take it easy, chief, take it easy."

"Alton?" Mitch asked hesitantly, recognizing the voice but not really believing his ears. He pushed the confused soldier aside and hauled his brother to his feet.

"It *is* you!" he exclaimed happily, pulling his brother into a powerful hug, lifting him off his feet, and laughed with unrestrained joy. Then he put Alton down and stood at arms length looking at the face he'd been sure he'd never see again. Roger Werts went and helped Nathan Squires to his feet.

"Mitch?" Alton asked in disbelief. He could barely recognize the man standing in front of him. "Is it really you?"

"Yeah, it's me, big brother," Mitch said with a laugh. Then he saw Nathan Squires for the first time.

"Nate!" he cried happily and gave him a hug, kissing the shorter man on his balding pate. Squires smiled dumbly and wiped his head.

Mitch turned to Roger Werts and Zeng-de's men.

"It's alright," he told Roger, leaving it to him to translate for the others. "This is my brother, Alton, and my friend, Nate."

"I can barely recognize you," Alton said when Mitch turned back to him. "Look at you! Where did you get all those scars? And those muscles?"

Then he put out his hand and touched his brother's arm, as if to make sure he was real.

"I can't believe we really found you," he said softly.

"I can't believe it either," Mitch said. "How'd you do it?"

"Long story, little brother, but Sandra's the one that had you brought here."

"I figured as much," Mitch said. Then he remembered the other members of his group and turned to Wanchese, embarrassed that he'd forgotten all about her in his excitement.

"Alton," he said, "this is my wife, Wanchese." He smiled at Alton's drop-jawed surprise. "And this is Roger Werts. The others are soldiers sent by a friend to protect us."

"Well, they're damn good at their job," Nate Squires said, finding his voice. "The bastards actually held a sword to my throat!"

Mitch laughed then turned to Wanchese.

"Wanchese, this is my brother, Alton."

"I'm very pleased to meet you," Wanchese said, surprised by her sadness. These men had come to take Mitchell home. She would be alone again.

"Pleased to meet you, too," Alton said. "But why would a beautiful girl like you marry this guy?" he asked, slapping Mitch on the shoulder. "Were you drunk?"

"No," Wanchese said, laughing.

"Not all of us need to ply our women with whiskey," Mitch said with a wink at Wanchese, who smiled.

"Speaking of whisky," Nate Squires said, running a hand up and down his neck, "I could use a snort right about now."

"Well, I haven't sampled any of the local brew yet," Mitch said, "but I believe Roger keeps a little handy." He raised a questioning eyebrow to Roger Werts, who shrugged and dug into his pack for his small liquor bag and handed it to Squires.

Nate looked at it dubiously.

"I was thinking of the booze back on the *SeaVista*," he said.

"You wouldn't insult my friend by refusing such a kind offer, would you, Nate?" Mitch asked with a smile.

"No, I wouldn't want to do that," Squires answered, taking the stopper from the back and taking a hesitant sip.

His eyes went a little wide as the liquid burned down his throat and into his stomach, but he refused to gag in front of a crowd.

"Interesting," he said hoarsely as he handed the bag back to a smiling Roger Werts.

"You came on the *SeaVista*?" Mitch asked Alton.

"Yup, she's over to the west about two miles. Tommy's got her."

"Could you have him meet us here?" Mitch asked. "I'd love to see how Zeng-de's men react."

"They're not going to shoot arrows at it or anything, are they?"

"No," Mitch laughed. "I'll warn them."

As Alton called Tommy on the audio link, Mitch turned to Wanchese, Roger and the soldiers.

"You've heard newcomers talk about coming here from places far off in the stars?" he asked.

"Yes," Roger answered.

"Well, you're about to see how they get here. It's a machine that flies."

Roger and Wanchese both looked at him uncomprehendingly.

"Just tell Zeng-de's men not to be frightened, Roger. Tell them I give them my word as a warrior that no harm will come to any of us."

Roger shrugged and turned to tell the soldiers what Mitch had said.

"This is what my people call a starship," Mitch told Wanchese as the faint whine of the *Sea Vista's* engines began to grow louder. "People can.fly between the stars with it."

"Alright," Wanchese said, still not understanding what he was talking about.

Then the ship came into sight, flying toward them at a height of twenty feet, coming to a stop near the stunned crowd where Tommy, ever the showman, put her into a hover and turned on all the exterior lights before gently lowering her to the ground.

"Incredible, isn't it?" Mitch asked Wanchese.

"Yes," she answered, staring wide eyed at the impossible thing before her.

"Would you like to see inside?" he asked.

"You can do that?"

"Yes," he answered with a smile. Then he took her hand and led her up to the ship, placing her hand on its smooth outer skin.

"Ask them if they want to touch it, Roger," he called over his shoulder. Soon Roger and Zeng-de's men were running their hands along the fuselage, talking back and forth excitedly. Their eyes almost popped out of their skulls when there was a sharp hiss and the outer door began to lower from the side of the ship.

Taking Wanchese by the hand again, Mitch led her up the ramp and into the ship. Roger and the others followed after a slight hesitation. Tommy met Mitch just inside the door and gave him a rough hug and a slap on the back before leading everyone on a quick tour of the small vessel.

"No one will ever believe us," Roger Werts said as he looked around in amazement.

"Probably not," Mitch agreed. "It might be better not to even tell anyone."

"I must tell my wife," Roger said.

"Would you like to go for a ride?" Mitch asked, and was glad he had when Roger's eyes lit up with excitement.

"We could do that?" he asked.

"Yes," Mitch answered. "Why don't you ask our friends if they'd like to fly."

Roger turned and asked the soldiers, using hand motions where words failed him. Many of the men looked doubtful but none of them wanted to be the first to refuse so they all ended up going for a short ride. Alton opened the side view ports and they all looked on in stunned silence as the ground sped past in a blur.

"What do you think?" Mitch asked Wanchese.

"I don't know what to think," she answered breathlessly. "It is impossible and yet I am here, seeing it and feeling it. It's like a dream, except I've never even dreamed that such things could exist."

"No," Mitch said, "I would never have dreamed of something like this either. But some men do. That's the first step in something like this being created, I think. Someone has to dream it before it can become reality."

Tommy set the ship down two miles south of Philip's village, having brought his passengers in ten minutes to a place it would have taken them three days to reach on foot.

"The village is only about two miles north," Alton said when everyone was off the ship.

"We've come so far?" Roger asked.

"Yes," Alton answered with a smile. "Not bad, huh?"

"No," Roger answered, smiling back. "Not bad at all."

"Roger," Mitch said, "explain where we are to the men and see if they'd like a ride back to where we were."

Roger spoke to the soldiers, listened to their answer and turned back to Mitch with a smile.

"They say it is impossible to have come so far, even in a flying house. They say they will stay with us until the village is in sight."

"O.K.," Mitch said. "Can't really say as I blame them. I wouldn't want to disobey one of Zeng-de's orders either."

"No," Roger said, "the warlord is not a man to trifle with."

Mitch turned to Alton.

"I need a favor, big brother."

"Why don't I like the sound of that?" Alton asked.

"Because you're not as dumb as you look," Mitch answered with a grin. "I need you to stay for a while and I need you to park this thing up in those sandy hills across the river from the village."

"Why?" Alton asked. "Can't we just go home?"

"I can't," Mitch told him. "I need to be here for this fight that's coming. And I want you here to take Wanchese to safety if things go badly."

"Of course I'll take her to safety. But why do you have to stay for this fight? You don't belong here, Mitch."

"I'm not so sure about that, Alton. I think I finally found myself here. And the man I've become can't just leave people who need him and still respect himself. I'm staying and I'd feel a whole lot better if I knew Wanchese was safe."

"Alright," Alton said, still not understanding. "You need a psychiatrist, but alright. I'll see that she's safe."

"Thank you," Mitch said, reaching out to touch his brother's shoulder. "This is important to me."

"O.K," Alton said. "I'll go tell Tommy where to park this thing and I'll walk with you."

"You didn't have to do that," Wanchese said softly when Alton walked away.

"Yes, I did," Mitch replied. "For my own peace of mind, I did."

"You shouldn't worry," she told him. "You will defeat the Inchasa and your brother will watch you. He doesn't understand yet who you are, I think. Perhaps this will help him learn."

"I like your attitude," he said, smiling at her. He was glad someone had confidence in him. He wasn't so sure himself. "And I hope you're right. I really hate to lose."

He was pretty sure he wouldn't be real fond of dying, either.

# CHAPTER 28

▼

# HONGZHI

Hongzhi was a tangled bustle of activity as Zeng-de entered from the west. This end of the small city was full of bazaars selling vegetables, smoked meats, cloth, clothing, tools, weapons, pottery, blankets, baskets and most anything else a person might need. There were even cloth tents where a man could buy the affections of a woman if he knew the right name to mention and had something of value to trade.

The buildings within the city were made of white stone and bright white plaster with doors and roofs of wood poles tied together and sealed with kilben pitch. The stone work was of excellent quality and many of the buildings were or two and even three stories. Many had awnings of colorful cloth over the entranceway, beneath which the inhabitants sold their wares and services ranging from blade sharpening to fortune telling.

Making his way through the jostling crowd, Zeng-de moved through the markets and deeper into the city where it was far more quiet and a good deal easier to get around. He traveled east and north until he came to an ancient, high domed temple with murals of men, women and beasts of burden scrolling across the white expanse of the dome. There he turned into a small side street and walked to a door at the far end. He knocked loudly and waited.

The door opened a crack and a wrinkled old face peered out at him.

"Ah!" the old woman gasped, "Zeng-de!" She threw the door open and put her arms around her youngest son. "What are you doing here?"

"I've come to speak to the elders," he told her as he returned her embrace. "I arrived late last night and didn't want to wake you so I camped outside the city."

"You should have come here," his mother chided as she stepped inside and motioned him in before closing the door. "It is never too late for one of my children to come home."

She led the way down a short hallway and into a spacious room that held cushioned furniture and an ancient loom that had been in her family for more than two hundred years.

"Sit, I'll get your father."

"You look well, my son," Sichu-de said as he walked into the room before his wife had time to go looking for him. "It's good to see you."

"And you, father."

"What brings you home?" Sichu-de asked as he took a seat on a long couch and motioned for his son to join him. Zeng-de's mother, Xian-de left to go prepare some tea.

"I'd like your advice, father," Zeng-de replied as he sat.

"Speak," Sichu-de said, a curious look on his face. It was unlike his son to leave his post for any but the most important matters.

"Tomorrow I go before the Council of Elders to oppose the words of Chin-Tsong," Zeng-de said. "I wish no offense to him or the Council but I think the Emperor should hear both sides of the issue."

"You sound as if your mind is already made up, my son. How can I help?"

"I need you to listen to what I have to say and tell me what you think. I'm afraid I may be blinded by the fact that someone I consider a friend is involved. I want you to help me see if I'm wrong, if I'm letting my emotions cloud my judgment."

"Of course," Sichu-de said, glad that his son was not too proud to seek the wisdom of others. Whatever it was Zeng-de had come to speak to the Council about was obviously very important to him, yet he was still open to the opinions of those he trusted. Not all men would be so open-minded.

"Thank you, father," Zeng-de said, then took a deep breath and explained what was troubling him.

"The evil ones to the west plan an attack. My scouts tell me they bring a large party, possibly as large as two or even three thousand men."

"So many?" Sichu-de asked, his face showing his surprise. The largest attack he had ever heard of had involved no more than one thousand enemy soldiers.

"Yes," Zeng-de answered. "They've built the shelters needed to hold enough supplies to support such a number. Their direct line of march leads to the people of the river, though it's possible they'll turn south and attack us. I don't think that's likely, but it's possible."

"If they are going to attack the river village," Sichu-de asked, "why are you so concerned?"

"Because a warrior came to the fortress and proposed an alliance between our peoples. He believes that if the river people are conquered, the sun worshippers will turn their eyes toward us next. I think he's right."

"And Chin-Tsong does not?"

"No. He says we will only raise the wrath of the enemy against us unnecessarily if we become involved."

"And this alliance, what do they offer and what do they want in return?" Sichu-de asked. It was unlike his son to disagree with his elders openly. Perhaps Chin-Tsong was making a mistake.

"They offer fifteen hundred warriors to fight with us if we are attacked now or in the future. They ask for the same number to fight with them in return."

"And the friend you spoke of?"

"The warrior who came to propose this alliance. He is an unusual man, father."

"He must be if you consider him a friend, my son. You don't use the word lightly as some men do."

The old man stroked his thin white whiskers. He could see no flaw in Chin-Tsong's wisdom as yet. They needed no help from the river people if they were attacked. They had more than enough men to defend themselves and what was theirs.

"Why do you believe this alliance to be in our best interest?" he asked.

"Because the sun worshippers have proven time and again to be an aggressive people interested only in war and death. The people of the river have been a people of peace, fighting only to defend themselves and their lands. They are interested in trade and the exchange of knowledge that would benefit both our peoples. And, most of all, because they made an offer of friendship. That has never happened before. It could be the beginning of much good will between us."

"All that you say is true," Sichu-de said. "But I would ask you this question. If your friend was not involved in the coming battle, would you still feel as strongly about this proposed alliance?"

Xian-de came in with the tea just then and Zeng-de had a moment to think about his answer.

"I don't know," he said as his mother poured tea into small cups of glazed clay. "That's why I came to you. I'm afraid I might be seeing things as I want them to be rather than as they are."

Sichu-de felt pride again in his young son. Not all men were wise enough to believe themselves fallible.

"You say the evil ones bring as many as three thousand warriors?" he asked.

"Yes, some of my scouts have even said four thousand, but I find that impossible to believe."

Sichu-de nodded his agreement.

"And how many men do you suppose the river people will send against them?" he asked.

"I can't say for sure," Zeng-de answered, trying to remember all that his scouts had reported to him about the river villages. "There are five villages of nearly equal size. I would say somewhere between two and three thousand men."

"And they know the attack is coming," Sichu-de said. "Which means they will prepare a strong defense. How many men would you say the evil ones will lose in this attack, my son?"

"A great many," Zeng-de replied, realizing as he said it that he had indeed been thinking with his heart and not his head. "Enough that they'll be unable to attack us in force even if they defeat the river warriors."

He lowered his head in dejection. Thank the heavens he had spoken to his father before making a fool of himself in front of the Council.

"I've been a fool," he said sadly.

Sichu-de placed a comforting hand on his son's shoulder.

"A man who wishes to help a friend is not a fool, Zeng-de," he said. "Merely a man worthy of friendship. What will you do now?"

"Go back where I belong," Zeng-de answered. He'd wasted enough time here. It was time he got back to his duties.

"Since you are already here," Sichu-de suggested thoughtfully, "perhaps you should stay and hear what the Council has to say on the matter. They may have some questions that you will be better prepared to answer than Chin-Tsong."

"That's true," Zeng-de had to admit. Would he ever seem as wise to his own children as this frail, hunched, grey-headed man seemed to him? "Thank you for your wisdom, father."

"It makes me proud that you are wise enough to seek it," Sichu-de said, giving his son's shoulder a squeeze. "Now, let us sit and enjoy some tea with your mother. She sees you so rarely."

*       *       *       *

Mitch and Philip heaved the final log into place atop the second defensive wall then stood bent over at the waist, their hand on their knees, catching their breath as others settled the log firmly in place. This second wall was one hundred feet behind and not quite as high as the first. The hope was that after the enemy managed to fight their way past the first wall, the sight of a second, and the fresh archers waiting behind it, would demoralize them enough to halt their advance and turn the space between the two walls into a killing zone.

"What next?" Mitch wheezed, sweat dripping from his face like water.

"We rest," Philip answered, shaking the sweat from his head and wiping his eyes. "It's almost mid-day."

"Music to my ears," Mitch said gratefully. He was enjoying the physical labor and could feel himself growing stronger with each passing day, but the heat became brutal as the morning drew to a close.

Still, he enjoyed the work and the connection and sense of purpose he shared with Philip and the other men working with them. It was a good feeling and they were good men.

"I'll go let Virgil and his crew know," he said before leaping over the narrow four foot high wall and walking across the open space between it and the first wall, which was five feet high and a full three feet thick, the rough logs caked together with thick mud and tied tightly in place with rope.

A trench three feet wide and three feet deep was being dug along the length of the front of this wall to prevent the Inchasa from getting a running start and leaping over it. That was where Alton and Nate Squires were being put to use.

The wall ran across the open ground where the waterless plain joined the flat, grassy approach to the river and Philip's village. Walking around the wall's western edge, Mitch found Virgil and his men lying on the grass beside the completed trench.

"Oh, great, you're done," he said. "Now you can start on the second trench, you know, the long one."

"Just shoot me now," Alton said wearily from where he lay flat on his back in the grass.

"Me first," Nate chimed in.

Mitch laughed and turned to Virgil.

"Philip says it's time for a break," he told the tall, hawk-faced warrior. "Looks like you guys have earned it. I didn't think you'd be done until the end of the day."

"Nathan inspires the men," Virgil said. "They feel guilty if they stop working and he keeps digging." Nate Squires had surprised both his friends and himself by proving to be a capable and tireless worker. He seemed to enjoy the physical labor as much as Mitch did.

"How is the second wall coming?" Virgil asked.

"Just finished."

"Good," Virgil said. "Good." If they lost this fight it wouldn't be for lack of preparation and effort. They would be ready when the Inchasa came.

"I think I'll go rinse off in the river," Alton said as he rolled over and pushed himself to his feet.

"Me too," Nate said. "I feel like I'm caked in mud. Digging and sweating are not a good combination."

"That would probably be a good idea for all of us," Virgil said and everyone began to get to their feet.

"I'll meet you there," Mitch said. "I want to see if Philip wants to join us."

When he leaped over the second wall again, he found the others already heading off toward the village, leaving only Philip, who stood leaning against the wall looking out toward the wide plain that would soon be filled with enemy warriors.

"The trench is finished," Mitch said.

"Good," Philip said, his gaze still fixed on the plain beyond the first wall. "We'll be ready soon. Then we can give the men some rest before the battle."

"You've got some good men, there," Mitch said. "I think we have a chance."

"Yes," Philip said, turning to face the man he had come to consider a friend. "Why do you fight with us?" he asked. He knew Mitchell had no reason to risk his life here with them. This was not his village and these were not his people. Yet he would risk the very real possibility of death or capture just as the rest of them would.

"Because I've seen what kind of men the Inchasa are," Mitch answered, having given the question quite a bit of thought over the past several days. "And because I would never be able to respect myself if I walked away without trying to help. I don't know how else to explain it."

Philip nodded. Some of the villagers were suspicious that a newcomer with no real ties to them would want to stay and fight. Thirty-seven of their own men had gathered their families and run off in the night rather than risk death or servitude and yet this man stayed. Some even suggested that Mitchell was one of those men who lusted for battle so greatly that they weren't interested in the opponent, only the act itself.

"You fight for yourself, then," Philip said, "rather than for us."

"I guess you could say that," Mitch answered, sorry that Philip though that of him. He liked this man. "For myself and the kind of man I want to be."

"A noble cause," Philip said. "I fight for the same reason. I wish I could just take my family away from here and build a new life rather than risk having them fall into Inchasa hands. But, then I would be of no good to them or myself. Sometimes a man has to risk all that he loves in order to be the man he wants to be."

"Yes," Mitch said, relieved that someone understood. "That's how I felt when I saw Wanchese facing the deathclaw. I couldn't just stand there and watch her die and still be the man I'd been telling myself I was."

Philip nodded his understanding. He hoped he would have had the courage to do the same.

"It's not an easy thing to be a man who is so honest with himself," he said. "But what in life that's worth having comes easily?"

"Not much," Mitch said. "And when it comes too easily, we seem to take it for granted anyway."

"Yes," Philip agreed as Mitch walked over to where his staff lay on the ground and picked it up. It was a curious weapon, but Wanchese had told him that Mitchell had killed five Inchasa in a matter of minutes with it, saving her life for a second time in the process.

"You will have trouble with Hunter Kane," he said as they began walking back toward the village. He had seen the way the two of them glared at each other. One day they would do more than just glare.

"Sooner or later," Mitch said with a shrug. "I'm hoping it will wait until after the battle."

"So am I," Philip said. Hunter Kane was respected enough as a warrior to have been charged with preparing the young and inexperienced warriors of the villages for the coming battle. What Philip thought of him as a man was something else altogether.

"I won't push it," Mitch said, not sure if Philip was trying to gently remind him there were more important things going on than his personal dislike of Kane, or simply trying to warn him that trouble was coming. "But I won't let him bother Wanchese."

"No, I wouldn't expect you to. I wish we didn't need him for the coming fight. He is a fool, but he is also a very strong warrior."

"Yeah, I've seen him working with the young guys. He's good."

"Yes," Philip agreed. "But not always the wisest of men."

"I've been thinking the same thing about a lot of the men from Secotan's village," Mitch said. "How could they have let Wanchese go unmarried. She's one hell of a woman."

"Perhaps that was part of the problem," Philip said with a smile. "Not all men want a woman who speaks her mind."

Mitch laughed. If there was ever a woman who spoke her mind, it was Wanchese.

"Besides," Philip added, "Secotan tells me she refused several of the warriors from his village. She wanted a man who would treat her with respect, I think. Wanchese was not always treated well by our people."

"Why?"

Philip thought about that for a minute.

"She was often teased about her eye and the scar on her face," he said. "That, along with the loss of her mother and father, caused her to become sullen and sharp tongued. It became easier to leave her alone than to deal with her."

"Oh," Mitch said with a smile. "I thought it was just me that brought out her sharp tongue."

"No," Philip said with a laugh. "She is actually far more pleasant since being wed. My daughter, Anna, has grown very fond of her."

"I know," Mitch said. "Wanchese is fond of her, too."

Philip nodded. He was glad the two had struck up a friendship. There was much his daughter could learn from Wanchese. Especially now that she had found some happiness. It would be a cruel twist of fate for her to lose the man who had brought her that happiness in a fight that was none of his concern. He prayed she would have better fortune now than at other times in her life.

"Virgil and the others went to rinse off in the river," Mitch said.

"A good idea," Philip said. "I must smell like the backside of a banebull after this morning."

The two of them walked to the river and into the cool water.

"How's the sunburn, Nate?" Mitch asked after diving in and coming up beside Alton and Squires.

"Still feels like my skin's on fire," Nate answered, but he was smiling as he said it. This active lifestyle definitely suited him. "But not as bad as yesterday."

"If you'd get out of your office once in a while and come to Teluride like you keep promising," Alton said, "maybe you'd actually get a tan."

"I just might do that," Nate said. "I'm even thinking about taking up hiking when I get back to Sylvas. The fresh air really does give you a lift."

"Next he'll be threatening to start chasing women," Mitch said with a grin.

"If I lose a few more pounds I just might do that, too," Nate said with a laugh, thinking for a brief second of Sandra Harvey's creamy white thighs and wondering if he should tell Mitch about all that.

"Well, you've got a free room at the SeaVista any time," Alton said. "There's usually a woman or two on the beach."

"Yeah, but I'd like one you haven't already screwed," Nate shot back.

"Oh," Mitch said with a laugh, "that could make things a little more difficult."

"Screw the both of you," Alton said with a smile as Philip and Virgil waded over to them.

"We should get inside or into the shade," Philip said and they all started out of the water.

"You are welcome to pass the heat in my longhouse," Virgil said to Nate and Alton. He had come to like and respect these strange newcomers with the odd clothing. They worked hard and kept the others positive with their friendly banter and humor.

"Thank you," Alton said. "I accept."

"Me, too," Nate said.

"I'll see you this afternoon," Mitch said then he and Philip too went their separate ways, Philip to his longhouse, Mitch to the shaded camp Wanchese had set up below a cliff at the northeast corner of the village. She was there, working on a second pair of moccasins for him, when he got there.

"Hi," he said.

"Hello," she responded with a smile. She'd been doing that a lot more lately. "How goes the work on the wall?"

"All done. The trench in front of the first wall too." He sat down heavily then pulled his pack to him, propped it against the cliff wall and leaned against it. "We'll be ready when they come."

Putting the moccasins down, Wanchese stood and walked out of camp toward the river. She came back a minute later with one of their water bags.

"I put it in the river to keep it cool," she said, handing him the bag.

"Thanks," Mitch said and watched her as she went back to her blanket and opened her pack. He didn't care how sullen she'd been as a girl, the men of Secotan's village were fools to let a woman like her get away.

"Will you sleep?" she asked as she pulled another blanket from her pack. She'd traded some of the hard to find roots and herbs she'd collected in the mountains for it so he wouldn't have to sleep on the hot deathclaw hide during the mid-day heat.

"Yes, thank you," he answered.

She spread the blanket beside her own and he stood and brought his pack and the water bag to it.

"You sound tired," she said.

"I am," he admitted. "Everyone is. It's a good thing we'll have a few days to rest before we fight," he added as he lay down on his blanket.

"The women are tired, too," Wanchese said. "Dare says she's made enough arrows to build a bridge across the river out of them."

Mitch chuckled. There *were* an incredible number of arrows piled around the village. They would be placed inside reed netting that would be strung along the inside of the two defensive walls so that each man would have a large supply ready to hand.

"If the Inchasa really bring five thousand warriors," Wanchese continued with a sly grin, "even you might be able to hit one of them."

Mitch laughed out loud. He hadn't caught on nearly as quickly as he'd thought he would and was still a lousy shot with a bow.

"That's a good strategy," he said. "I'll just aim at a big pile of 'em and hope."

"Choose a very big pile," Wanchese deadpanned.

Laughing, Mitch squirted water at her from the bag. She squealed with laughter as the water splashed on her shoulder and neck. Then a stick snapped in the trees to the south of the camp and Mitch instinctively grabbed his staff and rolled to his feet.

A young warrior came through the brush and into the camp. He was of medium height with long, dark hair and a thin build that had yet to fill out with the muscle of manhood. He stopped at the edge of the camp, his smooth young face looking embarrassed and a little afraid.

"I'm Raven Howe," he said tentatively.

"Hello, Raven. I'm Mitchell Harvey and this is Wanchese."

"Yes, I know. I've come to ask for your help," the boy said then stood a little straighter and met Mitch's eyes. "I want to learn from you, Mitchell Harvey. I want to be a strong warrior. Anna Granganimeo tells me you are the man to teach me."

"Why aren't you training with Hunter Kane?" Mitch asked. Maybe the boy was too young to and his parents were trying to keep him out of the battle. If that were the case, training him would be a very bad idea.

"I am," the boy answered, his eyes dropping to the ground. "He says I'm too clumsy, that I'll only get myself and others killed if I fight the Inchasa."

"That could be a blessing in disguise," Mitch said gently. "This battle is going to cost a lot of men their lives and young men like you will be needed to rebuild your people. Maybe it would be best if you didn't fight." This boy was too young to die.

"If they won't let me fight with them, I'll fight the Inchasa myself," the boy said with conviction. "I am of the warrior age. I will not dishonor myself and my family by not taking part in this battle."

Mitch nodded. He understood what the boy was feeling.

"Alright," he said after a minute. "Come back here after the evening meal and we'll see what we can do." Kane might be right and he might not. The boy deserved a chance. He was obviously willing to learn.

"Thank you," Raven said with a relieved smile.

"You're welcome," Mitch said. "I can't teach you all that much about the weapons your people use so keep working with Kane on those things. I'll see what I can do to help with your balance and footwork. And let's keep this between us. I don't want you to have any trouble with Kane."

"I will," the boy said then turned and headed back toward the main village.

"He'll probably wish he'd listened to Kane once the arrows start flying," Mitch said as he sat down again.

"Kane is a fool," Wanchese said. "Anna tells my that Raven is clumsy but strong. He deserves a chance. He would never be able to live with himself if he didn't fight."

"I know," Mitch said. He could understand the boy's motives very well. "I just hate the thought of someone so young being killed before he has a chance to really live."

Almost as much as I hate the thought of getting killed myself just when I'm starting to really live, he thought, glancing at Wanchese. Life could be a real kick in the ass sometimes.

# CHAPTER 29

▼

# THE EMPEROR'S
# CHOICE

"I think it extremely unlikely we are in danger of being attacked," Chin-Tsong said to conclude his briefing. "It would be a mistake to interfere in matters that don't concern us."

Many of the grey headed elders seated around the large, highly polished table of dark resa wood nodded their agreement as Chin-Tsong bowed to the emperor, who sat at the head of the long table, and took his seat.

"This is the first offer of friendship since our people came to this place so long ago," the emperor said, her voice soft but firm. "Is it wise to dismiss it so quickly?"

"It is an offer of friendship born of desperation," Chin-Tsong said. "I would be more inclined to listen if the people of the river had come to us in a time of peace."

"They have come to the outer fortress for three seasons running, have they not?" the emporer asked, turning to look at Zeng-de, who sat in a chair along the left hand wall of the council chamber with other spectators and those who hoped to be heard by the council.

Sensing that an answer was expected, Zeng-de stood and bowed politely.

"They have," he said. "Several of them have come during harvest time to trade with us and one man among them comes three times each year."

"That is trade," Chengua, a tall, thin elder said, his hands nervously wiping at his hairless pate as was his habit. "This is another matter entirely. They ask us to give them our young men, not herta corn and wu meat."

"And if we are not to be attacked," another asked, "what is it we will receive in return? What would we be asking our soldiers to die for?"

"A good question," Emperor Shizong said. "One which warrants further discussion. That is all I'm suggesting, that we consider this offer before rejecting it."

What was it that made her people so stubbornly resistant to change? she wondered. Their culture grew stagnant and old because no one sought out anything new, anything different. The entire northern section of their lands lay unsettled and unused because no one thought it worth the effort to explore it.

She had been trying for several years to snap her people out of their malaise and instill a new sense of exploration and curiosity. It was possible that extended contact with these river people could be a means to that end. If done carefully, of course. It wouldn't be wise to trust any outsider too much.

"Warlord Zeng-de," she said and he stood to his feet again, "it is you who would have to lead our soldiers into battle if we decided to help the river people. What is your thinking on this matter?"

"I have been in favor of this alliance," Zeng-de said. "But someone wiser than myself," he glanced at his father who sat beside him, "has made me see that my thinking may be affected by the friendship I feel for the warrior who came to the fortress and proposed it."

"What were your reasons for supporting it?" Shizong asked, surprised that Zeng-de would even consider risking his own life as well as the lives of his men for outsiders.

"A…ah…a combination of things, really," Zeng-de said nervously. He hadn't expected to speak to the council and hadn't taken the time to get his thoughts in order.

"I would like to hear them, please," Shizong said, and it seemed to Zeng-de that every set of eyes in the room suddenly turned to him.

"I think this could be the beginning of much good will between our peoples," he said, choosing the truth over concern for how his words might be construed. "Also, the river people have shown themselves to be a people of peace. We have never had so much as a minor conflict with them. I don't believe they have any ulterior motives and I think an exchange of goods and ideas could be a step toward friendship."

"Or a step toward conquest," Chengua put forth. "It is unwise to trust outsiders."

"They could no more conquer us than the evil ones to the west could," Shizong said. "We have too many men who could put down the plow and take up the sword for anyone to conquer us."

"That is what every empire thinks until someone proves them wrong," Chin-Tsong said. "It would be safer to refuse this offer and gradually continue to increase our trade with the river people in the coming years."

Safer, Shizong thought sadly. Are our spirits so filled with fear that we can think only of safety? Have we not grown past that point as a people?

"I doubt there would be anyone left to trade with," she said. "The river people don't have enough men available to them to survive the coming attack in any great number. If they survive at all. The evil ones will enslave them and take them away with them."

"I still don't see how that is any of our concern," Chin-Tsong said.

Emperor Shizong turned back to Zeng-de.

"Tell me about this man you call a friend, Warlord Zeng-de," she said.

Zeng-de hesitated. To talk openly of friendship with an outsider could well spend the end of his career. The emperor and the council had to have complete faith in the man in charge of the fortress that guarded the entrance to their land. Still, he was a man of truth and knew no other way.

"His name is Mitchell Harvey," he said. "He is a man of strength and wisdom, a man who seeks perfect balance at the start of each day and then lets that balance guide his actions. That is the way my father taught me a man should live if he wishes to find true peace and happiness and I take it as a sign of wisdom that he follow that path.

"He also has great respect for the arts of war and shows a far greater understanding of them than I would ever have expected of an outsider. He shows respect for our ways and our people. Not a man among my soldiers at the fortress has any but kind words to say about him.

"I cannot speak for other men of the river," he said in conclusion, knowing that he was taking a great risk, "but Mitchell Harvey is a man I am glad to call friend and a man I would trust at my back in the midst of battle."

This was the greatest compliment a soldier could give and even Sichu-de seemed surprised at his son's words. A heavy silence fell over the room as Zeng-de sat down and waited. Many of those around the hall showed shock that a warlord would speak so of an outsider. Shizong, however, looked at Zeng-de with admiration. Here was a man who was not ruled by fear.

"I would have been pleased to meet this man," she said, knowing it would further shock the elders. No outsider had ever been allowed beyond the outer fortress except by force. It was beyond imagination that one be allowed to meet the emperor. "Thank you for your honesty, Zeng-de."

She breathed in deeply and released a long sigh, her brow furrowed in thought. The elders around the table recognized this habit as a sign that she was about to make a decision.

"I thank you for your council, Chin-Tsong and Chengua, but I must disagree with you. Our people grow stale and uninspired because we seclude ourselves from all outside contact and it is time we begin to change that. I will allow War-lord Zeng-de to bring any of his own men who volunteer to go with him and fight with the river people. But they must agree of their own free will," she added, looking at Zeng-de sternly to impress the point. "I will send one thousand men back with you to reinforce the fortress and replace the men who choose to go with you. Understood?"

"Yes," Zeng-de said with a nod. It was far more than he had expected or even hoped for. If they got there in time.

The elders were not pleased but none of them dared say anything against the emperor's decision. Once she spoke all argument ceased.

"It will take several days to gather the replacements," Shizong said, "and repo-sition our forces so that Hongzhi is still well defended. You can leave as soon as all that is completed, Zeng-de."

"Thank you, Emperor Shizong," Zeng-de said, forcing back the argument that several days wait might make them arrive too late to be of any help. The emperor had given him a chance to help his friend as well as his own people. He would ask no more of her.

\*     \*     \*     \*

"On your feet," Manco snapped at yet another group of lounging warriors who had set up a rough hide lean to and were lying beneath it in the late after-noon sun. The men got to their feet and stood in front of the lean to in a ragged line.

"Take down this shelter and move to the edge of the plain," Manco ordered. "Find your captain and form up with your men."

Leruk walked up as the men began to take down their temporary shelter, mut-tering under their breath. He shook his head in disgust as the men gathered their weapons and packs and started moving north to where the army was forming at the edge of the valley. They would move out at first light the following morning.

"I hope the ten days of marching returns their spirit and discipline," he said.

"You think the celebration was unwise?" Manco asked.

"Feasting and celebration are for after the victory is won," Leruk answered, "not before the enemy is even in sight."

Manco looked at his brother appraisingly. It seemed he might not be a complete fool after all.

"But it makes the men love the Cuzco," he said. "I thought that was your philosophy, that the men will fight harder for a leader they love."

"Men will fight harder for a leader they respect," Leruk corrected. "A leader they know wouldn't ask them to do anything he wasn't willing to do himself."

"You think they don't respect the Cuzco?" Manco asked in surprise. It was unwise to speak that way of royalty. Even to your own brother.

"Respect is earned in battle," Leruk answered carefully. "The Cuzco hasn't had the chance to earn their respect yet."

What he wanted to say was that respect was earned in battle, not bought with food and wine. He wouldn't go that far, though. Not even with Manco.

"We will earn him his respect, then," Manco said. "We will defeat the enemy and bring him the glory he seeks."

"Yes, but it will be much more difficult than it should have been," Leruk said. "Because of my failure the enemy will be ready for us."

"Perhaps," Manco said. His anger at his brother's incompetence had faded over the last eight days as he'd watched Leruk's men retain at least some small amount of discipline and order during the celebration. Leruk had even gotten them to work with their weapons for a short time each day, something no captain other than Manco himself had been able to manage.

"It will make little difference," he continued. "We will win a great victory. The price we pay will be higher and the spoils earned fewer, but we will win a great victory. That's all that really matters."

They were quiet for a moment before Manco turned and faced his brother.

"I will know victory and live out my days in a city that bears my name," he said, "or I will spill my life out onto that battlefield. I will accept no other ending."

"I look forward to seeing that great city," Leruk said, not doubting for a minute that his brother meant every word. He knew it still rankled Manco that he and his men had been forced to retreat the last time they'd raided a river village. It would be victory or it would be death. And he doubted there was a man alive who could kill his brother.

"If the enemy meets us in force," Manco said as they continued walking, "we'll be forced to kill them. That will leave only the women and children to take captive. In the end, that may be for the best. Too many male slaves could become troublesome."

"True," Leruk said, impressed by his brother's insight. He hadn't thought of that. Large numbers of warrior slaves would be hard to control.

"We'll take their women and force them to bear our children," Manco said with obviously relish. "Their young boys we'll force to work in the mines and quarries until their strength is stripped away and their spirits broken. The young girls we'll find other uses for."

He smiled.

"Within a generation there will be no memory of the river people."

Leruk nodded. He didn't revel in the thought of killing off another people the way Manco did. But if that was the price of his people's greatness, he would do it, and gladly. The empire was what mattered.

Girak came trotting up to them.

"I think that's the last of them," he reported. "All of the others are either at the gathering point or on their way."

"Good," Leruk said. "Thank you, Girak. Have the men prepare a meal and set up a one man guard. We'll sleep in the open tonight. We'll have no time in the morning for breaking down shelters."

"I'll see to it," Girak said then turned and trotted after the last bunch of stragglers.

Manco nodded approvingly. He had already given the same orders for his men.

"We'll just have to wait for the rest of the men to break down their shelters," he said. The other captains would let their men sleep under cover unless the Cuzco himself ordered them not to, which he wouldn't.

"I know," Leruk said. "But I want to remind my men that even in the face of another's mistakes, they are to follow orders."

"A wise decision," Manco was forced to admit. "And have no fear, Leruk. The ten day march will restore the discipline of the others. As will the sight of the enemy. Not to mention the women to be won."

"Yes," Leruk agreed, "the march should sweat the food and wine out of them. And they're well trained. You've seen to that."

Manco nodded.

"They'll be ready when the time comes. And so will I."

\*       \*       \*       \*

Sandra Harvey swore as she tripped and almost fell for what seemed like the hundredth time since she'd started walking toward the cluster of buildings behind the wall. Demetrius Nestor had played her for a fool, leaving her on this waste hole planet even after she'd given in and slept with him. The bastard had promised to take care of her if she was "a good girl." Prick.

There was activity around the wall as she approached and a tall, muscular man dressed in nothing but a cloth around his middle, some sort of band on one arm and a disgusting necklace made out of bones from the look of it, stopped what he was doing and watched her curiously. He stared at her as she walked closer and broke out in a stupid grin when she got within twenty feet or so.

"Let me guess," he said, "you missed me so much you just couldn't stay away?"

What the hell was this half naked idiot babbling about? she thought. Then there was something about the smile and the eyes, especially the eyes, that made her catch her breath.

"Mitch?" she asked, looking in disbelief at the handsome man standing in front of her, his long, dark hair falling almost to his shoulders, sweat glistening on his tautly muscled chest and arms.

"The one and only," he said.

"Sandra?" another voice asked incredulously form her left.

"Alton!" she exclaimed. "What are you doing here?"

"Looking for my brother, you low life bitch. What the hell are you doing here?"

"I came looking for him, too," she lied instinctively, knowing he wouldn't believe it. There was something in the way he looked at her that told her he knew.

"You can save the bullshit, Sandra," Nathan Squires said, stepping past Alton and looking at her with disgust. "We know how Mitch got here and who paid for it."

She didn't know what to say. She was obviously in a good deal of trouble. But what were Alton and Nathan Squires doing here? If they came looking for Mitch they must have a ship. If they had a ship, why were they still here?

"What are you doing here, Sandra," Mitch asked.

She hesitated. Maybe there was a way she could make herself look like a victim.

"A black market thug, an awful man named Simon Bellotti, had me brought here when I refused to sleep with him," she said. "He tried to force himself on me and when I fought him, he had me brought here. I'm lucky to be alive, really."

Alton and Nathan Squires started laughing and Mitch had to smile.

"I think I like your gangster friend, Nate," he said, not believing Sandra's story for a minute. From what Alton and Nate had told him, Simon Bellotti was both rich and powerful. Not the kind of man Sandra would say no to. She would have been both willing and enthusiastic.

"I'm going to have to comp him at the SeaVista," Alton said. "That's a man who takes care of his friends."

The three men laughed while Sandra stood by looking furious and the river warriors looked on with curiosity.

"This is actually kind of convenient," Mitch said when he was able to stop laughing. "Nate, can you write up a divorce decree?"

"Sure, I've got a legal data pad on the ship."

"Good. Why don't you get one ready and then Sandra and I can sign it. I was planning on having you serve her when you got back anyway. This way I'll know it's done."

"I'm not signing anything," Sandra said defiantly. "Not unless there's a good amount of money transferred to my account."

"Oh, I think you'll sign it, Sandra," Mitch said with a cold smile. "And you'll never see another credit of my money. I don't like the things you spend it on."

"And just exactly why would I do that?" Sandra asked.

"Because if you don't, Alton will leave you here," Mitch said simply. "And if you do, he'll drop you somewhere where you can find a new sucker to sink your hooks into."

"You wouldn't leave me here," she said, trying to look helpless and pitiful. "You're not that cruel."

Mitch laughed again and her face turned red with anger.

"You don't know the first thing about me, Sandra," he said. "You never took the time. You can sign the divorce decree or you can stay here. Those are your choices."

His eyes were hard when he looked at her and Sandra knew he meant it. More than his body had changed since she'd last seen him.

"I'll sign," she said dejectedly. "But you have to drop me somewhere outside the Confederation. I don't want Simon Bellotti finding me."

"I'm sure you can find someplace, can't you, Alton?" Mitch asked.

"I'd rather throw her out an airlock on the way home," Alton said nastily. "She doesn't' deserve a second chance."

"No," Mitch said, "but I do. And having her officially out of my life seems like a pretty good start."

Alton nodded in agreement.

"Can't argue with you there," he said.

"Good," Mitch said as he punched his brother lightly on the arm. "Call Tommy and warn him not to let her onto the ship until we tell him to. She'd probably try to slit his throat and leave you two here."

"You sound as if you're not coming with us," Alton said with a questioning look.

"We'll talk later," Mitch said evasively. "I'll bring her into the village and see if they can find something for her to do."

He turned and walked away, motioning for Sandra to follow him.

"You look good," she said when they were out of earshot of the others.

"Don't expect any thank you's," Mitch said. "I damn near died my first day here."

"I wasn't looking for any thank you's, Mitch. I was just saying that you look good. I didn't recognize you at first with the long hair and all that muscle."

"That's funny," Mitch said. "I recognized you as soon as I saw you coming. Not too many women have a body like yours."

"They why do you want t a divorce?" she asked coyly, desperately trying to find a way out of her situation. Mitch had always had a weakness for her body. And it might even be fun now that he'd lost the flab. "You were a good lover before. I bet you're incredible now."

"Save it," Mitch said. "You never give up, do you?"

"I'm serious, Mitch," she said breathily. "I really want to make love to you." She quickened her step and ran her hand along his back. "These scars are kind of sexy."

Mitch stopped and turned to face her. She looked up at him and smiled, expecting a passionate kiss or at least an embrace. She got neither.

"I got those scars almost getting myself killed," he told her, wondering why he felt no real anger, "by a very big, very nasty animal that I should never have even known existed. But I met the big, nasty son of a bitch up close and personal because rather than try to be a wife to me, you paid someone to bring me here and leave me to die."

He looked into her soulless eyes and wondered how he could have been so blind and so stupid.

"I was a fool when I met you, Sandra," he said almost sadly. "I'm not a fool anymore. So keep your hands to yourself and save the sweet talk for someone who doesn't know what you are."

With that he turned and started walking again. After a minute, Sandra followed.

Wanchese was sitting with Dare and Anna beside Philips longhouse when she saw Mitchell walking into the village followed by a strikingly beautiful woman with the bright yellow hair that was so rare among the river people. Putting aside the cloth she'd been cutting into bandages, she stood to her feet and went to meet him.

"Hi," Mitch said uncomfortably when she reached him.

"Hello," she responded. "You're back early."

"I ran into a complication," he said, gesturing to the yellow haired woman. Then he looked Wanchese in the eye and stood a little straighter.

"Sandra," he said, "this is my wife, Wanchese."

The way he said it made Wanchese feel it was important to him that this woman know she was his wife.

"How do you do?" she asked politely.

"This is the woman I told you about," Mitch continued, "the one that had me brought here."

"Oh," Wanchese said in surprise. Then this woman was his wife also?

"She'll be leaving when Alton and Nathan do," Mitch said.

When Alton and Nathan do? Wanchese thought hopefully. Did that mean that Mitchell wasn't leaving?

"She'll stay in our camp?" she asked, hoping she wouldn't be.

"No," Mitch answered. "She can stay with Alton." His brother and Nate Squires had taken to sleeping on the ship. The nights were just too cold to be sleeping outside if you didn't have to.

"I'll see to her for you," Wanchese said, relieved.

"Are you sure?" Mitch asked. He really didn't want Sandra spending time with Wanchese.

"Of course. Go back to what you were doing. Dare and I will see to her."

"Alright," Mitch said, unable to think of a believable reason to refuse. "Thanks. I'll see you later then."

He reached out and touched her arm affectionately, hoping she wouldn't be offended enough to say something that would embarrass him. He wanted Sandra to think he was happily married. He wanted her to know that all her scheming had only brought him happiness.

"I'll be waiting," Wanchese said a little uncomfortably, confused by his affection but not wanting to show it in front of the yellow haired woman.

Mitch turned and left and Wanchese led Sandra to where Dare and Anna were looking at them curiously.

"This is Sandra," Wanchese said. "She is a newcomer who will be staying here until Mitchell's brother leaves. I told Mitchell we would keep her busy."

"Hello," Dare said with a nod of her head. "I am Dare Samuels and this is Anna Granganimeo."

"I'm Sandra Harvey," Sandra said, placing emphasis on the last name, "Mitch's wife."

"I see," Dare said though she didn't see at all. Mitchell had another wife? A newcomer?

"Mitchell doesn't seem to consider a wife," Wanchese said stiffly. "Perhaps you shouldn't introduce yourself as one."

"Well, we haven't seen each other for quite a while," Sandra said with a suggestive smile. "He'll come around." She wasn't divorced yet. There was still hope. Besides, she didn't like this snotty little one eyed bitch. Might as well make her wonder.

"Is your marriage even legal?" she asked. "I mean, with Mitch already being married and everything?"

"A man can have more than one wife," Wanchese answered. "He can also rid himself of them if he wants to." She didn't like this woman. She was beautiful, though. Perhaps that was how Mitchell had come to make the mistake of taking her as a wife. She remembered the young warriors who had suddenly found her full of wifely virtues once her young body had bloomed.

"How exactly did you and Mitch meet?" Sandra asked. Mitch hadn't really been here all that long. How could he have gotten himself married again already?

"He saved my life," Wanchese answered, then added proudly, "And I saved his in return."

"Oh," Sandra said, "you saved his life. So he married you out of a sense of gratitude, then, is that it?" Or maybe he felt bad for you because of your eye?"

"You would have to ask him," Wanchese said shortly, her face coloring with embarrassment and anger.

"I've seen the way Mitchell looks at her," Anna said in her friend's defense. "It's not gratitude or pity I see in his eyes."

Wanchese smiled at her young friend in thanks. She wished she could tell Anna and Dare the truth. But it shamed her too much. Mitchell might well have agreed to take her as a wife out of a sense of obligation or maybe even pity. She'd never thought of that. He was an unusual man, one she still found it difficult to understand completely.

"He's a good man and a good husband," she told Sandra. "It was foolish of you not to appreciate him." She would not accept this woman's insults. The fool had returned the love of a good man with treachery. She had no right to speak ill of anyone.

"Yes, you might be right," Sandra replied with a forced smile. "I hope he'll give me another chance. We can be so very good together," she said with a knowing smile, glad that her inferences to her and Mitch's past sex life seemed to cause the little cave girl such discomfort.

"How long have you been here?" Dare asked to change the subject, wanting to spare Wanchese any more pain. The girl had had enough of that in her life.

"Since this morning," Sandra answered. "I woke up over in that field and started walking this way when I saw smoke."

"Sit," Dare said, motioning to a space between herself and Anna. "We're making bandages for the coming battle."

"What battle?" Sandra asked, taking the seat offered her. The cave girl sat down across from her and started slicing thin white cloth into wide strips.

"Our enemy, the Inchasa, are going to attack," Dare said. "We're preparing bandages for the wounded."

"Oh," Sandra said, then shrugged and picked up a long piece of cloth. Anna handed her a small knife.

The four of them passed the morning cutting bandages, Dare answering Sandra's many questions while they worked, until the men began to return form their work loading arrows into the reed nets strung along the back side of the two defensive walls.

"It's almost mid-day," Wanchese said. "We'll stop now and wait for the worst of the heat to pass."

"What do we do until then?" Sandra asked.

"Rest and try to stay cool," Wanchese told her as Mitchell and Alton came into view followed by their friend Nathan who was talking with Virgil and Philip.

"I have to see to Secotan," Dare said. "I'll see you this afternoon."

Wanchese and Anna nodded and got to their feet as well. Anna smiled once at Wanchese and then went into her family's longhouse to get a cool drink. She was glad to get away from the newcomer woman. She had already decided she didn't like her and had a feeling that spending more time with her wouldn't change her opinion.

"You can come with us," Alton told Sandra as the men walked up to them, "if you don't mind being locked in a cabin. We're going back to the ship so Nate can get started on your paperwork."

"You don't have to lock me in a cabin, Alton," Sandra said. "I won't give you any trouble."

"I think I'll do it just the same," Alton replied, his voice hard. "I don't take chances with snakes."

Wanchese couldn't completely hide her smile.

# CHAPTER 30

▼

# ON THE MOVE

"Our forces will be divided into three separate prongs of advance," the Cuzco told his captains, who sat on the deep green carpet that covered the floor of his tent. His army was on the move and it was time for him to lay out his order of battle so that his captains could in turn lay it out for their men.

"The center force will be the main force and will consist of three thousand men broken into five detachments of six hundred men each. These will be commanded by: Sapa, Pitkel, Choque, Amaru and Quirau. The right hand prong will consist of one thousand men under the command of Manco with the left hand prong, consisting of the remaining nine hundred and seventy men, commanded by Leruk."

"The enemy will be massed and waiting for us. The two outside prongs will force the enemy to maintain a presence on each flank while our main body breaks through their center, dividing their forces and causing wide spread panic."

The Cuzco stopped and looked at each one of his captains to make sure they had all understood him. His battle plan was an inspiration from his visions and could only fail if his men didn't carry it out correctly. He would not have it fail because one of them was not intelligent enough to ask questions.

"Once that is accomplished," he continued when he was convinced everyone understood him thus far, "our main body will turn and destroy the enemy force placed between them and Leruk's force on the left. Once that group is subdued, we'll turn our attention to the force confronting Manco on the right.

"If we follow this plan exactly as I've laid it out for you, we will split the enemy forces right down the middle. That should cause enough fear and panic to allow us to still capture large numbers of slaves despite the enemy being aware of our coming."

"Questions?" he asked, looking around again to make sure his plan was understood.

"Your plan seems excellent, my Cuzco," Sapa, a tall man of medium build said, glad that his force would be part of the large hammer of victory while Manco and Leruk would be acting merely as a decoy. He'd never liked either of them.

"Wouldn't it be better to see the enemy's disposition before solidifying our plan of attack, my Cuzco?" Manco asked cautiously. He didn't want to offend the boy but he also had no desire to die for nothing. How could they prepare an order of battle for an enemy they hadn't even sighted yet?

"The enemy will be massed to meet us, Manco," The Cuzco said sharply. "That is all you need to know. Your continued lack of faith begins to concern me. Would you rather I give command of the right hand prong to someone else?"

"No, my Cuzco," Manco said, rage coloring his face and his teeth clenched against saying anything foolish. How dare this boy threaten to replace him after all he'd done to prepare the army for this battle? Did he have no sense at all? "That won't be necessary."

"We shall see," the Cuzco said, anger still evident in his voice. "Any other questions?"

There were none. If it wasn't safe for Manco to ask a question, it was even less so for the rest of them. Like him or not, he was the best of them and everyone knew it.

"Good," the Cuzco said. "What is the condition of my army, Sapa?"

"They do well, my Cuzco," Sapa answered in surprise. That was a question that would normally be asked of Manco. "Their spirits are high and they're anxious for battle."

The Cuzco nodded. He had expected as much.

"And our advance scouts?"

"They've traveled as far as the eighth supply shelter, my Cuzco," Sapa answered, grateful that Manco had briefed him and the other captains that morning, "and have had no contact with the enemy."

"None at all?" the boy asked. That seemed odd. Could the enemy truly be so incompetent as to let them come within striking distance unnoticed?

"None, my Cuzco," Sapa answered. "They have likely positioned men along the route of the final days march," he added, hoping to impress the Cuzco with his grasp of the enemy's thinking. "That would still give them enough time to position their forces before we arrive."

"Very well," the Cuzco said with a dismissive wave. "You have your orders. Each of you will be responsible for your own force for the rest of the march, with Sapa seeing to the assignment of each garrison as I've outlined. That will be all."

Each man stood and bowed to his king. Sapa bowed deepest of all. He had just supplanted Manco as the Cuzco's second in command.

*       *       *       *

Zeng-de paced anxiously at the head of his column outside the western reaches of Hongzhi. The last of the men he'd been waiting for had finally been outfitted and were moving across the city to meet up with him under the command of Ziaozong, the man who would be left in command of the fortress while Zeng-de was gone. Once these men arrived he could get underway. Time was growing short and he was afraid it might already be too late.

There would be fifteen hundred men making the journey to the fortress. The emperor had decided to send more reinforcements to protect against the unlikely event of the evil ones bearing south and attacking them. It was a wise precaution. Zeng-de was very impressed with the emperor.

He had spent a good deal of time with her while waiting for the necessary troops to arrive from deeper within the empire. She asked intelligent questions and showed a sharp mind for tactics as well as logistics. He had gotten the feeling that she understood the possible importance of the river people making a gesture of friendship, whatever their reasons.

Wu-zong, one of the replacement officers being sent to the fortress, walked to the head of the column and approached Zeng-de.

"Ziaozong has reached the marketplace," he reported. "He asks that we start moving out so he can form his men outside the city."

Zeng-de nodded curtly. Finally.

"Pass the word," he called loudly. "Move out!"

The order was called down the line and the column began to move. Zeng-de stepped off at a brisk pace. He would march these men hard. There would be plenty of time for them to rest when they reached the fortress. The column moved away from the city and was soon lost to sight as it moved down into a shallow valley that would take them to the Yaunzhang River, the first of two rivers they would have to cross on the way to the fortress. It was a wide but shallow river and would pose no problem for them. The second river, the Knizhou, was also wide and far deeper than the Yaunzhang. They would make that second, more treacherous crossing on the second day out from Hongzhi.

As the column moved down into the valley Wu-zong quickened his step and fell in beside Zeng-de.

"If one of your men at the fortress doesn't want to go with you, Warlord," he said, "I'd very much like to take his place."

"Why?" Zeng-de asked. Wu-zong was both young and inexperienced. He would have very little idea what he was volunteering for. And Zeng-de had no need for young glory hunters. Not even the son of an old and dear friend.

"Because you're going to need every man you can get if you hope to be of any help," the younger man answered. "And also because my father told me I would learn more in one battle with you than in twenty years of fortress duty."

Zeng-de smiled. He had fought with Wu-zong's father the last time the evil ones had attacked. Then it had been he who was young and inexperienced. Wu-zong's father, a gruff old veteran named Xi-zong, had shown him what he needed to know to keep himself alive. If Wu-zong became half the soldier his father had been he would do well.

"You could also die far from home," Zeng-de said. "With little chance of your body being brought home to be blessed by your family."

It was widely believed by their people that only a body blessed and consecrated by loved ones would be allowed to pass into the next life. Without the blessing, the soul would wander the afterlife aimlessly, unable to interact with those who had gone before him.

"Yes, I know," Wu-zong said. It was a chance he was willing to take.

"Has your father spoken to you of battle?"

"Yes. He's told me of the thrill and the fury and also of the fear and pain. I'd still like to go with you."

Zeng-de nodded.

"If one of my men declines you may come," he said. If Xi-zong thought his son was ready for battle, he was ready.

"Thank you," Wu-zong said. "I won't let you down."

Zeng-de nodded and quickened his pace. If they didn't get moving it wasn't going to matter who came with him. They had to hurry. He could feel it in his bones.

*    *    *    *

"What we discuss here today must go no further than these walls," Philip said solemnly to the members of the Grand Council. "Not even our wives can know what we speak of here. Do I have your word?" He looked at each man in turn and each one nodded his oath of silence. Philip hoped they meant it. The last thing they needed now was panic.

Nodding, he stood and went to the far end of the Central Longhouse. He came back followed by Virgil Crane. Philip took his seat and motioned for Virgil to sit beside him.

"Please tell everyone what you've told me, please, Virgil," Philip said.

"I've just returned from the camp of the enemy," Virgil told them. "What Mitchell Harvey and his woman say is true. I estimate there are close to five thousand warriors moving this way."

"Five thousand," Secotan breathed in despair. "You're absolutely certain?"

"I am," Virgil said. He'd gotten so close to the Inchasa camp that one of their warriors had almost tripped over him as he made his way out into the tall grass to relieve himself. Virgil knew what he'd seen.

"How many do we have?" Secotan asked.

"Twenty-four hundred and eighty one," Elan White supplied. "That includes the three hundred or so newly trained warriors."

"Newly trained boys, you mean," Secotan said.

"Were we any older when we first saw battle?" Manteo Hatarask asked.

"No," Secotan admitted. "But we weren't facing nearly five thousand enemy warriors either. We'll have to disperse the untried warriors evenly amongst us and keep them close to experienced men."

"Yes," Philip said with a nod, "that makes sense. We can see to that without too much trouble, I think. Have you all considered the battle plan Secotan and I have proposed?"

The other Councillors nodded that they had.

"It seems as good a plan as any," Ananias Dare said. "I only wish we had more men to put it into action."

"So do I," Philip said. "Unfortunately, that isn't going to happen. So here is what Secotan and I have in mind. My men will man the very center of our line behind the first wall. Secotan and his men will be responsible for the left flank, Manteo the right. Ananias and his men will be held in reserve to attack with the lance after the enemy has forced his way past the first wall. Elan and his men will then strike from behind the second wall before coming over the wall and engaging the enemy hand to hand."

"Wouldn't it be better to have all our men firing on the enemy from behind the first wall?" Elan asked. "We can always have them retreat behind the second wall once the enemy starts to over run the first."

"We could do that," Philip said. "But it's imperative that they retreat behind the wall before engaging the enemy. We want to be able to strike with fresh warriors just when the enemy thinks he has us beaten. We're hoping the surprise of being faced with a second wall will weaken their resolve and give us a chance to encircle them."

Elan nodded his acceptance of that.

"We can have them retreat as soon as the enemy reaches the first wall, then," he said. "But I think it would be a mistake not to have every available archer attacking them while they're out in the open."

"We hadn't thought of that," Secotan admitted. "I like the idea now that I've heard it, though. What do you think, Philip?"

"I'd have to agree. We should practice the retreat several times, though. It's vital that we have men behind that second wall when the enemy breaches the first."

"We'll practice it," Elan said. "What about the ancient crossbow?"

There remained in Philip's village one of the ancient six foot long crossbows built by their ancestors. It was thought of as a sacred relic more than as a useful weapon, but it could serve them well in the coming battle. It had a range nearly one hundred feet further than traditional hand held bows.

"Virgil will man the ancient bow at the very center of the first wall," Philip answered.

"Is that wise?" Manteo asked. "It could fall into the hands of the enemy."

"If we lose this fight, Manteo," Secotan replied, "we'll all fall into the hands of the enemy. We'll just have to risk the bow."

"True," Manteo said. "I suppose we need to keep that in mind as we make all our decisions. What about your families?" he asked the three men who had decided to keep their women and children with them.

"We're going to send them across the river," Philip answered without conviction, "along with all the dugouts. If we're defeated, the Inchasa won't be able to cross the river very quickly. The women and children will try to escape to the south."

He looked at the hopeless expressions of the other men. There was little chance of any of them escaping. They'd either be captured or die of thirst in the short grassed hills on the other side of the river.

"It's the best we can do," Philip said apologetically.

"Then we had better not lose this fight," Secotan said. He couldn't bear the thought of his wives and children being raped and brutalized by the Inchasa. There would be no surrender for him. He was determined to fight to the death.

"There is something else," Philip said, looking at Secotan uncomfortably. "Hunter Kane has renewed his efforts to have you removed as Councillor, Secotan. I doubt he'll have any success but I'm afraid of what might happen if you're killed in the battle."

"Forgive us for speaking of such a thing," Ananias broke in. "I pray with all my heart that no harm comes to you. We only wanted you to be warned. There are some who are unhappy with your decision to bring your families here, so he has gained some small support."

"You don't need to apologize," Secotan told him. He had come to terms with the possibility of his own death. He'd known a great deal of happiness in his life. And he had known about Hunter Kane's efforts for several days.

"You're afraid Kane will have the support to become Councillor if I'm killed?" he asked.

"Yes," Philip answered. "And I can't think of anyone less suited for the position. His anger too often controls his thinking."

"True," Ananias said. "And he has shown himself to be more interested in his own desires than what is best for the people of his village. What the fool tried to do to young Wanchese is proof enough of that. What can we do?"

"I'll speak to Mother Shaw," Secotan said, "and have her begin to quietly gather support for Geris or Nathaniel as a replacement should I be killed."

"That could be dangerous to your position if you survive," Ananias warned. He both loved and respected his niece's husband. He was a good man and a good Councillor. His village needed him.

"That's a chance I'll have to take," Secotan said. "I'd rather lose the position to someone like Geris than risk having someone like Kane gain power. I'll speak to Mother Shaw."

"How do we deal with Kane?" Elan asked.

"We don't deal with him at all," Secotan answered. "He's within his rights to seek my position. The fact that he's chosen to do so secretly will only hurt his cause."

"Very well," Philip said. "If that's all?" He looked around the circle of men to see if there was anything else they needed to discuss.

"May I speak?" Virgil Crane asked hesitantly. He knew he didn't belong here with these men. But he knew wrong from right.

"Of course," Philip said.

"You're wrong to keep the full truth of what we're facing from our people," Virgil said, hoping they would forgive him for overstepping his bounds. "They'll be more frightened by the sight of so many warriors coming against them if they aren't prepared for it. You should be honest with them and trust in their courage."

There was a long moment of silence as the Councillors thought that over.

"We're just trying to spare the women and children the fear of knowing what we face," Philip said. "But you're probably right, Virgil. Sometimes I forget just how much courage our women possess."

"Yes," Manteo said. "And it's possible that the sight of so many enemy warriors facing us could cause even worse panic if our people are unprepared for the sight."

"Alright," Philip said. "We'll tell our people what we're facing. Thank you, Virgil."

"I'll tell my wife, Leta," Ananias said with a smile. "By morning everyone in the village will know." Leta was the recognized gossip queen of the river villages.

The other men laughed briefly. Then a heavy silence fell over them as they thought of what the coming days might bring. They had done all they knew to do and were as ready as they could be. Now they could only pray it was enough.

# CHAPTER 31

▼

# RAVEN'S TEST

Wanchese moved around the small camp below the cliff keeping her hands, and thus her mind, busy taking care of small chores that needed to be done, though they could have waited until morning. Mitchell had been gone for over three hours. He had gone across the river to see Alton, Nathan, Tommy and "her", as she had come to think of Sandra Harvey.

The woman had been making a nuisance of herself since arriving three days earlier, spending as much time as she could arrange to with Mitchell, even going so far as to show up uninvited for meals and the mid-day break.

Mitchell was entirely too tolerant of the woman and Wanchese had begun to wonder if she had been able to fool him into accepting her again. There had been no outward signs that that was the case, but there hadn't been any outward signs of rejection either. She was only worried about Mitchell. He was her friend, after all.

The bushes on the eastern side of the camp, the side facing the river, rustled and she turned to face the sound, drawing her knife as she turned. She'd seen Hunter Kane watching her more than once and she was determined not to be taken by surprise again. She relaxed and put her knife away. It was Mitchell.

"Hi," he said wearily as he threw his pack to the ground and leaned his staff against the cliff. "Sorry I'm so late."

"You don't have to apologize," she said, not meaning a word of it. That was one of the things she admired about him. He was considerate of her.

Mitch dropped to the ground beside the fire and wrapped himself in his cloak.

"Is this more of that tea?" he asked hopefully, gesturing at a small pot boiling beside the fire. It seemed even colder than usual tonight. And that was saying something.

"Yes," she answered and he poured himself some.

"You want some?" he asked. She seemed colder than usual lately, too. He hoped they weren't going back to that again.

"Yes, thank you."

He poured her a cup and she sat down across the fire from him.

"How do people get divorced here?" he asked, deciding he might as well tell her this and get it out of the way. "They just take off the marriage bands?"

"Yes," Wanchese said stiffly. So, the woman *had* gotten to him again. So be it! She didn't need him anyway. It just would have been easier for her if they had stayed married until she could go back to the mountains. "Some people also burn the marriage bands."

"Where I come from," Mitch told her, "you have to say in writing that you don't want to be married anymore. That's what I was doing on Alton's ship. I had to sign the papers saying I didn't want to be married to Sandra anymore."

"Oh," Wanchese said, feeling as though a great weight had just been lifted off her shoulders. "She is no longer your wife, then?"

"She never really was," Mitch said. "Not in her heart. That's more important even than the piece of paper as far as I'm concerned." The whole process had brought back the memories of how foolish he'd been and what an ass he must have looked like to his family and friends. He was glad to have it over and done with.

"She signed her name to this paper also?"

"Yeah. She had to or else Alton would have left her here when he leaves."

"You say that as if you're not going with him," she said, trying to sound uninterested.

"I'm not. And I don't know how I'm going to tell Alton. He went to so much trouble to find me. I feel like I'm letting him down."

"Then why are you staying?" she asked, thinking she already knew the answer. And she did.

"Because, as crazy as it sounds, I'm happier here than I've ever been in my life. I feel like I'm alive and that even if I die tomorrow I will have lived more in the months I've been here than I did in my entire life back where I came from."

"The warrior life suits you," Wanchese said with a nod of understanding. "That isn't so surprising."

"I don't think Alton will be so understanding," Mitch said with a sad smile. "Or my parents. I can't go back, though. Not for them. If I did, I'd just be miserable."

"Your brother would want you to be happy," she said. "Perhaps you underestimate him."

"Maybe," Mitch said. "It wouldn't be the first time."

"Life is much different where you come from? Wanchese asked. "You have many machines like the one that flies?"

Mitch nodded.

"We have all kinds of machines that do all kinds of different jobs. Maybe we have too many machines. I had almost forgotten what it was to be cold or hungry before I came here. I think that takes away some of the joy of being warm and full."

Wanchese nodded but didn't say anything. Her trip on the flying machine was something she would never forget. The feelings were so overwhelmingly new and exciting. She wondered if Mitchell would miss such things in time if he stayed here.

"I wanted to thank you," he said, "for not threatening to slit my throat or anything when I touched you in front of Sandra." He looked embarrassed. "I wanted her to leave here thinking that I was...that we were...well...I wanted her to know that what she'd done had only brought me happiness. I wanted her to know that she'd lost, that all her plotting and scheming had only helped me."

"I understand. And you're welcome. I wanted her to believe we were happy, too. There is something about her that makes me dislike her very much."

"Join the club," Mitch laughed. "You should see how Alton's been treating her. I think that's why she's been spending so much time out here with us. She couldn't stand Alton anymore."

"She said she hoped to change your mind about ending your marriage to her."

"She tried," Mitch said. And she had. She'd done everything but take off her clothes and spread her legs. And she probably would have tried that if the opportunity had presented itself. She was really pretty pathetic now that he was looking at her with two eyes instead of one.

"Why?" Wanchese asked. "If she doesn't love you, why would she want to be married to you? Especially if you plan to stay here?"

"Well," he said, "it's kind of complicated. Probably the best way I can explain it is that where I come from I have a very nice longhouse, full of machines that make life easier and more comfortable. I also have enough wealth to get all the food, water and clothing a person might need. Sandra thinks that if she were still my wife all those things would belong to her if I stayed here. She wants them, not me."

Wanchese nodded her understanding. Sandra Harvey was a fool. She felt a little foolish herself now for having thought Mitchell could have been tricked by such a woman again. He wasn't a man to be taken advantage of twice.

"She has none of those things of her own?" she asked.

"No, not anymore. I left her with a good deal of wealth but she spent it all to have me brought here. She thought she'd be able to spend mine when her own was gone."

"She couldn't?"

"No," Mitch said with a smile. "I was already planning to divorce her even before she had me brought here. So I had made arrangements that kept her from being able to get her hands on my money, my wealth, without my permission."

"Is that why she came looking for you? To get your permission to spend your wealth?"

"She didn't come here looking for me. She was brought here against her will just like I was. I'm not sure why and I don't really care. I'm just glad she showed up so I could get her signature on the divorce decree." Signature and right thumb print actually, but why make things more complicated than they already were.

"Now I know it's done," he said with a satisfied smile. "I feel better knowing."

"What will become of her when she goes back?" Wanchese asked, wondering why she cared. But after all that had happened to her, she couldn't wish for any woman to be helpless, not even Sandra Harvey.

"She'll find another man to take care of her, I expect. Some of us men aren't all that smart," he said with a smile. "You might have noticed that."

"The evidence is all around me every day," she replied with a smile of her own. "I would have to be blind in both eyes not to see it."

Mitch laughed and was glad to see her smile. Whatever had been bothering her seemed to have passed. Then a shadow seemed to come over her face and her hand went first to her patch and then to the marriage band, and whatever thought it was that had crossed her mind brought back with it her distant coolness. She stood up and walked away from the fire. She barely spoke to him as they got ready to get some sleep and he fell asleep wondering what he'd done wrong.

She was already gone when he woke up which was unusual, though she had left his breakfast warming on the fire. He did his morning meditation, ate quickly, washed his bowl out and headed into the village to meet Philip and Secotan. They were going to check on the young warriors being trained by Kane to try to get an idea of just how much help they'd be.

He found them standing to the side of an open patch of grass where Hunter Kane was working with a group of thirty young warriors. Their training was nearly complete and Kane was having his students face each other in pairs with wooden swords. He would call two names and the students called would step into the loose circle formed by their fellow students and thrust and parry with the bulky, awkward weapons. The first to land three clean strikes was declared the winner.

Mitch saw that Raven Howe was one of the thirty and waited anxiously for his name to be called. Kane saved him for the last pair, pitting him against his best student, a tall, strongly made young warrior named Geah Winn. Once Geah made a fool of Howe in front of Philip and Secotan they'd have no choice but to let him discharge the clumsy boy from his class.

Geah and Raven picked up the wooden swords and faced each other, circling warily, their swords held in front of them in a two handed grip. Winn lashed out with the quickness of a striking snake but Raven Howe was ready for him. He'd watched Geah fight others during the past several weeks when Hunter Kane had refused to let him test himself against the other students. With so much time to watch the others he'd done his best to memorize each student's favorite strikes and blocks, just a Mitchell had told him to.

As Geah's sword slashed the air where he had been only a second before, Raven completed his perfectly timed step to the left and thrust a clean strike into Winn's exposed belly.

Surprised, Winn turned and attacked angrily, his dull weapon slashing through the air aggressively and forcing Raven back. But each strike met only empty air or Raven's sword as the once clumsy boy moved fluidly left and right, forward and back, always on balance and prepared for what Winn threw at him.

After a long, unsuccessful attack, Winn withdrew, too winded to continue pressing. Now Raven stepped to the attack and in his eagerness left his right side open. Winn's sword thrust out quickly, striking weakly against Raven's ribs.

The two broke apart then and circled carefully, each now aware that the other was capable of taking advantage of his mistakes. Then Raven saw Geah's left knee drop as he set himself to step forward and thrust, and without consciously thinking about it, his response having been ingrained in him by hours of thrust and parry work with his mentor, stepped to the side and slid his blade underneath Winn's thrust, scoring a clean hit on the other boy's chest.

Geah spat angrily and kicked that ground. He had never lost one of these matches and had rarely even been scored on. To lose to Raven Howe would be a disgrace. And he didn't even want to think about what Hunter Kane would do to him if he embarrassed him in front of Philip, Secotan and the stranger.

He decided to try his favorite move, one he'd practiced so often that he could do it without thought. Stepping back and to the right, he set up the proper distance then feinted a strike to the head to bring his opponent's sword up and which he planned to follow with a quick drop to one knee and a slash across Raven Howe's midsection. He never got there.

Even before his knee had hit the ground he felt Raven's blade knock his own aside and strike him solidly in the chest. Stunned, he threw his sword to the ground in disgust and roughly pushed his way through his fellow students, muttering angrily, his face colored with shame. How could he have lost to Raven Howe?

Raven, filled with pride and excitement, turned to look at Mitchell Harvey, his face beaming. Mitch returned his smile and gave him an approving nod that filled Raven with more pride than he'd ever felt in his young life. Seeing the exchange, Hunter Kane decided there must be some connection between Raven Howe's sudden improvement and the newcomer. Enraged that anyone would dare interfere with one of his students, he picked up the sword Geah Winn had thrown to the ground.

"What are you grinning about?" he bellowed at the boy. "You leave yourself open at every move. Don't think that you're ready to go into battle just because an incompetent boy like Geah Winn can't take advantage of your clumsiness. Stand ready. We'll see how you fare against a man."

Kane held his sword in a two handed grip and moved it through the air swiftly and smoothly. His eyes hard and an ugly smile on his lips, he feinted to his left and when Raven stepped to his own left as he'd known he would, he knocked the boy's blade aside with his own and landed a powerful thrust to the ribs.

Yelping with surprise and pain, Raven dropped his sword and clutched at his ribs with both hands, his face twisted with pain.

"Pick up your sword!" Kane screamed at him. "A warrior drops his weapon only when his arm itself falls to the ground! Do you think the Inchasa will give you time to pick up your sword, boy?" Turning, he smiled wickedly at Mitchell Harvey. Let the fool see what happened when he interfered in things that are none of his concern.

"Please, restrain yourself," Philip said, placing a staying hand on Mitch's arm. "There is no time for conflict amongst ourselves."

"Stop him, then," Mitch said through clenched teeth. "He's trying to hurt that boy."

"Warriors get hurt," Secotan said calmly. "Raven Howe wants to be a warrior. Better he learn this lesson now with wooden swords than later when an Inchasa plunges steel into his belly."

The wisdom of that got through his rage and Mitch forced himself to relax as Raven picked up his sword and turned to face the smiling Kane. Kane whirled his sword through the air and stabbed mockingly at the boy, laughing as he did it. There was cruelty in his eyes and an odd smile on his face. Raven did his best to ignore the laughter and the taunts, determined not to let Kane make a fool of him. He would not drop his sword again no matter what happened.

He braced himself for the pain he knew was coming and suddenly attacked. Kane easily blocked his strikes and let out another laugh. Raven ignored him and attacked again, this time trying to feint low and then strike high. His sword met only empty air and more laughter.

But the laughter stopped short as Raven, his sword never stopping, stepped immediately to his right and swung a waist high strike that Kane just barely managed to block. There were murmurs of surprise among the other students. Raven Howe had almost landed a strike against Hunter Kane!

Hearing them, Kane's eyes grew hard and he slashed a thunderous blow at Raven's sword. The boy hung on despite the shuddering pain that went through his hands and up his arms. He was on the verge of congratulating himself for having held on when Kane struck down on the back of his neck and everything went dark, a streak of terrible pain shooting all the way down his back the last thing he felt before dropping into unconsciousness.

"Enough!" Secotan cried, moving towards Kane with the fluid motion of a cat. "There's no need to injure the boy!"

"*I* will decide what is needed here," Kane spat back. "They are my students and I will train them my way."

The two men came together and stood face to face and Mitch was sure there was going to be violence. But Philip stepped between the two and pushed them apart.

"You will not strike one of these boys again, Hunter Kane," he said. "Your task is to prepare them for battle, not belittle and injure them. Do you understand me?"

It was a long moment before Kane answered and Mitch could see the struggle going on inside him. He desperately wanted to defy Philip's order but he also desperately wanted to avoid the dishonor of being removed from his position. If he was going to be Councillor he had to avoid that.

"I understand," he said finally. "But hear this," he continued, looking first at Secotan and then a Mitch. "When this battle is over I will seek out my enemies and destroy them." He turned on his heel and stalked away, his students nervously stepping out of his way, opening a path for him.

Mitch bent down and picked up Raven Howe.

"I'll bring him to Wanchese," he said.

Secotan picked up Mitch's staff and walked with him. Philip followed a short distance behind, wondering if he'd acted wisely. It might have been better for him to let Mitchell or Secotan kill Kane. And it would be a fight to the death if ever they came to blows, he had no doubts about that. The problem was he wasn't at all sure that either of them could kill Kane. For all his other faults, Hunter Kane was a dangerous warrior. If only he had as much sense as he did strength and ferocity.

"I'll bring him to our camp," Mitch said as they entered the village. "Could one of you send Wanchese? She's with Dare and Anna."

"I'll get her," Philip said and headed off toward his own longhouse. Mitch and Secotan continued on through the village and to the camp beneath the cliff. Wanchese came quickly.

"Get my pack," she ordered as she bent over the boy, who was now conscious and in pain. Mitch brought it and put it down beside her.

"Sit still!" she snapped at the squirming boy as she examined him quickly for any broken bones. She found none, though several of his ribs and the back of his neck were tender to the touch. She rubbed some of her healing ointment on his cuts and bruises and told him to lie still.

"He'll be fine," she told the concerned men. "He'll be sore for several days but it shouldn't last long. He's young and will heal quickly."

"I'll be ready for the battle," Raven said intensely. "Please let me fight, Philip. I'll be ready." He couldn't let himself be left out of this fight. He'd never be free of the shame if they didn't let him fight.

"I'll fight beside you proudly, Raven," Philip said. "Now, rest. And do whatever Wanchese tells you to."

"I will," Raven replied, tears of joy running down his cheeks. He could fight!

Just then the boy's mother and father came rushing into the camp.

"Raven!" his mother cried and ran to him. "Are you alright?"

"I'm fine," the boy answered, embarrassed to be treated like a child in front of the warriors in the camp. "It's nothing."

"It doesn't look like nothing," she told him. "Look at these bruises."

"What happened?" the boy's father asked coldly. He wouldn't stand for his son being abused. Someone would pay for what they'd done.

"I learned that I still have a lot to learn," Raven said before anyone else could answer. "And that I can never leave my opponent even the smallest opening. It's a lesson I won't soon forget, father. But that's all it was, a lesson I needed to learn."

Mitch had to smile. The kid was a fighter. And he had courage.

"You're a fast learner," he said. "It took me a broken jaw and three cracked ribs to learn that lesson."

Raven smiled. His teacher's opinion meant everything to him.

"Can I take him home?" his mother asked.

"Of course," Wanchese said. "Take this salve and spread it on his bruises each morning and at night before he goes to sleep." She handed the thick middled older woman a small earthen jar.

"Thank you," the woman said, taking the jar and then helping her son to his feet. Secotan and Philip went with the boy and his parents back to the main village, wanting to make sure the boy's father didn't try to confront Kane. There was no time. Not now.

"He's a good kid," Mitch said after they'd left. "And a quick learner. He almost had Kane there for a second."

"He's come a long way thanks to you," Wanchese told him.

"I just showed him what Zeng-de taught me," Mitch said. "I hope it's enough to keep him alive."

"Who broke your jaw and cracked your ribs?"

"Another student who was learning from my friend back home," Mitch answered, smiling at the memory of his cockiness and the valuable lesson he'd learned. "He looked like a harmless old man and I made the mistake of deciding I should go easy on him. He didn't mean to break my jaw. I stepped right into a punch by accident. The ribs I'm pretty sure he meant, though. My attitude seemed to offend him."

"And you learned from it?"

"Hell yes," Mitch said with a nod. "I learned a lot. Like not to judge people by looks and that taking anyone lightly can be painful. Now I assume that the person I'm facing is better than I am and deserves my best effort. That way I don't get any unpleasant surprises."

"You think Raven learned that today?"

"I don't think Raven has any problems with being overconfident. What he learned today was that any opening, even the smallest, briefest second of lost concentration can get you hurt."

Wanchese nodded.

"It was Hunter Kane who hurt him?" she asked.

"Yes. I think he saw Raven smile at me after he'd won his sparring session and made the connection between Raven's improvement and my sudden interest. He took his anger out on Raven."

"You will have trouble with him," Wanchese said, finally voicing what she'd known since the two of them had arrived at Secotan's village. "He'll hate you for many reasons now."

"I know," Mitch said, unconcerned. It would happen when it happened and his worrying about it now would only distract him from what needed to be done. He'd probably die in the battle anyway. That was why he'd asked Alton to take Wanchese back to the mountains if he was killed and Kane survived. He needed to know she'd be alright.

"Are you sorry we stayed?" he asked, wondering if she would have been happier going back to the mountains right away. Maybe he'd been selfish in wanting to stay.

"No, I'm glad we stayed. I've enjoyed spending time with Dare and Anna." It was nice to have friends. And to be treated with respect. Even if it was only because of who she was married to.

The story of how Mitchell had gotten the horrible scars on his back had quickly made its way through the camps and longhouses of the gathered villagers and he was looked on with curiosity and respect. She shared in that respect by virtue of their marriage. It had taken several days for her to get used to the polite greetings she received as she went about her daily business. And even longer to adjust to her stature as something of a hero to many of the young women who had long found the yoke of the old traditions hard to bear and who saw her as the reason at least some of them had been given freedom from that burden. What the men thought of her she could only guess.

"When the battle is over, what will you do?" she asked.

"I need to go back to the mountains and make Zeng-de a staff like mine. Then I'll bring it to him. After that, I don't really know."

"I would like to see Nang-de again," Wanchese said. "I was just beginning to understand her speech when we had to leave."

"We can go together, then," Mitch said quickly. He tried not to think about what Wanchese would want to do once this was all over but it was always there nagging at the back of his mind. He'd come to enjoy her company more than he would ever have imagined he could enjoy the company of a woman he wasn't having a sexual relationship with. He was hoping they could keep traveling as friends. It would be better than nothing.

"And on the way," he added, "I could teach you more of their language."

"I'd like that," she said.

Then her eyes grew narrow and hard as she stared past him and she drew her knife. He turned to see Hunter Kane standing at the edge of their camp.

"You are a fool," he said to Mitch. "The children's tricks you taught that boy will only get him killed."

"Then he'll die as a warrior," Mitch said, taking a step forward and a little to his left, placing himself between Kane and Wanchese. "He deserves that chance."

"I'm not interested in what you think he deserves," Kane said. "You should not have interfered."

He stepped to his right so he could look at Wanchese.

"If he lives through the coming fight," he told her, pointing at Mitch, "I'll kill him right in front of you. Then I'll make you wish I'd killed you too."

He smiled at her tauntingly.

"Why wait?" Mitch asked, stepping closer, his staff gripped in both hands, his heart filled with a burning desire to kill a man for the first time in his life. Always before he'd killed out of a sense of self-preservation. That he could feel the intense desire to kill a man simply for the satisfaction of watching him die frightened him. What kind of man was he becoming?

"Because you're not worth the trouble killing you now would cause me," Kane answered. "Your friends are in power now. They won't be for much longer. I'll deal with you then."

He turned and stepped back into the brush, leaving Mitch to fight the urge to follow him and end things now. Only the promise he'd made to Philip stopped him.

"It will give me great pleasure to watch you kill him," Wanchese said coldly.

"It will give me great pleasure to do it," Mitch said, ashamed that he meant every word. He'd never known real hatred before and it made him uncomfortable to feel it now.

They passed the rest of the day in camp, with Alton, Nathan and Sandra coming to see them right after the mid-day heat, spending the afternoon and eating the evening meal with them before heading back across the river for the night.

When night came and it was time to go to sleep, Mitch found himself unable to quiet his mind, his spirit wrestling with the morality of this sudden desire to take a life. It was only after Wanchese unknowingly rolled over in her sleep and rested her head on his chest that he was able to put his doubts aside and push them from his mind.

He lay that way for a long time, just enjoying the sensation of her closeness, the feminine smell of her, the soothing rhythm of her breathing. When next he opened his eyes it was morning and Wanchese was already up and moving around the camp getting the fire built up again.

He watched her for several minutes, wondering if she knew she'd spent part of the night in his arms. Obviously not, he decided. Otherwise he would have woken up with a knife at his throat. Then he sat up and started putting his moccasins on. They were going to need more firewood.

# CHAPTER 32

▼

# DRAWING CLOSER

Capac was disappointed to see that the long march was returning the strength and discipline to the Inchasa army. The high spirits and disorganized merriment of the first two days of the march had slowly given way to an air of quiet confidence and determination. None of the Inchasa warriors had forgotten the Cuzco's promises. Each one silently promised himself he would do great things in this battle, that he would come out of this fight draped in glory and live out his days in a city bearing his name.

"I'd like to walk a little now, Noref," Capac said.

"Alright," Noref answered. Then she stopped and lowered the litter to the ground. The Cuzco had decided that since Capac would never be able to walk the entire distance to the river village, he would have to travel on a litter most of the way. And since it would be the most degrading and embarrassing for Capac, the Cuzco had also decided that the litter would be a travois pulled not by a beast of burden or strong male slaves, but rather by Noref, Capac's woman.

"I'm sorry," Capac said for the hundredth time. "You must be exhausted."

"I'm fine," Noref said as she helped him to his feet. "Are you sure you want to walk?"

Capac nodded. He'd been walking a little more each day and had lost most of his limp. It was still painful and he had a long way to go before the scar tissue would be broken up enough for him to walk normally, but he was getting closer.

What bothered him more than the pain in his feet was the fact that Noref was with him. He had begged her to stay behind and go with the others to the island but she had refused. He had even risked a meeting with Javet to ask him to talk to her. But the old priest had told him that Noref was destined to travel with him and there was nothing anyone could do to change that. The Cuzco's decision that she would pull the litter had proven Javet correct. After that there was no way for Noref to slip away with the others.

And now she was here and there was nothing Capac could do to protect her. When the battle was over and messengers were sent to Pachacutec with the news, word would reach the Cuzco that the Lydacians had all disappeared and every single Lydacian traveling with the army would be tortured for information and then killed. Capac hoped that when the time came he would be strong enough to kill Noref before Manco got his hands on her.

It would have been much simpler if she had escaped with the others. Then he would have been free to carry out his plan. He would have waited until the moment of the Cuzco's greatest triumph, shown him what had been written in his precious Inchasa book describing his greatness in awe inspiring detail, and then thrown the book into one of the camps fires right in front of him. After that he could have died happily, having taken at least some small measure of revenge. But there was no way he could do that with Noref around to bear the brunt of the boy's anger.

"Take your time," Noref cautioned as she picked up the handles of the empty litter and hurried to catch up with him.

They were walking near the front of the long column along with the other servants and slaves. Behind them came the Cuzco's personal guards, now commanded by Sapa, then the main army and finally a small detachment herding the paccar cows that would provide the Cuzco and his captains fresh meat on the march.

"I'm alright," Capac told her. "It's almost time to stop for the night anyway. I can keep up this pace till then."

"Alright," Noref said, impressed with how much better he was moving now. But she was afraid he was pushing himself too hard. He was obsessed with the idea of walking normally again. She could understand that. Why he was so determined to do it before they reached the river village was still a mystery, though. Why the rush?

"Would you like some water?" she asked.

"No. I'll wait until we stop."

They walked on in silence for several minutes while Noref considered the best way to approach him with her concerns.

"Capac, what are you afraid of?" she asked, knowing that while he might keep something from her he wouldn't lie to her when asked a direct question. "What's going to happen when we reach the river village?"

"Nothing is going to happen when we reach the river village," he answered sadly, looking at her with sorrowful eyes that made her want to reach out and comfort him, something he would never allow out in public view. "It's what will happen after the battle is won that worries me. They'll send someone to Pachacutec with news of their victory."

"And when the messenger comes back," Noref said, now understanding, "he'll bring news of our people's escape. What will they do to us?"

"What do you think? They'll torture each and every one of us until someone tells them where our people have gone. Then they'll kill us. That's why I didn't want you to come, Noref. This can only end one way for us."

"That's why you're so determined to walk," she said with sudden insight. "You want to try and escape, to save me. That's it, isn't it?"

He nodded. If only he thought they had a chance. But where could they go that the Inchasa couldn't find them?

"There might be a chance for us to escape during the battle," he said. "It will probably be some time before they notice we're missing. They'll be celebrating their victory and might not even notice we're gone until the next morning."

That wasn't really true, though, was it? The first thing the Cuzco would want to do when the battle was over was to see that it was all written down in the book. And that meant having Capac write it. They would know he was gone and they would come after them.

"Why didn't you mention this?" she asked.

"I wanted to wait until we saw what the area around the river village is like. There has to be somewhere for us to escape to for us to have a chance, some kind of concealment, someplace to hide. I didn't want to get your hopes up. It might not be possible."

"It will be possible," Noref said confidently. "You'll find a way."

Capac smiled. If only he had as much confidence in himself.

"I hope you're right," he said as the advance scouts came into sight up ahead, gathered in front of the sixth storage shelter. "I really hope you're right."

The column reached the shelter a little more than an hour before darkness fell and quickly set to work gathering wood and getting fires started. Capac and Noref made their camp as far away from the others as the roving Inchasa guards would allow and settled down to eat a sparse mean of bread and thin stew beside the fire.

"I'm tired," Capac said when he was finished eating. "I can't imagine how you must feel."

"I'm tired, too," Noref admitted. "I'll get the bed ready."

Capac cleaned their utensils and banked the fire for the night while Noref prepared a soft bed on top of some trampled grass. They went to bed and quickly slipped into an exhausted sleep. Several hours later Capac awoke with a start, feeling his head beginning to swim as a vision came over him, the reality of his surroundings slipping away, chased from his consciousness by the powerful onslaught of his vision.

He saw himself standing in the middle of a wide open plain of green grass with nothing around him for as far as the eye could see. Then, suddenly, the man-huascar reared up out of nowhere to stand before him, looking down at him with its terrifying red-rimmed eyes.

"What do you want from me?" he heard himself ask in Lydacian.

"To hear what you have to tell me," the beast answered in the river language.

"If I tell you you'll kill me," Capac heard himself say.

The beast laughed then, turning its fang filled maw up to he sky. Then it turned its eyes on him again and pointed back behind where Capac was standing.

"It is you who wished to kill me," the beast said and Capac saw himself turn to see the entire Inchasa army coming toward them.

"I didn't bring them," he said. "They brought me. I mean you no harm."

"Then tell me what I need to know," the beast said.

Then the Inchasa army attacked and the beast began to fight with a joyous abandon that made Capac move away in fear and awe. He stood to one side, watching the battle rage back and forth.

Then Manco strode bravely from the ranks of the Inchasa and stood in front of the beast, his sword drawn and a smile of anticipation on his face. The beast turned then to face Capac once again.

"Tell me," it said, pointing to Manco with an outstretched foreleg.

"He is called Manco," Capac heard himself say, "the strongest of them. It is him you must kill if you wish to win this battle."

"Manco," the beast in Inchasa. Then the two of them lunged at one another with fierce cries of joy and fury, Manco with his sword swung back to strike, the beast slashing forward with its vicious talons.

And then the vision abruptly ended just as the two were about to tear into each other and Capac came back to himself, still lying beside Noref, a cold sweat clinging to his skin and his heart beating heavily in his chest.

He lay there for a long time trying to understand what it was the vision was saying to him and what the significance of the man-huascar could be. Its presence in all of his visions had to mean something, something he didn't understand. And his every instinct told him that it was important that he understand, that every-thing depended on his understanding. But what could it mean? What could it mean?

*       *       *       *

"The men may have fires," Zeng-de told Xiazhu, his second in command, "but small ones. The evil ones may have scouts probing this way." Especially if they've already over run the river village, he thought sadly. And Mitchell. Mitch-ell would be dead. He wouldn't allow himself to be captured.

"As you wish, Warlord," Xiazhu said. Then he and Zeng-de's other officers bowed and went off to relay his orders to their men.

Zeng-de and Wu-zong then sat down on a blanket and ate, shivering with cold despite their heavy woven coats. It would be another long night.

"We'll need to send our scouts further out from this point on," Zeng-de said, thinking aloud.

"To guard against ambush?" Wu-zong asked.

Zeng-de nodded. If the river people were already defeated, the evil ones might decide to march against his people. Victory can leave an army feeling invincible. They might decide to try their hand against another adversary before marching home.

"There is something the men have been wondering about?" Wu-zong said. "I've heard them talking. They want to know if we arrive in time to join the fight and the river people decide to surrender, will we surrender too?"

"No, Wu-zong, we will not surrender. If the river warriors do, we'll escape across the river and try to make our way home. I doubt they'll surrender, though."

"Why?"

"Because surrendering would mean watching their women and children forced into slavery. Would you surrender?"

"No," Wu-zong answered. "I'd die before I'd watch my family mistreated."

"So would I," Zeng-de agreed. "I expect the men of the river feel the same way. I know my friend does."

"You're afraid for him, aren't you?"

"No, not afraid. I know that if we're too late and the battle has already been fought, if he's still alive then he's won victory. He wouldn't survive in defeat. I think he would keep fighting even if both of his legs were torn from his body. There are some men to whom admitting defeat is more frightening than death."

"Men like you?" Wu-zong asked with a smile.

"Yes," Zeng-de admitted. "And men like your father. I saw him kill two sun worshippers with his sword in his left hand because his right was broken. The sharp edge of the bone was sticking out of his skin just above his elbow." He smiled at he memory. Xi-zong had the fiercest face in battle he had ever seen. Almost inhuman.

"He is a fearsome warrior," he added.

Wu-zong nodded. He had seen the scar many times. And his father had made him practice his weapons with both hands from the time he could walk. He had often wondered why until his older brother had told him the same story Zeng-de had just told. After that he had done whatever his father asked of him without question.

"My father has spoken to me often about war," he said. "He seems to view it with a mixture of fascination and revulsion."

Zeng-de looked at him, impressed. It was an astute observation for one so young and inexperienced.

"That's as good a description of the feelings that race through your mind and body during battle as I've ever heard," he said. "Killing another man brings with it some very complex emotions. On the one hand you're thrilled in an indescribable way because it's not you who has died, on the other hand, a man with any soul at all is saddened to have been forced to kill. There are those who can never overcome the guilt. The soldiers' life is not for everyone."

"How do you know if you're meant for the soldiers' life?" Wu-zong asked, suddenly afraid he might disappoint his father and Zeng-de.

"You can't," Zeng-de told him. "Not until you've watched the life drain from another man's eyes and seen his blood running down your sword. Only then can you know."

\*     \*     \*     \*

"Come on in," Alton called from the galley as Mitch and Wanchese came down the narrow passageway. "The grub's almost ready."

"Thank you for inviting me," Wanchese said as she and Mitch took their seats at the long rectangular table that took up most of the room. She liked Mitchell's brother very much. Nathan, Sandra and Tommy were already seated around the table.

"Thank you for coming," Alton said, oozing the charm that had made his guests feel so welcome at the SeaVista the past several years. He genuinely liked his brother's new wife. She had class.

"It's nice to see you again, Mrs. Harvey," Tommy said in part because he knew it would irk Sandra and also because he liked Mitch's new wife, too. She didn't talk much but she was always nice. And he liked the way she and Mitch talked to each other more like friends than as husband and wife.

"Thank you, Tommy," Wanchese said when she realized suddenly that he was talking to her. She hadn't thought about her last name being Harvey before. Everyone in the village had always just called her Wanchese. She smiled at Tommy.

"It's nice to see you again, too. And you, Nathan."

It was lost on no one that Sandra had been left out of her welcome.

"Same here," Nate Squires said. "Mitch causing you any trouble now that he's got so much free time on his hands?" Preparations were finally complete and everyone was resting up for what was coming.

"Only when he tries to cook," she answered with a smile. "Everything he makes tastes like moccasin bottom."

Mitch laughed along with Alton, Tommy and Nate. He should never have tried to help. Cooking had never been one of his strong suits, but moccasin bottom?

"Well this is going to be some good eating'" Alton said from the small range where he was preparing the food. "I followed your directions to the letter, Wanchese."

"I hope you follow them better than your brother," she said, wondering why she felt so comfortable with these men, ignoring Sandra's presence altogether. "Majta meat isn't easy to cook."

"Here, taste," Alton said, carrying a fork full of the roasted yellow meat to her. She took the fork from him and tasted the meat hesitantly. Over cooked majta meat tasted awful.

"That's delicious," she said, wide eyed with surprise before putting the rest of the meat in her mouth and chewing appreciatively. "Truly delicious!"

"Thank you," Alton said, beaming. "Not everyone in our family is bereft of useful skills."

Mitch smiled. It was good to see Wanchese enjoying herself. She obviously liked Alton and the others, discounting Sandra, of course, who had taken no part in the converstation so far. He could almost feel sorry for her. Almost.

"Mitchell has useful skills, too," Wanchese said in his defense, causing the men around the table to smile and Sandra to scowl. "I've never seen a warrior like him. And the speed with which he learns new languages is absolutely amazing."

Mitch smiled, flattered but also keenly aware of the doubtful looks on the faces of the others. He didn't blame them. He didn't think of himself as a warrior, let alone a good warrior. Why should they?

"Yes," Sandra said, finally breaking her silence, "I heard a wild story about you killing five men somewhere up in the mountains, Mitch. I never knew you were so...handy."

"Five?" Alton asked doubtfully. "What did you kill them with?"

"With his staff," Wanchese answered for him when Mitch didn't say anything. "And he was still not well at the time. He hadn't fully recovered from the deathclaw poison."

"That's the thing that tore up his back?" Tommy asked.

Wanchese nodded.

"It's a deadly beast," she said. "I didn't expect Mitchell to live. He's a stubborn man, though. But he was still not well when the Inchasa attacked us," she continued, warming to the subject. If Mitchell wouldn't tell these men the truth about himself she would tell them for him. "He killed five of them and let a sixth run away because he was just a boy."

"You killed five men with a stick?" Alton asked, looking at Mitch. "Remind me not to insult you anymore."

"If you stopped insulting me you'd never talk to me," Mitch said, smiling uneasily. He would have preferred not to discuss this particular subject. But if Wanchese thought Alton needed to know, he would keep his peace. Besides, it wasn't often she said nice things about him. He'd be smart to just shut up and enjoy it while it lasted.

Alton laughed as he placed a plate of roasted meat, baked worm root and mashed sibya gourd in front of Wanchese. Then he served everyone else and placed his own plate at his place, went and got some glasses and his last bottle of scotch.

"A toast," he said when he had poured everyone an inch or so and they all stood to their feet, glass in hand. "To my brother and his lovely wife," he toasted, raising his glass high. "May they have a long and happy life together and a whole shitload of kids so my parents will stop bugging me to get married and give them some grandchildren."

"Here, here!" Nate and Tommy said through their chuckles and Mitch could see the color rise in Wanchese's face as they all drank.

"What is a shitload?" she asked shyly as they took their seats. The men burst out in laughter and she smiled, wondering what she'd said that was so humorous.

"I'll explain later," Mitch said, smiling back at her. Damn! She was beautiful when she smiled.

# CHAPTER 33

▼

# CONTACT

Capac and Noref were walking along the side of the column so that Capac's slow pace wouldn't interfere with the Cuzco's litter and the guards surrounding it. They had fallen back from their usual position and were walking to one side of the royal litter when a messenger came and reported to Sapa excitedly.

"Our scouts have made contact," he said. "They've encountered a small enemy force approximately two hours from here. Two men were killed and another wounded. The enemy has continued to harass them ever since, retreating after each attack."

"Finally!" Sapa said, slapping the messenger on the back. "I'll send more men to deal with the situation. We'll send them running back where they came from like frightened children!"

Then he went to the Cuzco's litter.

"There is news, my Cuzco," he said and the Cuzco moved aside one of the cloth panels that enclosed him.

"What is it?" he asked irritably and Capac could smell the herb smoke even from twenty feet away.

"We've made contact, my Cuzco," Sapa said triumphantly, as though it was through his own actions that the enemy had been sited.

The Cuzco nodded wordlessly and let the cloth fall back into place. Of course the enemy had been sited. They were less than a day's march away. He wondered if he had been too compulsive in replacing Manco. Sapa had not lived up to his expectations. It was too late to change things now, however. Sapa would have to do.

"What did he expect?" Noref asked Capac as twenty warriors trotted by on their way to assist the forward scouts. "Of course they've made contact. We're almost there, aren't we?"

"Yes," Capac answered. "I'm surprised they didn't come across some resistance sooner."

"Then why is Sapa acting like this is such a surprise?"

"Because Sapa is an idiot," Capac said with a grim smile. "It must cut Manco to the heart to have been replaced by a fool like him."

"Good," Noref said. Manco could never suffer enough pain to suit her. "You had better get back onto the litter. Judging by the way he's strutting around with his chest puffed out, I'd say Sapa is probably going to start picking up the pace."

"Alright," Capac said with a wry grin. He waited for Noref to stop and lower the litter to the ground then let her help him onto it. He laughed quietly to himself when he heard Sapa shout the order to speed up the march. Noref lifted the litter off the ground and set off again, resuming their place near the front of the column.

They marched all morning and passed the mid-day heat at the site of the small battle between the advance scouts and the river warriors. The bodies of the two dead warriors had already been burned by the time the main body arrived and the sickly sweat smell of burned flesh made the two hours they spent resting seem much longer. It was with great relief that they resumed their march when the heat finally subsided.

Sapa came and reported periodically to the Cuzco, each time receiving no response other than a silent stare. The Cuzco seemed almost disinterested in what was happening until, late in the afternoon, as the last rays of the sun approached the southern horizon, the call came down from the column that the enemy village was coming into sight. Then the Cuzco ordered his bearers to bring him forward.

They brought him to the very front of the column and lowered him to the ground. He stepped from the litter and walked away with Sapa to look at the enemy position, his purple cloak wrapped around him tightly. The wall was a surprise. There had been no wall in his vision. But that was a minor complication at most. Everything else was exactly as he remembered. And the wall fitted perfectly with his three-pronged order of battle. Manco and Leruk would occupy the flanks while the main body fought their way over the wall. Yes, he decided, everything was just as it should be.

He looked with satisfaction at the long sweeping slope of brown grass that led to another expanse of shorter green grass. And behind that, the wall and then the enemy village. And behind the enemy village the river, the river and the high bank on the opposite side where the women and children would watch their men kneel before him tomorrow. He smiled expectantly as he turned and walked back to his army. It was time to begin.

"Bring me the slave," he ordered and Sapa sent a man to get the river woman.

She was tall and thin, her dark brown skin broken and scabbed over in many places where she had been disciplined with the switch. She wore a dirty dress of flimsy cloth and carried her soiled slave cloak in her hands.

"Capac!" the Cuzco called loudly. "Bring me Capac!"

Noref helped him from the litter and Capac walked to the front of the column, escorted by two of the Cuzco's personal guards.

"You understand the river speech?" the Cuzco asked him when he reached him.

"I do."

"Good. You will go with the slave and see that she says exactly what I tell her to say. I will hold you responsible if my message isn't delivered precisely as I say. Do you understand me?"

"I do," Capac answered, knowing that what the Cuzco actually meant was that Noref would be punished if his words weren't repeated exactly, though how the Cuzco thought he would know they weren't repeated exactly was a mystery.

"Sapa, you will go with them. I want you to take a good look at those fortifications."

"Of course, my Cuzco," Sapa said importantly.

The Cuzco turned to Capac.

"Tell her that she is to tell the enemy that the Cuzco of the great Inchasa people demands their immediate surrender. She will tell them that if they refuse we will kill every last man among them. Tell her now."

Capac spoke quickly to the slave woman and she nodded her understanding.

"She is to relay my words exactly," the Cuzco repeated. "She is to tell them that I demand complete surrender and servitude. They will bow the knee before me or they will die. Those are their choices."

Capac spoke to the slave again and again she nodded that she understood.

"She understands," he said.

"Go then," the Cuzco ordered and Sapa set out for the enemy village, marching off with an erect, purposeful bearing. The slave and Capac followed along behind.

It was a long, slow walk to the enemy camp and by the time they had covered half the distance a group of twenty or thirty enemy warriors had moved out from behind the wall and were waiting for them some fifty feet in front of it. Capac smiled to himself. So much for Sapa's good look at the fortifications.

As they came within sight of the enemy he heard the slave woman gasp and turned to her. There were tears running down her cheeks and he felt pity for her, thinking that the sight of her former home after so long a time away must be overwhelming to her.

Then a large, brown skinned warrior broke from the ranks of the enemy and walked toward them, staring at the slave and dropping to his knees in front of her when the small Inchasa delegation came to a halt.

"My daughter," he said, his voice a hoarse whisper, his entire body shaking with emotion.

"My father," the slave replied, reaching out a trembling hand to touch the kneeling man's face.

"What's happening here?" Sapa asked angrily. "Tell her to speak the words of the Cuzco, Capac. Tell her to speak them now!"

Capac reached out and touched the woman's arm gently, nodding for her to speak when she looked at him. She stood straight, her hand clasped tightly in those of the kneeling warrior.

"The mighty Cuzco of the Inchasa people," she said loudly but without emotion, "demands that you surrender to him and enter his service. He says that you will either bend the knee before him or die."

Capac sighed with relief and nodded to Sapa that the woman had spoken as she'd been instructed.

"Tell the Cuzco we will never surrender," someone said in Inchasa. "Tell him we would rather die than serve him."

Then the man who spoke pushed his way through the crowd of enemy warriors and stood in front of Capac and Sapa, looking at them with a challenge in his eyes. Capac felt bile rise in his throat and his chest grew tight. The cloak. The claws around his neck. It was the man-huascar of his dreams! It had to be. And he spoke Inchasa!

*      *      *      *

"Someone comes!" one of the young warriors called loudly to Philip, Secotan and the others who had gathered behind the wall to get a first look at the enemy. "Three of them."

"Let's go out and meet them," Philip ordered as he watched the small Inchasa delegation coming toward them. He didn't want them getting close enough to see the piled reeds, grass and branches that covered the shallow ditch in front of the wall. He wanted it to come as a complete surprise tomorrow.

"Virgil!" he called as he lifted himself onto and over the wall, "Run and get Mitchell. We'll need someone who speaks Inchasa."

"He is already coming," Virgil called back. He could see Mitchell moving through the grass beyond the edge of the village. His deathclaw cloak and black walking stick were unmistakable.

"Perhaps the sight of the defensive wall will make them reconsider," Elan White said hopefully.

"I wouldn't count too heavily on that, Elan," Secotan said. He seriously doubted the enemy had marched ten days only to be turned aside at the sight of some minor defensive positions. The Inchasa would know they still outnumbered his people nearly two to one. There would be no turning back.

The minutes passed slowly as the Inchasa made their way toward them. Secotan looked back and saw Mitchell climb over the wall just as the enemy came within easy view. Then he heard Philip gasp and turned to see what was wrong.

No! he thought in anguish. It can't be! Then a searing fire of anger and hatred exploded in his chest as Philip staggered forward and fell to his knees before his daughter, his first born, taken from him so long ago.

"My daughter," Philip whispered.

"My father," Phila Granganimeo croaked, reaching out a trembling hand to her father's face.

Then one of the Inchasa spoke angrily to the other man in the delegation, one with a black tattoo on his shaven forehead, and the man reached out to Phila, who looked at him then stood straight and looked at the river warriors gathered before her.

"The mighty Cuzco of the great Inchasa people demands that you surrender to him and enter his service," she said loudly. "He says you will either bend the knee before him or die."

Then someone spoke in the Inchasa tongue and Secotan turned to see Mitchell pushing his way through the crowd, his deathclaw cloak draped over his shoulders and his ever present walking stick in his hand.

He stepped out of the crowd as he finished speaking and stood in front of the Inchasa with the tattoo burned into his forehead. The man stared at him, his face frozen in fear, almost as though he were seeing a spirit or apparition.

Then the other Inchasa spoke to Mitchell violently, shaking his fist and gesturing back toward the huge Inchasa army. When Mitchell only smiled, the man grabbed Phila by the arm and pushed her roughly back the way they'd come.

Leaping to his feet with a guttural growl, Philip threw himself at the Inchasa, knocking him to the ground and taking Phila into a tight embrace.

"Lay a hand on my daughter again and I'll kill you with my bare hands," he raged, and the man with the tattoo translated his words for the other Inchasa, who leaped to his feet and drew his sword, his face red with anger and embarrassment.

Mitchell stepped forward, placing himself between Philip, Phila and the Inchasa. Secotan couldn't understand the words Mitchell spoke but the menace in his tone was easy to translate, as was the look of shock and anger that turned the Inchasa's face still another shade of red.

The man's eyes bulged angrily and he stood still for a long moment, his sword gripped so tightly his hands turned first red and then white. Then he spat something at the tattooed one and started back toward his own army. The tattooed one looked after him but didn't follow. Instead, he turned to Mitchell and looked at him appraisingly, the fear suddenly gone from his eyes.

"What is your name?" he asked in the village tongue.

"Mitchell. Mitchell Harvey."

"I am Capac," the other said.

Mitch nodded, not sure what was happening but sensing that this man meant him no harm.

"I am glad to have met you, Mitchell Harvey," Capac said. "I've seen you before, in my dreams, in my visions. I am not Inchasa. I am Lydacian. My people are a people of peace. The Inchasa conquered us long ago and made us their servants, just as they want to do to you."

"I'm sorry," Mitch said.

"Don't be," Capac said with a proud jut of his jaw. "My people are escaping even as we speak. While these fools are here trying to enslave you, we are slipping out of their grasp and starting over."

"Good," Mitch said. "I wish you luck."

"And I you," Capac said before being interrupted by Sapa.

"Capac!" he roared. "You will come with me this instant or I promise you that homely woman of yours will never see another sunrise!"

"I'm coming," Capac shouted back. "Let me at least try to convince them to surrender."

"We've already gotten their answer," Sapa said. "Now, let's go."

"Please, let me try," Capac said. "The Cuzco said to offer them a chance to surrender. We should do all we can to make sure we've satisfied his expectations. He may be angry with us if we don't."

"Well, yes, I suppose you may be right," Sapa said, the very thought of the Cuzco being angry with him enough to make him agree with almost anything. Capac hid his smile.

"There is one man you must kill if you want to have any hope of defeating them," he told Mitch quickly in the river speech. "He is the best of them, the strongest, the bravest, the most dangerous. You must kill him. That is what I dreamed I should tell you."

"How will I know him?" Mitch asked.

"You'll know him," Capac answered. "He's a full head taller than any of the others and he is more strongly built. His face is ugly and scarred. He wears his head cleanly shaven and moves like a ripper cat. You'll know him when you see him."

"Alright," Mitch said. "What's his name? Sometimes a man is thrown off guard when someone he's never seen before knows his name."

"He is called Manco," Capac said and Sapa was instantly suspicious.

"What are you telling him?" he asked. "Speak Inchasa so I can understand you."

"He told me that not all Inchasa are as weak as you," Mitch said. "And that if we don't surrender someone named Manco will kill every last one of us."

Sapa tried his best to think of a suitably biting reply but found none.

"We're finished here," he announced, and grabbed Capac by the arm. "They aren't going to surrender. Let's go."

Capac let him pull him along and the two of them headed back toward the Inchasa army, which was now busily setting up its encampment. He hoped he'd done enough. It had taken him a few moments to overcome his fear and remember that there was something he was supposed to tell the man-huascar. But he had told him. Now the rest was up to him.

"We should get behind the wall," Secotan said gently to Philip as Sapa and Capac made their way back across the open plain. "Their young king may be angry enough to order and immediate attack."

The others had been thinking the same thing and everyone turned and started back toward the wall.

"What exactly did you say to them when they demanded we surrender?" Virgil asked as they leaped onto and over the wall.

"I told them we would rather die than serve them," Mitch answered. "And when he pulled his sword on Philip, I told him he'd better start walking or I was gong to shove my staff so far down his throat he'd be picking splinters out of his ass. At least, I think that's what I said. I wasn't real sure about their word for ass."

Virgil Crane laughed at that, a rich, low rumble from his belly. None of the others could remember ever having heard him laugh aloud before and it made them laugh with him.

"An excellent reply," Secotan said with a grin. "He certainly took your meaning. I thought his head was going to explode, it turned so many colors."

Mitch laughed then turned to find the angry eyes of Hunter Kane on him. Not everyone appreciated his wit, apparently. He gave Kane a bright smile and went to help Philip and Phila make their way back to the village.

"Do you believe the tattooed one?" Secotan asked as they walked.

"Yes, I think I do," Mitch answered. "It can't hurt to spread the word, anyway. We'll keep our eyes open for a big ugly bastard with a shaved head and see if we can't take him out."

"What did he say the big one's name was?" Secotan asked.

"Manco," Mitch answered. "The man we have to kill is named Manco."

$$* \qquad * \qquad * \qquad *$$

The Cuzco was outraged when Sapa told him what had happened. He slapped Capac several times across the face and told him to get out of his sight and stay there if he wanted to live through the night. His displeasure with Sapa he hid so as not to open himself up to criticism for having promoted him.

He was sorely tempted to order an immediate attack. But his vision had been of a morning battle, with the sun glinting off his armor and the women and children of the enemy village watching from across the river. He would have to be patient. But they would pay for what they'd done. And he personally would kill the slave woman.

# CHAPTER 34

▼

# FINAL PREPARATIONS

It was still two hours before sunrise when Mitch and Wanchese made their way across the river in a borrowed dugout. The air was still bitingly cold and raw, their mood somber, neither knowing how they were supposed to act now that it was actually time to say goodbye, for a while at least. They were both very much aware that they might never see one another again and it was hard to know what to say. So, they said nothing.

As Mitch leaped ashore and pulled the dugout high onto the riverbank, a light switched on above them and Alton called out a hello. They could hear him making his way down the steep bank toward them and when he came into view they saw that Tommy was with him.

"Morning," Mitch said as he helped Wanchese from the boat. "Hope you guys weren't waiting too long."

"Not long at all," Tommy said, giving Mitch a friendly slap on the back and Wanchese a friendly smile. "Here, let me carry that for you," he added and took her pack from her.

"Morning," Alton said grudgingly. He wasn't feeling all that talkative. Watching the Inchasa army as it had set up camp out on the plain, it had suddenly struck home that these were real men; real men with real swords and arrows, and that his brother could very well be dead before nightfall the next day. And for what? He liked Philip and Secotan, too. But this was their fight. Why did Mitch have to be there? Did he really think one man could make a difference?

"Is the probe up?" Mitch asked as they walked up the bank. He had asked Alton to launch one of his high altitude probes over the Inchasa camp to monitor them and give him some warning when they started getting formed up for their attack.

"Yeah," Tommy answered. "It went up a couple of hours ago."

"Great," Mitch said then moved closer to Alton.

"You O.K?" he asked.

"Not really," Alton answered. "My little brother is about to go out and get himself killed and I can't figure out why. I really can't, Mitch. This isn't your fight. No matter how much you like these people, this isn't your fight."

"No, I don't suppose it really is," Mitch admitted. How could he make Alton understand? Should he even try?

"I guess maybe it isn't really about whether this is my fight or not. I just know I'd never forgive myself if I walked away. I don't know what else to say, Alton. I have to do what I think is right. Can you understand that?"

"No," Alton said angrily, "I can't. And I don't think Mom and Dad will either when I show up to tell them you're dead."

Whoa, Mitch thought, he must be really desperate. He's even pulling one of Mom's old guilt trip ploys. But this wasn't about trying to get him to go to church when he'd rather sleep or to Grandma's house when he'd rather go out with his friends. This was about who he was as a man and he couldn't let anything influence his decision. Not guilt, not fear, not even love for his brother. He had to stay.

"Just tell them I died happy, then," he said as they rounded a copse of trees and sighted the *SeaVista*. "And that I died knowing what it is to really live. I couldn't have said that a few months ago."

"That's just all the more reason to keep yourself alive, then," Alton said in exasperation as they walked up the ramp and moved single file down the narrow passageway. "If you're finally happy then why go off and get yourself killed?"

He punched a button on a small wall panel beside the door to his cabin and the door slid open.

"Put Wanchese's things in here," he told Tommy then stalked off toward the galley.

Mitch looked at Wanchese with a shrug and motioned for her to follow Alton then fell in line behind her.

"You got any more of that scotch?" he asked as he took a seat at the table. "A little nip to warm the blood sounds good right about now."

"Nate's bringing it," Alton answered. "I'm hoping you'll get drunk and pass out."

Mitch laughed. He had passed out at his bachelor party and Alton had never let him forget it.

"I'd like to see that," Tommy said as he followed Nate Squires through the door, a bottle in his hands and Sandra on his heels. "I missed that party."

"I missed most of it myself," Mitch said with a laugh.

Alton grabbed glasses and Tommy poured everyone a drink. Mitch stood when they all had a glass and had taken their places at the table. And then his mind went completely blank. What was he supposed to say now? What could he say, really, other than thank you? And that sounded so inadequate.

"I want to thank you guys for coming to find me," he said. "I still can't believe you actually found me. But I'm glad you did. And I'm grateful. Thank you."

He nodded to Alton, Nate and Tommy in turn then turned to Sandra.

"And I have to thank you, too, Sandra, for having me brought here." He raised his glass to her, enjoying the confused and slightly guilty look on her face. "I've known more contentment and real happiness these past few months here than in all the years of my adult life put together. I know that wasn't your intent, but that was the result and I thank you."

"And, contrary to what Mr. Positive Thinking here seems to think," he continued, motioning toward Alton with his glass and smiling, "I don't plan on dying today. I accept it as a possibility, but I don't plan on it. In fact, I've never wanted to live more. But this is something I have to do for me, for the man I want to be."

He locked eyes with Alton.

"I don't expect you to understand, but I ask you to accept me at my word that it's necessary and let me enjoy this time with you."

Alton lowered his eyed and nodded his head in acceptance of his brother's request. He would never understand, though, not really.

"Good," Mitch said with relief. "Here's to living!" He lifted his glass in a final salute then drained it before taking his seat.

"Quick, give him another one, Tommy. There's still time," Alton called out, but he was smiling and the anger was gone from his voice. If these were going to be his last moments with Mitch he wanted them to be good ones.

They passed three quarters of an hour retelling old stories and talking about everything except what time it was and how much longer they had before the sun came up. Then Mitch stood to his feet.

"I'd like a minute alone with you if I could, Alton."

"Sure," Alton said. "Let's go to my cabin."

It took them only a few seconds to get there.

"You're absolutely sure about this?" Alton asked when they were inside.

"Yeah, I'm sure. Now give me a hug, you pain in the ass."

Alton smiled and they embraced for a long time, not saying anything, just enjoying the bond of brotherhood and friendship.

"I meant what I said in there," Mitch said when they finally released one another and stepped back to look each other in the eye. "Thanks for coming for me."

"No big deal," Alton said. "You would've done the same for me."

"Yeah, I would have," Mitch said. "But I still owe you. And I need something else from you, big brother. I need you to promise me you'll get Wanchese away from here if things go badly. Even if we win but I die, take her away from here. There are people here who might want to hurt her."

"Of course," Alton said. "I give you my word. I'll take her out of here."

"Thanks. Take her wherever she wants to go, whether it's to the mountains, to the fortress southeast of here where she has friends or even back to Sylvas or Teluride. She's a smart girl. She'd figure things out back there. And I've already set it up with Nate so she'll get all my property if I die."

"No problem," Alton said. "Whatever she wants. I'm glad you found her, Mitch. She's the kind of woman you deserve, unlike certain others we won't bother to mention."

Mitch laughed.

"Yes, she is," he said. "And now I'd better spend some time with her, too. I'm running out of time."

"I'll send her down," Alton said then the two of them embraced again and Alton left. Mitch was waiting by the open door when Wanchese made her way down the corridor. He motioned her inside ahead of him.

"I want to thank you, too," he said uncomfortably once they were inside. "I would have been dead long before Alton ever got here if not for you. And I wouldn't have enjoyed my time here as much if I hadn't met you. I'm glad we ran into each other."

He smiled and braved a look in her direction. She looked as uncomfortable as he felt.

"And I want you to know that Alton will take you anywhere you want to go if the battle goes against us or I'm killed. You can go back to the mountains or to be with Nang-de or you could even go with Alton if you want to. I've set things up so that all my wealth will be yours if I'm killed, so you wouldn't have to worry about that. And he and Nate could teach you whatever you needed to know."

"Thank you," Wanchese said, her voice not betraying the confused jumble of emotions she was feeling. She wasn't really surprised that he would think of her even now on the morning of battle, but she was touched just the same. And she was suddenly very much afraid. She hadn't really considered the possibility that Mitchell might die in this fight until last night. The seemingly endless line of flickering Inchasa campfires had changed that. There were so many!

And now Alton seemed so sure that Mitchell would die if he fought today and suddenly she understood that it was possible that he would be killed and she would be alone again. Worse, she would be without him, which somehow seemed worse even than being alone. And she had no idea how to deal with those feelings or if she should even let herself feel them. It was all very confusing.

"You're welcome," Mitch said lamely, trying to decide whether or not she'd slap him if he hugged her. A sharp rap at the door made it a moot point.

"The probe just sent the alert," Alton said when the door slid open. "They're starting to form up."

"O.K," Mitch said, disappointed. He'd had so little time with her. And there was so much he should have said. "I guess I better get going."

Everyone walked him back to the river, though no one spoke. He gave Nate and Tommy a quick hug and embraced Alton tightly. Then he decided it would be worth getting slapped and hugged Wanchese too. Her hair smelled wonderful as he pulled her close and she surprised him by returning his embrace.

"Take care of yourself," he said softly.

Then he let her go, threw his staff into the dugout and pushed it out into the water. Jumping in, he gave a last smile and waved then started paddling away. It was still dark and he was quickly lost from sight.

As he reached the opposite shore, the women and children of the village were being loaded into every available dugout and sent across the river. Almost as soon as Mitch pulled it up onto the bank, the dugout was grabbed away from him and quickly loaded. He just had time to grab his things before the dugout was filled nearly to overflowing and sent on its way.

He walked away from the river and into the village where husbands and wives, fathers and daughters and brothers and sisters were saying tearful farewells. The sight of Philip hugging Phila to him and gently kissing the top of her head gave him a lump in his throat.

It began to grow light as he walked out of the village and started out toward the first wall. He saw Hunter Kane standing with several other men, going over last minute details.

"You take care of yourself, Kane," he called. "I don't want anybody but me killing your sorry ass."

Hate flared up in Kane's eyes and his fists clenched as he called back, "You should go back across the river with the women and children and let the real warriors take care of the Inchasa. There will be plenty of time for you to die later."

Mitch smiled. There was always plenty of time to die, just never enough to live. He felt a growing sense of anticipation as he ignored Kane and walked to his place behind the wall. His sword, bow and quiver were already there waiting for him, along with a small round shield made of bark that Virgil had made for him. He doubted he'd use it, but it was nice of Virgil to think of him.

"Good morning," a nervous voice said behind him. He turned to find Raven Howe standing there, his sword slung over one shoulder and a bow over the other.

"Good morning, Raven. You look like you're ready to go."

"I am," Raven said, trying very hard to believe it. The truth was that he was so nervous he'd been unable to keep his morning meal down.

"Where have they put you?"

"Behind the second wall."

Mitch nodded. It was as good a place as any, better than some.

"Keep your eyes open," he cautioned. "But don't get too distracted by what's going on anywhere else. Be aware of what's going on around you, but focus on what's right in front of you."

"I'll try," the boy said. "Thank you for all you've done for me. I'll never forget it." He held out his right hand and the two of them gripped forearms in friendship.

"You take care of yourself," Mitch said, glad he'd had a chance to help the boy. If Raven died today, he'd die a warrior. That was important among these people. And more importantly, it was important to Raven.

"I will," Raven said. "You, too."

"I'm gonna try like hell, Raven," Mitch said with a grin and Raven walked off with a wave of his hand.

Mitch glanced at the northern horizon and saw that the first glint of sunlight was cresting into the sky. He took off his cloak and laid it on the ground beside his quiver and sword. Once the sun came up it would get hot very quickly.

Philip and Secotan walked up as he turned around.

"Are you sure you still want to do this?" Philip asked.

"I'm sure," Mitch answered and Philip nodded. He'd known the answer but felt honor bound to ask just the same.

"I wanted to thank you for all you've done, Mitchell. You and your friends. I'm grateful. I pray we'll speak again when this is all over."

"Me, too," Mitch said. "Take care of yourself. You, too, Secotan."

"I will," Secotan said. "Is Wanchese safe?"

"Yes, she's over across the river with Alton. She'll be alright. How about you? Your wives and children all set?"

Both men nodded.

"We've sent them across the river with all the water bags we could find," Philip told him. "If the battle is lost, they'll flee into the wasteland and stay hidden as long as possible. Hopefully it will be long enough."

"Your brother and the others have a place to flee to?" Secotan asked. "Those wastelands are no place to get lost, especially without water."

"Alton has a place picked out," Mitch said, wishing he could tell them more. But the *Sea Vista* could only hold fifteen or twenty more people. How were they supposed to decide who went and who stayed?

"Good," Philip said. "Well, we had better see to our men, Mitchell. Good luck, my friend."

"Same to you," Mitch said and watched them walk away. He turned back and looked out over the wall. It wouldn't be long now.

$$*\qquad*\qquad*\qquad*$$

It was time, the Cuzco decided, and walked over to his bed where his armor and cloak were laid out for him. The precious gold and silver his ancestors had used in such huge quantities before being brought to this new place were very rare here and he had been forced to confiscate every gold and silver item in the empire in order to provide the armorer with enough to make his vision a reality. Looking down at it now he knew it was worth it. Today he would look like a conqueror.

Smiling, he called for Sapa, who marched in importantly.

"You will have the honor of helping me with my armor, Sapa," the Cuzco said.

"Thank you," Sapa said with a bow, silently thinking that he had more important things to do than help the Cuzco get dressed. The men were forming up out on the plain.

"Do the shin guards first," the Cuzco said and Sapa picked up the two guards from the bed and buckled them on. After that came the breastplate then the forearm guards. Along the bottom of the breastplate were more than three hundred small hooks. From these Sapa hung long, thin strips of gleaming gold. Each strip was one inch wide and hung down to the top of the knee. When all the strips were hung, they gave the appearance of a skirt of shimmering gold, yet allowed the Cuzco to move his legs freely. Last came the upper arm guards, which Sapa buckled on with care.

"Have you chosen men to guard the slaves?" the Cuzco asked as he draped his purple cloak over his shoulders and fastened it at the neck.

"Yes, my Cuzco. I've chosen men who are either too young and inexperienced or very old and no long able to stand the wear of battle. Fifty of them, as you ordered."

"Good. Choose the best of them and have him sent here. Send someone to bring me Capac as well."

"I will see to it, my Cuzco," Sapa said then left him.

The Cuzco reached down and picked up his royal sword, made especially for this glorious day. It was without a doubt the most beautifully crafted weapon he had ever seen, with precious gems of deep blue, shimmering green and blood red set into the hilt and all along the scabbard. It was a weapon worthy of him and he smiled with satisfaction as he laid it back on his bed beside his silver helmet.

Sapa returned quickly with the man he'd chosen and was followed almost immediately by Capac.

"What is your name?" the Cuzco asked the old but still well built warrior Sapa had selected for him.

"I am Karac, my Cuzco."

"You will take this slave to the edge of the forest, Karac, as close to the enemy as you dare, and have him climb the highest tree that will support him. I want him to see everything that happens here today so that he can properly record our victory for me. Bring his woman with you. Kill her if he gives you any trouble."

"I will see to them for you, my Cuzco," Karac said, silently thanking the spirits that he wouldn't be among the poor bastards trying to fight their way over that wall. He'd seen enough of battle to know that this wasn't going to be the quick, easy victory the Cuzco thought it was going to be. They would win, of course, but it was going to cost a lot of good men their lives.

The Cuzco turned his attention to Capac.

"Today you will learn just who it is you serve, slave. And the fools who face us will learn who it is they have chosen to defy."

\*　　\*　　\*　　\*

"Quickly!" Zeng-de snapped. The men were sluggish this morning, probably because of the early hour. He was getting them started well before sunrise despite the cold. They were within easy marching distance of the river village and he was determined to be there well before the mid-day heat forced a break.

He had just over one thousand men with him. Nearly all of his men had been eager to go with him, with Wu-zong and five others from Hongzhi replacing the six who had said no. It was a good sized force and they were good men. They would be of great help. If they reached the river village in time.

"Have the scouts been dispatched?" he asked on of his officers.

"Yes, Warlord, they just left. And I told them to be very careful and stay out of sight as they neared the river."

"Very well," Zeng-de said. "Tell the men we'll eat while we march. It's too cold to sit still anyway."

Another cold meal wouldn't go over very well with the men, but they would understand. And he had no choice. Every fiber of his being was screaming that he needed to move quickly and he had learned a long time ago to trust his instincts.

"Good morning," Wu-zong said as he walked out of the darkness, his hands stuffed deep into the pouch on the front of his heavy jacket.

"Good morning," Zeng-de replied. "You slept well?"

"As well as can be expected," Wu-zong answered. "It's not easy to sleep when your teeth are chattering."

Zeng-de smiled. It had been a long, cold night without fires. But they were too close to risk even a small blaze.

"Tonight we'll have warm fires and a hot meal," he said. "If we get there early enough, we might even have time to build some shelters."

"It will be good to get there," Wu-zong said. "I think everyone is tired of wondering if we'll get there in time."

"So am I," Zeng-de said. "And we'll know soon enough. Go back to the rear of the column and tell them we move out in five minutes. We have no more time to waste."

# CHAPTER 35

## A CLASH OF ARMS

When the sun had risen fully into the early morning sky, the Cuzco strode confidently from his tent. His armor glinted brightly in the new sunlight and the jewels of his sword hilt sparkled behind is right ear. He looked and felt like the conqueror he knew he would soon be.

"Is my army ready, Sapa?" he asked.

"It is, my Cuzco," Sapa answered. "The men await your orders."

The young Cuzco nodded, walked to the front of his massed forces and turned to face them when he reached the center of the main body. He looked with satisfaction at the thirty neat rows of one hundred that formed the main attack force, each man aligned perfectly with the man in front of and behind him as well as those to either side. They looked like warriors!

Manco and his men were formed to the right of the main body in ten rows of one hundred, Leruk to the left with nine rows of one hundred and one row of seventy. These two groups would split off from the main force as they neared the range of the enemy's arrows and position themselves to attack the right and left flanks.

Everything was just as he'd ordered. He wished he could tell these simple warriors just how great a new day had dawned, how proud they would soon feel to have been here on this day. But they would never understand. He would have to show them. It was time for them to learn just whom they served.

"Follow me!" he cried in a voice rich with authority, power and confidence. Then he turned and started toward the enemy, his eyes searching the area behind the village and growing bright with excitement at the sight of the hundreds of women and children massed high on the opposite shore just as he'd known they'd be.

He could hear his captains giving the order to march and he scanned the wall and the men behind it. They were all standing, bows in hand, waiting for he and his men to come into range. He smiled a knowing smiled. They had an unpleasant surprise coming.

He felt as though he were floating, as if his feet no longer touched the ground. Even the growing heat had no effect on him. Such minor inconveniences were the concern of mere mortal men and could no longer touch him. Today he had become a god!

Behind him he heard the order for Manco and Leruk's men to separate themselves from the main body as they reached a point some fifty feet before the invisible line that marked the effective range of the enemy.

Manco and Leruk shouted the order and their men broke into a trot, Manco's men moving to the right, Leruk's to the left. It was imperative that they occupy the enemy's flanks before the main force began its assault on the wall.

Suddenly a lone arrow leaped into the air, followed quickly by a second. The Cuzco thought at first that the enemy was simply too undisciplined to wait until they were in range. Then he saw the arc and velocity of the arrows and realized that they were indeed going to reach them. His advisors had been wrong in their estimates of the enemy's effective range. They would pay for that.

The arrows were well aimed and arcing down directly toward him. He was determined not to move or even flinch. This would be his greatest moment of glory, the instant when his men would see for themselves that he was now truly a god and not merely a man calling himself a god like his father, his father's father and all the other Cuzco's before them. After this, nothing would ever be the same again!

He smiled as he heard gasps of fear behind him as Sapa and the others realized that the arrows were going to strike him. He spread his arms wide, his palms facing up toward the sun and watched the arrows streak the last few feet toward him. Let the enemy see who it is they have chosen to defy!

The arrows struck one after the other, the first at the very center of his breastplate, the second slightly lower and to the left. He threw his head back and laughed as the arrows bounced harmlessly away and the frightened gasps of his men turned first to silent astonishment and them to cries of wonder and a roar of excitement.

He started forward again. They had to be within bow range when Manco and Leruk engaged the flanks. Another arrow flashed into the air and he laughed again. The fools couldn't understand. They were wasting their arrows.

And, as he'd known it would, this arrow struck him with the same result as the first two and his men let out a wild cheer as he turned to face them, a smile of pure joy on his face and the thrill of anticipation in his eyes.

"First line!" he called with all his strength and the first line of warriors ran past him, cheering loudly. They moved thirty feet past him and then dropped to one knee, arrows notched, bows raised, each one arms length from the other.

"Second line!" he called and the second line ran past him to take up positions behind the kneeling archers, each man standing directly behind the open space between two of the kneeling men. Notching an arrow of their own, they stood and waited.

The process was repeated with men falling in line on either side of these men until two lines of men, one kneeling and the other standing, spread across the length of the wall. A second pair of lines fell in behind these two until the entire main attack force was arrayed before the defensive wall.

Once the main force was in position, the Cuzco reached up behind his right shoulder, drew his sword and raised it high in the air, the pre-arranged signal for Manco and Leruk to engage the enemy's flanks. He heard the roar of battle cries from each side and knew his signal had been seen and his orders carried out.

"First line, fire!" he ordered and the kneeling archers let loose their volley. As soon as their arrows left their bows, the second line ran past and took up a position under cover of their fire. As the first volley began its downward arc, the second line stopped, dropped to one knee and fired, at which point the first line, by this time on their feet and moving forward with another arrow notched and ready, ran past under cover of the second volley, knelt and fired again. The third and fourth lines followed behind, executing the same attack plan as the first two.

In less than a minute, the entire main attack force was moving toward the enemy position, each line giving the other covering fire while also moving closer to the defensive wall. Men began to fall as they came into range and the river warriors began returning fire, but the Inchasa pressed on, moving ever closer to the wall.

On the right flank Manco and his men tried to force their way through a narrow strip of open ground between the wall and the bank of the river. On the left

Leruk and his men pushed their way through a line of trees that met the wall on that side.

Because of the small area available for their attack, Manco and his men took heavy fire. Leruk's group was hidden, but also slowed, by the trees and undergrowth they were forced to move through. They distracted the attention of a large number of enemy warriors from the main assault that was taking place against the wall itself.

There in the center, the first wave of Inchasa to reach the wall fell into the shallow ditch, breaking their momentum. Undeterred, they clawed their way out and started over the wall, discarding their bows and drawing slings, swords and hand axes as they leaped down into the midst of the river warriors.

They were terribly vulnerable between the time they reached the wall and when they jumped down on the defender's side and men began to fall, temporarily clogging the route of attack until they could either jump or were pushed off the wall by others coming up behind them. Many of the first line either never made it over the wall or were already wounded by the time they faced the enemy man to man.

Even so, they climbed over the wall in a steady stream and the second, third and fourth lines were soon clawing their way over the wall and joining the desperate hand to hand fighting. Just as the last of the warriors of the main attack force made their way over the wall and began to press the outnumbered defenders back, they were met by a second group of defenders, a good sized body of men, who attacked with the lance.

Surprised, Sapa became disoriented and ordered his men to stand and fight where they were rather than continue pressing forward. They obeyed, reluctantly, and stood firm where they were, defending themselves rather than attacking, until the Cuzco himself suddenly appeared on top of the wall.

"Attack!" he screamed vehemently. "Attack!"

✳    ✳    ✳    ✳

"A messenger," Wu-zong said, pointing to a far off speck on the horizon.

"Yes," Zeng-de agreed. "And coming quickly."

Without realizing they were doing it, the two of them began to quicken their pace. Even so, it seemed an interminably long time before the messenger finally reached them, stopping in front of Zeng-de, bent over at the waist his hands on his knees, his chest heaving as he tried to catch his breath.

"Bring this man some water," Zeng-de called and a water bag was quickly brought to him. The messenger drank gratefully. His own water bag had been empty for the last third of his journey.

"Take your time," Zeng-de said as the messenger stood straight and started to speak. "Get your wind back. I can wait another minute to hear what you have to tell me." He could wait as long as he had to. A gasping, disjointed report was of no use to him. Better to let the man recover and then hear what he had to say.

Finally the man took one last drink from the water bag, put the stopper back and handed it back to the man who had brought it to him.

"Thank you," he said. Then he turned and faced Zeng-de.

"I bring important news, Warlord," he reported. "The battle has begun, just this very morning. The river people have built a defensive wall and are defending themselves from behind it. But the reports we've heard are true. There are at least four thousand Inchasa, maybe more."

Zeng-de nodded. He'd been afraid of that. It was too many. Mitchell and the others would have no chance no matter how bravely they fought.

"How goes the battle?" he asked.

"I have no idea, Warlord. As soon as we saw that the evil ones were moving toward the attack, Song-li sent me to you with this report."

"If we move quickly we might still be of some help," Wu-zong said eagerly.

"Yes," Zeng-de said thoughtfully. "Or we might walk straight into our own death."

With only one thousand men they would be severely outnumbered themselves if the battle was already over when they arrived. Even if the sun worshippers lost half their force in the attack they would still outnumber him more than two to one. And he would not lead these men into a massacre. Not even for a friend. His first responsibility was to his men.

"Bring me another messenger," he ordered and a thin young man was brought to him.

"This man will tell you where to find Song-li," he said, pointing to the exhausted messenger. "Find him. Tell him that we are coming as quickly as we can and that he is to remain hidden until we arrive. He is to take no action until we get there. Understood."

"Yes, Warlord."

"Good," Zeng-de said, placing an affectionate hand on the young man's shoulder. He looked too young to be a soldier. "I need to be informed immediately if the river warriors are defeated or surrender. That is very important. I *must* know what we're walking into."

"I understand," the new messenger said.

Zeng-de turned to the first messenger.

"How far away are we?" he asked.

"Two hours march, I think," the man replied hesitantly. He had never been very good at estimating such things.

"Alright," Zeng-de said. "Tell this man where to find Song-li and then fall in at the end of the column. You've done well."

✳    ✳    ✳    ✳

Mitch was fifteen feet to the left of the very center of the three hundred foot wall. Raven stood beside him. He and the other men stationed behind the second wall would fire as many arrows as they could before the Inchasa reached the wall. Then they would retreat behind the second wall until Manteo ordered them to attack. To their right, at the exact center, Virgil Crane stood with the ancient crossbow supported on the wall, one arrow notched and ready, another held in his hand ready to be loaded as soon as the first one was fired.

There was complete silence as the men watched the Inchasa approaching through waves of shimmering heat. Each man felt fear to one extent or another and each of them dealt with it in his own way. Some were able to force the fear to the back of their mind, others embraced it as fuel for their determination and some simply ignored it, telling themselves that if they refused to acknowledge it the fear could have no hold over them. For his part, Mitch embraced his fear, convinced that it was both natural and healthy. It couldn't do him any harm unless he let it control him and he wasn't going to let that happen.

Scanning the approaching enemy, he could see the spectacularly dressed man leading the column and guessed that he must be the Inchasa king. The man had courage, he had to give him that. Many another man in his place would have left the actual fighting to his subordinates and commanded them from a safe distance.

Then two large groups broke off from the advancing body of men, each one veering away from the center and toward one of the vulnerable flanks. Mitch swore under his breath. They'd been hoping the Inchasa would ignore the flanks until at least one full frontal assault had failed.

At the head of the group moving toward the left flank marched a huge man. He was a full head taller than any of the men under his command and even at this distance it was obvious that he was built like a brick wall. Sunlight occasionally reflected off his clean shaven head as he moved ever closer to the open space between the wall and the river. Manco, Mitch knew. It had to be. But there was nothing he could do about it from here. Secotan would have to deal with him.

As he turned to look out at the main body of men marching toward them he heard Virgil's crossbow fire and two arrows quickly shot into the air, one after the other. They were well aimed and he could see that they were heading straight for the Inchasa king.

The man didn't even move! He just stood there, watching the arrows come toward him. At the last moment he even spread his arms wide and turned his face up to the sun. Then the first arrow struck dead center in the middle of his chest, followed almost immediately by the second, though that one hit a little lower.

It was a second before Mitch realized that the arrows had bounced off the man's armor and fallen harmlessly to the ground. He could see the Inchasa king throw his head back and laugh. Then there was a wild cheer from his warriors.

Virgil let loose another arrow but it was no more effective than the others.

Then the first row of enemy warriors sent up a wild howl and ran past the king to take up kneeling positions a good distance in front of him. They were quickly followed by the second line, which stopped and stood behind the first. This process continued until four lines spread across the entire length of the wall. It seemed to Mitch that the entire process took less than a minute.

And then the air was filled with arrows. As he watched, the second line of men rushed forward just as the arrows fired by the first line started raining down around him. Bending down, he grabbed the little shield he hadn't thought he'd need and stuck his head over the wall behind it. The Inchasa were moving forward quickly and he noticed with shame that the men beside him were returning fire while he was ducking like a frightened child.

Standing, he notched an arrow in his bow, aimed at the closest Inchasa and fired. Ducking back down behind the wall, he reached for his quiver, preferring to use his own supply before moving on to the ones stored in the reed netting that ran the length of the wall.

As he reached for another arrow his eyes fell on the tied bundle of five arrows treated in the black ooze and he cursed himself hotly. If he'd given those arrows to Virgil the Inchasa king would be dead now. Shit!

Ignoring the bundle, he grabbed another arrow and stood up. He got off three more shots before the first Inchasa reached the wall and fell into the ditch. It slowed them down but not for long. As Raven and Manteo's other men began a quick retreat behind the second wall, Mitch dropped his bow and picked up his staff as Inchasa began crawling over the wall.

A few of them tried to stand on top of the wall and fire down into the defenders at close range. They were shot down so quickly that the men behind them saw it would be smarter to just get over the wall and on the ground as quickly as they could.

Mitch jumped to the attack, striking men down as quickly as he could and moving on to find another target. It wasn't long before the entire Inchasa force had made it over the wall and he found himself facing two and even three of them at once.

And it made him angry, angry and excited. He launched himself at each new attacker with a mixture of hate and joy, his mind wanting to kill these men who had come to destroy and enslave, while his spirit felt free and alive amidst the life and death struggle they brought with them.

He was soon covered in sweat and splattered blood and breathing heavily. No matter how many Inchasa he killed, more seemed to take their place and leap at him. He fought viciously, destroying men with abandon, his staff leaping and thrusting with speed and power, breaking arms and legs, snapping ribs and fingers and crushing shoulders and heads.

He was a terror. The Inchasa facing him had never seen anything like him and many of them quickly started to avoid him, attacking others, men who used weapons they understood. Mitch was enraged. He started moving forward, stepping to the attack, knowing that if he let himself get cut off from the others he would be surrounded and cut to pieces. He didn't care. He attacked again and again, pushing the men who faced him back even as the rest of the Inchasa force began to push forward.

Then Ananias attacked with his five hundred lancers. The Inchasa had been unable to bring their lances because of the wall and Ananias and his men used theirs brilliantly, catching the enemy off guard and stopping their advance in its tracks. The Inchasa leadership seemed disoriented by the sudden appearance of more defenders and Mitch heard the call going down their line to stand where they were and regroup.

As the Inchasa warriors did as they were told, Mitch called for the men around him to follow him and went on the attack. Overcome by the fury of battle, he became someone his own detached mind had difficulty recognizing as he blocked and parried, lashing out at any Inchasa unlucky enough to cross his path. All fear was chased from his body and was now replaced by a searing hot lust for battle.

Inspired by the sight of him attacking the enemy so fiercely, the men around him rallied and began to press the attack. The Inchasa, suddenly forced into a defensive mode they were ill trained for, began to give ground, moving back toward the wall, waiting impatiently for the order to go back on the offensive.

Then, whirling to meet a left handed sword stroke, Mitch was shocked to see the Inchasa king himself stand to his feet on top of the wall. Blocking the strike and knocking his attacker's blade aside, he delivered a skull crushing blow to he man's head just as the enemy king started to urge his men back to the attack.

"Ten river women for the man who kills this one," he called, pointing to Mitch.

"Why don't you come down and try it yourself," Mitch called back and the Inchasa king looked at him in surprise. This was the one Sapa had told him about, the one who spoke Inchasa. He ignored the taunt. He was a king, not a common warrior. His men would deal with the man soon enough.

The sight of their king seemed to inspire them and the Inchasa went back on the attack, many of them throwing themselves at Mitch, hungry for the reward. For a moment it was all he could do to defend himself as Inchasa after Inchasa came at him. He killed three in quick succession and broke another's arms. Two more faced him together, one to the right and one to the left. Leaping between them, Mitch put the wall at his back and waited.

They attacked together but both went for an overhead strike. Stepping back and throwing his staff up to block both strikes, Mitch almost tripped over something lying on the ground but still managed to hold them off. Recovering quickly, he moved with smooth efficiency from the defensive to the offensive as one of the enemy warriors thrust at him with his sword, trying to get to him before he could recover his footing. He was too slow and Mitch brought his staff down hard on his exposed forearms. The man dropped his sword with an anguished cry that distracted his partner just long enough for Mitch to step close and send him crashing to the ground, his head a bloody, broken mess.

Mitch finished off the man with the broken arms and looked down to see what he had almost gotten him killed and saw that he had tripped over his own quiver. Then his eyes fell on the tied bundle of black arrows and his bow lying there beside them. Damn! Why hadn't he tried harder to learn how to use them?

# CHAPTER 36

▼

# THE BATTLE RAGES

Standing on top of the wall, urging his men on to victory, the young Cuzco could feel the very essence of life flowing through him. He found the sight of men killing one another intoxicating and knew that once this victory was won he would begin to plan for another. He would conquer the farmers to the southeast and then move against the people of the desert. He would conquer everyone his father and all the Cuzco's before him had been unable to defeat.

Waving his sword above his head, he urged his men to go back on the offensive. They responded, giving him a sense of power even the herb had never given him. He watched as his men began to push the defenders back away from the first wall and toward the unexpected second wall.

He saw that there was one enemy warrior his men were avoiding, a man who used a walking stick as a weapon. He was a terror, killing men so quickly that no one wanted to go near him. He couldn't let that go on. The man had to die.

"Ten river women for the man who kills this one," he called, pointing to the river warrior.

"Why don't you come down here and try it yourself," the man called back, surprising him. This was the man Sapa had told him about then, the one who spoke Inchasa. He wondered idly where the man could have learned the language but otherwise ignored him. He was a king, not a common warrior. His men would deal with the man soon enough.

Glancing to his right, he saw that Manco was driving the enemy hard on that flank. If he could push through there the battle would soon be over. Leruk was having a harder time of it and his attack on the opposite flank was stalled. Turning back to the battle in front of him, he could sense the tide was beginning to turn. His men were now driving the enemy hard, inflicting punishment he felt sure would soon break their will to fight.

New waves of warriors began throwing themselves at the river warrior with the walking stick and the Cuzco was stunned to see the speed and seeming ease with which the man killed or maimed any man who attacked him. It wasn't long before his men were avoiding the man again. What good were river women if you weren't alive to enjoy them?

Then the Cuzco had to laugh as he saw the river warrior notching an arrow in his bow. Would these fools never learn?

"Take good aim!" he called with a laugh. "I'm right here!" Then he spread his arms wide and stood tall, offering the man a perfect target. He laughed again as the river man tried to steady himself and take careful aim. These people were such dullards. They would be well suited to a life of labor.

Then the man released his arrow and the young Cuzco stepped to his right to make sure the errant shot would hit him. Let the fool see how useless it was to resist a god.

And then he screamed, a loud, high pitched, resounding shriek of pain and surprise as the arrow pierced his golden armor, drove through the soft flesh of his leg and imbedded its tip in the large bone of his right thigh. Dropping his sword, he stood there staring in disbelief at the black shaft sticking out of his body. This was impossible!

He never saw the second arrow. At least, not until it was sticking out of his chest and he was lying flat on his back, looking up at the bright, clear sky and the huge, unforgiving sun.

"But I am a god," he gasped in confusion as his life flowed out onto the logs around him. "A…god."

The Inchasa who heard his screams and saw their Cuzco die were momentarily shocked by what they saw. But there was no time to dwell on it. They were at war and it was kill or be killed. They could worry about he consequences of the Cuzco's death after they had won victory.

They kept pressing the attack, taking advantage of their superior numbers by isolating the defenders into groups of one, two and three and then attacking with a superior force, whether it be two attacking one, three attacking two or four attacking three. And as the center pushed the defenders back, Manco and his men finally managed to break through on the right flank, pushing their way past the edge of the wall to join up with the main attack force. Within minutes they were pushing the defenders to the brink.

At that point the remaining river warriors jumped over the second wall and joined the now desperate defense, again surprising the Inchasa, checking their advance and giving the defenders a chance to regroup. Sensing that the attack was faltering and finding no one in command of the main attack force, Manco stepped forward and took control. Moving along the rear of their line he urged them back to the offensive. He could sense how close they were to victory. They just needed to keep pressing forward.

Under his command the Inchasa quickly recovered from the surprise of the fresh reinforcements and regained the initiative. They pushed the defenders back again and again, the failure of Leruk and his men to break through on the other flank the only thing keeping them from surrounding the enemy and completely annihilating them.

✳    ✳    ✳    ✳

After killing the Inchasa king with what he freely admitted to himself was a lucky shot to the chest, Mitch threw down his bow and grabbed his staff again. The defenders who saw the Inchasa king go down gave a half-hearted cheer, but the Inchasa themselves showed no ill effects. If anything they seemed to fight harder.

Moving away from the wall Mitch fought his way back to rejoin the defender's line. It was desperate, life and death fighting again and he was surprised to find bleeding wounds on his arms, chest and side as he killed the last Inchasa between him and the rest of the defenders. He had no recollection of how he'd gotten most of his wounds.

He fell back as the others did, careful not to let himself become totally separated from the men around him. If that happened he was dead. They would eventually surround him and kill him. No man could stand alone forever.

Scanning the length of the wall, he saw that Philip and his men were holding against the right flank but Secotan and his men had been pushed back on the left, allowing the Inchasa force there to spread out and join up with the main force. It was at this moment that Manteo Hatarask made the very wise decision to commit the rest of the men waiting behind the second wall. For a moment their arrival seemed to turn the tide back in the defender's favor, but before long they were being pushed back again. Slower now, but still being pushed back.

And then he saw Manco stalking back and forth across the back of the Inchasa line, giving orders and driving them on. He had to put a stop to that or this was all going to be over real quick. He started fighting his way to the left, trying to get closer.

As he moved, he was shocked to see Nathaniel Whyte run out into the middle of the battlefield and pull an injured man out of the fight. He knew Secotan had forbidden Nathaniel to fight, telling him that he could do more good treating the wounded than he could with a sword, but was the man insane? Running out into the middle of this field of death unarmed and dragging wounded away?

Then he forgot about Nathaniel. He was close enough now and he decided to take a chance that Manco's vanity was greater than his good sense.

"Manco!" he screamed over the din of battle. "Manco! Why do you hide behind your men?"

The huge man spun around, a sneer on his ugly face and fire in his eyes.

"I hide from no man," he roared and began pushing his way through his own men until he stood face to face with the enemy warrior who knew his name.

"Now, I will kill you," he said simply, and launched into a powerful attack, his sword alive in his hands, his strikes landing with such force that Mitch had to move backward just to keep his balance. Manco pressed him hard, his blade slipping past Mitch's defenses to leave a bloody gash on his left thigh. Then the big man stopped and moved back, not wanting to become separated from his men.

"Come," he said with a smile. "Don't challenge me and then run away."

Smiling back, Mitch stepped to the attack and now it was Manco's turn to be surprised by the speed and power of his opponent. They moved front and back and side to side, switching quickly from the offensive to the defensive and back again as first one and then the other of them went on the attack. Warriors from both sides gave them a wide berth and began to hazard occasional glances in their direction, drawn by the strength and skill of the two combatants.

Manco's sword flashed suddenly and Mitch felt it slice him high up on the outside of his left arm. The sight of blood running down his arm and dripping from his bent elbow brought another smile to Manco's face. He ran a finger along his blade then put it to his lips, tasting the blood.

"You are strong," he said. "I think I'll eat your heart as a tribute after I kill you."

"Don't do me any favors," Mitch retorted hotly. "Besides, you couldn't kill me on your best day." This man was the strongest, most skilled adversary he'd ever faced and the challenge both frightened and exhilarated him. This was what it meant to be alive!

Waiting until he saw the big Inchasa's hands begin to move, Mitch threw his staff out straight, timing the blow so that his thrust began just as Manco was pulling his blade back to strike. The big man jumped back quickly and tried to bring his sword down to block, but it was too late. He managed to deflect most of the power of the blow but the hard—shelled tip of the staff struck him solidly in the chest and he jumped back, wincing in pain.

Mitch smiled tauntingly. He needed to make this man angry enough to make a mistake.

Roaring with pain and anger, Manco threw himself forward, raising his sword high over his head and bringing it crashing down toward Mitch's. Throwing his staff up horizontally, his hands held wide, Mitch blocked the strike, pushed the blade aside and ran his staff down its length and into Manco's exposed hands.

It was a glancing blow without much power but it still hurt and Manco yelped and leaped back as if he'd been stung. He began to circle warily. He would never have believed a man could so much as scratch him with nothing more than a walking stick. This man was a warrior! That would make the taste of killing him all the sweeter.

"I'm through playing with you," he said through gritted teeth. "Now, you die."

His sword became a flashing talon, darting and slashing almost faster than Mitch could follow. Several times Manco was sure he'd gotten through and sunk his blade deep into his enemy's chest only to find his sword knocked aside at the last second or his foe no longer standing where he'd been. He grew frustrated and pressed all the harder. Sooner or later he would land a stunning blow and knock the man's weapon from his hands. And then it would be over.

Mitch let his body flow instinctively, concentrating on keeping his balance and watching for an opening. There were none. Manco was an incredible swordsman. His speed and power were frightening. But he was angry now and in that anger Mitch hoped to find his opening.

"Is that the best you can do?" he taunted, knowing that he risked everything. If Manco didn't make a mistake soon there was a good chance he would. And then he would die. He saw anger flash in Manco's eyes and needled him some more.

"I thought you were supposed to be dangerous? Maybe they were talking about another Manco."

Manco leaped at him with a snarl, this time swinging a blow right to left from the side, forcing Mitch to step toward him and throw his staff out vertically to block it. As he stepped in, Manco let go of his sword with his right hand and swung a nasty backhand to the side of his head, sending Mitch staggering back. Stunned, Mitch just managed to recover and block the next sword thrust.

"Better?" Manco asked.

"Much," Mitch had to admit as he tried to shake the cobwebs from his head and clear his vision.

Manco laughed.

"What is your name?" he asked. "I think I will want to tell my grandchildren the story of how I killed you, and they should know your name."

"Mitchell Harvey," Mitch answered. "But you'll never have grandchildren, Manco. I'm going to kill you, right here, right now."

The two of them circled warily, Manco with his blade raised over his right shoulder in a two-handed grip, Mitch holding his staff in front of him, his right hand held high, his left low, the weapon running diagonally across his body in front of him.

Manco's left shoulder tensed and Mitch was moving before his mind had time to object. As Manco stepped in and swung viciously from right to left, Mitch stepped toward him and swung his staff to meet it, snapping it forward with all his strength. The two weapons came together with a ringing crack and the hardened steel of Manco's blade snapped halfway along its length, sending a jolt of pain through the hilt and up his arms.

The instant the sword tip went sailing past his left side, Mitch pulled his right arm back, the end of his staff catching Manco full on the jaw, breaking it with a loud crack. Without stopping, he slid both his hands down to the lower end of the staff, raised it high over his right shoulder and swung it like an axe, catching Manco at the back of his ankles, sending his feet flying out from under him and lifting him high off the ground. The killing blow crushed his skull even before his huge body came crashing to the ground.

Raising his staff high over his head in his right hand, Mitch let loose a wild, lustful battle cry, the hot thrill of victory and the inexpressable joy of being truly alive bursting from deep within his soul. Some small part of his mind tried to tell him he should be ashamed of what he was feeling but he knew he couldn't control it. He was what he was and he felt what he felt.

Just when the sight of Manco's broken, bleeding body threatened to crush the attacker's will to fight, Leruk and his men finally broke through and pushed to join the main attack force. The Inchasa quickly renewed the attack, trying to encircle the outnumbered defenders, sensing that victory was theirs for the taking.

And then, seemingly as in a dream, Mitch saw Zeng-de standing on top of the first wall, his sword in his hand. Then others joined him. Too many for Mitch to count before they leaped down and threw themselves at the Inchasa from behind, taking them completely by surprise.

A loud cheer went up among the river warriors as they saw their unexpected allies join the fight. But the Inchasa were far from defeated. They still outnumbered the defenders, though by a far smaller margin than before, and they fought fiercely.

Immersing himself in the general battle again, Mitch lost all track of time as he attacked Inchasa after Inchasa. He suffered several more small hurts as he defended himself and began to wonder how much more he and the others could take. It was with a great sense of relief that he whirled around to see who was behind him and found himself face to face with Zeng-de.

"You came!" he cried happily, realizing after he said it how silly it must sound.

"Yes, my friend," Zeng-de said, gripping his arm tightly. "And now we will fight together. I will protect your back and you will protect mine."

Mitch agreed with a smile and turned his back to Zeng-de. The two of them fought that way, each able to sense and anticipate what the other was going to do as if they'd been fighting together for years. They broke attack after attack and moved from the defensive to the offensive as often as they could. Each of them came to the aid of the other time and again as the enemy did their best to separate and surround them.

And then, suddenly, the Inchasa began to fall back, what was left of their attack force moving along the wall toward the forest. The defenders gave chase, their tired, sagging bodies energized by the sight of the enemy in retreat.

$$* \qquad * \qquad * \qquad *$$

The battle was lost. Leruk could see it in the eyes of his men. The arrival of the treacherous farmers from the south had been more than they could overcome. Moving down the line, he issued the order for the men to execute a fighting withdrawal, choosing some of the more experienced men to help him organize it. It would take all their skill to get them out of this alive.

He made his way down the length of the wall, fighting when he had to, and passed the word. The exhausted warriors were only too glad to obey. Their strength was used up and their spirits broken. They took comfort in the voice of command. They started an orderly and disciplined retreat, fighting as they moved down the wall toward escape. A few gave in to panic and tried to make it back over the wall. Some made it, most didn't and their deaths served as a deterrent to the others.

Leruk stayed at the tail end of the retreating forces, determined not to leave anyone who could walk behind if it could be helped. He joined together with several of Manco's experienced men and fought to delay the enemy while the rest of the men escaped into the forest and around the wall.

They were pressed hard and Leruk thought several times that their route of escape was going to be cut off, but each time men from his own garrison pushed the enemy back and kept the thin line of escape open. At last, after what seemed an eternity, Leruk stepped into the forest and ran for the open plain.

It tore his heart in two to see just how few men were left to escape. What had the Cuzco done to them?

$$* \qquad * \qquad * \qquad *$$

"What the hell is the matter with you?" Karac asked as Capac jumped down from the tree he'd been watching the battle from. "Get back up there."

"I've seen all I need to see," Capac said. And he had. He'd seen the Cuzco die and then watched as Mitchell Harvey had fought and killed Manco. It was all he could do to keep from breaking out in a dance of joy.

"I'll decide when you've seen all you need to see," Karac said menacingly. "Now, get back up there."

"I think maybe you should climb up there," Capac told him, "and have a look for yourself. The battle is over and your men are retreating."

"Retreating?" Karac asked. "The Cuzco would never allow it."

"The Cuzco is dead," Capac said. "And so is Manco."

"What?" Karac asked. "Don't talk rubbish!"

"You can go look for yourself," Capac said. "The Cuzco is dead and your army is retreating as fast as their feet can carry them."

Karac stared at him hard. If the fool was lying he would kill him with his bare hands. But he wasn't. There was no fear in his eyes anymore. He was telling the truth.

"But...how?" he asked, suddenly feeling old, weak and confused. The Cuzco dead? But he didn't even have an heir. Who would ascend to the throne? And what should he do now, stay with his prisoners or escape with the others?

Noref felt no such confusion. She immediately pulled a knife from the arm of her dress and plunged it deep into the old man's back.

"What are you doing?" Capac exclaimed.

"You don't think he was just going to let us go, do you?" she asked. "He may be old but he is still Inchasa. Now, come on, let's get out of here before someone comes looking for us."

"Where will we go?" Capac asked, still looking at the crumpled form of the old Inchasa uncomfortably.

"To the forest for now," Noref answered. "Lydacia City once everything has calmed down and we can travel again."

"Lydacia City," Capac said to himself and his mind was instantly clear again. Yes, Lydacia City. And Noref was right. Karac would never have let them go. He probably would have killed them so he could escape himself.

"Let's go," he said, taking one end of the litter and motioning for Noref to take the other. He might still need it for a little while longer. But he would walk into Lydacia City on his own two feet. He promised himself that.

▼

# CHAPTER 37

# THE AFTERMATH

Wanchese ran to the *SeaVista*, Alton close on her heels. She needed to get her pack, her medicines. Mitchell was hurt. She'd seen the blood. So much blood.

Alton pressed the remote to open the hatch and followed her onto the ship and to his cabin. She grabbed her pack as soon as the door was open and darted past him again, out the door and back down the passageway. Alton grabbed the second pack she'd brought with her just in case there was something in it she might need.

He ran after her, understanding her need to get to Mitch and feeling a sudden sense of emptiness as it struck him that no woman had ever been so devoted to him. Maybe playing it fast and loose had a price he'd never considered before.

He'd watched the tears roll down her cheek as Mitch had faced the huge Inchasa and he'd slipped his arm around her as she'd trembled with fear. He had no way of knowing that the man Mitch faced was the same man who had killed her parents and tried to kill her. He only knew she was more frightened than he'd ever seen anyone in his life.

And she had sobbed in his arms when Mitch had finally killed the big bastard then howled with glee when Mitch's friend, Zeng-de, and his men had climbed over the wall. And now she was obsessed with the need to get to the other side of the river and see to Mitch's wounds.

He'd run through a powerful succession of emotions himself over the past few hours. First came the fear as arrows started falling all around Mitch, and then the sheer terror as things broke down into close combat. That had been followed by disbelieving awe, as his brother had transformed into a quick, efficient killing machine.

Then the fear had come back as Mitch fought the big Inchasa. He'd thought he was going to watch his little brother die for sure, then. And it had been a close thing. But Mitch had come out on top again. And now there was overwhelming relief. It was over. It was over and Mitch was still alive.

Running past Nate, Tommy and Sandra, he followed Wanchese to the river and just had time to jump into the canoe before she shoved off without him. There were two oars and he helped her get across the river as quickly as possible.

"You go on ahead," he said when they reached the other side, throwing the second pack up onto the bank. "I'll go back for the others."

"Thank you, Alton," she said, giving his hand a quick squeeze before picking up the packs and running off. Alton started back across the river, wishing he'd paid more attention when his father had tried to teach him how to steer a canoe that summer he was thirteen.

Wanchese found Mitch and Zeng-de standing by the first wall, surrounded by a mix of river warriors and Zeng-de's men, all slapping each other on the back happily and laughing together, the language barrier having no effect on them. Words couldn't express what they were feeling anyway.

"Mitchell!" she called without realizing it and he turned and smiled when he saw her. She ran to him and dropped the packs, the terrible sight of his blood smeared body the only thing that kept her from throwing her arms around him when she got there. She told herself to get control of her emotions. She was going to make a fool of herself if she wasn't careful.

"It's not as bad as it looks," Mitch said when he saw the look on her face. "I'm fine."

"You are *not* fine," she said, picking up her pack and taking him by the hand. "Those wounds need to be cleaned and bandaged. Take that other pack and come to the river with me."

"I can't," Mitch protested, "not yet. There are too many others who need help more."

Still holding her pack, she stood in front of him and looked up into his face, suddenly aware that she didn't want to control her emotions anymore. She wouldn't say or do anything that would tell him what she could now admit she felt, but she was tired of not letting herself feel it. He might not feel the same thing for her that she felt for him but that was a chance she was just going to have to take. Whether it be pleasure or pain, happiness or sorrow, she was ready to feel again.

"Mitchell," she said softly, "I know how strong you are. But you've lost too much blood. Let me clean and bandage your wounds and at least stop the bleeding. Please."

She saw in his eyes that she had said the one thing that would change his mind. He nodded and told Zeng-de he would be back in a little while then let her lead him to a shady spot beneath a tree on the river bank. He drank long and gratefully when she handed him his water bag.

"I'll get a fire going," she said. "Rinse off in the river. I need to see where you're hurt."

He waded into the river and she quickly gathered fuel and started a small fire. By the time he came back she had a small pot boiling and was mixing in the herbs she needed to cleanse and disinfect his wounds. She examined each wound closely while the pot boiled. There were fewer than she'd expected and most of them were minor. Most of the blood must have been from the Inchasa he'd killed. She breathed a little easier.

"It might be easier if you sit on that rock," she told him, pointing to a boulder a few feet away. Mitch went and sat on it and she spread her blanket at his feet and laid her pack and the pot beside her.

"This is going to sting," she told him as she dipped a cloth into the herb mixture and gently cleaned the deep gash on his left thigh. "But it will clean the wound and keep it from getting infected."

"O.K," Mitch said, wincing a little as the warm water ran into the wound.

She cleaned the leg wound first because it was the deepest then moved up to the scrapes and bruises on his face before working her way down to his neck, chest, arms and abdomen. He was right. It wasn't as back as it had looked. Still, she felt better knowing the wounds were clean and the bleeding stopped.

She felt his eyes on her as she worked and looked up to meet his eyes. He seemed embarrassed to have been caught looking at her and quickly turned away.

"I wish I knew how Raven made out," he said quickly. "And the others: Philip, Secotan, Virgil, Roger. I haven't seen any of them since the fighting ended."

"I don't know about Raven or the others," she said, silently cursing herself for having been so hard on him that he was afraid to even look at her openly, "but Secotan was hurt."

"Bad?" he asked.

"Yes," she answered. She'd seen him get run through from behind. He was probably already dead, though she'd seen Nathaniel Whyte run out and drag him out of harms way. If anyone could help him it was Nathaniel.

"There will be trouble because of it, too," she added. "Kane and Saul Rivers were fighting at Secotan's back while he dealt with two Inchasa in front of him. I saw the two of them look back at him and then move away, leaving his back exposed. The nearest Inchasa stepped in and ran him through from behind. Nathaniel Whyte dragged him away and treated his wounds, but...." she shrugged her shoulders.

"You think Kane and Rivers left him unprotected intentionally?"

"I do. And if I saw it so did Dare and anyone else who was watching that part of the battle."

Mitch looked down at his hands and willfully controlled his anger. He had a new and profound understanding of just how important it was to be able to trust the man at your back in a fight. Could Kane really be that heartless that he would let a man get killed just because he didn't like him?

Just then Alton, Nathan, Tommy and Sandra came running.

"Is he alright?" Alton asked.

"Good as new," Mitch said.

Alton came up behind him and wrapped his head in a loose hug.

"If you ever do anything like that again I'll kill you myself, you stupid son of a bitch," he said emotionally.

Mitch laughed.

"Nice to see you, too," he said.

"I mean it," Alton said. "I was scared out of my mind today. I'm not sure if I was holding Wanchese up or she was holding me up. I thought I was having a heart attack a couple of times."

"I had a few anxious moments myself," Mitch teased. "But I'm sorry it was so hard on you."

"He is being a wise ass again?" Wanchese asked with a smile and Mitch laughed again.

"You're a bad influence, Alton," he said. "She never used to swear before she met you."

"Oh, I'd be willing to bet she had a few choice names for you long before she ever met me," Alton shot back and Wanchese smiled, thinking of the awful names she'd called Mitchell under her breath when they were first getting to know one another.

"One or two, perhaps," she said.

"Hey!" Mitch said. "You're supposed to be on my side."

Wanchese laughed.

Tommy and Nate came over and shook Mitch's hand.

"You are one *bad ass mother*!" Tommy exclaimed as he took Mitch's hand. "They teach you that shit in the military?"

"No," Mitch said, shaking his head and smiling. Tommy had always had a way with words. "A friend of mine taught me."

"Well, from now on it's gonna be 'Yes, sir, Mr. Harvey' and 'No, sir, Mr. Harvey' from me. I didn't know who I was messin' with."

Mitch chuckled.

"You start calling me sir, Tommy, and I'll definitely kick your ass."

"Alright, alright, whatever you say," Tommy said. "Just settle down. I don't want you breaking out into one of those Tarzan yells. I almost shit my pants when you let that thing rip." Then he let loose with a very poor imitation and even Sandra couldn't help laughing. Mitch took a playful swing at him from where he was sitting.

"Sit still," Wanchese told him, but she was smiling. She finished cleaning his wounds and went into her pack for her healing salve.

"I don't know what's in that," Mitch said as he applied it to his thigh wound, "but it's damn good stuff. The wound feels better almost as soon as you put it on."

"It's a salve my mother showed me how to make," she said. "But you need herbs that only grow high up in the mountains. That's why I collected so much of that red and white berry before we left there. I knew I wouldn't be able to find it down here."

Mitch nodded than let out a weary sigh as she applied the salve to a shallow three inch gash on his right shoulder and the stinging pain instantly subsided.

"Are you alright?" she asked.

"Yeah, I'm fine. I'm just tired. And it just hit me that it's really all over and I'm still alive."

He opened his eyes and looked at her.

"Don't tell Alton," he said with a conspiratorial smile, knowing that Alton could hear every word he said, "but I didn't really expect to live through this."

Wanchese smiled as Alton mumbled something under his breath. She shook her head and wondered why Mitchell had so little faith in himself. Why couldn't he see himself for what he was? Though it had looked bad before Zeng-de and his men had come. Mitchell and the others might very well have fought as bravely as was humanly possible and still been overwhelmed by sheer numbers. They would have killed a lot of Inchasa before they died, but they would have been just as dead.

"Would it be alright if I asked how your mother got the berries?" he asked. "Do you mind talking about her?"

"Not with you. My father brought her the berries whenever he went to the mountains with a hunting party. Or, if he wasn't going, he would have someone else bring some back for him. Then my mother would show me how to make the salve. Later on my father would make me repeat everything he'd told me about how to recognize the bush the berries grew on. They were always teaching me things like that and they were both very good teachers. I knew the bush as soon as I saw it, even after all these years."

"They'd be proud of you," Mitch said, "if they could see you now."

Wanchese's reply was interrupted by Nathaniel Whyte, who called her name as he came running toward them. Mitch couldn't help thinking that a breech-cloth wasn't the best choice of clothing for a man as thin and unmuscular as Nathaniel. That said nothing about the man's heart, however, and Nathaniel Whyte was one case where it would definitely be a mistake to judge the book by its cover.

"Wanchese," Nathaniel said breathlessly when he reached them, "I've been looking all over for you. Would you come help me with Secotan?"

"He's still alive, then?" she asked, surprised that someone like Nathaniel would ask her for help. He was the best healer in all of the river villages.

"Yes. But I've done everything I know to do for him and it's not enough. He's dying, Wanchese. Can you help me?"

"Of course. I just need to finish with Mitchell's bandages and I'll be right there. Where is he?"

"In Philip's longhouse. But can't you come now?"

"Go ahead, Wanchese," Alton broke in. "I'll finish Mitch's bandages."

"But his wounds need to be covered properly or they might get infected," she protested.

"It's alright," Mitch told her. "Alton's had training in how to do it. Go on."

She looked up at him, hesitating, not wanting to leave him until she knew he was properly cared for. The look of anguish on Nathaniel's face finally convinced her, though.

"Alright," she said.

She took some bandages from her pack for Alton to use, handed the second pack to Nathaniel and picked up her own. Nathaniel grabbed her by the hand and started back for the village.

"Nathaniel!" Mitch called out and Whyte and Wanchese stopped and turned back to him.

"I saw what you did out there today," Mitch said, pointing back toward the battlefield. "You were the bravest man on that field. Your family should be damn proud."

Nathaniel stood straight and nodded his head in thanks, not trusting himself to speak. Then he took Wanchese's hand and started off toward the village again. It meant the world to him that a warrior like Mitchell would respect what he'd done during the battle but it wouldn't lessen the pain if his friend died. He had to get Wanchese to Secotan, and quickly. Still holding her hand, he broke into a run.

"Alright," Alton said, pulling the little group's attention back to him, "stand your sorry ass up and I'll get some bandages on you. I always knew that first aid course would come in handy some day."

Mitch stood and Alton quickly and deftly bandaged his wounds, having practiced his technique dozens of times during his yearly first aid refresher courses. For the first time he was glad he was required by law to have someone first aid certified at the resort year round. He finished the bandaging despite Mitch's protests that he didn't need to wrap him up like a damn mummy and then they all made their way back toward the plain.

The battlefield was still a tangled mess of human debris with old men, women and children helping their loved ones to shelter or mourning over a fallen father, brother, husband or son. Wounded Inchasa had been finished off and were being dragged out of the way with the other enemy dead. Mitch, Alton and the others went out to see what they could do to help. Even Sandra seemed affected by the scene and pitched in.

A few moments later a loud argument broke out back by the second wall and Mitch went to see what the trouble was. He found Dare Samuels and Geris Quick facing Hunter Kane, Saul Rivers and their friends. Philip stood to one side looking worried but not interfering.

"I *saw* you!" Dare screamed as Mitch got close enough to hear. "I saw both of you deliberately leave him unprotected. You might as well have stabbed him yourself. But you didn't have the courage to try that, did you? You're nothing but a couple of cowards!"

"Mind your tongue," Kane said, bristling.

"She can say whatever she wants," Geris Quick said. "If you don't like it, tell her she's lying. Tell me she's lying. Tell the hundred other people who saw the same thing she did that she's lying."

Kane drew his sword and stepped toward Geris.

"No man calls me a liar," he said with an angry sneer.

Geris drew his own sword and stepped forward to meet him, cold fury in his eyes.

"I saw it, too," Rolf Wind, another warrior from Secotan's village said, stepping forward and drawing his sword. "And I say you're a liar, Kane."

"So do I," another man said, stepping forward.

Kane turned and glared at the two of them and was on the verge of telling them he'd deal with them when he finished with Geris when, one by one, another fifty men came forward, weapons at the ready, angry determination on their face. There were some things you just couldn't allow.

Afraid that another battle was about to break out and not wanting to see any more men die, Philip stepped in and stood between Kane and Geris.

"Wait, please," he said. "Enough men have died today."

"Not yet," Geris said. "There are two more who need killing. Don't interfere, Philip. You didn't see what the cowards did."

"No," Philip admitted, "I didn't. But I know you well enough to know you wouldn't make an accusation like this if you weren't absolutely sure."

He turned to Kane and his friends.

"And I know you well enough, Hunter Kane, to know that you think only of yourself. I have no doubt that you did just what Dare says you did. I think you and your friends had better leave. I don't care where you go, but get out of my village. If you're not gone in ten minutes, I'll not only let Geris and these others kill you, I'll help them do it. I want you gone. Take your families with you."

"This is the thanks I get for helping you?" Kane said angrily. "You just throw me out without even hearing my side? If it weren't for me an Inchasa would be bedding your wives and daughters right now! I killed more Inchasa than any of you. And now you just throw me out because of the words of a hysterical woman? I don't think so. I'll leave when I'm ready to leave, not before."

"You will leave now," Virgil Crane said, stepping out of the crowd of onlookers. "You will leave right now or my men and I will help them kill you."

Kane spun around to face Virgil and found the men of Philip's village pushing their way forward to stand with the hawk faced warrior, swords and lances in their hands. He couldn't fight them all. His body shook with anger as he glared at the crowd impotently.

"Fine, we'll go!" he spat. They would set up their own village and live by their own rules. They didn't need these fools. Putting his sword back in its scabbard, he turned and walked away.

"Kane!" Virgil called and Kane stopped and turned back to him. "Don't flatter yourself. For every Inchasa you killed, Mitchell Harvey killed five."

"Ten!" another man shouted.

A sneer on his face, Kane turned and stalked toward the village, his friends following behind.

"Choose ten men, Virgil," Philip said when they were gone. "Follow them when they leave. Stay out of sight and don't get into anything with them, but follow them. I want to know where they are."

Virgil nodded.

The crowd broke up quickly and everyone went back to work. Mitch and the others passed the rest of the morning moving the wounded and dead and then passed the mid-day break in the shade of a tree by the river. When the heat let up Alton and the others went to see what else they could do to help. Mitch went to check on Secotan and found Wanchese and Nathaniel busily applying her healing salve to an ugly wound on the right side of his back. Wanchese looked up and he saw in her eye that things weren't looking good.

He barely spoke to her over the next two days as she and Nathaniel stayed with Secotan, working, hoping and praying, though he did stop by every few hours to see how things were going. In the meantime, he helped Philip communicate with Zeng-de and was glad to see the look of gratitude on Zeng-de's face when Philip announced that the trench in front of the wall would be deepened and enlarged and used to bury the men Zeng-de had lost in the battle. All sixty-three of them would be buried there with the wall remaining as a memorial to their sacrifice.

Philip also had Zeng-de write down the names of all sixty-three men and gave his word that as long as he lived those sixty three names would be read allowed in tribute every year on the battle's anniversary. Mitch could see in his friend's face just how much that meant to Zeng-de and that it eased the weight of his burden just a little. It wouldn't make it any easier to tell the families of the fallen that their loved ones were dead, but it would give them at least some small solace.

The second night after the battle all the work was finally done and the entire village gathered for a huge celebration, with food and drink, singing and dancing and tributes to the men who had died and those who had distinguished themselves in the fight. Philip presented the Inchasa king's jeweled sword to Zeng-de and asked him to give it to his emperor with a letter of thanks and appreciation. Mitch smiled as the entire village cheered.

And he laughed out loud when Roger Werts insisted that Nate and Alton come out into the middle of the huge circle of celebrants and dance with him. He laughed even harder when Alton heard him laughing and gave him the finger. The celebration lasted most of the night and ended with Philip and Elan White reading off the names of all the men who had given their lives, including Manteo Hatarask and Ananias Dare. In all there were thirteen hundred and eight names, including Zeng-de's sixty-three men.

When the celebration broke up Mitch went and checked on Secotan again. Wanchese was sleeping while Nathaneil watched over their patient. Mitch spread a blanket beside her and laid down for some rest himself. He awoke several hours later to learn that Secotan had regained consciousness briefly during the night. Nathaniel and Wanchese looked hopeful for the first time and he could see the relief on Dare's face when she smiled and said good morning.

"You look tired," he said to Wanchese when she looked up at him with a smile.

"I am," she admitted. "I'll get a full nights sleep tonight. I think the worst is over."

"Good," Mitch said. "I'm going to head out and see Zeng-de off. He and his men are leaving right after the morning meal."

"I'll go with you. I haven't had a chance to see him, to thank him."

They told Nathaniel they'd be back and headed out to find Zeng-de.

He wasn't hard to find. It seemed the entire village had had the same idea they had and Zeng-de and his men were surrounded by a throng of well wishers, many of whom were giving individual soldiers small gifts of food and trinkets. Mitch smiled as they walked up to the sight of Mother Shaw bending Zeng-de's face down to her and kissing his cheek.

"I see we're not the only ones who wanted to see you off," Mitch said in Chinese.

"No," Zeng-de replied with a smile. "But I'm glad you came. We haven't really had a chance to talk, have we?"

"No," Mitch said. "I guess we haven't. And I've spent the last couple of days trying to think of a way to thank you but there aren't any words that would cover it. We owe you and your men our lives."

"You owe your lives to your own strength and your own abilities. I saw the way you and these men fought, Mitchell. Your friendship is thanks enough for me."

"You know as well as I do that we couldn't have held on much longer without your help," Mitch said. "Thank you."

"You're welcome, my friend. It was an honor to fight beside you."

"Same here," Mitch said with a smile.

Zeng-de reached out and touched Mitch's staff made of the strange wood that could break bone and steel without suffering so much as a scratch.

"Don't forget your promise to bring me some of this wood," he said.

"I won't," Mitch said then turned to Wanchese and took her by the hand. "Wanchese wanted to thank you, too."

"Tell her there is no need," Zeng-de said. She is Nang-de's sister in my wife's heart and so, in my heart also. She is family to us and we need no thanks for helping our family."

Mitch translated and watched as Wanchese's eye swelled with tears.

"Thank you," she said softly and gave Zeng-de a hug.

"It's time for us to go," Zeng-de said when she let him go. "Come and see us when you can. You are always welcome in my house. I look forward to telling my sons the story of the day I fought beside you."

# CHAPTER 38

▼

# FINAL CONFRONTATIONS

"Do you still have trouble believing you are a warrior?" Wanchese asked softly as they watched Zeng-de and his men march off.

"No," Mitch admitted, liking the feel of her standing close so no one would overhear what she said. "I guess I can accept that now."

"Good," she said. "I was beginning to wonder if you would ever see yourself for what you really are."

He smiled.

"And what about you?" he asked. "Do you still have trouble believing you're beautiful?"

She thought about that before answering.

"I believe you think I'm beautiful."

"Well, that's a start, Wanchese," Mitch said with a smile. "That's a start."

"I also think your eyesight is suspect," she said, smiling back at him, "but I believe you mean it when you say it."

"I do mean it," he said, laughing. "And my eyes are fine."

She smiled again. She liked the way he laughed. She liked the way he looked at her, too. That was how she knew he thought she was beautiful. A man's lips can lie to you about that sort of thing but his eyes will tell you the truth. Mitchell's eyes said she was beautiful.

"We need to talk, I think," she said. "We haven't really had any time together since right after the battle."

"No, we haven't," Mitch agreed, suddenly worried. Had he said too much? Did she know how he felt about her? Was she going to gently remind him that she wasn't interested in anything other than friendship?

"I really need to get back to help Nathaniel," she said. "He's been up all night with Secotan. Maybe we could spend the mid-day break together at the camp?"

"Sure," Mitch said. "That sounds fine."

"Alright," Wanchese said then smiled and walked away.

Mitch watched her go. If she had figured out that he was in love with her at least she didn't seem pissed about it. She seemed softer somehow since the battle. Not weaker, just softer. When she was inside he headed for the southern edge of the river, took off his bandages and waded in for a bath. He washed, scrubbed and rinsed his breechcloth and rubbed his face with locaram to get rid of the stubble that was just starting to grow. When he was done, he put everything back in his pack and headed back to the camp. He was just sitting down to meditate when Alton, Nate, Tommy and Sandra came crashing through the shrubs and into camp. He didn't like the look on Alton's face.

"What's wrong?" he asked.

"I just heard from Terluride," Alton answered. "One of the mine shafts caved in. At least twenty-five dead, maybe more. They won't be sure until they excavate."

"Shit, I'm sorry, Alton," Mitch said. He knew how close Alton was with most of the miners and he could see how shaken his brother was.

"Dari Cole was in the shaft," Alton said softly and Mitch closed his eyes and lowered his head. "He's one of the twenty-five confirmed dead."

"Damn it!" Mitch said angrily then walked over and hugged his brother.

Dari Cole had been Alton's first customer on Teluride and the reason all the miners had first started giving Alton their business. He was also Alton's best friend. Alton had offered him a job at the SeaVista more times than he could count but Dari was a miner through and through. It was all he knew and all he wanted to know. The best Alton had been able to manage was getting Dari to live at the resort rent free on the weekends so the two of them could party and chase women together. They'd been so close that Mitch had almost been jealous.

"I have to get back," Alton said. "I have to be there for the funeral. I'm sorry."

"There's nothing for you to be sorry about," Mitch said, letting Alton go and looking at him. "You've been away too long as it is. When are you leaving?"

"As soon as we say goodbye. I didn't want to leave without seeing Wanchese, Philip and Virgil."

"Wanchese's at Philip's place so we can probably catch both of them at the same time. Virgil's out keeping an eye on Kane and his friends. I have no idea when he'll be back."

"Damn," Nate said. "I really wanted to say goodbye."

"So did I," Alton said. "But we don't have time to go looking for him. Let's head to Philip's."

They walked quietly out of camp toward the main village. When they reached Philip's longhouse Mitch went inside. Wanchese was talking with Dare while Nathaniel slept. Secotan was doing better but was still out most of the time.

"Hi," Mitch said. "Could I talk to you for a minute?"

"Of course," Wanchese said, her face showing her concern.

"Is Philip here?" he asked.

"No. He went to the river to bathe. He should be back any minute."

Mitch nodded. They walked outside and he took her hand and led her to Alton and the others.

"There's been an accident back on Teluride, Alton's home. Quite a few people have died, including Alton's best friend, Dari. They've got to leave and I knew you'd want to say goodbye."

Wanchese went to Alton and touched his arm.

"I'm sorry, Alton," she said.

"Thanks," he replied, reaching up and giving her hand a squeeze. "And thanks for taking such good care of this moron," he added, pointing at Mitch. "I know he can be a real handful."

"He does tend to get into trouble," she said with a smile and Alton nodded his head and grinned.

"I'm so glad I got to meet you," Wanchese said.

"Same here," he said. "You take care of yourself. You're the kind of woman Mitch deserves. Knowing he's with you makes it a lot easier for me to leave him here."

Wanchese didn't know what to say to that so she gave him a hug and then went and said goodbye to Nathan and Tommy.

"I can't wait any longer," Alton said. "You'll have to say goodbye to Philip and Virgil for us. It's time to go."

They headed back to the camp and then across the river to the ship.

"Come back and see us," Mitch said as he gave Alton one last hug. "You too, Nate, Tommy." He embraced both of them.

"We plan to," Alton said. "Which reminds me. Tommy, you got it?"

"Right here, boss," Tommy said, pulling a small syringe from his pocket and handing it to Alton.

"Locater microbes?" Mitch asked.

Alton nodded.

"It's alright," Mitch told Wanchese. "This will make it easier for them to find us when they come back."

Alton injected the microbes into Mitch's left arm then held his hand out to Tommy who handed him a second syringe.

"This is going to sting a little," he told Wanchese. She nodded and he gave her the injection.

"You're welcome at my place anytime, Wanchese," he said. "I mean that. I want you two to come visit me. You take care of yourself."

"I will," she said, giving him a kiss on the cheek.

Mitch said goodbye to the others again, even including Sandra, then stood with Wanchese as the others boarded the ship. They watched as Tommy lifted the ship a few feet off the ground and headed east. Mitch pointed out the ship as it finally climbed high into the air a little over a mile away.

"Alton must really like you," Mitch said. "I thought he was going to give me a hard time about staying."

"He knows you're happy here. Asking you to go would have been selfish. He's not a selfish man."

"No, he's not."

"He's a lot like you and yet a lot different, too. I like him very much."

"The part that's like me or the part that's different?"

She laughed.

"Both."

Mitch smiled. She wasn't going to make this easy for him. He was going to have to come right out and ask her where they stood.

"Do you need to get back to Secotan?" he asked as they made their way back to the river.

"No. Dare can watch him while Nathaniel sleeps. She knows where to find me if anything happens."

"Uh oh," Mitch said. "With the battle over, Secotan doing better and Alton gone, you're going to have to spend more time with me. You think I'll start getting on your nerves again?"

"Probably," she said as she climbed in to the dugout. He splashed water at her. She laughed and splashed him back.

They paddled back across the river, pulled the dugout up onto the bank and went to their camp. Wanchese spread their blankets side by side, sat down on hers and motioned for him to join her.

"Time for our talk, I take it," he said a little nervously.

"Unless there's something else you need to do," she said.

"No."

He sat down across from her and immediately wished he hadn't when she reached over and started untying his marriage band. She had just taken it off his arm when the hair on the back of his neck stood on end and he instinctively rolled to his feet, his staff in his hand.

There was nothing there. He waited, wondering if he was imagining things. Then Hunter Kane and Saul Rivers stepped out of the trees on the western edge of the camp.

"I wondered when you'd come," Mitch said, surprising himself. It was true. He hadn't given it any conscious thought but had known in the back of his mind that Kane would come sooner or later.

"I thought you'd be man enough to come alone, though," he added.

"I'll fight you man to man," Kane said, stung by the accusation. "But not with that." He pointed at the staff then tossed a sword to the ground at Mitch's feet.

"Let's see how you fight with a real warriors weapon," he said. "Or aren't you man enough to fight me without your stick? It's the stick that is fearsome, not the man. Anyone could kill with a weapon like that. What kind of warrior are you without it? That is what I've been asking myself while I listen to all those fools back there talking about how fierce you are and how many Inchasa you killed. Was it you who killed them or the stick that breaks bones like twigs? A real warrior can kill with any weapon. Pick up the sword and show me what kind of warrior you are."

Mitch smiled. It was a good speech. But he wasn't going to fight Kane with a sword. He'd be dead in thirty seconds. He handed his staff to Wanchese and motioned for her to stand out of the way.

"A real warrior needs no weapon but himself," he said. "Put down your sword and show me what kind of warrior *you* are, Kane. Do you have the courage for that?"

Now Kane smiled.

"This will only make your death slower and more painful," he said, throwing his sword to the ground and stepping closer.

"If you interfere I'll kill you," Wanchese said and Mitch turned to see her looking at Saul Rivers.

"He doesn't need my help," Rivers said. "I'm only here to watch him kill you later."

With that Mitch and Kane began to circle warily. Then Mitch snapped out a quick left hand that split Kane's bottom lip. But it had no effect on him. He just ignored it and swung a vicious kick to the deep wound on Mitch's left thigh. He smiled when Mitch winced in pain.

Mitch faked another jab and then threw an overhand right. Kane dodged the punch easily and landed another kick to the thigh. Then he threw his shoulder into Mitch's chest, knocking him off balance, and landed a driving right hand to the side of the head. Before Mitch had time to recover, Kane landed another painful kick to his thigh.

There was a taunting smile on Kane's broken lips now and he faked another kick to the thigh just to make Mitch react. Then he threw a jab of his own. But Mitch knocked it aside and swung a wicked left to Kane's ribs that he followed with a short left to the chin. Kane grunted in pain but never stopped moving and drove in low, wrapping his arms around Mitch's waist and knocking him off balance. Mitch locked his arms around Kane's head and the two of them fell to the ground in a jumbled heap.

They rolled around on the ground with first one and then the other of them gaining a slight advantage and landing a solid blow to the head or body. Then Kane momentarily got the upper hand and got his legs underneath him. He pushed Mitch's head to the ground and drove his left knee down on top of it. The blow landed hard and Mitch felt his head explode with pain but instinctively used Kane's momentum against him and was able to send him over his head and to the ground.

The blow to the head had hurt Mitch but it had also struck a spark inside of him and the battle lust began to surge in his gut. He felt the adrenaline surge through his body, the aches and pains of his wounds suddenly disappearing to be replaced by a surge of power and joy. There were no weapons but this was a fight for his life and it made him feel supremely alive!

He smiled when Virgil Crane stepped out from the brush behind Saul Rivers, having tracked he and Kane there. Now Rivers would be out of it for sure.

Ignoring Crane altogether, Kane drove low again, trying to get his arms around Mitch's legs and knock him to the ground again. But Mitch jumped back with his lower body while driving the weight of his upper body down through his elbows and into Kane's back. He heard the big man grunt as he fell to the ground on top of him. He jumped back to his feet and hit Kane three times in the head before he could get to his feet.

They circled again and Mitch noted with satisfaction that Kane's smile was gone. He'd hurt him that time. Kane tried to step close again and Mitch lashed a right to the bridge of his nose then stepped to his right and landed a short left to the same spot. Stepping in, he hit him full force with his left shoulder and sent him crashing to the ground. Kane scrambled up quickly but was now favoring the right side of his ribcage. Mitch feinted another right to the face and then landed a hard left hand to the ribs when Kane lifted his hands to block.

Grunting with pain, Kane drove in, swinging wildly, just wanting to get close. He needed to get Harvey on the ground again. He had an advantage there. If he could get his arms around the man's neck he'd choke the life out of him.

But Mitch was having none of it and smoothly stepped to the side, driving a right hand into Kane's left kidney as he went past. It sent him to the ground in a heap.

"Get up, you useless piece of shit," Mitch snarled, stepping back to give him room. "I'm not finished with you yet."

Howling with rage, Kane pushed himself to his knees and then stood. In his right hand he held his hunting knife.

"Coward!" Mitch sneered. "I should have known you'd try something like that."

He thought briefly of pulling his own knife. He had the beautiful dagger Zeng-de had given him on his belt. But he was no knife fighter. He was as likely to hurt himself as he was Kane. No, he decided. He'd said he would fight with no weapon but himself and that was what he would do.

Kane lunged in and jabbed with the knife, insane fury burning in his eyes. Mitch knocked it aside and stepped out of the way. Kane lunged again and Mitch jumped back. The blade grazed his chest and he felt the sting as it left a bloody scratch. Kane came at him again, mad with the lust to kill. He was like a wounded animal, bent on killing the thing that had hurt it.

He slashed with the knife again and Mitch jumped back just in time. Kane slashed again and Mitch caught his hand and fought for the knife. But Kane ripped it away and slashed wildly, ripping another gash in Mitch's right arm.

Mitch stumbled back and fought to regain his balance. Kane lashed out again and Mitch stepped back. Kane came again and this time Mitch moved his body and front foot back but kept his back foot exactly where it had been, giving the illusion of having moved back just as he had before while actually leaving the distance between them the same. The only difference was that now his body was coiled to strike.

This time when Kane lunged, Mitch knocked the knife aside with his left hand, stepped forward with his left foot and unleashed his right hand at Kane's throat, grasping his larynx in the same vicious, vice like grip he'd used so many weeks before on Sylvas, and pulled back with all his adrenaline enhanced strength, tearing Kane's throat open with a quick, terrible ripping sound.

Kane stiffened and his eyes went wide as he struggled to breath. His hand opened and his knife fell to the ground. Mitch let him go and he followed it to the ground. Mitch threw the bloody lump of flesh to the ground in front of Kane's face so it would be the last thing his eyes ever saw and turned to Saul Rivers.

"You still have a problem with my wife, Rivers? Let's settle that now, too."

"No," Saul Rivers said, his face looking sick as he stared at Kane and listened to the rasping torment of his last breaths. "No, problem. I don't want any trouble."

"Then get the hell out of here," Mitch said. "And don't let me see you again. The next time I see you, I kill you."

Rivers ripped his eyes away from Kane, looked at Mitch and then turned and headed back into the brush to the west.

Mitch turned and started toward Wanchese. Suddenly all the strength drained from his body, his cuts and bruises started to ache again and he felt unsteady on his feet. Wanchese ran to him, throwing his arm over her shoulder.

"Virgil, help me get him to the river," she ordered. "I need to wash his wounds."

"I'm alright," Mitch said. "I can make it to the river. I just need a drink of water." He really didn't want Virgil there to see Wanchese take the marriage band back. It hurt bad enough as it was without having to be embarrassed in front of a man he liked and respected.

Virgil walked over and gave him his water bag. Mitch drank long and deep then gave it back.

"Thanks, Virgil. I'm alright. You don't have to stick around."

Virgil looked at Wanchese and when she nodded her agreement, bent down, threw Kane's body over his right shoulder and walked out of camp.

Wanchese helped Mitch to the river, waded in with him and washed his wounds. Then she helped him back to camp and they sat down on their blankets so she could treat him.

"You must be getting pretty tired of doing this," he said with a weary smile as she gently wiped his chest wound dry. "I don't blame you for wanting the marriage band back. I was hoping you wouldn't, but I understand."

She looked at him for a long time then looked down, shaking her head.

"No," she said. "I like taking care of you. I wouldn't mind if you went a few weeks without almost getting killed, but I like taking care of you."

He smiled sadly. It was time for the "Let's be friends" speech.

"I'll see what I can do," he said.

She smiled and gave him another drink of water. Then she took a deep breath and plunged ahead.

"I didn't take the marriage band back because I was tired of taking care of you. I took it back because I wanted to offer it to you again and really mean it this time. I wanted you to mean it when you accepted it, too."

"I really meant it the first time," he said, suddenly unable to take his eyes off her. Could she really want him?

"I need to do it for myself, then," she said shyly.

He nodded and she reached out and put the band around his arm.

"I, Wanchese Hawkins, offer you this marriage band," she said, tying it back on his right forearm.

"I should offer you yours again," he said. It was suddenly very important to him that she accept it and mean it. She untied the band and gave it to him.

"I, Mitchell Harvey, offer you this marriage band," he said, and she lifted her hair out of the way so he could tie the band in place.

"Are you sure?" he asked.

She smiled.

"I'm sure."

He smiled like a happy idiot but couldn't think of a single thing to say.

"Do you remember when you said my mother and father would be proud of me?" she asked.

He nodded.

"Well, they would be proud of you, too. They would have hated Kane for what he tried to do to me and the big, ugly Inchasa you killed is the one who...did this." She gestured toward her eye.

"Manco did that to you? And killed your parents?"

"If that was the big Inchasa's name then yes, he killed my parents. I think it would please my father that it was my husband who avenged him."

"It pleased me, too," Mitch said and felt a little ashamed that he meant it. He never would have believed he was capable of being glad he'd killed a man. But he never would have believed himself capable of feeling a lot of things he'd discovered inside himself here. He decided he liked himself anyway.

And he liked the way Wanchese said "husband." It sounded permanent and he liked it.

"I'm sorry your parents were killed, Wanchese," he said. "I wish I could have been there to help them, and you. I'm glad Secotan and Geris got there before Manco could kill you, though."

"So am I," she said. "I used to wish I had died that day with my parents, but now I'm glad I didn't."

His heart beating like a teen aged boy putting his hand up a girl's shirt for the first time, Mitch reached out and took her hand. When she didn't pull it away he tried desperately to think of something romantic to say but, as usual, drew a total blank.

"I wish I could think of something to say," he told her with an embarrassed smile, giving her hand an affectionate squeeze. "I'm not very good at this sort of thing."

"I think you're doing fine," she said shyly, smiling back at him.

"Really?" he asked, reaching out and pulling her closer to him. "Does that mean you wouldn't threaten to slit my throat if I kissed you?"

Wanchese laughed out loud and moved her face closer to his.

"No," she said much less shyly. "I don't think I would."

And she didn't.

# THE END